A COUPLE OF QUICK FOOTFALLS WERE DAX'S ONLY WARNING BEFORE NEMI BURST OUT OF THE SHADOWS.

She came in swinging and shouting, and it took all of Dax's reflexes to jump out of the way.

"Nemi, wait!"

But the younger woman did no such thing, attacking like a feral animal. Her flurry of swings battered Dax's forearms as she struggled to block them. Dax knew close-quarters combat well—she practiced regularly in the holosuites, continuing the study of Klingon martial arts that Curzon had begun. The fighter before her was vicious, quick, and professional.

"Nemi, it's me!"

"I know," she said, sinking a sidekick into Dax's gut—right in her symbiont.

Dax's eyes bulged and her vision went blurry as she stumbled backward against a bar top. She ducked away from Nemi's nasty right hook, knocking over a stack of glasses and shattering some. Her assailant snapped up a piece of the drinkware and hurled it, hitting Dax in the shoulder when she ducked away. The blow stung like a brick.

Dax fended off another wave of frantic punches, kicks, and elbows. "Stop! I don't want to hurt you."

"That makes one of us."

STAR TREK™
DEEP SPACE NINE

REVENANT

ALEX WHITE

Based on *Star Trek*
and *Star Trek: The Next Generation*
created by Gene Roddenberry
and
Star Trek: Deep Space Nine
created by Rick Berman & Michael Piller

G

GALLERY BOOKS
New York London Toronto Sydney New Delhi

G

Gallery Books
An Imprint of Simon & Schuster, Inc.
1230 Avenue of the Americas
New York, NY 10020

This book is published by Gallery Books, a division of Simon & Schuster, Inc., under exclusive license from CBS Studios Inc.

First Gallery Books trade paperback edition December 2021

GALLERY BOOKS and colophon are registered trademarks of Simon & Schuster, Inc.

Interior design by Kathryn A. Kenney-Peterson

Manufactured in the United States of America

10 9 8 7 6 5 4 3 2 1

Library of Congress Cataloging-in-Publication Data is available.

ISBN 978-1-9821-6082-1
ISBN 978-1-9821-6083-8 (ebook)

For anyone who needs to be believed.

In Memory of Lisa Banes
(1955–2021)

HISTORIAN'S NOTE

This story takes place in 2372 after the Klingon assault is repulsed from Deep Space 9 ("The Way of the Warrior") and just before Major Kira Nerys leaves to search for crash survivors from the *Ravinok* ("Indiscretion").

1

Absence

"What about that guy?" Jadzia Dax asked.

Jake Sisko's irrepressible smile boiled over. "Kemocite smuggler."

The captain's son was a gawky, dark-skinned teenager, perpetually looking for the next adventure. Maybe that's why Dax always found him on Deep Space 9's Promenade mezzanine, people watching. Everyone on the station had to pass through there at one point or another, and that meant the diversity of occupants was always on display.

The science officer narrowed her eyes. "I'm pretty sure he works in the Replimat."

"That's only as a front for his insidious activities," he said. "Pick another."

"Okay, her." Dax surreptitiously pointed to a robed Bajoran woman passing underneath.

"She's on a secret mission, carrying . . . isolinear rods with"—he paused to search his thoughts, eyes glittering—"the names of Cardassian double agents."

Dax couldn't restrain a laugh. "A *Bajoran*?"

"That's why you wouldn't see it coming." Jake tapped his temple.

"Oh. Well, I don't know how I missed that."

"You've got to think of these things if you want to be a mystery writer."

Dax folded her arms and leaned on the handrail, looking for the next interesting target. "I thought you wrote poetry."

He demurred. "Sure, but it never hurts to play around with other genres. What if I'm not good at poetry?"

"Then you're like most poets."

"Don't get me wrong. I like poetry, but I think making up stories is, well, more fun."

"Show me what you've got, then."

A crowd dispersed into the Promenade beneath the pair—a ship unloading its passengers into the ring. They were well dressed, the tailoring reminiscent of Dax's homeworld. Some of the newcomers turned to talk with one another, excited to be able to stretch their legs, and she noted a few spotted necks; these were her people, the Trill.

Jake pointed to the fellow in the center of the pack: a silver-haired, pale-skinned Trill dressed in pleated finery. His was a diplomatic style, emblematic of grace and propriety.

"Take that guy right there," Jake said. "He's looking for someone important, and I bet it's—"

"Etom!" Dax called down to him, and the man turned to find her. "Etom Prit!"

The older fellow's face lit up with a familiar warmth. "Well now! Jadzia Dax! I was hoping to run into you!"

"I'll be right down." Then, to Jake she added, "You were right about him looking for someone important."

Jake gave her a cocky shrug. "Call it writer's intuition."

"Be good, Jake," Dax said. "I've got to go say hi to an old friend."

"Of course. See you around."

The shops were just starting to get crowded, and Dax had to fight through a small throng to get to Prit. When she reached him, she could scarcely believe her eyes.

It'd been more than five years since she'd seen the man, but Prit hadn't changed a bit. His mahogany irises were still sharp. Kindness and smiles had worn wrinkles around his mouth and eyes. He wore his suit stiff, and not one hair was out of place on his coiffure, nor his short, white goatee.

"Etom!" She threw her arms around him, and he gave her a quick squeeze before pulling back. "What an incredible surprise! What brings you to Deep Space 9?"

Prit's gentle, age-roughened voice warmed her heart. "Oh, is this Deep Space 9? We must've taken a wrong turn!"

The other members of his cohort tittered with laughter.

"Can't a fellow pay a visit to his favorite Dax?" he asked.

"I'm not sure Curzon would appreciate you saying that."

"No, I suppose you're right. He never liked being in second place." He elbowed her. "But he's not here!" Then he turned to his small group. "Friends, I'd like you all to meet Lieutenant Commander Jadzia Dax. We go way back. Jadzia, these are the members of the Trill Shipwrights' Council. We're here to discuss a mutually beneficial arrangement with the Bajoran government."

Officially, Prit was the commerce commissioner, charged with overseeing the Trill government's economy. His job was high stress, high pressure, and mostly on the homeworld. It certainly didn't involve sticking his nose into regular trade missions.

Dax shook hands with each of the party in turn. They were an odd crew, mostly older Trill, with a few middle-aged folks. Though some of them seemed like they could stand to get out of the boardroom more often, they were generally amenable.

Dax cocked her head. "You're leading a delegation?"

"Never too old to go into the field, I say!" Prit said, spreading his hands. "Speaking of which, you're pretty far flung yourself!"

"What do you mean?"

"Feels like the edge of space out here. Middle of nowhere, wouldn't you say?"

Benjamin Sisko's rich tenor cut through the noise of the Promenade. "A lot can happen in the middle of nowhere."

Dax turned to find her commanding officer approaching, a wide grin on his face. He was dressed in his usual: a command uniform without a speck of dust on it. He was more hands-on than most captains, appreciated decorum, and always looked his best.

"Commissioner Prit," Dax said, "this is Captain Benjamin Sisko. Captain, this is Trill Commerce Commissioner Etom Prit. He's a friend of mine—and Curzon's."

The captain shook Etom's hand. "You knew the old man too?"

"It was a mixed blessing." Prit winked, and Dax batted his arm.

"Any friend of Dax is a friend of mine." Sisko folded his hands behind his back and nodded. "Welcome to DS9, Commissioner. I know the commander will give you a tour. You'll find there's more to this place than meets the eye."

Prit nodded. "There would have to be to keep Jadzia interested. What do you do out here?"

"Science officer," she said. "And I can assure you, we're never bored."

Prit's laugh took her back many years. "Of that, I have no doubt!"

"Do you have time to look around?" she asked.

"We need to get settled in and set up for talks, but I'd like to take you up on your offer." He gestured toward the way he came. "My ship, the *Steadfast*, is a fine vessel, with an even finer chef."

"Ah." Sisko raised a finger. "I don't think I've ever seen Jadzia turn down a gourmet meal."

She winked at Prit. "Hard to say no when your captain insists on cooking for you."

"You haven't complained about my gumbo even once," Sisko said.

"And I wouldn't dare." Dax held up her hands in surrender.

Prit's eyebrows knit together. "What's gumbo?"

"Unless you want to be here all day, that's the second-worst question you can ask Captain Sisko," she said.

Sisko's hands fell to his hips. "And the first?"

Dax shrugged. " 'What's baseball?' "

Prit's delegates began to move, beckoning him to come with them. "I really must be going, but I'd love to hear more about this gumbo. Captain, you're welcome to join us."

"You know"—Sisko's mischievous smile told Dax she was in for a long evening—"I think I might."

That night, they ate and drank, discussing philosophy, politics, literature, and, of course, baseball. The *Steadfast* was just as beautiful as promised, with sleek Trill design at its heart. The meal was a bounty of nostalgic flavors, not only to Jadzia, but her previous hosts. Curzon's favorite dishes were there, along with some of Torias's and Emony's.

After a rousing recount of the 1959 World Series of baseball, Sisko excused himself, wishing both Dax and Prit a fond farewell.

"Here," Prit said, passing Dax a syrupy purple bottle and a glass. "*Lidashk*. Helps with digestion."

Dax resisted the urge to pat her overfull stomach and took the liquor, pouring herself a glass. "Oh wow. Haven't seen this since the last time I visited my uncle."

"Where do you think I ordered it from? As the trade commissioner, I like to support small businesses."

Once they both poured their viscous *lida* fruit cordial, they raised a glass to each other and drank. The liquor coated Dax's mouth in potent sweetness, finishing with a toasted vanilla bite.

"I appreciated the baseball lesson," Prit said. "I never knew statisticians had a sport."

Dax laughed. "It's a little different in person. I'm sure he could show you in a holosuite—if you have another century to stick around."

"Alas, I could scarcely conjure the time to participate in this trade mission. I'm so busy nowadays."

"You've been busy my whole life—and most of Curzon's."

Prit sighed, lounging in his high-backed chair. "You're right.

I never have enough of myself to spare for the things that truly matter. I need to fix that before it bites me."

Dax set her glass on the table. She knew two things about Etom Prit: his heart was a wellspring of kindness, and he always had an agenda. No way he was required for such a minor mission.

"I got so caught up in seeing you again that I almost forgot to ask." She folded her hands across her lap. "How is your family?"

"That's why I'm here." A pained smile played across his lips. "It's Nemi."

Over Dax's long life, there were triumphs and tragedies, and Prit's granddaughter, Nemi Prit, was both. She used to hang around his office, a spunky teenager excited to see the universe. It'd been Nemi who'd encouraged Jadzia to change history and reapply after she'd washed out of the initiate program. She'd pushed Jadzia to overcome Curzon's assessment. Nemi dreamed of being joined one day, too, following in Jadzia's footsteps.

Except when it was her turn, Nemi couldn't handle the pressure. It'd been heartbreaking for Dax to watch her fail, and when Nemi needed a reference to reapply, Dax had happily obliged. However, when she washed out a second time, there was no way to fix it. Nemi Prit, who longed to be joined more than anything, would never experience it.

In the subsequent years, they grew apart. Nemi's behavior became erratic. Her failure had been traumatic, and she couldn't stand to be reminded of it by being near a joined Trill.

"She's vanished." Prit's words snapped Dax back into the moment.

"Etom, I—" Her heart raced. "Have you contacted the authorities? Do they have any leads?"

He gave her a sour look. "Not like that, I'm happy to report. No, my granddaughter took off in our family yacht, and she's flaunting our wealth with her new club."

" 'New club'?"

"Yes," Prit said. "The *Kael'tach* or something like that. She met them through a friend who also . . . who also didn't make it through the initiate program. I thought it was a support group, but they almost seem proud of their failure."

"What do they do?"

He shrugged. "Commiserate, I suppose."

"She told you all of this?"

Prit's face turned a little red. "Well, no . . . but when she disappeared, I accessed her journals. Don't look at me like that, Jadzia. I couldn't find her, and I was getting desperate."

"But you know where she is now?"

"Yes. We tracked the yacht offworld and found her at a place called the Avendawn. The staff confirmed she's there."

"What's that?" she asked.

"A casino on Argelius II."

Dax wrinkled her nose. "Oh. That doesn't sound good . . ."

"Indeed. Not a great place to occupy time with one's anger and failures."

"How bad is it?"

"I have no idea. It's her latinum; she has her own accounts." He shook his head. "It's just—those funds were supposed to secure her future, and she's wasting them on a petulant fit."

Dax didn't appreciate his characterization. Nemi was many things, but petulant wasn't one of them. Prit always had a blind spot for his granddaughter, treating her like a child well into her teenage years—for good and bad. That meant lavish gifts, with extensive restrictions. She didn't envy Nemi on that front.

"She's been through a lot," Dax said.

"I can accept that, and I'm willing to do whatever it takes to help her conquer those demons. I've procured for her the most advanced therapies out there. I've sent her back to college."

"How did that go?"

"She dropped out."

"Sorry."

"Twice. It . . . hasn't been easy. Her parents would've done a better job, rest them."

Dax poured herself another glass of *lidashk*. Prit was twenty years younger than Curzon. The morose man before her, however, seemed impossibly old, his diplomatic facade strained and exhausted. Things with Nemi must've gotten even darker after she stopped talking to Dax.

"Etom," she said, "I know this is hard, but she's an adult. You and Curzon got up to a lot of mischief when you were her age."

"That's exactly what I'm afraid of!" His glass sloshed a little over the side, and he muttered a curse. "She's been gone for weeks. She won't answer my hails."

"But, she's okay?"

"Yes. I was able to bribe a staffer into checking up on her." Same controlling Etom, unfortunately.

Dax covered her reaction with a sip from her drink. "She's going to have to get this out of her system."

"Could you go and talk to her?"

"Me . . . ? Etom, I have responsibilities here. Doctor Bashir and I have experiments in process that I can't simply abandon. Why don't you go?"

"She doesn't want to see me right now."

"But she'll be happy to see me? A joined Trill?"

He shifted uncomfortably. "There are other reasons I need to send someone else. The Avendawn isn't the sort of place a trade commissioner can visit without scrutiny. The owner is notorious, and we've had to levy sanctions against him. I have my reputation to consider. Even Nemi being seen there is . . ."

Ah, reputation. That's his game.

"So that's why you took this trade mission, isn't it?" Dax said. "To talk me into fetching Nemi."

"No! Well . . . fine, yes, but it's out of concern for her well-being. She's an impressionable young woman."

"You're talking about her like she's still a child."

Prit suddenly found his *lidashk* very interesting. "Of course I am. She's my granddaughter."

"How old is she now?"

"Twenty-one."

And still with a short leash. Dax and Curzon both knew Etom Prit to be a sweet fellow, but he could be entirely beyond reason about certain things. He'd been like a brother to Curzon—even using his business to assist in espionage and statecraft when required—but he had his faults. He often tried to badger people into shape, and clearly Nemi was no exception. She probably saw an opportunity to get away from him and took it.

Dax locked eyes with him, mustering as much sympathy as she could. He was trying so hard, but if he kept using his power to push Nemi around, it wasn't going to work. Dax knew better than anyone that Nemi couldn't be shamed into being responsible.

"Etom, listen to me. You can't save someone from being twenty-one years old."

"So . . . you won't go?"

"No. I'm sorry."

He smiled. "I understand how busy you are. I'm sure you're right. Now, let's kill off this bottle of *lidashk* in your uncle's honor."

"I wish I could help with Nemi."

"Think nothing of it. I came all this way to see you. Perhaps we can share lunch tomorrow before I leave?"

"Of course."

Dax left Prit's ship that night with a fuzzy head and the warmth of nostalgia. They'd stayed up talking about the old days until he started to fall asleep. She remembered what it was like to be eighty years young; she didn't miss it.

The silent corridors of Deep Space 9 stretched before her, a final challenge before bed. She wasn't stumble-drunk and certainly not Klingon-drunk, but the liquor tugged at her limbs, beckoning her toward soft sheets and utter darkness.

She thought of Nemi and sighed. Prit had been so good to

Jadzia when she needed him, taking her in after Curzon's rejection during the initiate program. Had it been wrong to refuse?

He was just being paranoid. That was all. Nemi would eventually get past this and find her place. She was young and bright, if a little mercurial. And brash. And impetuous.

Curzon definitely would've washed her out.

To her shame, Dax had known Nemi wouldn't make it when she'd endorsed her for a second run at the initiate program. Nemi wasn't joining material, but Dax hoped she could inspire her. Unfortunately, she'd been wrong.

A patter of footsteps interrupted Dax's thoughts, and she cast about for the source, finding no one. Perhaps she'd only imagined it, or the *lidashk* was stronger than she thought. Curzon had been a drinker, a vice that occasionally got Jadzia in trouble.

Another set of steps went thumping past, and Dax jolted in surprise. Those sounds were in the same corridor, mere centimeters from her own position. It sent a chill up her spine, and she wished she had a phaser—though she was more likely to drunkenly stun someone.

She tapped her combadge. "Dax to security."

"Go ahead, Commander," came the officer of the watch's reply.

"Are you reading any life-forms near my location?"

"Negative, sir."

That didn't actually make her feel better. Deep Space 9 could get weird; prophetic visions, subspace disruptions, or time ghosts weren't out of the question.

Dax kept her breath steady and her hands relaxed. If something was amiss, she'd be ready to meet it. After a few seconds, nothing came, and she chided herself for being so jumpy. She'd been in plenty of tough scrapes, and hearing footsteps in a corridor wasn't one of them.

She continued heading for her quarters while her heart rate returned to a reasonable pace. It'd be nice to get some sleep—exhaustion could contribute to hearing things. Her schedule was light the next day, so she could stay in, enjoy some tea, and perhaps a book. Jake had made a few recommendations.

While considering her next read, she almost ran face-first into Nemi Prit.

It'd been three years since Dax saw her, but she hadn't changed much. Her platinum hair was tied in a bun, two loose strands falling across a sun-speckled forehead. Her icy blue eyes hadn't changed at all, and her lips were quirked in a knowing smile. She wore a white gown, its seams gently flowing at her sides.

"Nemi!" Dax blinked. "What are you—I, uh . . ."

Her friend smiled, but the light was gone. Nemi seemed to stare through Dax, hands clasping and unclasping at her sides. Her right eye began to twitch, and a single teardrop of blood emerged, flowing down her cheek. Nemi listed on her feet, then fell backward, robes billowing like a pale jellyfish.

Dax went to grab her, but all she found was air. Nemi was gone, and Dax was left in the corridor, stunned and alone.

"You've already lost something precious to you," came a low, male voice.

Dax turned to find a man bearing down upon her like an ill wind. She'd recognize that swept-back blond hair, stern brow, and predator's eyes anywhere. Her insides writhed at the very sight of him, and she took a step back. Dax had never wanted anything to do with this man ever again; she didn't even like thinking of him.

Joran Dax—the murderer, and former host to her symbiont.

"What do you want?" she asked.

"A memory." His voice echoed throughout the corridors.

The lights around her began to flicker, several of them going out. Shadows fell over the hall, distant at first but coming closer. Raw fear coursed through Dax, but she held fast. Joran wasn't real. He couldn't hurt her.

The rumble of the station rose in pitch, becoming a whine, a terrible sound like a drill. Joran smiled as the darkness engulfed them both. Dead whispers carried on the air, unintelligible and longing, reaching for Dax like drowning victims.

And then, nothing but an empty corridor.

She calmed her quivering breath and swallowed before straightening and smoothing down her uniform. Joran Dax was a part of her, but dead—a bad dream, a memory. There was nothing to be afraid of—

—while she was awake.

2

Elevated

Rather than wait until morning, Jadzia Dax headed to the infirmary. She didn't want to suffer through a night without answers, and hallucinations could be a sign of a serious problem with potentially lethal side effects.

"Commander Dax!" blustered the sleepy Bolian nurse as Dax came dragging into the infirmary. "Are you all right? What brings you here?"

"I need to check on my isoboramine levels," she replied. "Not feeling too good."

Isoboramine was the neurotransmitter responsible for keeping her body in sync with her symbiont. Trill that had a sharp drop in their levels often experienced hallucinations. Once, her levels got so low they almost had to remove the symbiont—which would've killed her.

"All right," said the nurse. "We'll have a look, and I'll let the doctor know you're here."

Dax frowned. "We don't have to wake him. I'm sure Julian values his sleep."

The vertical ridge of the Bolian's blue face split her smile. "Nonsense. That's his job. We'll make it easy for him by getting your vitals before he gets here."

The nurse directed Dax to a biobed, did some prep work, then paged Doctor Julian Bashir. He'd been a close friend of Dax's ever since Starfleet started running Deep Space 9 for the Bajorans, and constantly fussed over her whenever something was wrong. Sometimes he gave her the calm words she needed; other times he was outright annoying.

At the moment, her hallucinations were relatively minor. She'd had worse ones before her *zhian'tara*, when she'd discovered the existence of Joran. With those isoboramine fluctuations, she experienced violent outbursts and constant visions. She'd only been able to conquer it by accepting the murderer as part of herself—even the parts she hated, like his temper.

One vision wasn't the sort of thing to treat as a medical emergency, but Bashir would almost certainly make a big deal out of it. As predicted, he came rushing from his quarters, striding into the infirmary like he was prepping for emergency surgery.

Bashir was on the short side for a human male, slim with light olive skin and carefully coifed hair. He was sharp and maddeningly observant, with a pair of sympathetic brown eyes that caught the light like jewels.

"You know, I was having the most incredible dream," he said, coming to her side at the biobed.

"Sorry to wake you." Dax sat up, resting her elbows on her knees.

He smiled. "Not to worry. I wanted to check on our experiments anyway."

"In the middle of the night?"

"You're here. I'm here. What's stopping us?"

"A hangover, pretty soon," she said.

"Now that's just a Wednesday for you, so what else is the matter?"

Dax recounted the story of her vision, starting with her meal on the *Steadfast*. Bashir listened intently, occasionally taking notes on his padd. He took an interest in every detail; his interview was exhaustive.

"Well," he said, passing a hand scanner over her forehead. "Your isoboramine is a little depressed, but not by much. Frankly, it's your blood alcohol content that worries me."

"Ha, ha, Julian."

"I'm not joking. Given your neurotransmitter dip, the *lidashk* could've played a role in your vision. It contains several hallucinogenic compounds that might've built up and interacted."

She was already exhausted, and this line of inquiry sounded more exhausting. "I've gotten drunk with Klingons."

"Be that as it may, we're going to keep you a few hours for observation. Don't want to miss something important." He tapped his chin absentmindedly. "And I think we'll give you a dose of benzocyatizine to keep things stabilized."

She frowned. "A few hours?"

"You're already in bed. Perhaps use the time to catch up on sleep? You never get enough, and you're running yourself ragged."

"I napped too much when I was an old man."

He dimmed the lights. "Doctor's orders, Jadzia. I'll be by to check on you in a few hours. Call the nurse if you need anything."

She nodded, a little disappointed that she had no more answers than she had come in with. "Okay. Thank you, Julian."

"It'll be all right."

When he left, she felt no better. She couldn't get the image of Nemi from her mind, nor could she explain the profound darkness she sensed swirling inside. When fatigue finally swept her to unconsciousness, she fell into a deep sleep.

It was a lovely day at the Prit estate for moping over one's failures—bright and clear with almost nothing on the agenda.

Jadzia had spent her morning out on the back patio, sunning and enjoying the processional of fluffy clouds. She'd replicated a swimsuit and sunglasses, along with a large fruit drink. She lounged atop a wavy chair, periodically snoozing.

Etom Prit's mansion had a view that was close to perfect. Before her, a long pool of pristine blue water gave way to rolling hills of grain. Snow-capped mountains crested the horizon, fringed at the base with a beard of dark forest. From the other side of the house, she'd be able to see the lights of the distant capital, inviting her to participate in all the exciting activities she'd denied herself as an initiate.

Her past year employed by Etom Prit's shipping company had gone well, and for all her hard work, he'd invited her to visit his family over vacation. Prit took a personal interest in Jadzia, unable to resist his paternal instincts. Sometimes, his doting and interfering bothered her, but she tried to take it as a compliment that he considered her a second granddaughter. She was highly regarded, impactful, and appreciated, three things she'd never felt during her disastrous time in the initiate program.

A program that was in the process of passing judgment on her for a second time.

She'd been a fool to reapply; there was no point. No one ever got readmitted, and even if she did, would she still want to go back? The first time had been such a grueling ordeal that she couldn't imagine doing it again. But then, she also couldn't imagine giving up on joining.

"Jadz!" a young woman called for her, muffled by the walls of the house.

She closed her eyes. Jadzia didn't feel like being cheered up, and she wasn't keen for another pep talk from the fifteen-year-old Nemi.

Prit's granddaughter had become her shadow since Jadzia started working in the office. Nemi's parents had passed a couple of years ago and she had few friends, so the young woman looked to Jadzia for companionship. They went on camping trips and explored the nearby forest, and Jadzia taught her how to identify fungi and survive in the wild. Nemi became obsessed with her overnight.

The same Nemi had pushed her back into the initiate program. At her urging, Jadzia wasted all that time filling out the forms and going to interviews again. Of course, none of those efforts mattered, since the Symbiosis Commission was going to reject her. It was foolish to assume otherwise. Her personalized dismissal by Curzon Dax made clear that Jadzia was nothing special.

"Jadz . . ." came Nemi's voice, directly behind her lounger.

"Yes?" she asked, never opening her eyes.

"Did you hear me calling?"

"Yes."

"And you just decided to lie there?"

"Yes."

"Don't you want to know why I was calling you?"

Jadzia smiled at Nemi's forming exasperation. "Yes."

"And how were you going to find out?"

"My strategy was to lie here until you came and told me. Mission accomplished. I'm a genius."

"Get dressed," Nemi said. "I just talked to Pawpaw, and we're going out to dinner."

Jadzia took a deep breath, savoring the fresh mountain air. "Is there any way that you two can go without me?"

"You're moping."

"I'm fine."

"You've been moping since you got here."

"I think I've earned the right to do that."

"You haven't until they reject you."

"I did those humiliating admission interviews, then I did your grandfather's quarterly forecasts. Now, I'm on vacation." She absently pawed the nearby table for her drink. "There's no force on this planet that will get me out of this chair."

Nemi hefted the lounger from the back, and Jadzia went sliding into the pool along with the cushions.

Frigid water engulfed her, stealing her breath away. Her sun-warmed skin went so cold she nearly leaped out of the pool. She broke the surface, sputtering to the sound of Nemi's wild laughter.

"You little monster!" Jadzia splashed at her, but the teenager ducked out of range.

Nemi was wearing shorts and a puffy cream chemise—not exactly pool clothes. Jadzia sloshed out of the water after her, grinning viciously, and Nemi took off with a shriek. She was going to soak this kid.

Jadzia chased her through Prit's statue garden, into the conservatory, past the study. Nemi, wearing shoes, was a lot faster, but Jadzia was determined to get her revenge. Nemi burst through the kitchen door, and Jadzia came sliding through after.

Colorful streamers hung from the ceiling in curling spirals, and a huge red cake stood atop the kitchen island. Iced across its side was the word *Congratulations*.

"Surprise!" Etom Prit shouted, and Jadzia nearly slipped onto her rump.

She hugged her wet skin and looked around in shivering confusion. This had to be about her application, but it couldn't be. That was a silly dream. Only kids like Nemi believed in that stuff.

"What's happening?" Jadzia asked.

Nemi took her by the shoulders, beaming. "They accepted your application. You did it."

"I did?" She almost didn't want to believe it. This was too large, too beautiful a truth to exist in her reality. "How did . . . you know?"

"I have my ways. Computer, towel, hot." Prit fetched a fuzzy cloth fresh out of the replicator and draped it around Jadzia.

The seeping warmth was almost as surprising as the cold, and it broke down a barrier in her. She'd wanted this for so long. She'd fought and fought, and when Curzon Dax took it away from her, she'd given up. Somehow, Jadzia had gone from the limitless child who dreamed of sharing the ancient wisdom of a symbiont to an office drone. It was a gentle nightmare, and one that could've haunted her until the end of her days.

But looking into Nemi's shining eyes, seeing her exuberant smile—she was finally awake again. Her life had been wrenched back into its rightful shape, and Jadzia found herself overwhelmed by the chance she'd been granted.

She tried to speak, but the words wouldn't come through trembling lips. She wanted it to be true.

As if Nemi read her mind, she said, "Yes, really."

Prit patted her back through the towel. "Hey, there, now. No need to cry."

Jadzia wanted to tell him that she wasn't crying, but all that came out was a broken sob and a sniffle. Nemi rushed in and hugged her tightly, pressing her cheek to Jadzia's and comingling their tears.

"I'm so proud of you!" she cried. "You did it! You made history!"

Jadzia slowly slipped to the floor in the arms of her friend. Nemi held on to her, whispering encouragements and smiling until she finally realized—

She was going to make it. No matter what, Jadzia was going to become joined.

Jadzia Dax opened her eyes, her first thoughts of Etom and Nemi Prit. The commissioner was genuinely frightened for his granddaughter. She'd been wrong to turn him down.

The bustle of the Promenade's morning foot traffic filtered into the treatment room, and she sat up with a start. How long had she been out? It felt as though no time had passed at all.

"Rise and shine," Bashir said, fetching his scanner and coming to her side. "I'm looking at the results from the night, and there are no anomalies. Healthy, deep sleep."

Dax smacked away her dry mouth, head cottony with a hangover. "I was out cold. What time is it?"

"Close to noon. I let you rest."

"Julian!"

"You needed it," he said. "And it gave me a chance to tabulate the data from the biomatter matrices we set up."

"I thought we were going to go over those together."

"Jadzia, you need to relax. You're taking on more responsibilities than you have time for. I called the captain, and he cleared you for leave."

"Why wouldn't he? It was my day off."

"All I'm saying is that you should let me take care of the matrices for a while. I'm grateful for the collaboration, I am—but I'd like to see you exercise a little self-care."

Doctor Bashir was the epitome of the human aphorism "Kill them with kindness." Once he dug in, he could be unbearable. If she argued with him, she'd be there all day, so she said what she always did when she needed him to stop talking.

"All right. You make a good point."

"Good."

"Were you in here all night?" she asked.

"Part of it. I had trouble getting back to sleep, and I hoped some coding would do the trick." He shrugged. "Alas."

He may have said he was there to check the experiment, but Dax knew him too well to believe that. He had a soft spot for her, favoring her with all sorts of attention. If she was in a treatment bed, he'd be nearby.

"Doctor Bashir," the nurse's voice came over his combadge.

"Go ahead," he replied.

"There's a gentleman out here asking if Commander Dax is present. He said his name is Etom Prit."

Dax kicked herself. She hadn't told Prit that she wouldn't make their lunch date.

"Please, send him in," she said.

Prit came bustling through the door in his business attire, face overcast with worry. "Jadzia!"

"I'm so sorry, Etom," she said. "How did you know where to find me?"

He idly wrung his hands as he spoke. "I got worried when you didn't make our appointment. Since our lunch date was nearby,

I thought I'd check the infirmary—and here you are! What happened? Are you all right?"

She gave him a reassuring smile. "I'm fine. Just . . . exhausted is all."

Prit's eyebrows knit. "I'm so sorry. I never should've added to your burdens with Nemi's nonsense. Surely you're right, and my granddaughter will come to her senses."

Joran's voice whispered in her memories. *You've already lost something precious to you.*

"Etom, I—" Dax began, trying to figure out how to explain her vision to him. Joran was a secret that few knew, and she liked it to keep it that way. Worse still, her vision brought with it a feeling of violence, of evil. She couldn't tell him what she'd experienced, or he'd do something rash.

"I'm worried about Nemi," Dax said. "I think I want to go check it out."

"You don't have to do that," Prit said. "I didn't come to guilt you, and you're here sick."

"I have a feeling that Nemi . . ."

Prit's eyes locked onto hers, and she saw a little of his old spark.

"She could probably use a friend," Dax finished. "I'll make plans to visit the Avendawn. I've got some time off."

"Hi, Doctor Julian Bashir," the human cut in, shaking Prit's hand. "Do you mind if I have a quick word with my patient?"

"Uh, not at all," Prit said, gesturing toward the door. "Shall I wait outside?"

Bashir clasped his hands together. "Yes, thank you. It'll only take a moment and then she's all yours."

As soon as Prit was out of the room, Bashir said, "Nemi was the girl from your visions, yes? The one you told me about?"

"Yes."

"Do you really think it's wise to chase a . . . a hallucination?"

She looked into his eyes, wishing she could explain what it was like to be joined, to know truths from other lives. "Julian, I have to. There's something going on, and I won't forgive myself if I ignore it."

"How do you know it's related, and not simply your subconscious assembling it out of nearby stimuli?"

He might be right. It could've been a drunken dream caused by any number of interactions. She'd felt guilty at refusing Prit's request. After all, she owed so much to the Prit family.

These dreams couldn't be ignored. She needed to investigate. As a science officer, Jadzia Dax believed in facts, but as a joined Trill, her vision was important. She didn't need hard evidence to chase this down. A warning from Joran was enough. Bashir would just have to understand.

He pressed on. "And it's probably nothing. As your doctor, I have to object to this course of action."

She regarded him coolly, lips pressed together in annoyance.

"Julian, I'm going to a casino resort. You told me to take a vacation. You don't get to tell me how."

"But—"

"And you said it yourself. You don't need my help with the matrices. You can handle them on your own."

"That's not quite what I had in mind when—"

"Wish me luck." She smiled and squeezed him on the shoulder before hopping off the bed. "And it's 'probably nothing,' right?"

Without giving him a chance to object, Dax strode out to the infirmary foyer. Prit stood listlessly near the intake console. He turned to her, eyebrows raised in expectation.

"Etom," she said, "I'll talk to Nemi. I don't know what I was thinking, turning you down. You'd never do that to me."

"Oh, my dear, I appreciate it, but are you going to be all right?"

"Yes, but I'm not going in there blind. I want to talk to her friends in the *Kael'tach*. Do you know who they are?"

He took a deep breath and nodded, resolute. "I'll send over everything I have."

Dax's cabin on the commercial cruiser *Amity* was anything but comfortable, with just enough room to sit in bed and read. There were no amenities, since few pleasure vessels departed Deep Space 9. The worst part was the light scent of milled metal and body odor from some previous resident. She already missed her quarters back on the station.

She'd packed light for the trip, just a duffel with a few changes of clothes, a padd, her tricorder, and a phaser. She hoped she wouldn't need the weapon, but her time in Starfleet had proven one thing: a phaser was always handy.

She eventually had a transfer to Argelius II, though for the moment, she had nothing but time. Dax activated her padd, pulling up the information that Prit had sent over on the *Kael'tach*.

Or in the common tongue, *The Elevated.*

Dax didn't know why that phrase bothered her, but the words had a synesthetic effect, like someone running a finger up her spine. Her world seemed palpably darker just thinking about them, and she tried to imagine the sort of group that might convene under such an appellation.

Dax visited the *Kael'tach*'s online presence, but found only a logo with a stylized eye and feather. Nothing she tried would get her past security. Without the proper credentials, it'd be impossible to proceed, not to mention illegal. Dax was looking into the *Kael'tach* for a friend, not as a Starfleet officer, so her hands were tied.

The logo had a small motto at the bottom: *Lives realigned. Potential realized.*

It looked like a recruitment agency. Prit had said the members were all washouts; Dax imagined herself finding this group after being cast down by Curzon. She'd been so bitter and broken in those days, having suffered through the traumas of the initiate program and the Symbiosis Commission, only to be thrown out.

Curzon had tried to rob her of her potential out of lust. She could still remember the guilt in his expression, the shame in his posthumous admission during her *zhian'tara.*

"You were so lovely . . ."

He'd infantilized her, berated her, destroyed her self-respect, all because he "loved" her. Curzon didn't think of it as sexual harassment, but he'd ejected her from the opportunity of a lifetime because he couldn't control himself. Jadzia had no other words for it. If she'd known the truth back then, she would've signed on with the *Kael'tach* in a heartbeat. Maybe it was a support group?

Her padd contained the preliminary dossiers Prit compiled on Nemi's friends: basic, publicly accessible facts, but exceedingly thorough. Prit had been an ally of Curzon's, occasionally using his vast holdings in service of the state's diplomatic intrigues. Just like Curzon, Prit knew people who could get all sorts of information.

Dax tapped through the pictures of Nemi's friends. Aia Keteel was a promising biomed student most of the way to a doctorate. Seval Gep had a minor warp-dynamics breakthrough to his name and dreamed of being a ship designer. Bani Moxern was an accomplished soldier, with a valorous decoration from the Federation.

These young people were rising stars, exemplars in their fields the way Jadzia Dax was in hers. It took a special sort of person to become an initiate, so it wasn't surprising that they were all accomplished. Washouts were often snapped up by prestigious institutions—the Symbiosis Commission even had a career placement office to help take the sting out of failure. That was how Jadzia met Prit before she was joined—he collected Curzon's cast-offs for his company.

Prit's dossiers only went so far. They didn't say how Nemi's friends failed, or when or why. They only contained a few former addresses, contact information, and employment records. Prit managed to get Aia Keteel's transcript somehow, and Dax found that disconcerting, but not out of character. The man knew how to dig.

From time to time, Dax served as a field docent, evaluating initiates as Curzon had. A failure typically ended their chances of being joined. Her decision would alter the course of an initiate's entire life, so the Symbiosis Commission gave docents all the tools they needed to research a candidate.

Dax still had her field-docent access. It wasn't technically against the rules.

She connected to the database to see if she could find the reasons for their dismissals. Seval Gep had made a pass at his docent, and Bani Moxern had attempted suicide—an instant disqualifier for someone about to be trusted with another life. Aia Keteel hadn't been dismissed by a docent; an abnormality in her abdominal cavity *might* preclude her from being joined. Dax already knew why Nemi had been dismissed—abusing stimulants to get a neural edge.

When Dax got to the placement section for all of them, it was blank. There were no listings of current employment, and no psychiatric screenings for well-being, either.

It'd been horrible for Jadzia to be kicked out by Curzon, and the only thing that made it bearable was the help she'd gotten. Etom and Nemi saved her life. None of Nemi's friends appeared to have received anything.

The lights flickered overhead, and Joran's cold anger leaked into her thoughts.

Kael'tach.

She brought up their info on her padd one more time, staring at the logo. The eye and feather didn't spur any memories. The name bothered her though. The longer she looked, the more the twin pressures of rage and indignation built inside. She was always so calm. Why couldn't she get control of her feelings?

The light flickered again, disrupting her thoughts.

Dax waited in silence for things to get spooky, but they remained cramped and vaguely smelly instead. She returned to her research, continuing late into the ship's evening. Curzon used to spend hours poring over dossiers of diplomatic opponents and stakeholders. She brought that training to bear on Nemi and her companions, trying to assemble a picture of their relationships until she was finally exhausted.

The room darkened, and she thought she could make out the distant strains of a piano—Joran's instrument. Maybe it was an electrical issue, or perhaps she'd been awake too long. One thing was certain: Dax wasn't in the mood to play games with a ghost. She took out the small benzocyatizine injector, placed it to her neck, and shot a dose into her bloodstream.

She hated this feeling—her uncertainty and anger. Joran probably didn't know anything, but he liked to cause trouble. He was a vicious manipulator in life. Dax hadn't known about him before last year, when he'd emerged in her consciousness through hallucinations and fury. That's when she learned that she'd been lied to by the Symbiosis Commission.

They'd concealed his existence and installed a memory block in the Dax symbiont to silence him. When that block started to deteriorate, Jadzia thought she'd lost her mind. Her inability to acknowledge Joran's existence desynchronized her with her symbiont, to near-lethal effect. Understanding her past hosts was just as critical to the symbiont's survival as eating and drinking. Joran was a part of her. She'd come to accept that, just as she accepted and forgave Curzon's sins.

Within a few minutes, the benzocyatizine stabilized her thumping heart, and sleep beckoned her to put the padd down. She had a long trip to Argelius II, and it was probably best to catch up on her rest.

This was, after all, supposed to be a vacation.

3

Shore Leave

The Argelian chief city of Luminox sparkled into being before Dax. Never was there a more magnificent introduction to a place than by transporter. A splendid gem of arts, music, dancing, and far more hedonistic pastimes, Luminox was a welcoming port long trod by Starfleet. Dax found herself in the center of the city's Marble Hill Plaza, overlooking an emerald bay. From the rise, a lush public garden spread before her, its fountains and foliage giving way to the twisting city streets beyond. The Avendawn rested in the distant waters, its flowing alabaster form illuminated by lights.

Of course they'd beamed her into the wrong part of town. She hated traveling private.

Dax took a deep breath of fresh air, shouldered her duffel, and began the long walk through the city. The sea breeze braced her tired heart as she made her way down the cobblestone streets. Tourists wandered from one site to the next, enjoying the food, drink, and one another, filling the evening with laughter. Colorful lanterns hung from multifoil arches, and Dax stopped to admire the intricate carvings on many of the columns.

The whole planet seemed to breathe with life, from the alabaster gaming halls to romantic parks teeming with floral delights. Dax stopped to purchase a pack of Argelian sweet buns, her mouth watering at the thought of the warm, honey-flaked dough. She'd scarcely paid for them before she dipped into the bag for one.

Buttery sugar crust broke over her tongue before she'd even tasted the moist, chewy center. She intended the sweet treats to last the whole walk, but they didn't survive a block. With gratitude kindled in her heart, Dax was fortunate to have a long stroll ahead of her on a near-perfect night.

The closer she got to the water, the less people were wearing. Moonlight bathers packed the beaches by the seaside cafes, frolicking in the temperate streams where they rejoined the ocean. Glamorous bars rose from the rocky shoals, bonfires aglow and spits fully loaded. The scent of grilled meat drifted on the salty breeze, and Dax cursed her stomach for not having more room. Luminoxi cuisine focused on takeout, and their beach breads came highly recommended. She was considering picking something up for later when she arrived before the majesty of the Avendawn.

Up close, the casino would stun a jaded architect. The gambling den was built from the bones of an old, beached star freighter, heavily modified. White sails stretched from its sides like fish fins, underlit with flowing gold. Glimmering stripes ran across its hull in jewel tones, demanding attention. The pier to the ship was equally festooned with flame-lit lamps of all sizes, and shops promising everything from enticing liquors to priceless antiques (priced reasonably) lined the edges.

It woke her old soul, looking at the place. Late-night hands of *t'Sang* with Klingon friends had been a part of Curzon's life—even now she could not resist a match. Only a few of Dax's past hosts enjoyed adding currency to the equation, but Jadzia loved it. True risk with real consequences gave the game an edge she could scarcely avoid. Starfleet provided plenty of thrills, but there were long streaks of boredom. Gambling, on the other hand, was never dull.

Dax had latinum and leave. She'd make this a fun vacation, and Joran could stuff it.

She took in the sights on the pier, noting that many celebrants were dressed in formal attire. Her Starfleet uniform was comfortable, but too functional in the sea of high fashion. It wouldn't stop her from getting into the premises—a Starfleet officer was always welcome on Argelius—but she wanted to be upgraded at the gaming tables.

A diaphanous gown fluttered in one of the windows, arresting her gaze. Drapes of pale, waxy fabric faded to violet like the petals of an *enkeela* flower. An elegant neckline circled to a plunging back, with shoulders adorned by twin crests of iridescent feathers.

The right dress could stun a Dax—albeit for different reasons. Emony would come alive thinking of the way it flowed. Curzon would see a woman wearing a garment like that as a rival, a romantic interest, or both. For Jadzia, it was the way the clothes made her feel.

Dax went in and chatted with the designer while they fitted and replicated a gown for her. It set her back a bit of latinum, but only a week's winnings at *tongo*. After adding on a matching clutch and heels, she thanked the artisan and had the dress sent to the Avendawn under her name.

Duffel in hand, she walked the rest of the distance to the fabulous casino, passing beneath its coruscating arches into the lobby rotunda. Hanging gardens drooped overhead, vines bursting with pink flowers. Nautical blues intertwined with cream and gold in the floor's spiraling mosaic. A long, swept wing desk occupied one wall, staffed by smiling Argelians in flashy, embroidered uniforms. Jets of water leaped overhead in wide arcs, shot from fountains hidden among statuary.

This was going to be expensive.

Dax had to stop thinking like that. She wasn't a hundred years old anymore; it was time to live a little.

She checked in and ate dinner at the palatial grill, enjoying succulent meats, roasted and arranged atop bitter leaves with a sweet chutney. It would've been fun to bring Kira here. The major didn't like gambling as much as Dax, but she certainly knew how to enjoy a meal. Like Jake Sisko, Kira was a keen observer of people, and always had the funniest things to say.

Well fed, Dax visited her room to see what her latinum had gotten her.

Not as much as she'd hoped.

For all the soaring opulence of the lobby, her room was small. The casino wouldn't make money if people sequestered themselves, so they designed the quarters to be boring. At least there was a balcony where Dax could take in the view of the bay. Pleasure craft raced up and down the waves in the moonlight.

The Avendawn staff had left her dress on the bed, boxed in enameled chartreuse with a dark green ribbon. She opened it, pulling aside the tissue paper and scintillating ribbons to find the treasure wrapped inside. Her breath caught once more, and she held the garment aloft to admire it.

In a scrape, Dax was unstoppable with a Klingon *bat'leth*. In this arena of cards and dice, the dress would provide her a lethal edge.

Curzon had been a skilled manipulator. Joran was less subtle, but much more craven. Either one of those men would've killed to have Jadzia's advantages. She went into the bathroom to freshen up, applying an orchid-purple lipstick to set off her blue eyes and brown spots. She stuffed her clutch with the tricorder, though the phaser wouldn't fit.

A scanner was always useful. A weapon? Not so much.

Dax stopped in front of the mirror on the way out to admire her handiwork. Satisfied, she blew herself a kiss and headed out.

The gaming floor was a wide disc of clear material, through which the waters of the bay were visible. Undersea gardens waved in the currents, their enchanting depths lit with a symphony of colors. Machines and tables jingled with the clash of chips and merriment, dreams made and bank accounts broken. Chandeliers dangled from above, long rods of pure light spilling over the scene.

Dax headed to the cashier, trading some of her latinum for a decent stack of chips. If she was going to succeed in finding Nemi, she would have to take on the high-stakes tables.

Walking through the aisles of games, she quickly learned the limits of her budget. The starting bids at some of the tables were outrageous, but she should've expected that—the daughter of Trade Commissioner Prit would choose somewhere expensive.

Dax was perusing the high-roller territory when she located her quarry.

Nemi was transformed from the woman Dax once knew. Wan elegance replaced bubbly exuberance. Dark liner traced her icy eyes, and her platinum hair was cut short. She was sheathed in a knockout black skirt and strapless top, which showed off her long trails of Trill spots. Judging from her stack of chips, she was cleaning out the other players at the *tongo* table.

Dax felt guilty for not knowing Nemi even played *tongo*. It'd been too long since they'd spoken.

Nemi leaned over and whispered something to the Andorian next to her, and he laughed so hard he nearly spilled his drink. She shrugged and smiled with a languid energy Dax had never seen in her friend. As a teenager, Nemi was equal parts silly and melodramatic. The woman before Dax was more like a noble, commanding the world with her magnetic presence.

The assembly of players groaned as Nemi tossed down a hand, claiming the pot. The Ferengi running the game gleefully announced her victory, grabbing the house rake. As she reached down to scoop up her winnings, Nemi made eye contact with Dax.

It was an acknowledgment—nothing more. Nemi went on about her business, and if she felt any affinity for Dax, it was lost in translation. Dax walked to the table's leather rail and stood behind Nemi's chair.

"Hey," Dax said, starting off with a smile, "long time."

"Jadzia Dax," Nemi replied, affect flat, "what a surprise."

Despite the dismissive tone, Dax kept her polite mask in place. It hurt to be greeted like that by the girl who used to run into her arms. It'd been a long time since Dax had stayed with the Prit family, but Nemi was always the highlight. They'd discussed so many things, been inseparable.

In that moment, however, Dax might as well have been a stranger.

She waited for Nemi to show any other response, but the action continued around the table, and her eyes returned to the game. The other players were good, if a bit surly at their bad luck: a lovestruck Grazerite couple, the Andorian with striking cerulean skin, and unexpectedly, a Klingon. The Grazerites were too distracted with each other's affections to be effective, and the Klingon's space was littered with empty goblets of bloodwine. That left Nemi and the Andorian.

The venture cards in the market were balanced—all growth—so the index was on the rise. The Grazerites indexed and acquired small margins—safe maneuvers, but hardly profitable. The Andorian evaded, keeping a soft hand on his holdings while he waited for the market to turn sour. The round came to the Klingon, whose portfolio was so burdened with high-risk investments that he had no capital.

"It'd be wise to retreat," Nemi said, pressing her fingertips together. "Maybe sell a few—"

"A warrior does not fall to an accountant," he slurred, pointing at her with a sharp-taloned finger.

Her eyes sparkled. "Throats are cut in more places than the battlefield. Fight me, and learn."

"The gentleman will state his action," prompted the Ferengi dealer.

"My action?" He stood, heaped his remaining pile of chips onto the golden tray, and shouted "*Confront!*" so loudly that patrons at the nearby tables jolted.

Nemi spread her cards on the felt—a full consortium.

"*Damn your spots!*" he bellowed, raising his most recent goblet like he was about to throw his wine. He then thought better of it, sniffed the cup, downed the contents, and proceeded to wordlessly slouch off in the direction of more fruitful pursuits.

Nemi pulled her earnings in, stacking them neatly into marbled-resin towers. She kept each one precisely sorted, rapid-counting them in the way Dax had seen Ferengi dealers do. That was a fairly advanced table technique, and Dax had never mastered it.

Dax decided to try speaking to her friend again. "That was well played!"

"It was," came Nemi's curt response as she finished arranging her winnings.

The Andorian barked a crass laugh.

Dax gave him a poisonous look, then returned her attentions to her friend. "Nemi . . . I've come to find you."

She nodded. "Well done. And you can now tell Pawpaw you did."

"I'm not here because of him. I'm here because of you. We're all worried."

"Yes, as you can see, I'm doing terribly." Nemi checked her thick stack of thousand-credit chips. Her winnings would dwarf any pot at Quark's.

Dax looked into her friend's eyes, trying not to be betrayed by the dismissal. It wasn't working. "Surely we can catch up? You can tell me what's . . . what's been going on with you."

"Players, ante up," called the Ferengi dealer.

Nemi's polite veneer vanished. "There's only one group of people that I want to talk to right now, and they're sitting at this table. If you'll excuse me."

She returned to play, tossing in a few chips, along with a tip for the dealer. The others at the table eyed the pair of Trill women, but rejoined the festivities when it was their turn. Dax stood by, nursing her wounds and wishing for all the world she had a drink.

The Klingon's space was empty, save for the depleted goblets of high-proof bloodwine. A member of the waitstaff descended upon the mess immediately, scooping the cups into a large bin. When it was clean, Dax sat down across from Nemi and stacked her chips on the felt.

"New player joining the market," said the Ferengi, flipping her a marker.

"Jadzia"—there was a warning in Nemi's eyes—"I'm not going to play nice."

Dax looked at her own tiny stack versus the mountain of currency at the table—her vacation fund would last her three hands in this game. If she lost two of them, she'd have to quit, because there wouldn't be any leverage against the competition and she'd just get bullied out of the market.

She tossed a nauseating amount of chips into the pot—the minimum bet. "Let's play."

The Ferengi slid her a pair of cards to get her portfolio started, and around the wheel they went. The Grazerites, roused by Dax's appearance, ceased focusing on each other to aggressively acquire moderate-risk ventures. The Andorian went big on a high-buy in the sweet spot. Dax had only picked up a small margin before Nemi's declaration came.

"Confront," she said.

Despite the cold-hearted nature of *tongo*, it was bad form to confront a startup player. It took time to build a diverse portfolio, and Dax's little ventures could scarcely hold their own. She could index the market and hope to get lucky, or she could evade, and let Nemi take a slice of her meager war chest.

Of course, if the dice came down on Dax's side, she'd take a sizable chunk of Nemi's money and get off to a good start.

"Index the market," Dax said.

Nemi cocked an eyebrow, but kept quiet as the dealer passed Dax the dice. Their polished bone inlays glistened in her hands, and she blew on them before tossing them onto the table.

The result couldn't have been worse, and Dax got to watch in agony as her old friend snapped up her ante—and her ventures. It was only the first hand, and she already had to buy back in.

The dealer took her chips, smiling politely. "We have some twenty-cred *tongo* tables over there, you know," he said, gesturing with his head.

Dax took her cards and cleared her throat. "No, I'm fine here, thank you."

"Maybe you shouldn't spend it all in one place." Nemi casually ran a finger up the sides of her rectangular chips, producing a set of satisfying clacks. Her glare was like ice. "Spread the fun out a little—somewhere else."

Dax looked Nemi in the eyes, trying to piece together some reason for the animosity. She'd come expecting resistance, but nothing like outright hatred. Weren't they still friends? Dax had been looking forward to talking with her, reconnecting after so long.

She refused to believe this was the Nemi she once knew. There had to be something wrong here.

Which meant Joran was *right.*

Nemi took a sip of her wine. "Seriously, you don't have the latinum to play at the big kids' table. Just looking out for you, *Jadz.*"

Dax fixed her with a flinty gaze as the other players received their cards. "I have enough to take *you* on."

Nemi blew a breath out, suppressing a laugh. "I'm not even going to notice adding your chips to my pile."

Around the wheel again, and this time, fortune favored Dax. The Grazerites had taken on too much risk, making them ripe for forced retreats and hostile takeovers. Dax acquired like a bloodthirsty Klingon, startling them out of their ante with large bets.

She didn't have to confront Nemi directly—not until she'd cleaned out a few of the other players at the table.

Over the course of an hour, Dax amassed a small fortune of safe investments, staying out of Nemi's way when she could. She employed the empathy of an accomplished diplomat and her lifetime love of math, skewering her fellow players whenever possible.

The Andorian was the first to fall, which surprised Dax. She'd taken him to be a shrewd player, but he often missed solid strategies. After Nemi eliminated one of the Grazerites, the other one followed, leaving the table empty but for her and Jadzia.

Dax had done well playing against the others, but Nemi was in a class of her own. She whittled down Dax's holdings, always one step ahead. She had a preternatural sense of Dax's cards, like Nemi could see right through her portfolio.

After a particularly tense exchange, a waiter came to take drink orders. The house was doing well off Dax's duel, and they wished to send compliments.

"Vulcan port," Nemi said.

Part of Dax didn't want to drink while she was exhausted, stressed, and in an isoboramine dip. Unfortunately, that part didn't include her mouth, which said, "Klingon bloodwine. Um, please."

That's when she noticed Nemi's friend Bani Moxern out of the corner of her eye. He'd taken up a spot on a couch some distance away, watching the action unfold at her table. From where he was sitting, he could've glimpsed Dax's cards once or twice.

"Hey," Nemi said. "Are we going to finish this?"

Dax had to be careful not to tip her hand when she fetched her cards. "Absolutely."

The wheel spun, and it was time to act. Nemi acquired with everything she had, going for the all-out assault. She intended to buy up the board, choking off any avenues of decent betting. It was an old style of play, flashy and bullying—and heavy on investment. That left Dax's ventures little room for growth, but the potential to pick up a lot of money if she won.

Dax squared her cards and put them face down. "Index."

The dealer passed her the dice, and she rolled, picking up two more cards at high risk. Her heart skipped a beat as the first card hit her hand.

Nemi flicked her fingers at Dax's chips. "How much have you got there? Twenty-five? Twenty-six large?"

"Thereabout"—Dax smirked—"if you can take it."

Nemi pushed her pile of chips forward. "Converting reserves

to all in. How about you retreat and give me what little you've got on the table?"

Dax pushed her own chips forward. "Confront."

Nemi scoffed. "Are you serious? You barely own the board."

"The lady wishes to confront," said the dealer, along for the ride at this point. "Do you retreat?"

"Of course not." Nemi scowled. "Let's have it. I've got basically everything."

"But I've got a total monopoly," Dax said, matching her cards to the dice.

She hadn't realized how many people had been watching her game until the wave of wild shouting bowled her over from behind. She leaned back in her chair and took a heady draft of her bloodwine.

It was almost as sweet as the look on Nemi's face.

"Okay," Nemi said, reining in her shock and rising from her chair. "I see."

"Nothing personal," Dax said, glancing back at a furious Bani Moxern. "Just business, right?"

Nemi snapped her finger for a porter to come and get her tray of remaining chips. The fellow was quick fingered, racking them into formation while Nemi donned a silky shawl.

"Have fun playing with yourself."

"Listen, can we talk now?" Dax stood, organizing her winnings. She'd withstood the assault, and now she was sitting on a fat stack.

Nemi's frosty eyes locked onto Dax's, and she scowled. "I have nothing to say to you. Or any other joined, for that matter. I'm happy now."

"I was just about to comment on how happy you were." Dax's sarcasm was the wrong response.

"Let me tell you something—if Pawpaw wants the yacht back, he can come and get it himself."

Nemi stormed off into the crowd, the porter shortly behind.

4

Signal

Dax quickly finished racking her substantial winnings and passed them to a porter for deposit. He nodded, handing her a cryptochit for the cashier, and she took off after Nemi.

She clocked Bani Moxern out of the corner of her eye, getting up to head deeper into the gaming floor. Given her sudden luck after she'd hidden her cards, they must've been collaborating somehow. If he was here, there was a good chance that some of the other *Kael'tach* were too. It seemed smart to stay out of his sight.

Nemi had fallen a long way from the initiate program if she was running cons in a casino. It wasn't likely to end well, and Dax resolved to get her friend to stop before she ended up languishing in a prison. Love might've been the basis of modern law on Argelius II, but in a former era, the Argelians were brutal murderers and torturers. It wasn't wise to test their justice system.

Dax ducked down a row of *makra* machines, their spinning dials singing in her ears. It wasn't the most inconspicuous activity, skulking around in a dress, but she needed to try to stay concealed. Nemi exited the casino floor by the distant cashier booths, and Dax scurried after her, picking up her skirts as she ran.

After the cacophony of the gaming area, the exit corridor was a muted bass boom. Huge, gold statues of Pyrithian bats flanked the carpeted walkway. A couple of gamblers made their way toward the main floor, laughing and joking with each other about the entertainments to come.

Up ahead, Nemi slowed down—giving Dax just enough time to duck behind one of the statues before she turned. Dax remained hidden, and as the approaching gamblers passed, she took her compact from her clutch and pretended to check her makeup. After they were gone, she used her mirror to peek around the corner and watch Nemi leave.

Nemi's trail led Dax out onto a vast wooden dock that stretched along the ship's starboard side. Villas sprouted like mushrooms, wide roofs atop glassy facades. The bay lapped at the western edge of the dock, where dozens of bright waveskimmers bobbed in their slips. Strings of colorful lanterns hung overhead, providing just enough illumination for Dax to see the path and Nemi's silhouette.

This section was specifically for the high-stake gamblers, those who could afford to rent an entire house within the casino. Wood smoke called to Dax from every chimney, and she glimpsed the celebrants inside their villas, drinking and partying. It looked like fun, and she missed Kira once again. Julian Bashir could be entertaining, too, though he might get the wrong idea from the romantic setting.

Several times, Nemi glanced around, and Dax had to duck into the shadows. The formal dress added some difficulty, but she remained undetected. Once, she was forced to huddle into a clump of bushes, which snagged on her gossamer skirts.

"Really?" she whispered, pulling her dress free to find a jagged rend in the fabric.

She'd been so upset about the tear that she almost lost Nemi in the darkness. Dax hustled after the woman nevertheless, stopping when Nemi entered one of the larger villas. The door slid closed behind her, and she disappeared inside.

Nemi's lodgings were massive, a multilevel villa overlooking the bay with a majestic view of the nearby mountains. Panoramic windows offered a look into the structure, and Dax saw no sign of activity. She slipped into the garden walkways surrounding the structure, finding plenty of places to hide.

Circling the villa, she arrived at a pool with a garden and private dock. The glass walls at the rear of the villa's second floor were open, panes folded to one side to bring in the full sea breeze. Nemi emerged on the balcony, drink in hand, and Dax hunkered down behind a massive planter of reedy bushes.

Nemi didn't look happy; her fingers quivered as she brought the full tumbler to her lips and took a huge swig. Whatever it was, it was stiff, because Nemi coughed upon the liquor hitting her throat. She put the glass down and massaged her hands to steady them. When they wouldn't stop shaking, she went back inside.

Dax had to strain to see what happened next, nearly falling out of cover. Nemi took a small device from a table, put it to her neck, and sighed. An injection?

The poor kid. What had she gotten herself into?

Maybe it was nothing, and Dax was overthinking it. Perhaps she simply hated Dax for being joined, and the shot was a regular prescription.

It wouldn't do to stand there guessing in the bushes. Dax could hack the hotel lock in no time flat with her tricorder—but using Starfleet equipment to break into the villa was foolhardy. If she got caught, it was a court-martial offense. Two days ago, she didn't want to come here, and now she was thinking of risking her commission.

Nemi came back outside, leaning on the railing of the balcony, and Dax squeezed deeper into the shadows. She forced her breath to remain steady, ignoring her pounding pulse. She was so focused on staying still that she almost didn't see the lights flickering behind Nemi. They seemed to be shorting out, but Nemi took no notice at all.

There was movement in the flat, and Joran emerged onto the balcony beside her to glare down at Dax. His thin lips parted, and he mouthed the word—

Kael'tach.

The name was like ice in her bones, and she did what she could not to shiver. Nemi had to be in danger. A dark cloud hung over her, and if Dax didn't figure out what it was, she was certain her friend would wind up dead. If breaking and entering was required to get to the bottom of that mystery, so be it.

Several Daxes had experience getting into restricted areas, and Jadzia capitalized on that. She searched the balconies for a vulnerability and found it immediately. The easiest way up was a thermocrete trellis near the pool, connecting the garden level to the open second-floor balcony.

She probably wouldn't fall and break her neck.

Dax waited an hour in the darkness, listening to the slap of the waves against the piers. This wasn't her first time doing this—Curzon had hidden in dark hotel bushes more than once after a narrow escape. After a while, the lights went out, and Nemi left through the front door.

Though Dax wouldn't use her tricorder to break a lock, she figured a quick scan wouldn't hurt. Running a sweep found no lifeforms present inside the structure, save for a few house plants. This was probably her best chance to get inside; the tables on the distant casino were in full swing.

Dax scurried across the deck to the mass of vines growing up the trellis. She wasn't sure what they were, but they looked firmly attached. There was no way she could climb in her dazzling evening dress, so with a deep feeling of regret, she tore the long petals of fabric from the bottom, leaving a ragged hem at her knees. She kicked off her heels, seized a couple of vines, and tested their strength; they held firm. Slowly, she pulled herself up, hooking her foot into a gap in the trellis. Only twenty more steps to go.

Halfway up, some of the vines began to break free, and Dax scrambled to grab substitutes. Once she was stable, she frantically tucked plants back into the latticework, lest the break-in be obvious.

Finally reaching the balcony, she unceremoniously threw herself over the railing, flopping onto the floor. She sat up with a grunt, rubbing her hip where she'd hit the ground. "Going to leave a mark."

Dax glanced around, finding a large outdoor entertaining space with a couple of chairs and a table. The living room beyond the balcony was an elegant arrangement of maroon and gold furniture to complement the dark wood of the villa. She spied a serving area with a replicator, flanked by some stylized onyx bats similar to the ones in the main casino. In the center of the room, on a small table, lay Nemi's injector.

Dax padded across the darkened room to the table and picked up the hypo, inspecting the readout: one hundred twenty-two doses remaining of hexacyclosporine MK. The prescribing authority was listed as the Path of Sky Institute.

She double-checked the screen. The drug was an extremely specific immunosuppressant, only replicated in small batches for one purpose: to reduce symbiont rejection pains. Before HMK, the process of joining could be agonizing for some and uncomfortable for all during the first year. Dax, herself, had used it.

The Nemi of years' past wasn't a jaded gambler; she was a sweet kid who had hopes of becoming someone important. She *loved* Dax. There was only one explanation.

Nemi had to be a joined Trill.

A couple of quick footfalls were Dax's only warning before Nemi burst out of the shadows. She came in swinging and shouting, and it took all of Dax's reflexes to jump out of the way.

"Nemi, wait!"

But the younger woman did no such thing, attacking like a feral animal. Her flurry of swings battered Dax's forearms as she struggled to block them. Dax knew close-quarters combat well—she practiced regularly in the holosuites, continuing the study of Klingon martial arts that Curzon had begun. The fighter before her was vicious, quick, and professional.

"Nemi, it's me!"

"I know," she said, sinking a sidekick into Dax's gut—right in her symbiont.

Dax's eyes bulged and her vision went blurry as she stumbled backward against a bar top. She ducked away from Nemi's nasty right hook, knocking over a stack of glasses and shattering some. Her assailant snapped up a piece of the drinkware and hurled it, hitting Dax in the shoulder when she ducked away. The blow stung like a brick.

Dax fended off another wave of frantic punches, kicks, and elbows. "Stop! I don't want to hurt you."

"That makes one of us." Nemi knocked the shade off a lamp and picked up the metal stem, brandishing it like a club.

Dax clutched her gut, controlling her breathing as her attacker approached. Her symbiont felt like a huge bruise, and her arms already smarted from blocking blows. That lamp might cave in her skull.

Could Nemi kill her?

Would she?

The second Nemi tensed to swing, Dax sprung and trapped the lamp against her body. She seized both ends and twisted, ripping it free before shoulder-checking Nemi backward. She threw the weapon aside and held up her hands.

"Come on, don't do this," Dax said. "We're supposed to be friends."

Nemi sized her up from head to toe, evaluating Dax's stance. This woman wasn't some doe-eyed kid; she was a seasoned fighter. Dax watched for the change in her eyes, the steely moment when she'd decide to attack again.

There!

Nemi took a swing, and Dax blocked it before smashing her elbow across Nemi's temple. The woman went from charging beast to slack body in a heartbeat, sprawling out across the carpet. Dax stood huffing for a moment before rushing to her friend's side.

"Nemi, I'm so sorry." But Dax's murmured apologies fell on unconscious ears.

She fetched her fallen clutch and pulled out her tricorder before returning to Nemi. The device powered up, and Dax initiated her medical scan. Pulse, good, oxygen, good, heart rate, okay, brain waves—

Dax blinked at the tricorder's readouts, trying to make sense of it. She ran it over Nemi's body, double- and triple-checking. There was one healthy signal, from the symbiont living inside Nemi's abdomen.

Nemi's waves were dead flat.

"No . . ."

Dax's eyes burned with tears, and she hit the side of the tricorder, hoping some percussive maintenance would fix it. This couldn't be. Her old friend wasn't her friend, but something much more sinister. The tricorder readout blurred in Dax's vision as she stared at Nemi's flatline.

Nemi, who'd cheered her back into the initiate program.

Who'd been like a little sister to her.

Who'd lost her way.

Dead as a puppet.

The lights flickered, and Dax looked up to find Joran standing over them both, hands dripping with blood. He wasn't smiling as usual. Rather, he had an air of weariness, shoulders slumped and eyes sunken.

Jadzia gave him a bitter look. "Don't start with me."

He said something, but she couldn't make out the words. His speech was disjointed, slurred, as in a dream, or a nightmare. The edges of his form distorted, and then he blew away like so much dust.

Why couldn't she hear him? The old memory block? It was supposed to be gone.

What memories were still obscured?

Nemi's eyes shot open.

Dax balled up a fist and wrapped her free hand around Nemi's neck. "Stay down, if you know what's good for you."

Nemi gently grasped her forearm. "Dax."

All of Dax's muscles went titanium taut as electricity coursed through her body. She couldn't breathe or move. Her vision whited out, ears ringing, jaw clenched so hard she thought her teeth would break.

The symbiont writhed with pleasure.

When the current stopped, Dax's body went slack. Her head thunked against the floor, and stars danced in her eyes.

Sight fluttered into darkness.

The sun warmed her eyelids, and Dax opened them against her better judgment. Spears of light cut into her optic nerve—almost like she'd downed a glass of bloodwine and then gotten a hefty shock. The first thing she saw was warm gray—until she realized there was a piece of paper on her face.

Dax tried to reach up to take it, but her arms were seized so tight she could hardly extend them. She took a deep breath and rolled over. The paper fell off, but she didn't care with her level of injury. She was pretty sure she'd pulled all of her muscles. That had to be some kind of record.

Or was it? The pain was as familiar as it was heinous. There was something about the particular blend of dry mouth, swollen eyes, and muscular agony that triggered a memory. Someone had done this to her before.

In Jadzia's life, she'd gotten blackout drunk, had a concussion, been stunned, punched out, and electrocuted. Nemi's touch felt similar to that last one, but it was off. It was Joran who recognized the feeling. As she ruminated, her muscles slackened enough that she could move, and she got to her knees in agony.

Nemi's villa came into focus, with the fight of the night before still writ large. Dax reached down and took the slip of paper that had fallen to the floor.

Red ink scratched an elegant hand across a cream-colored sheet.

Dax,

I was fond of you once.

I won't be fond of you twice.

5

Wake

Dax replicated herself a glass of hot tea and sat down at her hotel-room desk. She huffed the steam, letting the fine Argelian leaves and spices soothe her senses. After she'd had a moment of peace, she pulled the computer over. She had a lot of unpleasant calls to make, so she might as well get started.

First up: the Symbiosis Commission. They were responsible for all joinings, as well as keeping tabs on the symbionts. They had betrayed her once before, so she wasn't keen to talk to them.

"Hello?" Doctor Renhol's angular features appeared on Dax's desk screen. *"Jadzia! What happened to your face?"*

The doctor had been Dax's attending physician while she was at the Symbiosis Commission. She hadn't changed much from their last contact a year prior: light skin, brown hair swept back, a subtle shade of mauve on her thin lips to match her uniform. Her brows were perfectly pointed—if it weren't for her Trill spots, she could be mistaken for Vulcan. She had to be on the young side of fifty, though Dax wasn't sure. Despite her stern appearance, Doctor Renhol had a kind voice and compassionate demeanor, the very picture of a medical professional.

Dax forced a smile, trying to ignore the citrus stinging of her split lip. "I have something to report to the Commission."

"Oh—okay. I see. Are you all right?"

"No."

Renhol recoiled. *"Tell me what's happened."*

Dax recounted the whole tale, from the moment she heard Prit's request to when Nemi stunned her. She included everything: the vision, the gambling and drinking. The doctor listened, taking notes and occasionally interrupting to ask questions.

It almost made Dax forget the ease with which Renhol had once lied to her. She'd been part of the cover-up of Joran—an act that had nearly killed Jadzia and Dax.

When Dax reached the part of her story about the brain waves, Renhol grew serious.

"Are you absolutely certain you were reading it right?" she asked.

"I'm a Starfleet science officer. I know how to read a tricorder."

"Jadzia, I don't know what to say. What you're describing . . . It shouldn't even be possible."

"I work next to a wormhole. I've seen plenty of impossible things on Deep Space 9." She let out a sigh. "Is this something the Commission has seen before?"

"Not in my experience."

Dax searched the doctor's eyes for any deception. Renhol could be dangerous. The doctor's first loyalty would always be to the Symbiosis Commission, but she seemed genuine this time.

"I'm going to need you to brief the Commission. We can set up a conference—"

"I'm coming to Trill," Dax said. "I want to go through the Commission archives myself."

"Oh, I see." Renhol tapped her chin, deep in thought. *"Very well. I'll have a room prepared for you."*

Dax loved being a joined Trill, but hated her time in the Commission. Years of invasive testing, grueling studies, and betrayal didn't foster pleasant feelings or a longing to be there. After she'd dedicated her life to being joined, they had abused her trust.

Joran hated the place, too, though it was probably because he died there.

"Thank you," Dax said, "but I'll be staying at the Capital Arms Hotel. I can be there in four days."

"All right. I'll make the arrangements for the debrief. Anything else to add?"

"No."

"Be safe, Jadzia. I'm glad you're okay."

She smiled. "I will, Doctor."

Dax terminated the call and regarded the blank screen for a long time. She dreaded what came next, but it absolutely had to be done. Despite the early hour of the day, she replicated herself a shot of Scotch and downed it in one. Then she retook her seat with her more reasonable mug of tea and commed Etom Prit.

He answered, eyes bleary and ringed with dark circles. A tuft of white chest hair poked out between the folds of his robe. He'd been asleep, but he was wide-awake upon seeing Dax. He took in the state of her face with growing recognition that bad news was on the way.

After a painful pause, he asked, *"What's happened?"*

She opened her mouth to speak, but the words died in her throat.

"I don't know how to tell you this." It came out a whisper.

He looked into her eyes, nodding. He seemed so noble to Dax in that moment, steeled for whatever came next. She wouldn't have wished this on her worst enemy, much less a dear friend. She wanted to linger in the moment before he knew the truth—a time where he wasn't yet heartbroken.

Prit swallowed, slicking back his sleep-wild white hair. *"Spare me nothing."*

It felt like standing at the edge of a vast cliff. All Dax had to do was step forward, and the fall would take care of itself. "I found Nemi, and she . . ."

Has become an abomination?

Isn't coming home again?

"She's dead . . . isn't she?"

Prit's simple question opened a floodgate within Dax, and she explained the whole situation though bitter tears. What had happened to Nemi was sick and cruel, a profoundly unfair turn of fate—the sort of thing that destroys faith and joy. It was evil.

Dax needed to tell him, even though it hurt. He was the only man in the galaxy who could understand what she was feeling. In a previous life, he'd been a confidant. In this one, a mentor. She could always count on his kindness and gentle heart.

But when she looked at the man on the screen, he was anything but soft. His eyes had gone icy, his jaw set. He wasn't aggrieved yet; he was cold as the grave, a blush of fury lurking beneath.

She finished her briefing, and after a long pause, he asked, *"What else do you know?"*

The only thing she hadn't told him was about the name on the injector: the Path of Sky Institute. Etom Prit may have been Nemi's grandfather, but Dax had an obligation to the coming investigation. If she told him where Nemi got the drug, he'd almost certainly act on his own.

And Dax knew his darker side. He'd done things for Curzon, carried messages, smuggled spies to and from Federation embassies, engaged in economic manipulation. Prit had deadly friends in high places, and Dax couldn't risk him destroying the only people who could give her answers.

"I'm going back to Trill," she said at last. "This has to be discussed with the Symbiosis Commission."

"They ruined Nemi—" His anger burbled over, and he struggled to control himself. *"They kicked her out twice, and now they want some say in what happens?"*

"It's a case involving a symbiont. They have to be the ones to handle it."

He closed his eyes. *"Do you know which one? Which symbiont?"*

"I don't."

"Do you have any clue?"

"No."

But she did.

Joran knew something, but she couldn't trust Etom with that knowledge yet.

He seemed to age ten years. The lines of his wrinkles deepened with his pain, and his skin went sallow.

"*I knew those people from the* Kael'tach *were . . .*" He searched for the word. "*. . . were rotten. I'll make them regret this. Every last one of them. I know who her little friends were. Can start digging there.*"

"Etom, I know how you feel, but—"

"I'll see you when you get to Trill."

The connection went dead, and Dax deflated in her chair. That hadn't gone well, but she couldn't imagine a reality where it did. Prit had an unbelievable amount of clout, and he was never going to sit back and let the authorities handle things.

Dax closed her eyes and nursed her cooling tea. She still had one last call to make, to DS9. This leave was going to be longer than she anticipated, and she needed the captain's approval.

Her transportation would be in-system soon, and she'd need to beam up. Perhaps it was best to call him from the ship. She didn't want to waste any more time getting off this planet.

With Captain Sisko's permission to continue, Dax pored over her tricorder data in the stateroom of her ship. Luxury liners plied the lanes between Argelius II and Trill, and Dax splurged on the best lodgings she could get. She deserved it after the horrors of the past day, and she had the latinum after her night in the casino.

Her stateroom was decked out in emerald and gold with hardwood accents. Traditional Trill design values gave the place a familiar air with just enough decadence to feel pampered. The space was simultaneously extravagant and meditative, a careful balance to achieve. There was also plenty of room to pace, and Dax wore a trail in the carpet as she considered the situation.

Nemi's vital signs had been good, but her brain waves were flat. Her body was receiving all of its signals from the symbiont. That also meant that Nemi's persona still existed in that creature, an imprint of a departed soul. Her body had been stolen.

Dax pulled out the note and stared numbly at the handwriting. Nemi knew her, but what about the symbiont? The joined could meet endlessly across lifetimes. There was something strange about the way it addressed her.

Dax.

Nemi had known her before she was joined, so she typically called her Jadzia. It was an odd change to call her by her symbiont's name.

And why had the electric shock felt so familiar to Joran?

Dax sat down at the computer on the curved desk and used her field-docent access to download the roster of joined Trill. It seemed impossible that Nemi could've gotten joined without the Symbiosis Commission's knowledge, but she had to double-check.

As expected, they had records of Nemi's failures, but not of her being joined. Just to be sure, Dax looked up Bani Moxern, Aia Keteel, and Seval Gep. Nothing. What if they were joined too? What if they were puppets?

Was it even possible to be joined outside the confines of the Symbiosis Commission? Starfleet had performed joinings to save the symbiont, but only in dire circumstances. Questions swirled in Dax's mind about the source of these creatures. What had Nemi known going into the procedure? Perhaps she had been kidnapped, coerced, or tricked before she'd been joined and murdered.

No, Dax couldn't call it murder, yet. She wasn't sure what it was. Before yesterday, she wouldn't have thought it possible for a host to be brain-dead, operated by a symbiont. It was like a ghost story.

She wished she'd had more time with Nemi's body. If she could've done more scans or genetic analysis of the symbiont, she'd have some answers. Nemi's sudden revival and electroshock powers had caught her off guard and left her at a disadvantage.

The next avenue of inquiry was the Path of Sky Institute, but Dax came up with very little. The organization was a Symbiosis Commission–accredited healthcare provider, servicing on-world joined. All of their records appeared to be in order, and they were in good standing with the Federation Medical Association. They were authorized to dispense prescriptions—though the injector might have been stolen. She had no way to access Nemi's medical records, and that seemed like crossing a line anyway.

Most joined only needed hexacyclosporine MK for their first year. Symbiont and host could be killed by an overactive immune system, but that was easily managed with medication. No one had died from rejection in five hundred years, and even in the worst-case scenarios, hosts only needed an injection once a day. Dax had managed to get off the stuff in her second month. Nemi's joining was almost certainly recent if she was still using it.

The lamp began to flicker.

Joran's voice came through fragmented, like a sound on the breeze. She only caught the word *"Emergence."*

Dax immediately injected herself with benzocyatizine. "No, thanks."

She wasn't in the mood for spooky visions, regardless of how informative they might be. Joran was restless, angry and dying to say something, but he couldn't seem to put a coherent sentence together. Every time Dax saw a new piece of evidence, she shook loose a bit more of the dust from her mind. She hoped that something would jog Joran, but what if the original memory block was the problem?

After a few more minutes of research, the benzocyatizine began to take hold. It calmed Dax's stress-strained heart and raised her isoboramine levels, eliciting a series of yawns. She hadn't slept enough. Every part of her body still ached from Nemi's assault. Simply staring at the screen wasn't getting her anywhere, and perhaps it was best to sleep.

After what felt like the longest day of her life, Dax stripped off her clothes and crawled into her soft, luxurious sheets, grateful for a moment's respite.

The piano was an Oppan Twenty-Eight, one of only three in existence. One was on Earth, in Carnegie Hall. Another belonged to Klavis Blou, the Risian octogenarian composer. The third one lived in the Ea'elle Opera House on Trill, inside an acoustic paradise.

Long boards ran the length of the stage, which bulged into the audience to allow performers more room to work. The seats were empty, their velvety blue upholstery spotless. The faces of famous composers and poets lined the proscenium, carved from white marble and lit in aquatic hues. The curtains were open, violet draperies spilling down either side like waterfalls. A row of lights at the apron nearly blinded her as she walked to the piano and sat down.

Brassy fittings enclosed a set of resonance drawbars, and white keys shone in the spotlight. They called to her, compelling a song from her tired body. A familiar ache seized her hands, and she rested them in the ready position.

Except they weren't hers—the fingers were longer and thicker, youthful, but with knobby knuckles. Blond hairs grew from the digits like shoots of new grass. Pronounced veins ran up the back. These hands were strong, confident, and precise, beautiful in their own way.

They were Joran's hands.

She pressed lightly to bring forth a chord. It suffused the space, reflecting and doubling upon itself before fading with the entropy of the strings. When she let go, silence returned to the theater.

A set of soft claps echoed from the audience, and Jadzia looked up to see a lone woman sitting in the middle of the auditorium. The face was impossible to discern, blurry and ever shifting, and she wore a strapless dress so black it absorbed the light. Her pale skin bore Trill spots, tracing a line along her collarbone and up her neck. Quicksilver hair spilled down around her shoulders, adorned around the top with a sapphire circlet.

She inspired a maelstrom of conflicting feelings: love, anger, fear, and lust. The longer Jadzia stared at the blurred visage, the more of it resolved until she could almost discern the identity. It was like trying to peel away a mask, and she'd only uncovered the lips when the figure moved. The mystery woman raised her arm high in the Trill gesture for an encore.

Jadzia's long, masculine fingers tickled a melody, and a phantom trumpet joined in, bolstering it with an elegiac solo. A full orchestra blossomed around her, brass, strings, and woodwinds. With the majestic accompaniment at her back, she played Poltus Wennit's *Adagio in Summer*, a Trill symphony dating back a century.

In the audience, the woman gave a restrained smile. Dark silver lined her upper lip, a contrast against the deadly red of the plump lower half. Jadzia knew that mouth somehow—she'd kissed it many times, but when? As whom?

Fingers flickered over the keyboard, going ever faster. She slammed down the ends of phrases with manic energy, her hits echoing through the empty theater. She struck a hard chord, and her knuckles stung. Fingers ached. Muscles failed. The tune reflected her chaos, faltering with every other note.

She couldn't keep up, but she couldn't stop. She had to play for the woman in the audience, even though she couldn't understand why. When she looked out at the stranger, the woman was on her feet, hands clasped before her as if in delight. Her predatory grin burned beneath a blurry visage.

Jadzia tried to pull back, but some force held her firm, smashing her hands, shooting pains rocketing through her forearms until she couldn't take it anymore. She screamed as the piece reached its crescendo, and the lights dimmed low in the sudden death of the music.

Only Jadzia's ragged, whimpering breaths broke the stillness. Her hands were ruined—too used up to ever play piano again. Shaking, she looked out into the audience. The stranger's vicious smile went wider, like she could distend her jaw and swallow someone whole. Jadzia focused through the pain, trying to tear away the gauzy mesh shielding her identity.

A pert, thin nose came through, followed by two delicately arched eyebrows and sparkling green eyes. All at once, Jadzia recognized the face of Elta Vess, one of Curzon's old flames. It'd been a fast, hot relationship in his early days as a diplomat, but one that rocked his world. What Curzon and Elta had was special—until she'd brutally dumped him. He'd always had complicated feelings about her.

Indignity boiled up inside Jadzia, anger with Joran for daring to use someone so intimate to make a point.

A distant rumble of thunder was the only warning she got before a bolt of lightning blasted the piano. The assembly exploded into molten metal and smoking sticks, and she went flying backward. She bounced across the stage boards, smashing her face, unable to shield herself with her broken hands. The piano lay in flaming splinters a few meters away, and Jadzia regarded it with swimming eyes.

Heavy footfalls approached. She rolled over to find a pair of bare feet. Joran looked down at her, eyes wild, hair askew. He wore a patient's gown.

"You need to listen to me," he said, reaching down to grasp her by the throat.

He hoisted her one-handed, and she thought he might snap her neck from the clicking of her spine. She groped at his arms with broken fingers, desperate to free the air in her lungs. Her cheeks prickled and her strength faded as he lifted her over to the edge of the stage.

He looked into her eyes all the while, accusation in his gaze. "This is what's coming to you."

When he released Jadzia, she should've fallen into the orchestra pit. She gasped, braced for a ground that never arrived.

Windows streamed past—the side of a high-rise. Jadzia plummeted from the top of the Trill Symbiosis Commission building. She screamed one last time before the pavement knocked her back to consciousness.

6

Commission

Jadzia spent the next day furious. Curzon had loved Elta Vess, a joined Trill, since the day he'd met her. They'd been an odd couple—the hotshot diplomat and the older psychiatrist, but it hadn't mattered to Curzon. The joined knew love no matter the age.

The pair made waves in the capital, Curzon's rising star magnified by Elta's socialite status. They'd broken rules and indulged their passions for each other in creative ways. Curzon's political friends adored Elta, and she was at home at every gala and soiree. She'd captivated him in a way no other woman had, and even after she left him bereft, he'd harbored an unrequited flame.

A few years after she'd broken up with him, Elta vanished from the public eye, sparing Curzon the continued agony of seeing her at events. Then he learned why: she had Fventik's Disease—a terminal illness affecting both host and symbiont.

Elta and her symbiont, Vess, died, and so passed one of the greatest symbionts of all time. In its many lives, Vess had been a racing daredevil, an accomplished soldier, a famed author, an ascetic, an activist, and a brilliant psychiatrist. Symbionts were the cultural memory of the Trill, and Vess's loss was a blow.

For Joran to use Elta for his twisted purpose was unconscionable.

After vacating the pleasant splendor of her starliner, Dax stood before the doors of the Symbiosis Commission, conflicted on every axis.

She hated the place. Curzon liked it, and so did Torias. Emony didn't care one way or the other. Audrid was a Symbiosis commissioner for years, so she enjoyed it. For Jadzia, the Commission brought up memories of her painful trials: physical, intellectual, and emotional. She'd been remade in this building, forged into something harder than the innocent child who'd applied. Joran loathed the building most of all. It was the site where he'd committed a brutal killing and died fleeing the scene.

He had, however, enjoyed the murder.

The Symbiosis Commission operated from a tall, golden building of three towers, interlinked in an L shape atop a broad pediment. The campus was situated beside the N'Ladix Reflecting Pool, a public park dedicated to the Trill spirit and their partnership with the symbionts. The Capital Bay spread behind the building, with the North Bank Entertainment District beyond. The gardens surrounding the Commission were sparse, designed to encourage meditative introspection, but Dax found no comfort in the beauty.

Joined Trill protected the memories of all the hosts of their symbiont. As the sum of these lives, these individuals discovered amazing things, traveled boldly, and advanced Trill civilization. The first Trill to break the warp barrier had been joined, the culmination of a sculptor, a mathematician, and a physicist. One who carried a symbiont inside them also carried the hopes and dreams of every Trill for a better future.

The balmy summer's day did nothing to buoy Dax's spirits. She approached the doors, which parted in a puff of cold, clinical air. The scent of the place was so aggressively neutral that it dulled the senses. Living there had been maddening, like spending years in a hospital.

The lobby was an expanse of polished stone, more like a concourse in a spaceport than a foyer. Along every wall, slanted windows spilled daylight across the shiny thermocrete floor. Teachers, mentors, docents, administrative staff, and initiates went about their business, heels clacking endlessly in the cavernous enclosure.

Ground level housed the offices that dealt with the Commission's interactions with the general citizenry, such as Public Relations and Career Placement Services.

The underground offices were dedicated to symbiont needs. The first few subbasements housed laboratories and medical treatment facilities. Beneath that, there was tighter security and the Caves of Mak'ala—the birthplace of all symbionts.

One level above the lobby was Host Services, home to the majority of the Commission's medical doctors. Every two years, Dax was required to return for routine checkups. Above Host Services were the initiate levels, forbidden to most outsiders. It was supposed to feel like school, but Dax found it was more like prison. The isolation from her family while in the initiate program had been unbearable.

The very top levels contained the transplant facilities, where Jadzia would die one day, if everything went according to plan. She found it hard to avoid thinking about giving up Dax whenever she visited. The previous hosts had different experiences with death, and Jadzia intended to delay hers as long as possible.

She greeted the receptionist at the front desk, a tan young man dressed in a gray Commission uniform.

"Jadzia Dax here for Doctor Renhol."

"It's good to have you back with us," he said. "Welcome home."

"Nice to be here," she lied.

She waited until Doctor Renhol summoned her, taking the turbolift to Host Services. There, she was ushered into a room where she found a panel of joined Trill waiting for her behind a long table. Doctor Renhol introduced them as Commission investigators and gestured to a chair in the center of the room. Dax was reminded of her thesis defenses. She hoped this wouldn't be as pedantic.

When she saw Bentis Brac, she knew that hope was in vain.

Councilor Brac was a lanky, light-skinned Trill, with droopy cheeks and a thin neck that scarcely filled his high collar. He was a background investigator with the initiate program, and Dax pitied anyone who had come under his lens. The Brac symbiont was only on its second host; the first one had been a prominent justice. Sophomore symbionts could be prematurely world-weary and judgmental, and Brac comfortably inhabited that stereotype.

"Jadzia Dax, thank you for coming to speak with us in person," he said, putting on a pair of glasses to look at his padd. "We understand you've had something of an adventure."

"Councilor. I appreciate the opportunity to come and share," she said. "This is very disturbing."

"I'm sure. It can't have been easy to deal with Joran's memories and interference." He looked to the others and nodded. "For that reason, this is a sealed debriefing. Commission eyes only."

He tapped his padd a few times, and the ring lights around the doors went red.

Dax glanced at Doctor Renhol, who shifted uncomfortably in her chair. She'd told the doctor everything because Renhol was still her physician—and she knew about Joran. Her honesty might be used against her. How much about Dax's mental state had been shared with Brac?

"Jadzia," Renhol began, "my colleagues are here because of the extremely sensitive nature of your case. For everyone's best interest, I think you should recount what happened in your own words."

She'd hoped for a warmer welcome and more collaboration. "Absolutely, Doctor."

Yet again, she went through the tale of her friend's tragic demise. It didn't get easier this time, but she'd gotten better at hiding her grief. If the Symbiosis Commission was going to be this icy, Dax had to be in absolute control of herself. To that end, she minimized Joran's involvement. She stuck to the facts of the case—ironclad evidence she had from the scene, things she could easily prove.

She finished her story, proud that she hadn't cracked even once in describing the macabre fate of her friend.

"Now, Doctor Renhol tells us you've been suffering from hallucinations," Brac said.

"Yes, but I'd rather talk about Nemi," Dax replied. "Her situation is—"

"Yes, I know . . ." He held up a hand, and her temper flared. "And we'll have time for that later. I'd like you to tell me the nature of these hallucinations. Do they feel . . . prophetic? Are you at the center of them? Is there something you're supposed to do?"

She put on a thin smile so she wouldn't scream. "That is irrelevant. We're here to discuss what Nemi has become. I have the recordings on my tricorder."

"Well, that's exactly it." Brac leaned on his chair's armrest, propping up his chin on his hand. "I'm trying to establish the mental state of the person *conducting* the readings."

Surely, she hadn't heard him right. "*My* mental state?"

Brac idly tapped his cheek with his index finger. "Let me explain the situation for you from our perspective."

"Councilor—" Dax began.

"I hope you'll hear me out—I can see I've agitated you." He gave her a thin smile of his own, and she bit back her immediate reply.

"My friend is dead. I think we can acknowledge that's an emotional subject." Dax crossed her arms.

"And I wish to proceed with utmost sensitivity, I do."

Dax's smile faltered like shields under fire. "I came here for help. I could've reported this to the Argelian authorities as a murder, but I wanted to keep things within the Commission."

"Nemi Prit is a private citizen," Brac said. "We failed this girl out of the initiate program twice. Her psych profile afterward was a nightmare. Now you're asking us to get involved with her again?"

"Because she's become a monster!"

"That's what *you've* told us."

"I have good evidence—"

"That you recorded one set of brainwaves after drunkenly breaking into her domicile. I'll point out: that happened *after* you assaulted her while hallucinating."

"Stop interrupting me, Councilor. You don't have to believe me, but a tricorder can't lie."

"An instrument is only as accurate as its wielder, and you were in a compromised state. According to Doctor Renhol's report, you were mixing . . . bloodwine and benzocyatizine was it?"

"That was synthehol."

"Are you sure?"

She wasn't, but that was beside the point. Dax knew exactly what she'd seen.

"Councilor, I'm the chief science officer on Deep Space 9. I don't make the kinds of mistakes you're talking about."

He steepled his fingers. "Oh, yes. We know all about Deep Space 9. Wasn't it your Captain Sisko who extorted the Commission by threatening to leak our most protected secret?"

A look of shame passed over Renhol's face.

"I had no part in Captain Sisko's actions, but I supported them," Dax said. "I had a right to know about Joran, and the Commission hid it from me."

"You are, of course, correct," Brac said, spreading his palms. "That's why we never pursued action against you and your captain. But now you're here, asking us to investigate a fantastical claim. I'm truly sorry that the Commission hid Joran from you. No host should ever be burdened as you have been."

She waited for him to finish, seething.

"But we also have to recognize your limitations because of it."

"Okay, why don't you go—" She caught herself before letting him have it. Joran was a tough serpent to wrestle, and she'd be damned if he made her lose her cool. "We aren't focusing on the most important matter at hand. Who is this other symbiont? How did it get control of Nemi?"

Looking across the faces of the panelists, she knew she'd lost them. They were all wondering if Brac was right. It was easier to believe that a host with a fractured personality hallucinated sometimes and tore up a hotel room. If they accepted that a symbiont could kill its host, it'd probably break their heads open. It was too frightful a possibility to consider.

"Are you going to find Nemi?" Dax said at last. "That would prove what I'm saying."

Brac looked to his fellow panelists, reaching some nonverbal agreement. "We'll contact you regarding this investigation as needed."

"Councilor—"

"We do want to speak to Nemi Prit," Brac said. "We'd like to know how she feels about your entry into her rooms. And if she's willing, we can scan her brain waves and put the whole matter to rest. Aside from that, you are not to approach Nemi Prit anymore."

Dax glared at this vole of a man. Two lifetimes weren't enough to teach him how to pull his head out of his ass. He wasn't going to take her seriously, and the rest of the panelists would follow his lead. She could see it in their faces.

"I think we're adjourned," Brac said. "We'll keep you apprised of any updates."

They gathered up their things and filed out. Dax followed them into the hall.

"You can't ignore this," she called after them. "It's bigger than your grudge against Captain Sisko."

"Jadzia—" Doctor Renhol began, holding up a hand.

"No." Dax cut her off. "I'm telling you something really foul is going on, and you're not listening. I cannot be clearer about that."

"But I am listening, Commander Dax," Brac said, turning on her with a sigh. "And what I'm hearing is, quite frankly, nonsense. Hosts occasionally die with a symbiont inside, yes, but their bodies don't get up and walk around. They certainly don't go play *tongo*."

She waited for him to finish making a fool of himself.

"They can't do anything without a living host." He smacked his lips dryly. "That's why we call them symbionts, you know."

"I have a masters in exobiology and could tell you a dozen ways that you're wrong," Dax said. "You need another life or two to get that arrogance out of you."

Brac scoffed, but it was a direct hit—insecure about his age. He was so easy to read, and if she couldn't change his mind, she'd push his buttons.

"We're trying to handle things the proper way," Brac said. "We can't always send in our commanding officers to blackmail people."

"He was trying to save my life."

"I hope you'll feel free to submit any additional evidence you have to my office. Good day, Dax."

He turned and left, mumbling something about lunch.

"I'm sorry," Doctor Renhol said.

Dax wanted to yell at her, but she needed the doctor too much. She couldn't lose all of her allies in the Commission in one day.

"Please, just—" She blew her frustration out between parted lips. "Don't be sorry. Help me. You believe me, don't you?"

"I'm sure something is wrong with Nemi."

Dax stared at her. "I know what I saw. What about the electric shocks?"

"I don't know. We have to investigate, it's true."

"I need you to believe me."

"I'm trying, Jadzia."

Bentis Brac didn't want to help, but Dax had other avenues at the Symbiosis Commission she could hit up for information. One of her past hosts, Audrid, had been a Symbiosis commissioner, so she knew the bureaucracy intimately. Sure, some things might have changed, but her insights would be valuable. She would start her research with herself, and summon Audrid with the Rite of Emergence.

Before that, however, Dax intended to talk to one of the Guardians of Mak'ala. All the symbionts were born in the caves, and the

Guardians tended to their every need. The Trill of that organization were obsessive and vigilant. It fell to them to keep an entire species alive and thriving, and their knowledge of symbionts was encyclopedic. They knew not only the biology, but also the mythology, and that made them her most valuable resource.

So when Dax was denied entry to the caves, she was outraged.

"I-I'm sorry," the gate operator, a nonbinary Trill with a dark complexion, stammered. "Your security file says 'Escort required.' "

The official gate to the Caves of Mak'ala was an array of scanners and guard stations. Those who wished to enter had to submit to all manner of imaging and decontamination, and access was carefully controlled. The ecosystem it shielded was delicate, and any infections could prove catastrophic.

Crossing her arms, she said, "I'm Dax. Since when is an escort required for a joined Trill?"

"Again, I'm sorry," they replied. "That's just what your access says. I can't change that from here."

"That makes no sense."

"I wish I could help you, but—"

"No, I understand." She didn't mean to get snippy with some random security guard, but she didn't want an escort listening to her conversations. The Commission was acting cagey, keeping her at arm's length. They might try to interfere with her interviews or censor them.

"If I did want to get an escort . . ." she began, and the guard tapped their interface a few times.

"Certainly. The next appointment is in eight days."

"Eight?!"

"Apologies again," they said, and they looked like they genuinely meant it. "My supervisors have scaled back the number of visitor slots and—"

"It's fine. I get it." She shook her head in disgust. "Well, let me sign up for the appointment in a week."

"Okay. I've got you down for thirty minutes next Tuesday."

"Thirty minutes?" She grimaced, and they looked like they were going to melt under her gaze. "Fine."

Dax left the Symbiosis Commission stymied and angry. She'd come there hoping for answers but found disappointment instead. She made her way across town toward the Capital Arms Hotel as storm clouds gathered over the skyline.

Warm summer rain fell in sheets, and she ducked inside a restaurant to take shelter. The scents of fresh vegetables, crusty breads, sauces, and meats won her over. She paused to have a peaceful lunch at a window counter. The food wasn't special, but it was serviceable, and that was what mattered most.

She stared morosely out at the cityscape, haloed by the daytime downpour. There was no way to help Nemi now. She was dead, and only Dax's sense of justice remained. She considered her next action while she ate. How could she investigate Nemi's condition? She needed to talk to the Guardians, but they were inaccessible for eight days. As long as the Commission controlled the entrance, she'd never be free to get the answers she wanted.

But Dax knew someone who excelled in getting past checkpoints. With this person at her side, the Commission didn't stand a chance.

It was time to call in Major Kira Nerys.

7

Houseguests

Dax slouched into another hotel room, slinging her duffel to the bed. She'd already enjoyed luxury and suffered economy this trip and found the room at the Capital Arms Hotel blessedly average. The place was owned by a retired Starfleet officer, and her uniform guaranteed she'd be well cared for. And all the interfaces were LCARS, so she already knew how to use the replicator and personal appliances. Hotels varied a lot from world to world.

After freshening up, she unpacked her bags and tested the replicator with a *raktajino*. She'd only taken a single sip before imagining Doctor Bashir chiding her for drinking an honorable amount of caffeine.

"Caffeine creates anxiety, and that's bad for isoboramine."

She didn't want to give up her Klingon coffee, so she took a blood scan with her tricorder. Curzon had to do the same thing three times a day toward the end. He hadn't enjoyed getting old, and Jadzia felt annoyed at having to test her levels just to have her treat.

She checked the time, waiting for the third watch on Deep Space 9 to be over—a few hours to kill. While she sat, she studied any publicly available article she could find about symbiosis and brain death in the Federation. Unfortunately, there was little info, and her motivation waned alongside the *raktajino*'s effects, until neither remained in Dax.

It was one in the morning on Trill when she finally caved.

"Computer," she said, and the system chirped. "Contact Major Kira Nerys on Deep Space 9."

"Warning," the computer replied. *"You are at the local time of oh-five-hundred."*

"That's fine," she yawned. "Connect me."

The screen against the far wall flickered on with an animated icon.

"Hailing," the computer said.

Kira Nerys appeared onscreen, eyes shining. Her auburn hair was already swept aside and in place, her makeup done. Her nose had a row of Bajoran ridges, and when she smiled, it was like she had a secret. When she sneered, she could strike fear into anyone.

"Wow. You're chipper," Dax said. "I was worried I was calling too early."

Kira raised a cup of steaming-hot tea to her already-painted lips. *"I always look like this."*

"Really?"

"I get up at oh-four-thirty, to keep a tight schedule."

On the surface, the two women had little in common. Dax loved to party, but Kira wasn't much of a drinker or gambler. Dax regularly visited Quark's holosuites, but Kira would only participate if they were fighting something. Dax had loved her childhood on Trill, while whole parts of Kira's had been spent in a Cardassian camp. Dax liked to dismantle mysteries, but Kira treasured their sanctity.

Despite all of the differences, they were close friends who had the utmost respect for each other, personally and professionally.

"Well, you're making me look like a slacker," Dax sighed.

Kira's eyes crinkled with her smile. *"I make everyone look like a slacker. Why are you calling me at this hour? You're supposed to be on leave."*

"I am. It's just . . . not going well."

Kira frowned and leaned closer to the screen. *"Oh, no. A guy?"*

Dax laughed bitterly and turned away. "Nothing that bad."

"Aw. Tell me what happened."

She started to tell the story, but lost steam before even the first words left her mouth. "My friend is dead. I need your help."

Kira nodded quickly. *"Where are you? Are you safe?"*

"It's not like that. I'm at the Capital Arms on Trill. My friend, she . . ."

"It's all right, Jadzia. You don't have to tell me everything right now." Kira looked like she wanted to jump through the screen to hug her, and Dax wished she could. The past few days had been an interminable nightmare, and she could use some support.

"You do have to tell me one thing," Kira said.

"What?"

"Where you want me to show up."

"Thank you, Kira." Dax sniffled, hoping it wasn't too obvious. "I'll send you coordinates to the hotel."

"Hang in there. I can get to you in two days."

"I knew I could count on you."

Kira smirked. *"I'd be mad if you didn't ask."*

They chatted for a while, with Dax asking how things were going on Deep Space 9. Kira was almost certain to get her leave approved if she wanted to check on Dax. Captain Sisko was worried about her, as was Bashir. Worf, the new Klingon strategic operations officer fresh from the *Enterprise*, asked where she'd gone. That tickled Dax somewhat. He was cute, if a little stern.

"All right. I have to let you go so I can pack," Kira said. *"Are you going to be okay?"*

"Yeah. Talking to you helped a lot."

"Don't worry. I'll hail you from the ship once I've booked passage."

"You don't have to," she laughed, and it felt nice. "I hope I'll be asleep by then."

"Good." Kira nodded, giving her a reassuring smile. *"Just remember you're not alone."*

"I'll see you soon."

That night, Dax slept like a baby. When the sun rose, she stayed in bed until her body started to ache and her stomach rumbled. The hotel replicator had Andorian fry cakes with any flavor of jam she could imagine, and she treated herself to whatever she wanted. She needed to be pampered for the ritual to come.

The Rite of Emergence had never been one of her strong suits, so she rarely used it. She wasn't particularly good at the joined-Trill esoterica, something she considered a personal failing. It'd been taxing enough when performing her *zhian'tara*.

But Audrid might know another way into the Caves of Mak'ala.

The serpentine caverns went on for kilometers, and a new branch had been discovered only a hundred years ago. There had to be other entrances, and the Guardians always knew a joined Trill on sight. If Dax could get inside, they'd speak to her, help her in any way they could.

She had a right to be in those caves. The Guardians were sworn to aid all joined Trill. The fact that the Symbiosis Commission was throwing up barriers was unconscionable. She was going to visit the caves, if only to make a point to that upstart Bentis Brac—his reach wasn't limitless.

After a second plate of fry cakes, she ventured out onto the balcony for a bit of midday meditation. The hotel had placed a few big pots of Trill foliage for her, a nice touch in the classically human décor of the Capital Arms. She popped open the balcony sunshade, spread a mat down, and got into a breathing rhythm.

Everyone always said the Rite of Emergence was easy. She wished that were true. It was never "easy." It required absolute concentration and wholeness of being, and Dax was bad at freeing herself from distractions. With the proper prep, however, she could perform the ritual and keep it going for days.

That evening, she planned to be contorting her mind into two people.

The Trill capital's daily rainstorm swept through, washing the streets around the hotel. Dax ducked inside from her patio perch, soaking wet, and jumped straight into the shower. Even after the rain stopped, the sky still contained a smattering of fat clouds, ripened and ready to burst. So much for a peaceful stroll in the early evening.

She commed Doctor Bashir, who berated her for not checking in sooner. She asked after the biolattice experiment, but he only wanted to talk about her. Dax assured him that she and Kira could handle things, and that Deep Space 9 needed its chief medical officer.

Evening finally arrived, and with it, her self-imposed deadline. After a day of rest, she was in the best possible state of mind.

Except for all the psychological and physical trauma she'd recently endured.

Dax had loved Nemi like a little sister. Jadzia's historic achievement in the initiate program had been—in part—because of Nemi. When things seemed impossible, Dax had imagined letting her informally adopted little sister down. It had powered her in harsh days under the unwavering scrutiny of the docents. Dax wouldn't start disappointing Nemi in death.

Dax replicated four tallow candles, placing them on saucers around her mirror. The flickering of the flames enabled better concentration, and she needed all the help she could get. A tingle formed in her abdomen as she looked into the mirror. She needed to unspool her thoughts, to create absolute calm inside. Once she was blank, she could become any previous host.

She focused on Dax's memory of Audrid's face. Ginger with wavy hair in her prime, she had a bright smile and boisterous laugh. She was built thick, with pale skin that showed an easy blush, as it did when she celebrated. In her later years, she struggled with drink a bit, buckling under the weight of being on the Symbiosis Commission. It'd been hard for her to be as kind as she was and control the lives of thousands of initiates. Atop all of that, she bore the burden of helping decide when symbionts were transferred to the next host, effectively ending the lives of the former.

Audrid was a wonderful person who put her all into a thankless job, and Jadzia treasured everything that she'd added to Dax's experience. Audrid's thoughts came easier with each passing second, and Jadzia began to feel her presence in the room. It was like hearing an old song, or catching the scent of a favorite treat. A deep and abiding familiarity settled over her body as she began to speak. *"I'nora, ja'kala vok . . . 'za Jadzia . . . zhian'tara rek . . . pora'al Zheem Dax . . . Tanas Rhem Audrid. 'za Jadzia Tanas Rhem Audrid. Audrid Tanas Rhem. Vok Jadzia Audrid Tanas Rhem."*

She studied the mirror for any changes. It always started in the eyes; she should've noticed her irises beginning to shift color, their surfaces transmuting to someone else's. From there, it'd go to her hair, her posture, and finally her face.

"*Vok Jadzia Audrid Tanas Rhem*," she said more insistently, trying to coax out the former host. Instead, the candles began to go out one by one, and quiet yet insistent words pushed their way into her consciousness like a sharp pin.

"Call to me."

Dax blinked, and the candlelight returned as if nothing had happened. Cold sweat tickled the back of her neck.

A fist slammed against the mirror from the other side, and Jadzia's visions of Audrid vanished. She backed away as Joran banged on the glassy surface, eyes like stone.

This was exactly what she was afraid of. She needed to think of Audrid, but she'd never concentrate with his behavior. Joran was far more dominant in her fears, going as far as to stalk her dreams.

He smashed his hand against the glass, and the surface wobbled—a hard hit, but not nearly enough to break through. Jadzia needed to reclaim her thoughts. She couldn't have him taking up residence there, or she wasn't sure what might happen to her.

He'd murdered three people. They'd had to pull Dax out of him to save it from his corrosive influence. What sort of imprint had he left on the symbiont?

Brac treated Jadzia like she was poisoned. Maybe he was right.

Joran smashed the glass again, and this time a hairline fracture split the mirror. The other side was a seething cauldron of rage and fear. Joran's fist impacted the surface once more, and the glass spider-webbed. He was happy to toy with her at her *zhian'tara*, so of course he would corrupt the Rite of Emergence.

He shouted, voice refracted by the shards. It dipped in and out like a broken comm unit, and "our death" was all she could make out. Dax had heard the old Trill myths of host personas possessing someone and running off into the night. The biologist in her knew there hadn't been any documented cases.

The anthropologist in her knew that all legends came from somewhere.

The mirror crashed into the hotel room, and Dax stumbled backward onto her rump. Joran's body spilled out of the frame, animated in angry, jerking spasms. His head snapped up to lock gazes with her, and Dax jolted. Unnatural contortions brought him to a crawling state, fingers lengthening, eyes growing darker. This was what she knew him as—a predator. Dax's breath caught in her throat as he crept toward her, head swaying with each lumbering motion.

The door chimed, and his gaze snapped in that direction.

Dax blinked. Joran was gone—no glass fragments, nothing else amiss. She sat on the floor, chest heaving, alone.

The door chimed again.

"Who is it?"

"Ensign Colin Hart."

"Onscreen."

Her desk screen lit up with a light-skinned human male in a Starfleet security uniform. She crossed the room to get a closer look. He had to be in his early twenties, with a mop of dusty orange hair and high, hollow cheekbones. He stood at ease, with his hands folded behind his back, clearly expecting to greet a lieutenant commander.

Dax shook her head and climbed to her feet. A professional call at this hour had to be important. Maybe she was being recalled to the station? No. They would send a message. A secret mission? More bad news?

"One moment," Dax replied.

She checked her reflection in the unshattered mirror to make sure she looked like an officer and not a sweaty, hallucinating Trill. She was about halfway there.

Oh, well.

"Come in," she called, and the door slid open in the foyer.

Hart walked around the corner, and his arm swung up holding a type-2 phaser.

Dax dove as his first shot missed her. He tried to line up another, and Dax charged him. As long as he had distance, he had lethal advantage.

She slammed into his gut in a bear hug, and her assailant groaned in pain. He brought his elbow down on the back of her neck, and stars danced in her eyes, knocking her free. She lunged and grabbed his phaser before he could bring it to bear on her again. She was quick, but his strength won out and he pushed her off.

She closed the gap with a fierce sidekick, planting a heel directly into his gut. Her attacker screamed, and blood coated his teeth. He fired at her again, but the shot went wide, etching a burned line across the far wall. The weapon was set to kill, no doubt about that.

He wheezed and grimaced as a small red stain began to spread on his abdomen. She hadn't stabbed him, just rushed him. It seemed like he had a preexisting wound—so she kicked him again in the same spot. Dax took apart her assailant, swapping between body blows and trying to tear away his weapon.

When she finally got it loose, she brought her elbow across his face, sending him spinning back into the balcony glass. She switched from kill to stun, but before she could fire, the man opened the balcony door and slipped around the corner. She dashed out into the rainy night just in time to see him leap over the railing.

Three stories from the ground.

Dax rushed to the edge, peering into the storm and blinking away the pouring drops. Her attacker had landed on the street below. He clambered upright and limped along the road toward the urban sprawl. She aimed the phaser, but she didn't shoot. There were civilians in the road, and at this distance, a miss was possible.

She bolted out the door, weapon in hand. He was badly wounded in two places—legs and torso. If she could run him down, stunning him would be child's play. Then she could get some answers.

Down she went, rushing through stairwells as fast as her legs would carry her. She burst into the lobby, where the hotel bar was packed. She scanned the crowd for anyone who might help her, and her eyes fell on a dark-skinned woman with short, natural hair in a Starfleet security uniform. She'd probably just come off duty.

"Ensign!" Dax shouted. "With me!"

The woman did a double take. "Sir?"

"Now!" Dax went jogging past.

"Yes, Commander!"

The women ran out into the street, where several bystanders gawked. It was a busy city thoroughfare, but pedestrian traffic had died down for the evening. Neon blue lights blared from the shopping district across the street, washing the whole avenue in monochrome.

"We're after a man from Starfleet security," Dax shouted. "He shot at me!"

"Copy," the woman replied.

"Did anyone see the guy who jumped off the balcony?" Dax called to the confused crowd, and a few of them pointed.

Her companion acknowledged and bolted up the street with impressive speed. Dax trailed after, following them both down a drainage path.

With a grace Emony would envy, Dax leaped the barrier into the thermocrete canyon. The slick ground sloped to catch the runoff, and water gushed around her feet from the deluge. A bloody handprint stained the clean stone closest to her, the rain eroding its presence by the second. Up ahead, her companion splashed farther into the culvert after their prey.

It was hard to make out her backup in the near darkness. Very few lights serviced the drainage system, which grew more perilous the deeper they got. The sewers were towering accomplishments of engineering to deal with the daily squalls, and waterfalls joined the path from other runoffs. Dax leaned on the wall as she sloshed along for fear of slipping.

"Colin!" the woman ahead cried out. "Stop!"

Dax redoubled her pace. She couldn't leave her backup without backup.

She caught up with them at the lip of a wide outflow overlooking a churning pool. The woman had her phaser firmly fixed on the man's chest, and he stood at the edge of a sharp drop. He clutched his gut, pale skin growing more bloodless by the second.

"Colin, what's wrong with you?" asked the woman, tensing up her grip.

Dax's attacker stepped closer to the perilous drop, peering over. He didn't look disturbed or distressed in any way. Rather, he struck Dax as bored. Blood leaked around his hand, drenching his front. That wound wasn't pretty.

He swayed once, then slipped quietly over the edge. Dax hurried to the drop-off, just in time to see him hit a catwalk on the way down. His body spun with a bang, then vanished into the churning water far below.

"*Colin!*" The woman slid to her knees.

Together, they searched the waves until they were sure he was gone.

Dax spent the next six hours going over exactly what happened with Trill investigators in one of the hotel conference rooms. She told them about the fight and chasing Colin Hart into the drainage system with the ensign later identified as Keisha Rush.

Rush told them about Hart, an ensign and a fellow security officer at the nearby Federation science outpost. It was a small installation, a prototyping facility for a new starship power system. Rush and Hart were supposed to meet at the Capital Arms after work for a drink. He'd showed up late and was acting strange. He then excused himself, and that's when he'd gone to Dax's room.

The investigators then took Dax aside and combed through her story again. The ensign's bloodstained uniform was the first point of interest. The second was the phaser he used in the attack. It should have been locked up at the end of his shift. When investigators checked, Hart's phaser was gone, logged out sixteen hours ago. That was after Dax visited the Commission.

Dax and Rush were both thanked for their cooperation and dismissed. The pair came slogging into the lobby as first light broke, and the ensign turned to her.

"Sir, what made Colin do it?"

"I'm sorry, Ensign?"

"Colin wasn't, like, some super assassin. We worked together for eight months. He was a sweet guy." Rush pinned Dax with her piercing hazel eyes. "Do you think he *chose* to go to your room and kill you?"

Dax didn't want to share the details of her Symbiosis Commission case, but there was no way to dodge the ensign's question.

"No. I don't."

"I didn't think so," Rush said. "I have a few questions for you."

"Ensign, I'm not sure this is appropriate—"

"Colin was studying to be criminal investigator. He was up for a promotion. He has—had—a cat. Someone needs to check on Noodles. Starfleet is going to have to tell Colin's mom and sisters he's dead." Rush shook her head. "He had a whole life in front of him, and now he doesn't."

She was so young. Dax wondered if it was the first time Rush had lost a colleague. Starfleet was a beacon of hope, a place for explorers and a force for peace—but it was far from safe.

"Ensign Rush, I'm sorry about your friend. I will try to get to the bottom of this—but that's also why I can't discuss it with you."

"You're a science officer, blue." She pointed to the cerulean shoulders of Dax's uniform. "It's not your job to get to the bottom of crimes."

"I'm on your side."

"Glad to hear it, Commander. I want to know who killed my friend. Surely you can understand that."

"I can." Dax looked into her eyes, trying to project compassion. "More than you know."

"If you get what I'm saying, then you've got to tell me what's going on. In my place, would you be satisfied giving a statement to the authorities and walking away?"

"No."

"All right then. Tell me why you're here, and I'll leave you alone."

Dax sighed. "How much time do you have?"

"I'm on my second wind. Let's get some coffee."

8

Gathering

Ensign Rush pried most of the details out of Dax. They spent much of the morning discussing the case over eggs and toast in Dax's room and got to know each other. Rush was an Earth-born human, waiting for her appointment to the Judge Advocate General to come through. Both of her parents were alive and happily married, though she was estranged from her sister.

Dax shared a bit of her own background, and Rush was curious about how joining worked. Joined Trill were always expected to be ambassadors for the Symbiosis Commission, and Dax hid her weariness as she obliged the ensign.

After a few hours, Rush bade her farewell, adding, "Sorry about your friend."

"Yours, too."

When she finally shut the door, Dax was totally spent. They'd moved her to an interior room, with holowindows. She could easily keep the door locked and her phaser at her bedside. The extra measures helped Dax to relax.

Just a standard, phaser-at-the-bedside vacation.

Her voice was gravelly. Her clothes felt like she'd jumped in a lake. Dax wandered into her secured bedroom, with its holowindows depicting a Trill forest, ready to pass out. The images of the outside world faded to orange sunset, then purplish evening as woods became capital skyline. She stripped off her uniform and climbed into bed, greedily snuggling into the blankets.

Her alarm seemed to go off immediately.

Groaning, Dax rolled over and slid out of bed.

"Computer." She rubbed her eyes and shambled into the bathroom. "End alarm."

The room acknowledged with a chirp, shutting off the chimes. It'd been days since she'd gotten anything approaching normal sleep. Her body was still smarting from her encounters with Nemi and Ensign Hart, but there was no way she was willing to get medical care at the Commission—not until she knew who'd attacked her.

After freshening up, she descended to the picturesque lobby to wait for Kira. The major was supposed to be arriving any moment, and Dax eagerly watched the transporter zone through the front windows. After a half hour of waiting, Kira sparkled into being.

The Bajoran woman hefted her bag and headed inside, immediately running and hugging Dax the moment they made eye contact. Kira pulled back, eyes raking the bruises on Dax's face and neck.

"Did you get in another fight?" she asked.

"I honestly can't remember who punched me where this week," Dax replied. "Can we just get some lunch?"

"Let me stash my stuff. What are you in the mood for?"

"I miss Klingon food. I'm dying for some fresh *gagh*."

"No thank you," Kira said. "But I could have *krada* legs."

They got Kira checked into her room, then set off for a little Klingon place in the lower garden district. Dax filled Kira in on the way, giving her all the details of the attack.

The major was furious at Dax for failing to let her know when it happened.

"Look, it'd been a . . . a long day," was all Dax could muster in her own defense.

The two of them arrived at the cozy Klingon restaurant, its walls awash with red and copper tones. They took seats at a battered metal booth, listening to the head chef serenade everyone from the open kitchen. The opera was lovely, but lousy for conversation, so they moved to the outside tables.

"Kicking that guy in the wound, nice." Kira took a sip of her tea. "I can't believe he jumped."

Dax savored a fermented-root digestif, a practice she'd acquired from Curzon. He'd sworn it warded off the gas that Klingon cuisine brought on. Dax knew it to be his excuse to have a drink before a nap.

"Ensign Hart never intended to live." Dax looked over the menu. "I'm sure of it."

"What makes you say that?"

"First off, the path he took led straight to the underground master drainage." Dax lifted her shot glass by its tiny handle and sniffed the earthy contents. "Hart couldn't have chosen a worse place to run to—unless he wanted to jump."

Kira shrugged. "I've chased down plenty of Cardassians. Some of them did strange things before the end."

"Ensign Rush said Hart's behavior was off, and I believe her. I'm not sure any decision Hart made was 'his' decision." Dax crossed her arms. "Second, there was the wound. Whatever was wrong with Hart, he came into my room that way. It looked like he'd been stabbed."

"Why would you attack someone and jump off a balcony if you were bleeding out?"

"If you weren't in your right mind . . ." Dax stared at the patterns in the hammered metal table, trying to force some sense onto the mess.

Why would he jump into the drainage system?

"You okay?" Kira asked. "You kind of zoned out for a minute there."

She sighed. "This feels like it's getting darker by the minute."

"I'm here to help."

"I appreciate that."

"Where do we start?"

"Well—" Dax leaned back in her chair and took a pull of her syrupy drink. Its bitterness washed over her, rattling her back to life after a rough couple of days. "I need to get into the Caves of Mak'ala—but the Symbiosis Commission is stopping me."

Kira's eyes lit up. "Interesting. If you're trying to figure out how to make . . . an alternative entrance, we can rig up some explosives—"

"Not like that," Dax said.

"Oh, so more like we grab an insider and force them to let us in?"

Dax stared at her.

"What? You can take a girl out of the resistance, but . . ."

"I was thinking of something a little less violent."

"How was I supposed to know that?"

"I appreciate the enthusiasm."

"You know I'd dispose of a body for you." Kira gave her an innocent smile.

"I believe it."

Their food arrived, fresh and spicy enough to swell Dax's lips until they tingled. They both took a few bites in silence to blunt their hunger.

"This isn't as good as on DS9," Kira said.

"You'd better not let the chef hear you—it would insult his honor."

"If you didn't call me to blow something up, and you don't want my opinions on Klingon food, what *do* you want?"

"Yet," Dax said, holding up a utensil. "I don't want those things, yet."

"I'm listening." Kira took a bite of her food.

"Trying to get through the Symbiosis Commission entrance is out of the question. Security is extremely tight, and I've been denied access. But Audrid was a Symbiosis Commissioner, and she knew a way—the Guardian Road."

"Wait. Don't you have her memories?"

"It's not that easy. I need to bring her forth with the Rite of Emergence."

"Then you can ask her where this road is?"

"Exactly." Jadzia nodded.

"You needed me for this?"

"Joran has been . . . interfering."

Kira frowned, and her Bajoran nose ridges added some annoyance. "Ugh. I hate that guy."

Dax bristled a little. "Hey, *I'm* that guy."

"Sorry. You know what I meant."

"Anyway, there's this ritual, but when Joran causes trouble, I'm not able to do it. I need someone to lend me strength. Someone I trust." She smiled at Kira. "I can't think of anyone better."

"Count me in."

They'd spent the better part of the afternoon taking in the sights of the capital. Just like before, Jadzia pampered herself, resting her mind for the ritual. Kira made that easy, suggesting all manner of things to see and foods to try. She was always game to explore.

They took in the North Shore Greenway, and for a second, Dax was simply enjoying a stroll with one of her friends. It was what she should do, if she ever took leave. Dax savored the feeling, trying to forget the reason for her return to her homeworld: Nemi's death.

Relief gave way to grief as reality set in. Eventually, Nemi's fate weighed too heavily on Dax, and they decided to return to the hotel. The Rite of Emergence wasn't going to conduct itself, and Dax was eager to make some progress.

She started laying out the implements of focus: flame and a mirror.

"You know what's nice about Deep Space 9?" Dax lit a candle

beneath her hotel-room mirror. "No one bothers me about my joined rituals."

Kira sat cross-legged on Dax's bed, munching a fruit she'd bought from the Summer Market on the way back. "Why would they?"

"You know how humans can be. Some of them want to deconstruct anything you can't read with a tricorder."

"True. The people on the station aren't like that though. I always figured Starfleet was pretty accepting."

"You haven't dated much in Starfleet." She lit another candle. "Anyway, it isn't perfect, but . . . Deep Space 9 just might be."

Kira almost choked on her fruit. " 'Perfect'? I think you're going to have to run that by me again. You know Quark is there?"

"He's not that bad."

"He followed me around with a holoimager so he could make a simulation for a creepy customer."

"I'd forgotten about that." Dax leaned against the dresser. "No, I was thinking about my *zhian'tara*. Some people have trouble accepting my identity. You, Odo, Benjamin, Julian, Leeta, Chief O'Brien, and even Quark—accepted parts of me into themselves. You all make me feel . . . celebrated."

"What brought all of this on?" Kira grinned. "I mean, I don't mind the compliments, but . . ."

"Nemi. We were close. Not recently, but once. I keep thinking of that little girl, and all the things she was good at. She should've been a sculptor. Or a track star. Or an engineer. If she'd never joined the initiate program, I think she'd be thriving. Happy." Dax's gaze fell. "Sometimes I think it's my fault. I wrote her that letter of recommendation. I vouched for her twice."

"And if you hadn't, she would've hated you forever."

"She'd still be alive."

"Listen to me. I *chose* to join the Bajoran Resistance. It could've gotten me killed. Prophets know I had too many friends that didn't make it . . ." A little sigh escaped Kira's lips. "But you know, that was my purpose. And I would've done anything to be there, defending my people, fighting to free them. From what you've told me, Nemi thought she found her purpose in becoming joined. Nothing could keep her from that."

Dax nodded. "Yeah."

"Not everyone is born ready to meet their fate. Nemi had to try, and you had to support her."

"I know."

"Let's summon Audrid and get some answers." Kira hopped off the bed and came to Dax's side. "What am I doing here? Do I need to light a candle too?"

Dax laughed. "No, but you need to be fearless. Shouldn't be a problem for you."

"I'm brave, but I'm not fearless."

She looked into Kira's eyes. "Then I hope you like being terrified. Ready?"

"As I'll ever be."

Dax placed a palm to the mirror and took Kira's hand. "Do what I do."

Kira nodded and copied her, placing her free hand against the mirror.

Dax closed her eyes, candlelight flickering across her lids, and focused on the warmth building in her abdomen. Kira's hand was soft against hers, the comfort of a capable friend by her side. If Joran came, no matter what he did, they'd be together. "*I'nora, ja'kala vok . . . 'za Jadzia . . . zhian'tara rek . . . pora'al Zheem Dax . . . Tanas Rhem Audrid. . . .*" Dax began.

Kira copied as best she could, her sincere effort bolstering Dax's spirits. She imagined herself speaking Audrid's name into a pool, drawing forth her memories.

Dax repeated her incantation, and the pool grew brighter.

Kira jerked and gave a sudden shout. When Dax opened her eyes, Joran stood over both of them with a surgical drill. Rain-drenched patient scrubs stuck to his pale, wet skin. Cold light coated him like a sheen of ice.

"Don't look," Dax said. "He's not real. Just think of me."

"Right. Yeah." Kira shut her eyes, and Dax did the same.

Joran's presence passed through her like a shade, sending shivers up her spine. He was trying to disrupt the process, but she wasn't going to let him.

That's when the smell hit.

It wasn't rot, but something much fouler—a fresh kill. Steaming blood clouded her nostrils, and she tried not to gag. Joran brought on the grisliest memories he could, awakening violent urges inside Dax.

"I've been in a Cardassian prison, you know," Kira said, chuckling. "You're going to have to do better than a little stink."

Had a Guardian been administering the rite, they would've been appalled at the outburst. Yet in this makeshift setting, it'd been exactly what Dax needed to hear.

That's right. He's nothing but a shadow.

Joran diminished inside her, disarmed by the outburst. This had been the sort of thing Audrid would find funny, and she did. Dax sensed her presence long before she saw anything.

Audrid's floaty, ringing laugh came to mind first. She found the humor in everything. She loved long walks through the parks around the Symbiosis Commission campus, especially in the fall. She was a passionate spouse, and she'd loved her husband dearly.

At least, the first one.

She'd had two children, but one had died and the other was estranged. She couldn't bear to have more, but loved all children for the rest of her days. She'd tried to make the Symbiosis Commission more humane, to make the initiate program less grueling so that future generations might enjoy participating. Those reforms took a lot out of her and tore her family apart. When Audrid finally passed on, she hadn't been surrounded by friends and family, but Commission staff who'd served with her for years.

As Audrid blossomed inside Jadzia, Joran wilted. Dax took solace in Kira's friendship, and her fear receded like the tide. It would be okay. Nothing could harm her in this place.

"Hello!"

The voice was strained, older and female. Jadzia opened her eyes to see Audrid standing behind her in the mirror. When she turned around, it was as though the woman was in the room with them.

"Hi," Dax said, dropping Kira's hand.

"Did it work?" Kira asked. "I thought I saw an old lady."

"It did." Dax looked her honored guest over.

Audrid was shorter than her, with puffy cheeks and a round chin. Silver strands dominated her dusty red hair, which hung in ringlets around her head. Audrid's nose had swollen in old age, with a blush tip at the bottom like she'd been drinking—which she often had. The life of a commissioner involved making a lot of uncomfortable decisions about others, and she suffered from a nightmarish case of empathy. Every night, Audrid had taken her failures to bed with her, only to wake thoroughly tangled in them.

"Well, you called?" Audrid said with a smile.

"Yes!" Dax replied. "Sorry, I'm so glad it worked. Joran has been a problem."

"I know." Audrid frowned. "You must be careful of that one."

Dax shook her head. "He can't hurt me."

"Don't underestimate him," Audrid said. "When he was joined to Dax . . . he kept us repressed."

"Should I be doing something, or . . . hearing something?" Kira asked.

"Oh, sorry! You can't see Audrid, but I can talk to her as though she's in the room with us."

"Tell her I said hi," Audrid said.

Dax gestured to where Audrid stood in the middle of the room. "She says hi."

"Hey." Kira waved at the empty air. "I've got to say, this is one of the stranger introductions I've had."

"Audrid," Dax said, "I've called upon you because I need to find the Guardian Road."

The older woman straightened. "The Guardian Road . . ."

"Yes. I want to get into the Caves of Mak'ala so I can speak to a Guardian. I need to know where the path is, and you can tell me."

Audrid stared at her, eventually breaking into a tired smile. "Oh, dear."

Dax blinked. "What?"

"The Guardian Road isn't like a secret walkway with sidewalks and cordons. It's a set of twisting caverns with hundreds of branching choices, deadfalls, and unstable tunnels."

"I thought you knew the way," Dax said.

"I knew of a *way. I was seventy years old when I ran the Commission." Audrid shook with laughter. "Those old caverns weren't what you might call accessible. I had them surveyed and guarded. Jadzia, I don't even know where the entrance is."*

Dax's heart sank. Without a secret path to the Guardians, she was flummoxed, and whatever conspiracy was forming might pass her by.

"What? What'd she say?" Kira asked.

"She can't help us," Dax replied.

Audrid tapped her index fingers together in front of herself. "I can point you to a map, though."

"Okay," Dax said. "Where is it?"

"Across the park from the Symbiosis Commission building—in the Grand Archives."

The Grand Archives were the records storehouse for the Commission—an impossibly large building dedicated solely to tracking the health and exploits of the joined. Their records dated back hundreds of years, covering every conceivable topic about the symbionts, along with biological samples in cold storage. Dax had done some research there for her exobiology degree. The classically stylish building wasn't nearly as impenetrable as the Commission.

"If my Commission access is limited at the main building, it'll be limited there too," Dax said. "How are we supposed to get in?"

Kira cleared her throat and raised a hand. "We could, um, break in."

Despite the copious replicator offerings available in their rooms, Kira and Dax ordered a delivery of *kesht* balls. They were oat dough, stuffed with flaky red fish and pan-seared with an oil-salt crust. The dish was popular in the capital, but Dax never saw it offered anywhere but Trill.

"Okay." Kira bit off a hunk of stretchy dough, revealing a steaming pink core. "This is good. I like the sweet note."

"I know." Dax sat at the hotel-room table and unwrapped the paper from her own *kesht*. "I could eat this every day."

"Oh, thank you for having this." Audrid greedily watched Jadzia take a bite.

The thin, crispy exterior gave way to chewy dough. An herbal brine infused the cakes, drawing Dax's mind to a life on the shore. She let out a happy sigh, which Audrid copied in turn.

"You really should get them more often," the older woman added. "You could probably program this into your replicator on the station."

"I'll think about it," Dax said. But, it wouldn't be wise to have such a delicacy within easy reach. It might become mundane.

"From what you're telling me," Kira said, "we need to break into the Grand Archives, get a copy of the Guardian Road map, and get out."

Dax put her food down and wiped her fingers. "If we get identified, I'll be court-martialed. You won't be welcome to serve with Starfleet. Is that a risk you're willing to take?"

"The attempt on your life happened the same day you briefed the Commission on Nemi. It's related," Kira said. "They're interfering with your access to the Caves of Mak'ala. Do you know what we did to the Cardassians who kept us away from our temples? Let's just say we weren't polite."

Dax grabbed some savory vinegar sauce and poured it into her *kesht*'s core, staining it brown. "I knew you'd understand. We can't trust the Commission to do the right thing just yet. If we break in correctly, no one will ever know."

"Solid plan, but"—Kira shoveled some blanched greens from the takeout containers onto her plate—"you're really going to be okay if they catch you in the Caves?"

"Yes. Those people are sworn to serve me. That's enshrined in Trill law."

The gall of the Commission, locking her out. It was clear that they were holding a grudge against her and Captain Sisko over the Joran incident. Brac had gone out of his way to be hostile—and someone had showed up to kill her that very evening. Was he in on the assassination attempt, or just a bad person?

Whoever's feathers she was ruffling, she needed to figure it out before they caught her off guard.

Dax fetched the computer and brought it to the table, looking up the Grand Archives in a local database. It had historical information, a rough approximation of blueprints, operating hours and more—but nothing they could use to break in.

"See, the thing about these old buildings," Kira said, "is that they all have structural weaknesses. Easy breaching points."

"'Structural weaknesses'? That young woman over there needs to slow down." Audrid laughed. "There are plenty of ways to get into the Grand Archives without blowing it up."

"Kira, we're trying to avoid property damage," Dax said. "Especially anything traceable."

Kira rolled her eyes. "I didn't mean it like that."

Audrid raised a finger. "If I may."

Dax held up a hand for Kira to pause. "Sorry, she's telling me something."

"This is an old water maintenance hatch." Audrid pointed to the

blueprint. "We had a terrible fight about it one year on the utility appropriations committee. That whole area was prone to flooding, so we had to install pumps to drain the tunnels. The locks on the substations are all manual, because it was cheaper."

Dax shifted in her seat. "Do you know if they're still there?"

"How much do you want to learn about appropriations committee politics?"

"Is there a short version?"

"My colleagues, as a 'compromise,' got locks that were rated for a thousand years. They said that should make 'even someone like Audrid happy.'"

Dax frowned. "This is the sort of stuff you remember from your days as a commissioner?"

"The bureaucracy and infighting? Dearie, what else do you think a commissioner does?"

"That sounds miserable," Dax said.

Audrid smiled kindly and nodded. "It was."

"I always thought you were proud of your work there."

"Oh, I was proud of my work. I gave the best years of my life to that den of vipers. Loved the job, but most of the people could jump off a cliff."

"I'm . . . sorry to hear that. These are manual locks?" Dax said, pointing the entrance out for Kira.

"Yes," Audrid said. "Those corridors date back centuries. Installing decent security down there proved too expensive, so we just . . . didn't. I doubt it's changed."

Dax turned to Kira. "She's saying these utility tunnels will get us in if we can break the locks."

"That's great," Kira replied. "Manual locks don't set off the alarm grid."

Audrid sighed wistfully. "I warned those old fools that someone could break in if they did it this way."

"So"—Kira pointed to the exterior shots on the screen—"we go in through the utility tunnels, come up alongside the mains, get into the database, and get out the same way?"

"And all we have to do is melt one lock," Dax said.

"And get past any guards—" Kira added.

"Archivists—" Dax interrupted.

"—without being spotted. And we can't stun anyone, because that would be assault. You need to leave your weapon here. If we're caught breaking and entering, I don't want to be doing it armed."

"Could've used someone with her brains on the appropriations committee," Audrid said.

"If we get attacked," Dax said, "we'll be defenseless."

Picking at her dinner, Kira said, "Let me worry about what to do with security."

Kira had more tactical experience, so Dax decided not to pursue the question further.

"Is there a day of rest coming up?" Audrid asked.

"Tomorrow night," Dax said.

Kira almost spit out her food. "What about tomorrow night?"

"I was telling Audrid that's the day of rest," Dax said.

Kira nodded. "I see. And no one wants to be stuck in a library on their leisure time."

Dax frowned. "I love libraries."

"Of course you do," Kira said. "This is good. Fewer people means less risk."

Audrid piped up. "Actually, it should be closed, except to staff."

Dax gestured to the empty air where she stood. "Audrid thinks it'll be closed."

"There we go," Kira said. "I've broken out of a Cardassian prison camp. We can handle a library on a day of rest."

9

Retrieval

The next night, the three of them made their way through the streets of the capital toward the Grand Archives. Dax and Kira wore dark, comfortable clothes, waiting to flip up their hoods until they got to their destination. Audrid wore her favorite flower-print dress and a flashy hat, since she was invisible and it didn't matter.

Housed at the site of the original Symbiosis Commission, the Grand Archives was much older than the surrounding buildings. Classical Trill statuary adorned the columns, figures carved in white marble reaching for the heavens. Curling inlays of twisting vines and flowers ran across the ground in bright mosaics.

"This place is impossible to maintain," Audrid said as they passed into the shadowed colonnade. "Honestly, I argued that we should sell it off. 'Old' is not the same thing as 'significant.'"

"Would you mind keeping it down?" Dax whispered.

"I'm only in your head, dear," Audrid said.

"But you're distracting me."

They circled around the Grand Archives complex toward the maintenance entrance. A service ramp took them into a basement level before they cut across to the utilities tunnels. So far, everything perfectly matched up with the maps and Audrid's intel.

When they reached their intended point of entry, however, they found it had been sealed. Age streaks painted the thermocrete surface—it had to be decades old.

"That's one way to fix the flooding issues," Kira said.

"Audrid." Dax rubbed the bridge of her nose.

"It's not my fault. I've been dead for nearly a century."

Dax bit her lip. "I thought you said the locks were rated for a thousand years."

"Yes, but they'll last longer encased in thermocrete," Audrid said. "I have to say, we didn't even discuss doing this. It's a smarter choice."

Dax nodded. "I'm sure it is. Kira, we're not getting in this way."

Kira stood with her hands on her hips, inspecting the sealed entrance. "I can see that."

"Got any other ideas?" Dax asked. "Should we regroup and come up with something else?"

Kira shook her head. "There'll be another way in, and security here is a joke."

Audrid raised a finger. "It's a library, not a fortress."

"What are you thinking? Break a lock?" Dax asked.

Kira laughed. "No. You want a structural weakness."

"Kira, we can't blow up—"

"Not what I meant," Kira said. "This is a centuries-old building with a storied history. It's going to have old windows and doors everywhere. There are probably sections of the roof that are open to the elements. We need ancient hinges, weak joints, that sort of thing."

Dax knew very little about the building's exterior structure. Her time in the archives had been focused on databases and historical records, not security gaps.

"There's an office on the top with a cupola." Audrid got a wistful look. "I used it for a while when the Symbiosis Commission was evacuated for some minor contamination. That Grand Archives office was spectacular. You could open the cupola with a lever, and the breeze would sort of swirl down through the space. Just what the doctor ordered on difficult days—"

"There's a cupola on the roof we can get into," Dax said. "We just have to get up there."

Kira rubbed her hands together. "Now we're talking."

They wound around the exterior, looking for any way to get to the building. Too bad they couldn't just beam up to the roof. Even if they could find a transporter, that would leave a log.

"There," Kira said, pointing out a renovation scaffold.

The skeletal metal construction stretched up the side of the building, black gauzy material surrounding it to protect people below from dropped tools. Ladders crisscrossed its interior, barely visible behind the gently swaying fabric.

Dax traced the path they'd have to take from the ground all the way to the top; it looked safe enough. "If we get up there and that cupola won't open, we need to scrub the mission. We're already off script, and if anything goes wrong . . ."

"We'll get in and out before you know it," Kira said. "Audrid knows where to find the map of the Guardian Road, right?"

"If nothing has changed in the past century," Dax said, and Audrid shot her an annoyed glance. "Let's go."

They approached the scaffold and found a basic lock on the door to the workers' area. Kira flipped out a blade and cut a person-sized slit through the nearby mesh, opening a path around the barrier. She slipped through, holding the flap open for Dax to follow.

One floor at a time, they made their way up the side of the Grand Archives. Inside the scaffolding, they found a half-dozen restoration sites, statues in various states of repair. A pang of nostalgia struck Dax; she'd seen these statues in many lives, and it was odd to see them so degraded.

"I always liked that one." Audrid pointed to a plump fellow with a face like a satisfied house cat.

"Who is it?" Dax whispered as they passed, and Kira shushed her.

"Haven't the faintest," Audrid replied. "Doesn't he look silly?"

Dax kept her voice as low as she could. "A little."

Kira wheeled on her. "I'm going to need you to stop talking to Audrid while we're committing a crime."

"Sorry," Dax mouthed, but Kira just shook her head and kept climbing.

After too many flights of steep, shaky stairs, they reached the roof. The women had to clamber over the parapet, the edge of which was filthy with decades of urban dust. Audrid, being a mere figment of the imagination, was already on the roof when Dax got to her feet, brushing herself off.

"That looks tiring," said the older woman.

"It is." Dax bit back a snide comment. "Where's the cupola?"

Audrid pointed in the direction of the front of the building, and Dax spied the silhouette of their target. Hidden by the parapet, the rooftop was a jungle of climate machinery and building subsystems. Dax and Kira climbed over pipes and under conduits to cross its wide expanse. An electrical buzz suffused the air, the product of huge old power hookups.

They reached the cupola, a copper dome with four stained-glass windows. The abstract designs were more for filtering the light than anything else, with random patterns in the glass. Up close, the copper cladding on the windows was starting to fail in places, with some parts being little more than crunchy flakes of green patina.

"Structural weakness," Kira whispered, flipping out her knife and slipping it into a seam. She worked her way around the glass, eventually pulling it free, then she reached inside and flipped a catch, opening the window.

Audrid laughed, marveling at Kira's ease. "I told them to sell this building. Inefficient, always needing renovation, no security."

"I think it's nice. Storied," Dax said. "Besides, you're the security hole."

Audrid crossed her arms. "I'm just saying I was right."

"All good over there?" Kira cut in.

"Yeah, sorry," Dax replied.

About two meters beneath the cupola was a maintenance walkway secured by hanging cables. Kira went in first, landing with impressive silence. She hunkered low and dashed into the darkness like a cat. Dax hung her legs over the edge of the window and gauged the jump.

It wasn't a difficult maneuver—but there were consequences for failure. The cupola sat atop the main office—which was at least ten meters down. A fall from that height onto the marble floor would certainly shatter something, if not everything. Dax pushed off from her perch, going from trespassing to breaking and entering.

She landed harder than she'd hoped, but she hit the ground moving. Within seconds, she'd followed Kira into a side door and down a flight of stairs.

"Right." Kira checked up and down the stairwell. "Which way to the map?"

"I don't know. We need to look around," Audrid replied.

Dax's eyes went wide. "What do you mean you don't know?"

Kira threw up her hands. "She doesn't know?"

"I'm trying to remember." Audrid frowned. "We're in a stairwell, and it's been a while since I've been here. If I could look around a little bit more . . ."

"She needs to look around," Dax whispered.

"Yeah, by all means. Let's sign up for the tour." Kira shook her head, tonguing the inside of her cheek.

"Please tell your friend I'm sorry," Audrid said.

Dax gave Kira a contrite expression. "She's sorry."

Kira sighed. "Where does she need to go?"

"I just need to look, uh, around," Audrid said. "It'll come back to me."

Dax said, "Anywhere we can go safely."

"Fine." Kira opened the door a crack to peer out, and a shaft of light spilled across her eyes. "Let's move. Stay with me."

The pair crept into a wide corridor, supported by flying buttresses of ivory material. Every few meters, some piece of brilliant Trill artwork stood on display, a reminder of the talent produced by joined Trill. Dax wished she could stop and look at a few of them. She'd never paid attention when she'd studied here, wrapped in her ambitions.

"Oh!" Audrid said, and Dax's heart jumped a beat. "It's this way. This way!"

Dax made a quiet hiss to get Kira's attention, then bade her follow. They turned and headed the other way down the corridors, delving deeper into the complex. Every shadow seemed darker, every noise they made louder, and Dax jumped at any movement—real or not. She prayed Joran wouldn't decide to make an appearance, because she wasn't sure she could handle him.

"Almost there," Audrid said. "I promise it's this way."

They turned a corner to find a sign marked SPECIAL COLLECTIONS. It hung alongside a thick, hermetically sealed door. A keypad softly glowed beside it, awaiting input. Neither the lock nor the door were particularly new.

"Yes!" Audrid clasped her hands together. "It's still here. I was wondering if we were ever going to catch a break."

"This doesn't look like a break to me." Dax pressed a palm to the solid metal.

"What's the code?" Kira said.

"Try two-six-five-three-five-two-two," Audrid replied. Dax entered it.

The lock pad cycled green, and the door came unbolted with a resonant *thunk.*

Audrid preened at her success. "That was the default admin code. We used it because ours were too hard to remember."

"Terrible security." Dax stepped into the darkness beyond.

"Do I even want to know?" Kira asked, and Dax shook her head.

The room on the other side of the door came to life—a wide, white hall with hundreds of smooth, lacquered drawers lining the sides. Dax had heard about this place but never had the occasion to visit. Her work in the Grand Archives had been focused on chemistry and exobiology; this section housed sociological and archaeological discoveries. It contained items dating back to the first joinings.

Kira surveyed the massive array of drawers. "Going to need some guidance here. Where to?"

"Audrid?" Dax turned to her.

The older woman nervously tapped her fingers together. "Uh . . . oh, right. I think we have to use the index terminal over there." She shuffled across the floor to a carrel. "It should be here!"

Dax followed her into the nook and found a screen awaiting input. "What do I search? Guardian's Path? Guardian Road?"

"I don't know," Kira replied. "Oh, you were talking to her again."

Audrid pondered for a moment. "Try 'South Bank Surveys Section B.'"

"Catchy name." Dax typed in the query and read back the result, "This one? 'Section B South Bank Surveys Final'?"

The former commissioner snapped her fingers. "Those surveys have the Guardian Road. I always wanted to go down there myself, but they weren't easily accessible. I'd ordered everything surveyed for the archives, which is probably why you thought of it, Jadzia."

"We'll need climbing gear for the Guardian Road." Dax punched the retrieval code, and one of the drawers popped open across the room.

"My kind of mission," Kira said with a smile. "Let's get the information copied."

Dax went and pulled open the collections drawer, finding hundreds of isolinear optical chips in cradles. The one they wanted flashed green, and Dax removed it from the drawer. She checked the serial number on the chip. The last four digits matched up with the catalog.

Dax slotted it into her tricorder. "Copying the files now . . . got them."

"Great," Kira said. "Back up to the roof."

They replaced the chip, then Dax lead the way to the door. She opened it, and found Doctor Renhol on the other side, clutching a padd, face in shock. Audrid gave a startled shout, and Kira ducked back out of sight.

"Jadzia! I—I'm sorry, I was just surprised to see anyone at this hour. Much less you." She looked like she'd been headed somewhere down the hall.

Dax's heart caught in her throat. This was the worst-case scenario, a person intimately familiar with her discovering her in an unauthorized area. At least she hadn't seen Kira. If Dax could think of something clever, maybe she could save this terrible situation.

"I was just leaving." Dax couldn't even convince herself with that one.

The doctor's lips were stiff as she gathered her courage. "Brac . . . told me he was revoking your clearance. I . . . I know you're not supposed to be here."

"Why would he do that?" Dax searched Renhol's eyes.

"He says you're unstable at the symbiont level. That Joran—"

"Joran is a part of us," she snapped, and Renhol recoiled. "Sorry. It's just . . . disrespectful. He's a part of Dax. And we're fine."

"Apologies."

"Do you believe me? What I said about Nemi? What she was?" Dax suppressed a shudder.

Renhol stared at the ground. "I might."

"I wasn't drunk. I wasn't hallucinating. I know what I saw."

"I know. That's . . ." Renhol's eyebrows knit together. "That's why I'm here. I came to see what research existed on the subject."

Dax smiled. So Doctor Renhol thought something was fishy too.

"I'm not saying you're right." The doctor raised a palm. "But I wouldn't bet against you."

"Thank you." Dax checked the hallway up and down.

"That doesn't explain why you're here," Renhol said.

Dax wanted to tell her, but she couldn't. She didn't know how the killer got to her hotel room, but it wasn't a random act of violence. Someone had to have sent him. If it was . . .

Dax, I was fond of you once. I won't be fond of you twice.

Nemi's symbiont was making good on its threat.

"I—" Dax probably should've prepared a cover story.

If Renhol was a co-conspirator, she'd just have Dax arrested for trespassing. She hadn't called for help yet, so maybe there was a chance.

"I need to get into the Caves of Mak'ala," Dax said, and she could heard Kira sigh in disappointment. "Brac was wrong to bar me from there, and he had no right to."

"He said you needed an escort because you were unstable. The caves are the singular treasure of Trill."

"What is he afraid of? That I'd harm my own?" Dax scowled. "Or that I'd keep looking for answers? Doctor Renhol, I need you to forget that I was here."

Renhol blinked. "I have a clearance. You know I can't do that. If it's discovered there was a breach and I didn't report it, I'll be just as guilty as you."

"Someone tried to murder me, Doctor." Her anger flared at speaking the words aloud. "I think it's related to Nemi and my report to the Commission."

Renhol appeared genuinely shocked, thank goodness. "What?"

"Someone inside the Commission wants me stopped, and they want me dead," Dax said. "I can't sit around and wait on an escort appointment. I need to talk to the Guardians." Dax took Doctor Renhol's hand. "An arrest would be catastrophic for me. It could end my career. Doctor, please forget you saw me."

"I . . . I believe you." Renhol sighed. "I've always felt terribly for what happened. With Joran. We shouldn't have . . ."

"I could have died. The Commission treated me like a husk."

The doctor drew in a sharp breath, eyes fluttering and growing moist. "I agree."

"You'd been my doctor for a decade. How could you?"

"I know I failed you."

"*Help me*. Turn around and keep walking."

"Okay." Renhol swallowed and nodded. "Okay. I'll leave."

"Thank you. Truly."

Awkwardly, Renhol turned and kept moving. Dax waited until the coast was clear, then signaled Kira to come out. The Bajoran straightened up as she drew close.

"I didn't expect that to work," Dax said.

"You don't know that it has. She might be calling for help. Let's get out of here."

Quiet as the breeze, they headed toward the roof. Back in the spacious main office, Dax noticed a few busts against the back wall—polished stone atop bronze pedestals. She approached, finding them all to be noteworthy figures in Commission history.

Then her gaze locked on Doctor Elta Vess, and it was like her world turned sideways. The nightmare came sweeping back—broken fingers bashing piano keys—as cold nausea overtook Dax. She shuddered and stumbled to her knees, her vision blurring at the edges.

"What's happening?" Audrid asked, but her voice came out broken and drifting.

The Rite of Emergence was faltering.

Such a rage burned inside of Dax, but she didn't know why. Her heart raced, and she clutched her tightening chest. Another wave of nausea washed over her, and she retched.

A haunting melody rang out like a dirge. She smelled ozone, and the building rumbled with distant thunder. Dax took a hard swallow, trying to keep her dinner down.

Kira's hands were around her shoulders, voice gentle. "Jadzia, tell me what's wrong. What's happening?"

"Isoboramine dip." Dax swooned as she tried to stand, and Kira kept her upright. "I need my benzocyatizine injector."

"Where is it?"

Dax smiled weakly. "Back at the room."

"Damn."

"I can make it. Just . . . help me get out of here."

"Don't worry. I'll carry you out if I have to." Her eyes sparkled in the darkness. "Stay conscious, for my back's sake."

"Will do."

Together, they hobbled out of the rooftop exit, down the scaffolding, and into the humid night of the Trill capital.

"Hey, now," Kira murmured as the lights came on in Dax's suite. "You're okay. Let's take it easy."

Dax's nausea had only grown worse on the long trek back from the Grand Archives. Dizziness dogged her steps, and every bright light was like a glass shard in her optic nerves. She'd done really well not to throw up on Kira in the taxi.

Her retching had provided the major with a good cover story; Dax was drunk and had to sleep it off. No need to offer medical attention. Kira did all the talking, and Dax stumbled along. The major had supported her under one arm, smiling like they'd been partying the whole night, and that got them upstairs to Dax's room.

Audrid had disappeared. The Rite of Emergence was broken by more of Joran's nonsense. Dax tried not to be bitter about that, but she'd worked so hard at relaxing.

Kira shrugged Dax onto the bed with a grunt. "Been a while since I dragged a body around."

"Ha, ha." Dax's forming migraine weakened her voice. "Computer. Lights off."

The room plunged into darkness.

"I need to be able to see if I'm going to find your injector," Kira said. "Computer, lights one-quarter."

The room grew just bright enough for Dax to find it annoying. Photosensitivity could come with an isoboramine drop, and she wanted nothing more than to hide in the darkness and sleep.

Kira tossed the room, looking for the injector and making frustrated grunts the whole time. She was trying to act tough, but it didn't fool Dax. Her companion was tired and frightened for her.

"I think it's . . . I think it's by the replicator," Dax said.

"Ah! Finally." Kira marched over to it and grabbed the device. "You take it in the arm, or . . ."

Dax had a dry swallow and pointed just above her collarbone. "The neck. I'll do it."

She took the injector and pressed it to her skin. The device gave a pneumatic whisper as it delivered the drug, and Dax's headache blunted immediately. She took slow, calming breaths, hoping to get her heart rate under control.

"Now what's happening?" Kira asked. "What do I need to be doing? Do I call a doctor?"

"Sit down over there." Dax rubbed the bridge of her nose. "No doctor, just . . . just stay with me until this passes."

Kira went and sat in the darkened room, pulling up a chair beside the bed.

"I'm going to be fine," Dax said.

"I know. It's pointless to worry about you."

"Totally."

Kira rested her elbows on her knees. "What happened back there?"

"Joran."

"I thought so."

Dax lay back and closed her eyes for a moment. The hallucinations were getting worse. If she needed to go to the Commission for help, she couldn't trust what they might do.

The last time she'd experienced isoboramine fluctuations like this, Joran had been trying to break through Dax's memory block. That personality's struggle for emergence nearly killed them both, and the more she ignored it, the worse it got.

She opened her eyes and stared at the ceiling. "I can't avoid Joran forever. I need to listen to him."

"The murderer?"

"I wish you wouldn't call him that," Dax said.

"Sorry. You haven't told me much else about him."

"I don't know that much. He had a brother, and they didn't get along. Yolad is still around, but an old man. When I tried to call him, he wouldn't talk to me. He and Joran were long estranged, and he wanted to keep it that way. I got the impression they had a troubled childhood together."

"Do you think Joran was evil?"

"I don't like to think of him in those terms. He was a failure as a joined. As a member of society too." She rested her hands on her abdomen. "Evil always comes from somewhere. I never found out why Joran did what he did. But I can tell you this: he didn't think of himself as evil."

"Neither does Gul Dukat, but we both know better," Kira said. "Villains never know they're villains."

"There's something I can't quite get over about Joran's imagery: it's not about harming other people. It involves violence befalling a host. Usually me." She frowned. His visions were harrowing on her psyche, and she wasn't sure how much more of his abuse she could handle. "There must be some reason he's obsessed with death."

"Well, he is a murderer."

"Yes, but in my visions, I'm not doing any killing. I keep getting hurt, sometimes catastrophically."

"How did he die?" Kira asked.

"He was . . ." Dax began, but trailed off. "I'm not actually sure. They said he was killed trying to escape the Symbiosis Commission after murdering some people. I don't remember the exact manner of his death. They captured him and removed Dax."

"You die if they remove your symbiont, right? If they took it out of Joran for killing people, that was an execution."

"I never thought of it that way. In the records I saw, it said, 'Dax symbiont recovered from host.' "

"But you don't remember anything about the circumstances?"

"No. I know so little about him. And it's hard to tell what was a dream and what wasn't. The memory block distorted him, broke him somehow."

"I'm so sorry that happened to you."

"Thanks."

"Did he fight back? Maybe there was a trial."

"There definitely wasn't," Dax said. "Joran became unstable after joining—physically compatible, yes, but not mentally. The Symbiosis Commission wanted to bury his secret after he killed those people. If they'd had a trial, the public might've found out."

Kira shifted in her chair. "Doctors at the Symbiosis Commission conspired to put this guy to death without so much as a trial?"

Dax thought about it. "No, because they wouldn't have the authority to do that. You're right. It would've been murder. Something like removing Dax would've required the opinion of a magistrate."

"And do you remember ever receiving such a pronouncement?"

"No . . ."

Kira sniffed. "Was Joran alive when they took the symbiont out of him?"

Dax tried to remember, but it was like trying to see through thick mist. No details resolved themselves, only sweeping outlines. "I don't know, but there's one way to find out."

"How?"

"Another ritual, at a special location."

"Uh-oh."

Dax laughed. "Don't worry. We don't have to break in. Any joined is welcomed there."

"Where is this place?"

"We call it the *morden'oct*," Dax said.

"Meaning?"

"Death House. Get some rest. You can come with me tomorrow night."

"Whoa, whoa, whoa," Kira said. "We've still got to do the Guardian Road!"

"We've got a busy day tomorrow, then."

Even on the highest-pressure diplomatic missions, Curzon Dax was a master of relaxation. The Splendor of Aet'act was a gorgeous hotel, the sort of place one could get lost. Tourists from all worlds came to see its towering atriums, which housed a few kilometers of artificial rain forest and romantic walking paths.

Despite the wonders, Curzon had barely made it out of his hotel room. He'd been holed up with the lovely Elta Vess all weekend, and that was exactly how he liked it. But all good things had to come to an end, and with the closing of the week, Curzon was due in strategy meetings.

They always cut into his limited personal time. He'd much rather have stayed in the hotel room with Elta for the rest of eternity.

"I'm afraid I'm not going to be able to make it to our dinner date tonight," Curzon said, pulling on his tunic.

"Oh?" Elta sat up in bed, clutching the silk sheets close. "I had arranged something special."

"The chancellor called a meeting."

"You just found out about this?"

Curzon looked himself over in the mirror, fluffing his hair. "It's recent. He's the chancellor. You know how it is."

He'd actually known four days prior, when the chancellor handed him the itinerary. Even though he'd never admit it, he'd accidentally double-scheduled with Elta.

"Really? Because I found your itinerary lying out on the dresser," she said, and his stomach dropped. "We need to talk."

"Elta, my dear," he said, turning to her, "I apologize. I forgot about the chancellor when I agreed to come with you."

"You've double-booked the last three dates I planned." She cocked an eyebrow. "I'm starting to wonder if you only show up for the things you want to do."

"What?" He came and sat beside her on the bed. "I did no such—"

But he had.

He took her hands and ran a thumb over her knuckles. That was where she showed her age the most, and he traced the routes of her veins. Time had only made her more beautiful, and he already regretted disappointing her.

"I'm sorry, darling," he said. "I didn't mean anything by it."

"You know it's okay," she patted his hand. "The life of a diplomat requires a lot of selfishness."

"Elta—"

"You lied to me, then you automatically tried to deny it. Curzon, I love you"—she stroked his cheek—"but you are a bastard."

He drew up short as she took her hands away, smiling kindly.

"Don't be upset. You need to be selfish." She looked out the window at the snow-capped mountain. "It's your job and a major part of your psychology. It's who you are."

Curzon gaped, heart racing. He hadn't realized she harbored these feelings, and it looked like the situation was spiraling out of control.

"Hold on a minute," he said. "I'm not all that bad."

"Curzon, can you not understand? You don't have time for me. How good or bad you are in a relationship doesn't matter if you're never here." She got a distant look, hugging herself. "When you're with me, truly *with* me, you make me feel like I'm not alone for the first time in forever. The way you carry yourself, the way you look at me, touch me—"

He couldn't stop his eyes wandering at those words.

Then she locked him down with a stare, and it was like being caught in a tractor beam.

"You make me feel like my old self again, Curzon. *Alive*."

He'd always treated their relationship as a casual fling, expecting her to end it at any moment. They'd agreed it was only physical attraction, no strings attached. That was why he hadn't taken it seriously before . . . but now he saw.

She'd fallen in love with him. She was something precious and special in his hands, something no man could ever have possessed, and he should've paid more attention.

But he watched the candle burn low, then go out in her expression.

"Which just makes me your fool." She slipped from the bed, padding over to a robe and donning it. "I don't know how much I want this anymore."

His mouth went dry at the words. Elta was perfect for him. She was the sort of woman he needed: beautiful and confident, capable of captivating galactic dignitaries for hours on end. With her at his side and the Accords under his belt, he was unstoppable.

"Oh, no, no, no," he said, "let's not do anything rash. We could discuss this over a romantic meal."

"Sure," she said. "How about dinner tonight?"

Curzon gave her a wounded look. "That was unfair."

"I'm not trying to bring you down. I'm simply stating a fact. Your star is on the rise. You don't have time for us, and I'm okay with that."

"I regret making you feel that way."

"Oh, so they're just feelings? I'm imagining it, and you *do* have time for me?"

"I—"

"This behavior right here—using an apology to distort reality—is one of the reasons I can't be with you, Curzon. When it comes down to it, you have a pattern of not respecting my intellect."

"I'm sorry." He shook his head, spreading his arms for a hug. "You're right."

"I know. That's why I'm leaving you."

He'd thought things were going so well. He'd become quite smitten with Elta over the past months, even telling her he loved her. The prospect of losing her eyes, her smile, her soft lips, her scent—it was almost too much to bear.

"Elta, please—reconsider."

"No. You treat me like an accessory, and if it weren't for your substantial . . . talents, I would've left you weeks ago."

He tried to raise a point in his defense and take credit for the compliment at the same time—and his brain shorted out.

"You're more than—than that to me," he stammered.

It came off weak and melodramatic, and she winced.

"Search your heart, Curzon. You don't think of me as a peer."

He followed her to the dressing room. "I absolutely do. You're as important as any ambassador. The groundbreaking work that you've done on—"

"Would you cancel an appointment with the Klingon ambassador at the last minute and then lie about it?"

"No, because that could start a war."

"So you keep your engagements with him. You have no choice."

"Exactly."

"But you have a choice with me—so you cancel." She walked to the closet replicator. "Computer, Lorenzo Vittal dress, red. Matching heels."

The garment it spat out was painfully gorgeous, twisting Curzon with longing.

"I'm sorry, you're absolutely right." He tried again, working his charming smile as hard as he could. "Let's start over."

"We've already done that once before, but you've apparently forgotten." She pulled the dress up over her body, securing the magnetic straps into place. She pointed a thumb at her back. "Fasten me?"

"What? Oh, sure." He tapped the fasteners at the rear of her dress. Was he never going to get to hold her again? "Elta, please. I promise I truly am sorry. You're everything I've ever wanted in a woman."

She turned to him with a sad smile. "So true. And you're about sixty percent of what I've ever wanted in a man. Please don't take it personally."

"'Don't take it . . .' You're criticizing my personality!"

"And there are plenty of people who love you." She brushed off the shoulders of his tunic, resting her fingers on his collarbone. Even in that moment, her touch was enough to set him humming with delight. When her eyes locked onto his, his heart skipped a beat.

"—just not me. Goodbye, Curzon."

10

Mak'ala

Dax had been awake only for a few minutes when the call came in. Captain Sisko's angry face filled the screen.

"What were you thinking? To fail to report an attack like this to me is unlike you, old man."

Dax and Kira sat helplessly in Dax's hotel room, absorbing a tirade from their commanding officer. He knew of the attempt on Dax's life because local Starfleet personnel reported it to him as a matter of procedure.

It could've been worse. If Sisko found out what they'd done in the Grand Archives, they'd be ordered back to DS9 and Dax would be facing a disciplinary hearing. She could only hope Renhol would keep her secret.

"I cannot believe you left me in the dark," Sisko said.

"I'm sorry, sir," Kira interjected. "I also knew, and I didn't report it immediately."

She was obviously trying to take off a little of Dax's heat, but she knew Sisko better—he could burn hotter than a star.

His eyebrows shot up. *"I know. Don't think you're out of the woods on this one, either, Major. You may have gone to Trill to deal with a personal affair, Dax, but now that you've been targeted, it's* my *business."*

Dax nodded. "Benjamin, this is important to me—"

"And a member of Starfleet was killed," he interrupted. *"We have a method of doing things, and you know that. We're going to deal with your case, but we're going to do it the* right *way. No more risks."*

Dax exchanged glances with Kira, who asked, "What do you mean, sir?"

"Jadzia, your health is fluctuating, and I understand you've set the Commission against you."

"Benja—"

"I'm sending Doctor Bashir."

That was bad. Bashir would get in the way, and he wasn't the felonious sort.

"And because your life is under threat," Sisko continued, *"I'm sending Lieutenant Commander Worf. He will oversee the remainder of this off-the-books operation, while ensuring your safety and survival."*

Kira brightened. "That's great, Captain."

"Glad you approve, Major," he said. *"Then you understand why I'm cutting short your leave and recalling you."*

Kira balked. "What?"

He gave her a thin smile, his eyes widening with restrained furor. *"I have deployed my chief science officer, my chief medical officer, my strategic operations officer, and you, my Bajoran liaison. I have almost no command staff. You need to come back, or I'll be running the station with Odo."*

"Sir, you want me to just leave Jadzia alone?" Kira asked.

"Not until Lieutenant Commander Worf and Doctor Bashir arrive, but then you will depart immediately." Sisko leaned back. *"Your capable seconds have already been pulling double duty for days. Deep Space 9 is on the edge of a war zone. Strangely, I find the station is more important than a personal vendetta."*

Dax frowned. "Benjamin, this isn't just revenge."

"If I were in your shoes," Sisko replied, *"it would be."*

Dax shifted in her seat. "I appreciate your support."

"I've done what I can," he said. *"Be careful, and see that you return in one piece, Commander."*

"I will," Dax said.

His frightful smile returned—polite, with a threat just beneath the surface. *"Don't make me regret my magnanimous nature. Sisko out."*

The captain disappeared from the screen, and Dax exhaled.

Kira said, "I should've reported in."

"Me too."

"So . . . what do we do?"

Dax said, "We go to the Caves of Mak'ala, then the *morden'oct*."

"You don't think he'll object?"

"Benjamin? If he'd wanted us to stay here, he would've said so. Duty required him to chew me out and he did it."

"I guess. What do we do first?"

"Caves. The *morden'oct* is only open at night."

"Can we get dinner in between?"

"Oh, definitely," Dax smiled. "Can't confront my own mortality hungry."

Dax and Kira trudged through the streets of the capital, heavy packs weighing them down. The morning sun warmed the pavement beneath them, turning the dewy rains into a cloying steam. They wore civilian clothes, looking more like tourists than Starfleet officers.

Kira pushed up her sunglasses and checked her tricorder. "The entrance is supposed to be near an old citadel."

"That's *the* Old Citadel. It's a major landmark," Dax said. "It was a fortress that stood on the site of the capital in ancient times."

"Where?"

"These four or five city blocks," Dax said, gesturing around. "It was huge, but it's long gone."

Kira smacked her lips. "How can it be a major landmark if it's gone?"

Dax pointed to a low stone wall that ran beside the sidewalk. Every few meters, there was a brass plaque, inscribed with the symbol of the Old Citadel.

"It's here," Dax said. "That stone wall is the shape of the original building."

"So according to the map"—Kira pointed to her tricorder—"the entrance is next to this corner here."

Dax shaded her eyes as she looked over the busy street for anything that might suggest an entrance to the Guardian Road. She found shop fronts, cafes, and lodgings—nothing that would indicate a secret beneath them. They wandered along the symbolic wall, trying to get a better sense of the fortress's shape.

Past the shops was an old Trill "municipal station," a traditional washing house and toilet dating back a few centuries. The buildings weren't commonly used for anything except their sewage functions, but were maintained as historical curiosities.

The exterior was made of polished, laser-cut marble, its walls faceted to catch the sun. Colored glass ran in ribbons up the sides of the structure, sparkling with an oily sheen. The copper roof was like a dollop of cream, puffy and round.

Dax and Kira entered, gazing up at the high ceilings as they did. The interior was a large, circular space, with a row of stall doors lining the walls. Sinks stood around a central column, arranged like a decorative fountain. The windows filtered sunlight into rainbow streaks, adding texture and interest to every surface.

As lavs went, it was extremely fancy, but not clean.

Kira pointed to a steel-grated door, which blocked the path to a spiral staircase. "Where does that go?"

"It must lead to the bathhouse. Doesn't look like it's in use anymore."

"I think we need to get down there," Kira said.

"Why?"

"We're trying to get into some caves. Caves are down."

Dax shrugged. The logic was solid enough. When she approached the door, she found it locked.

"Let me," Kira said, breaking out a small set of picks. "Mechanical locks are easy."

Dax watched her click around inside the lock for a few seconds before opening it with a metallic snap.

"That was fast," Dax said.

Kira smirked and tucked away her picks. "It's a bathroom lock, not one of Dukat's booby traps."

They wrenched open the bars, rusty after so many years. Beyond, stone steps stretched into the darkness. Black streaks of mildew ran along the walls, and the scent of ancient mold grew stronger the deeper they went.

"This reminds me of Bajor," Kira said.

"Oh?"

"We have lots of tunnels—especially under the temples, adapted from the original sewer systems. Looks like you've got some too." She pulled out a lantern and held it aloft. "Those tunnels made it hell for our occupiers to keep tabs on us."

Even in the tiny stairwell, incredible details came out under the lantern light. Gold chips sparkled in the ceiling, forming a swirling field of stars. Every step was covered with detailed ornamentation, though much of it was streaked with mold.

Chlorine and steam tickled Dax's nose, the air growing thick with moisture. They came to a landing where glossy white tiles formed the floors and walls—less filth here. Water dripped in the shadows, the sound omnipresent and echoing.

Glass bricks in the ceiling allowed in natural light from the floor above, revealing a wide, green pool, tiled with alternating stripes of blue and gold. The water rippled ever so slightly with each drip to hit the surface, but other than that, it was still. Algae gathered in the corners; this bathhouse needed cleaning before anyone took a dip.

"I bet this place was something special back in its day," Kira said. "Have you ever been to the bathhouses on Bajor?"

"I keep meaning to. I wasn't sure if they were for non-Bajorans."

"You'd be welcome. The ones that survived are beautiful."

They traversed the room, taking note of the three exits. The first door had a sign designating it a supply closet, not a way forward. The next had a soft chugging behind it, some mechanical system.

The door on the far side of the pool was cool to the touch, and a gentle breeze ushered from the crack underneath.

The breath of the planet.

Dax lit up inside at the scent, something oddly nostalgic to her: wet stone and lichen. The birthplace of the symbionts was somewhere below.

She pointed to the door. "This is the way in."

"Okay." Kira inspected the locking system. "Electronic, but it's not too complicated."

"You had to open a lot of locks in the resistance?"

She smirked. "Had to get out of places as often as I had to get in. I'll hack this thing open in a second."

"I wish I could do that."

Kira shook her head as she worked. "You don't want to need this skill."

Quick as a wink, she popped open the console and rewired the lock. The door slid open, revealing a sloping stone pathway heading into darkness. The inviting scent of the depths called to Dax. A metal sign protruded from the rough-hewn wall, old Trill letters etched into its surface.

"What does it say?" Kira asked.

"It's a warning," Dax replied. "Basically, 'No one comes down here. If you keep going, you're on your own.' "

"Anything else?"

"Anyone not joined may be subject to lethal force."

Kira held up her hands. "I don't enjoy being 'subject to lethal force.' "

"First of all, you're in my care. When we encounter a Guardian, they'll understand that. Second, you are one of the four toughest people I know."

"One?"

Dax gave her a sincere look. "There were these three Klingons Curzon knew . . ."

"I'll take it," she said.

Dax stepped into the claustrophobic passageway, its ceiling low enough that she had to duck. Based on her calculations and the data from the map, the hike would be six kilometers. She hoped it would open some so she could stand up straight.

They came to a branch and pulled out their tricorders. It was easy to reconcile their location.

"We go right," Kira said.

"See?" Dax huffed. "It's not so bad."

"I've seen the map. We both know the worst is yet to come."

"Not the worst. The most challenging," Dax corrected.

"You should take up politics."

"Been there. Rewarding, but draining. Not in this life."

The first few forks weren't so bad, but as time went on, the pathways became more complex. The caves weren't just left and right turns—Dax and Kira had to rappel down jagged cliffs, through treacherous chutes, along precipices, and above underground rivers.

The caves branched like a nervous system with tons of cramped splits. The pair hiked through most of the day, stopping only to admire an underground lake while snacking.

When Dax spotted the mottled stones of the inner chambers of Mak'ala, she put a hand on Kira's shoulder.

"Put out your light," she said, and Kira did.

In the absence of the lantern, azure clusters of glowing lichen came to life, shedding their cool luminance over the cavern. Dax stood in the darkness, reverent.

"Exquisite," Kira said.

A warm glow filled the tunnel ahead along with approaching footfalls. Dax crouched reflexively—though she wasn't in danger. She had every right to be here.

A tall, thin man came ambling around the bend, staff in hand. The top section glowed like a lamp, shedding light across his path. He was a tan-skinned fellow in middle age, with a strong nose and pronounced brow. He had shaggy, short hair, with a wild bit at the top like the stalk of an onion. His uniform was a creamy brown dress with simple patterns sewn into the piping.

He regarded Dax with coppery eyes. "Who are you?"

"Jadzia Dax."

"'Dax.' Welcome home. I am Guardian Olome." He gestured to Kira. "Is this your guest?"

Dax nodded. "She is, Guardian."

He clicked a button on his staff, and it emitted a descending whine. A weapon powering down?

"Welcome to you, as well," Olome said. "I didn't expect to be answering a call to the Guardian Road today."

He waved for them to follow and turned to walk away.

"Answering a call?" Dax fell in behind him as he shuffled up the tunnel. "You knew we were coming ahead of time?"

"No." He laughed. "We have motion detectors all through here. You couldn't have picked a longer path in."

"Your sensors are well hidden," Kira said. "I normally spot that kind of stuff."

"Thank you," he said. "I'd pass your compliments to the man who did it, but he died a long time ago. No one uses this road anymore."

"I can see why," Dax said.

She was filthy after a long day of slogging through dangerous, muddy caves. It'd been fun, but she hoped it'd be a once-in-a-lifetime experience.

They wound around the corner and found the greatest wonder of Trill yawning before them: the Caves of Mak'ala. Luminous pools of milky fluid hummed with electricity, and little bolts of static crackled out every time a symbiont broke the surface. More of the glowing lichens carpeted the roof with velvety luminance.

This was the place symbionts were born, where they returned if they needed to await a host, where they could be nursed if ill, and where they sought respite, if the grief of losing their host was too much to bear.

"It's beautiful," Kira breathed. "This is where you're from?"

"Part of me," Dax replied, smiling.

"What's that?" Kira pointed to one of the discharges across the surface of the water.

"That's how the symbionts communicate," Dax said, "when not in a host body."

"Through electric shocks?"

"Yes." Dax watched one of the symbionts emit a jolting flash before submerging again. "And they can be quite powerful."

Olome nodded and grinned. "Young symbionts occasionally express their displeasure with us with enough power to give us a good shock. It's an informal rite of passage for a Guardian."

He dipped his staff into pools as they passed, watching the light along the top turn green, blue, or yellow. When it went yellow, he pulled out a little padd and jotted down some thoughts.

"What brings you to us, Jadzia Dax?" He searched his notes, muttering to himself about salinity.

"Well, I . . . My friend died recently."

"Oh." He frowned. "I'm so sorry to hear it. Is that what has you so conflicted?"

She considered his question. "Conflicted?"

"Fractured, maybe?" He plunged his staff into another pool, and it went green.

"You can tell that just from looking at me?" Dax asked.

Olome straightened, holding up a bony hand. "May I?"

She nodded.

He spread his fingers wide across her abdomen and closed his eyes, inhaling. He made a pained expression. "You are out of balance."

"That's true." Her insides relaxed under his touch, and she let out a relieved breath.

"You're suppressing something—a fact you're not ready to face."

"I want to. It's honestly getting frustrating." She rubbed her temple. "I . . . I think it has something to do with the way Joran died."

His face went grave. "You should free those memories."

"I will. Tonight." She glanced at Kira for strength before continuing. "My friend who died . . . she was joined."

He narrowed his eyes. "Has this death been recorded?"

"No," Dax said. "And neither has the joining."

He took a sudden breath, growing deadly serious. "I need to know."

She proceeded to tell Olome the story of meeting Nemi, of how different she was, about the *tongo* game. He listened, rapt, never doubting a word coming out of her mouth. She hadn't realized how good it would feel to be believed. This was a man who knew everything there was to know about the symbionts, and he took her word as the absolute truth. When Dax got to the part where Nemi shocked her into unconsciousness, Olome breathed, "*Lor'inor.*"

Dax leaned closer. "What?"

"*Lor'inor*—the Lost Lights."

The name tickled something in the back of her memory. She'd been dealing with that sensation too much recently.

"Hillian Qilaa," Olome began, "was a joined Trill who lived centuries ago, when our species first took to the stars. He fell one day while hiking alone in the mountains, suffering a diffuse axonal injury. The man known as Hillian Qilaa died instantly, but his heart still beat, and his lungs still drew breath. Qilaa, his symbiont, was able to continue the functions of the host for its own survival."

Dax swallowed. "It's true. I was right."

"Any symbionts who suffer such a fate should return to the caves for trauma assistance and rehosting, but sometimes that doesn't happen. Occasionally, a symbiont becomes trapped inside of a dead body. The ones who embrace their host's fate are called *Lor'inor* or Lost Lights. Often, they don't want to return."

Dax's eyes grew wide with the revelation. "That's horrible."

"Qilaa spent six months stranded in the wilderness. The man that emerged was different—he had all of the memories, but none of the compassion. He was aggressive, manipulative, and dangerous."

Dax tried not to despair, but every sentence out of Olome's mouth confirmed her suspicions about Nemi.

"His family eventually had him examined, where the truth was uncovered." Olome sighed. "That was when he attacked, killing the doctor, his wife, and son. Qilaa expressed . . . abilities. The symbiont's electrical discharges were magnified through a dead host, giving him a powerful weapon. He disappeared after the attacks, killing three of his pursuers from the Commission. It took five years to catch him."

"What did the authorities do?" Kira asked.

"The symbiont was removed and placed into stasis, along with others of its kind in the archives. We keep them there in the hopes that we can one day rescue them."

"In the Grand Archives?" Kira asked.

Olome nodded.

"That place needs some security upgrades—"

Olome peered past Dax at the major. "What does she mean?"

"I'm sure it's nothing," Dax said. "Guardian Olome, how often do these . . . Lost Lights happen?"

"Thankfully, they're few and far between. The precise nature of the injury must kill off specific parts of the host. Only an ill turn of fate can create a *Lor'inor*."

Nausea swept through Dax, and she doubled over. Olome gently placed his palm on her abdomen, pushing her back from the nearest pool. He closed his eyes and took a deep breath.

"Dax, you're struggling." His voice was gentle as rain. "I can feel something trying to come loose, like a snarl in your fabric."

She heaved breaths, hanging on to his arm. "Oh, something feels like it's coming loose."

He tensed, clearly ready to drag her out of there for the sake of the symbionts if she started vomiting.

"I'm good," she said. "I'm good."

"Tonight," Olome said, "you will address this snarl. Please, you must, for your health."

"Yeah . . ." She swallowed before blowing out a breath. The nausea receded, and her heart slowed. "Tonight. I promise. Thank you, Guardian."

"Thank you, Jadzia Dax. Take care of yourself." He supported her while she straightened. "Why did you come via the Guardian Road?"

"Someone in the Commission cut off my access. Said I was dangerous because I was having hallucinations."

A ridge of concern appeared between his thick eyebrows. "But that means you need care, not contempt."

"I thought so too," Dax said.

"I'll speak to the other Guardians. This is unacceptable."

Kira raised a hand. "Guardian, we still don't know how Nemi was joined. Jadzia said it wasn't official, and the Commission didn't have a record."

"That is most troubling of all," Olome said. "Perhaps your mystery symbiont is one who is shunned, forbidden from rehosting."

"Like they're cast out of Trill society?" Kira asked.

"Yes. We have several such crimes. Reuniting with a lover from another life. Symbiocide."

"That's one reason to work outside the system," Dax said.

"Some exiled have taken that path," Olome said. "It's highly illegal."

Dax straightened. Perhaps that was the type of symbiont Nemi had inside her.

"What can I do for Nemi?" Dax said.

Olome placed a hand on her shoulder. "Mourn. Now, what else can you tell me about your friend?"

11

Death House

Though Dax asked Olome more questions, she learned little else. He cautioned her against pursuing Nemi, reiterating just how dangerous a Lost Light could be.

"They are shrewder than you could possibly imagine."

Thankfully, the Guardian Road wasn't the only way out of the Caves of Mak'ala. Modern Guardians had their own "road," and it was a lot shorter and safer—because it was a simple lift. When one of them would leave the caves to conduct a *zhian'tara*, they had a special egress away from the Commission. It was more convenient, and Guardians preferred not to walk the Commission halls.

Olome took Dax and Kira to this exit, ushered them through security, and bid them farewell. The pair emerged at a mass transit station a few hundred meters from a platform. They nervously eyed the darkened tunnel for any sign of a train.

"Whew!" Kira said as a confused bystander helped her up onto the platform. "Thank you."

"You shouldn't . . . be down there," he said.

"Good advice," Kira replied, walking out of the station with Dax. "I'll keep it in mind."

They returned to the surface as the sun draped the ample clouds in evening gold. The short hike out, combined with the grueling trek in, sapped their strength, and they both plopped down on a nearby park bench. Dax shed her pack onto the grass and leaned back.

"I think my bruises are going to have bruises tomorrow."

Kira laughed. "Come on, that was fun. Nobody shot at us, and you got some answers."

"The caves are really something."

The bench looked out on the North Bank, known for its night life. Speckles of holograms and laser light dotted the skyline—nightclubs and music venues beckoning to patrons in the lively streets. Dax's hotel was over there, on the other side of the Capital Harbor—too far to walk. She desperately wished to crawl into bed.

"You know how you promised me dinner?" Kira said. "You can skip that. I just want a nap."

Birds called to one another, sailing on the harbor breeze. Water lapped at the dock, and pedestrians passed by, idly curious about the two sweaty, disheveled women on the bench.

Dax closed her eyes, and she could sleep right there.

"Nope." She forced the cheer into her voice. "We have plans, remember?"

"Aw."

"Yeah. We have to go back to the hotel, get clean, and get dressed up before we go to the *morden'oct*."

"Dressed up? Tell me you're kidding."

"No, you have to look your absolute best," Dax replied.

"Why?"

Dax gave her a sidelong smile. "Because this is a date with death."

Every joined Trill knew death like an old friend.

They'd greeted it time and again, sometimes as a sudden, rushing doom, other times as a quiet visitor in the small hours of the morning. Dying was as much a part of life as getting wrinkles or going bald, and joined Trill were always prepared to meet their fate—though some liked to do more research than others.

Those with morbid curiosity could find the answers they needed at a *morden'oct*, where they could relive a previous host's final moments.

Dax and Kira's autotaxi shot across the gloaming sky, bumping with minor turbulence. The ride was old and uncomfortable, but they wouldn't have to bear it for long. They headed for the swamps out of town, where the city gave way to wilderness. Everyone from the capital thought the countryside was nice, but Dax knew it better. Jadzia had camped there as part of the survival qualifications for the initiate program. She'd seen another side of that dank forest, and she hated the bayou as much as the Symbiosis Commission.

They'd replicated traditional garb for their destination: dark-blue funeral attire. Dax's dress sleeves came to umber frills like a late sunset. Kira chose a slim suit like her Bajoran militia uniform, curling floral patterns embroidered into its cloth. Dax had done dark eyeliner and lipstick to match her somber outfit, but Kira was more subdued.

"This, uh, Death House . . . sounds a little creepy," Kira said.

Dax gave her a daring look. "Not scared of the afterlife, are you?"

"No. It's just . . ." She gave a little shrug. "If you say *death house* to a Bajoran, that has a pretty grim connotation. I'd like to know what I'm getting into."

Dax dropped the grin immediately, giving Kira's hand a squeeze. "Sorry. It's not a gory place, but it can be frightening. For me. Which is why I'd like you there. We just call them death houses because there isn't a good translation of *morden'oct*. The concept is particular to a joined Trill and our language."

"There are lots of words like that in Bajoran. *Prophets* is a major oversimplification, but no other short phrase translates. I'm glad *death house* is the same."

Dax nodded. "Absolutely. The connotations of the original word are a little dark, but beautiful. We joined have a different relationship with mortality. Symbiosis is an embrace, but every host will have to let go one day. *Morden'oct* refers to the melancholia of leaving one's home, never to return. This ritual isn't very popular with my kind."

Kira rested her elbows on her knees. "Most of us don't like thinking about death, much less our own."

"The symbionts shield newly joined from the immediate knowledge of all former deaths. It's harmful to feel the grief of so many hosts at the same time." Dax looked out the window at the passing trees. "Being joined gives me glimpses of Dax's other hosts when I need them. Sometimes those are nightmares like Joran."

"I'm sorry. He sounds terrifying."

"And I'm about to become him." Dax's shoulders fell and she let out a long breath. "I don't want to do this."

"Then we can go back."

"No. I need to see what he wants me to. It's literally killing me."

"Killing you—"

"It's not that bad, yet," Dax said. "But the farther out of sync I get, the lower my isoboramine goes. If I can't resolve this . . . the Symbiosis Commission will remove Dax. I *have* to do this."

"Okay." Kira took her hand. "I'm here for you."

The autotaxi settled down onto the landing pad of the *morden'oct*, engines washing the nearby trees. Kira climbed out first, then held the door for Dax.

The major looked their destination up and down, rocking on her heels. "This is some place."

An obelisk of black glass rose among the ferns and tall swamp trees like a gateway. The edifice stretched at least three stories high, crystalline surface glittering gold with a thousand cuts in the evening sun. The scientist in Dax wanted to pull out her tricorder and study the material composition of the building—

But where she was going, perhaps it was best to preserve the mystery.

The existence of the "death houses" was an open secret. They arose from an old tradition, one that made many people in the Symbiosis Commission nervous. There had always been tension between the Commission and the *morden'octs*. The medical establishment cautioned against older Trill indulging the service because there had been fatalities. Sometimes, very rarely, a young joined Trill would succumb to shock at a *morden'oct*, restarting the evergreen debate at the Commission over whether they should be allowed to operate.

For the time, though, *morden'octs* were sacred cultural institutions, and any joined Trill who wished to chance their own demise could see someone else's.

The courtyard that housed the landing pad was a restrained affair of laser-cut hedgerows and viridescent grass. A flat, circular fountain housed a barrage of jets, which suspended a mirrored ball atop a bed of water. Lamps came to life in the nearby woods like glowing toadstools, casting pools of light across walking paths. Dax spotted a lone Trill in the forest, clad in dark blue robes, sitting on a memorial bench.

"Shall we?" Dax asked, offering Kira an arm and a smile.

"Why not?"

They made their way up the steps to the obelisk, and its doors parted for them. The foyer was frigid, a crystalline palace housing a spectacular chandelier. Warm light seemed to rain from the ceiling, running down long strings, terminating just above the circular reception desk.

Seated behind the counter was a grinning Trill woman, aged like a tree—hard weathered, yet upright. Dark gray hair fell around her pale face in webs, and she regarded Dax with unblinking, icy eyes. She wore the traditional Trill blue, but an extravagant, layered outfit of velvet and lace that gave her a ghostly air. Silhouettes of trees intertwined across a high collar of clear material, like candlelit stained glass. Her plunging neckline showed her Trill spots, leading to a gold-boned bodice. A cascade of glittering scales flashed along the length of her gown, and the train slid like molten metal. Gold chains stenciled her tight, deep blue sleeves, broken only at her bare shoulders, and intricate nets of jewelry encrusted her hands.

Though Dax drew closer, the woman never moved. "Uh, hello."

"Greetings." She bowed her head slowly. "What's your name, traveler?"

"Jadzia Dax."

"And why have you come?"

Jadzia uttered the phrase she'd been taught as an initiate so long ago. "To see beyond life."

She'd always considered visiting a *morden'oct*. The thought of exploring death was no different in the abstract than exploring a wormhole—probably safer, even. Now that she had the very real need to experience death, every muscle in her body was steeped in dread.

"Welcome, Dax," the woman said through stained teeth. She tapped a few buttons on a hidden console. "We've been expecting you."

Dax glanced at Kira, then back to the woman. "Glad to hear it. Thank you for making time."

"Anything for the joined. Follow me."

The mysterious greeter turned and exited her desk, retreating to the far wall. Its smooth surface parted before her, revealing a corridor into inky darkness. She passed inside, stopping at the entrance to wait for Dax.

"I need my friend with me," Dax said.

"Yes," said the woman. "You will."

Their host seemed to glide into the shadows, vanishing. Dax and Kira followed her, crossing under the crystal archway into the dim beyond.

The walls in the corridor were the same dark, cut glass, layered so many times that their lines created infinite strands in the reflections. The only tones were black and honey gold, and the million facets shivered with the group's passage. The illusion was imposing;

the space seemed to go on forever, reacting to their presence, drawing them inside.

It was easy to imagine eternity in this beauty.

They moved through the entrance corridor slowly, enabling Dax and Kira to take in every detail of its fractal complexity. Kira openly gawked at its magnificence, eyes darting to each new spectacle. Dax wondered how big the corridor was; so much of it seemed an illusion. She longed to reach out and test her hypothesis, but she didn't want to fingerprint the walls.

Their escort led them through the mirrored maze like she knew it by heart, and Dax was glad. It was entirely too easy to imagine walking into a sharp wall, and the only thing worse than a fingerprint on the pretty crystal would've been her blood.

Chimes rang out in mournful tones from the unseen hollows of the complex. A low drone filled Dax's ears, a triad of notes meant to calm the soul and straighten the mind. Bells tinkled overhead, their tiny voices adding to the spectrum of noise. To Dax, it already felt as though she was passing from the mortal realm into whatever came next.

They finally arrived at a pair of tall, coppery doors, inscribed with the epitaph of a great Trill poet: *Death is the only true peace. Silence is our greatest treasure.*

"What does it say?" Kira whispered.

Given Kira's trepidations, Dax lied, "I'm not sure. It's too dark to read."

Their guide gestured for the doors to open, and they stepped aside. Beyond, they found an intimate room, scarcely lit by a dim globe hovering beneath the ceiling. The space contained a thick, bed-sized transparent slab, which rose from the smooth floor. One side of the solid mass had a scoop in its surface where someone could rest their head. A chair of clear glass, like molten bones, stood behind the headrest.

Dax gulped, looking at the place where she would feel death firsthand.

The woman waved a hand over the bed, indicating Dax should come and lie down.

"May my friend stay?" Dax asked.

The woman's lip curled in a slight smile, and she beckoned Kira inside. "Wouldn't have allowed her back if it was a problem. Join us, friend."

"I'm Kira Nerys."

She arched an eyebrow. "And I'm *Wynth*."

"Nice to meet you," Kira said.

Dax didn't want to tell Kira that *Wynth* wasn't a name, but a Trill word. It referred to the unfolding of the mind, the final moment of relaxation when all facets of a person dislocate.

"Have a seat here, Kira Nerys," Wynth said, gesturing to a small pedestal of crystal beside the bed.

Kira nodded and complied.

Wynth smiled wide, sweeping a hand over the slab with a little bow. "And now you, Jadzia Dax."

Dax flexed her fingers to keep them loose in the cold. "Of course."

It wasn't like she was actually going to die, she told herself. But then, if the experience was exactly the same to her mind—she was. A familiar fear crept over her, something she'd possessed the day before she was joined.

This experience could fundamentally change her. What was she doing?

Wynth took notice of her trepidation and laughed. "You can learn what it's like to die now or later—but you will find out."

Dax sat down on the slab. It was as cold as the rest of the room, and she shivered a little in her dress. If she'd known it'd be this way, she would've replicated something more substantial.

From her new vantage point, the place seemed much darker. Only a few golden strands sliced the black, vectors in every direction. The room was both small, and limitless.

"Lie flat." Wynth gently guided Dax's head into the hollow

in the slab, and it lit up underneath her. The woman placed two devices, each no bigger than a thumbprint, onto Dax's temples.

"What are those?" Dax asked.

"Monitors," Wynth replied. "In case I need to pull you out."

"Pull me out? Wouldn't I just wake up?"

"I hope so." The older woman touched a hidden display on the wall, and it came to life. "Are you ready?"

"What will I see?" Dax asked.

"Only what you must to understand your fate," Wynth said. "Dax knows."

Kira wound her fingers into Dax's, leaning over her with a kind smile. It was nice to have a trusted friend so close by. Was this what Curzon had felt before they took the symbiont from him?

"I'm here," Kira whispered.

"I'm grateful." Dax shut her eyes and took a deep breath. "And I'm ready, Wynth."

The older woman nodded, tapping a few buttons on the console, and a new wave of shivers swept over Dax. Was the room getting colder?

"Which of your past lives do we wish to recall?" Wynth asked.

"Joran," Dax answered.

Wynth raised her arms and her gaze. "*Vesti keth oul Joran zhian vok*."

Dax winced, waiting for the ceremony to begin, but nothing happened. Not wanting to be rude, she remained still and quiet.

And so cold.

The whole room was like a freezing storage unit, though Dax's breath didn't fog up. The shivers got worse, and Kira squeezed her hand.

"It's r-really cold in here!" Dax tried to keep her teeth from chattering as she spoke. "Are you not cold?"

Kira grew concerned. "No. I'm fine, but is that supposed to happen? Wynth?"

"*Vesti keth oul Joran zhian vok,*" the older woman repeated. "*Estul qet Joran.*"

The temperature inside Dax plummeted, and her shaking became uncontrollable. This new sensation was underscored by a creeping numbness—like she would never get warm again. She looked into Kira's eyes on the verge of panic, and Kira stood up halfway.

"Wynth," she said. "I'm not sure—"

"Vesti keth oul Joran zhian vok!"

The shakes penetrated every part of Dax, and Kira had to pin her shoulders to the slab. Dax's eyes went wide, and panic took over. What'd she been thinking? She needed to get up and run. This ritual was going to kill her.

Kira's fear did nothing to comfort her. The Bajoran was helpless to stop whatever was happening, and she glanced from Dax to Wynth in rising terror.

Wynth leaned over Dax, intense eyes boring into her. "The first lesson you must learn, Jadzia Dax: even with your friend beside you—" She reached over and tapped another button on the console.

"Everyone dies alone."

Dax's temperature fell through the floor, and her muscles shut off all at once. It was like falling backward off a cliff. Her mind unfolded, and darkness swallowed her whole.

12

Last Witness

Joran's hotel room was dark, save for the glow from his screen. His brother's face appeared, blinking and bleary.

"Joran? Are you okay?" Yolad asked him that every time he answered. So patronizing.

"I'm fine," Joran said. "You don't seem happy to hear from me."

"I am."

"You're a terrible liar."

"Please don't be like that." He squinted, probably trying to figure out where Joran was. *"You look good. Different."*

They hadn't spoken in two years. Of course he'd changed.

"I *am* different. I've been joined."

The look on Yolad's face made the lie so much sweeter. In truth, Joran wasn't to be joined until the next day, but he was eager to put a down payment on his gloating. After his joining, he could cut his family out of his life for good.

"That's . . . that's great, Joran! I'm proud of you."

"The Belar sons." Joran gave a wry grin. "May we outshine our worthless parents."

"Don't say that. Mom misses you."

"And Dad?"

"Joran, I—"

"Does he even ask about me?"

Yolad looked away. *"I'm sorry for how he's treated you."*

Joran needed to control his temper. A joined Trill would be

more confident. "Yes, well, I've grown beyond caring about such things. He can watch my star rise from the ground."

Yolad nodded, smiling. *"He'll come around. He'll see what he's missing."*

"I don't care. I don't need his approval anymore."

The smile faded. *"Of course. Would you come home? Let us see you in person for once?"*

"I wouldn't want to be a drain on you and Teelo."

"I'm sorry she called you that."

"It's forgotten, Yolad."

"Glad to hear it. I miss you."

No, he didn't. Yolad missed having someone to make him look good. His brother won awards and got into a prestigious music academy. He pretended to encourage Joran, but he had stolen ideas for his compositions. Yolad didn't want a brother. He wanted a mirror who'd reflect his brilliance back onto him.

However, Joran had his own successes. He'd composed for three orchestras, traveled to many worlds to play *his* music. Joran's family had only ever made him feel inferior, held him back, but with his joining, he would cement his independence. It was time to get rid of the dead weight in his life, and joining was as good an excuse as any.

"Now that I'm joined, I have a lot to sort out," Joran said. "You might not hear from me for a while."

"Oh, um, okay."

"I need to be on my own. To process."

"Of course, I . . . Will you check in with us from time to time?"

"Be well, Yolad. I don't think we'll meet again."

The words felt great leaving his mouth, so perfect and true. And tomorrow, he'd have his symbiont, and his haughty attitude would be fully justified with a superior intelligence.

"Who is the symbiont?" Yolad asked.

"Excuse me?"

"What's your new name?"

12

Last Witness

Joran's hotel room was dark, save for the glow from his screen. His brother's face appeared, blinking and bleary.

"Joran? Are you okay?" Yolad asked him that every time he answered. So patronizing.

"I'm fine," Joran said. "You don't seem happy to hear from me."

"I am."

"You're a terrible liar."

"Please don't be like that." He squinted, probably trying to figure out where Joran was. *"You look good. Different."*

They hadn't spoken in two years. Of course he'd changed.

"I *am* different. I've been joined."

The look on Yolad's face made the lie so much sweeter. In truth, Joran wasn't to be joined until the next day, but he was eager to put a down payment on his gloating. After his joining, he could cut his family out of his life for good.

"That's . . . that's great, Joran! I'm proud of you."

"The Belar sons." Joran gave a wry grin. "May we outshine our worthless parents."

"Don't say that. Mom misses you."

"And Dad?"

"Joran, I—"

"Does he even ask about me?"

Yolad looked away. *"I'm sorry for how he's treated you."*

Joran needed to control his temper. A joined Trill would be

more confident. "Yes, well, I've grown beyond caring about such things. He can watch my star rise from the ground."

Yolad nodded, smiling. *"He'll come around. He'll see what he's missing."*

"I don't care. I don't need his approval anymore."

The smile faded. *"Of course. Would you come home? Let us see you in person for once?"*

"I wouldn't want to be a drain on you and Teelo."

"I'm sorry she called you that."

"It's forgotten, Yolad."

"Glad to hear it. I miss you."

No, he didn't. Yolad missed having someone to make him look good. His brother won awards and got into a prestigious music academy. He pretended to encourage Joran, but he had stolen ideas for his compositions. Yolad didn't want a brother. He wanted a mirror who'd reflect his brilliance back onto him.

However, Joran had his own successes. He'd composed for three orchestras, traveled to many worlds to play *his* music. Joran's family had only ever made him feel inferior, held him back, but with his joining, he would cement his independence. It was time to get rid of the dead weight in his life, and joining was as good an excuse as any.

"Now that I'm joined, I have a lot to sort out," Joran said. "You might not hear from me for a while."

"Oh, um, okay."

"I need to be on my own. To process."

"Of course, I . . . Will you check in with us from time to time?"

"Be well, Yolad. I don't think we'll meet again."

The words felt great leaving his mouth, so perfect and true. And tomorrow, he'd have his symbiont, and his haughty attitude would be fully justified with a superior intelligence.

"Who is the symbiont?" Yolad asked.

"Excuse me?"

"What's your new name?"

closing his abdominal cavity. They glanced at him with reassuring smiles.

The symbiont wriggled into place, and more static jolts rocked Joran's body. The creature was attaching to the most critical nerve endings, intertwining with him. Electrical pops sparkled through Joran's form from inside to out, and his breath quickened.

Then came the voices.

They were quiet at first, like a babbling brook—whispers of lives long past. They seeped into his mind from outside, spilling between stress fractures. Growing louder, they flooded his psyche, deafening him, drowning out all reason.

And in that moment, Joran finally understood joining for what it was: a terrible mistake.

His mind contorted under the influence of the symbiont, thoughts becoming slippery and strange. One moment, he was calm. The next, he was thrashing about on the bed, surgeons shouting at one another to hold him down.

He was Joran, but he was also Torias, Audrid, and others. It was wrong, unnatural. A joining wasn't supposed to be like this. Joran was a fully realized individual, an achiever—he could never share himself as an equal with anyone. He craved control, and this was the exact opposite.

They wanted him to do things, these past hosts: say words that weren't his, think dead thoughts. He was being invaded, taken over, converted. There was only one thing on his mind: flight.

Joran threw an elbow, catching one of the doctors squarely in the nose with a crunch. She reeled, surgical mask blotting with blood. He sat up, squirming free of the other medical staff and tearing the surgical tent off.

"Get him! Get him!" shouted one of the nurses, reaching for his arm.

Joran pinwheeled his wrist, easily breaking free as adrenaline surged in his veins. Doctors groped for him, and he stood atop the bed. Mustering his panicked strength, he leaped over them, his feet

Joran didn't know. He only possessed two facts: the former host had died suddenly in an accident, and the symbiont was being prepped for implantation tomorrow. As an initiate, it was Joran's duty to be there for the symbiont, a host whose legacy would carry on for generations to come. If he didn't accept that fact, they might cull him from the initiate program.

"Take care, Yolad," he said with a smile, and closed the connection.

Then Joran went to bed, knowing that on the morrow, his life would change forever.

Joran Belar's death truly began at the moment of his rebirth.

The surgeons slipped the Dax symbiont into him, filling him up. His eyes widened as it pushed deeper into his belly, feeling out his spinal column. It probed around his organs, attaching nerves and rewiring him. He'd studied the biology enough to know the mechanics of the act, but experiencing it was another thing entirely.

With this, he could finally become what he was meant to be. The strength of the past hosts would be added to him, and he would secure his place in history as one of the greatest pianists of the modern age.

His parents, his brother, everyone who'd doubted him would be proven wrong with this achievement: the first Belar to be joined.

The operating theater at the Symbiosis Commission was clean and bright white, with high ceilings. The medical staff were top-notch, entrusted with taking care of the geniuses and super-achievers of Trill. Now Joran would be recognized in that same rarified air.

"Joran Dax, can you hear me?" one of the doctors asked, and he nodded.

The first tendrils of connection were a static shock, rippling across his entire being. The doctors worked diligently on him, closing his abdominal cavity. They glanced at him with reassuring smiles.

The symbiont wriggled into place, and more static jolts rocked Joran's body. The creature was attaching to the most critical nerve endings, intertwining with him. Electrical pops sparkled through Joran's form from inside to out, and his breath quickened.

Then came the voices.

They were quiet at first, like a babbling brook—whispers of lives long past. They seeped into his mind from outside, spilling between stress fractures. Growing louder, they flooded his psyche, deafening him, drowning out all reason.

And in that moment, Joran finally understood joining for what it was: a terrible mistake.

His mind contorted under the influence of the symbiont, thoughts becoming slippery and strange. One moment, he was calm. The next, he was thrashing about on the bed, surgeons shouting at one another to hold him down.

He was Joran, but he was also Torias, Audrid, and others. It was wrong, unnatural. A joining wasn't supposed to be like this. Joran was a fully realized individual, an achiever—he could never share himself as an equal with anyone. He craved control, and this was the exact opposite.

They wanted him to do things, these past hosts: say words that weren't his, think dead thoughts. He was being invaded, taken over, converted. There was only one thing on his mind: flight.

Joran threw an elbow, catching one of the doctors squarely in the nose with a crunch. She reeled, surgical mask blotting with blood. He sat up, squirming free of the other medical staff and tearing the surgical tent off.

"Get him! Get him!" shouted one of the nurses, reaching for his arm.

Joran pinwheeled his wrist, easily breaking free as adrenaline surged in his veins. Doctors groped for him, and he stood atop the bed. Mustering his panicked strength, he leaped over them, his feet

12

LAST WITNESS

Joran's hotel room was dark, save for the glow from his screen. His brother's face appeared, blinking and bleary.

"Joran? Are you okay?" Yolad asked him that every time he answered. So patronizing.

"I'm fine," Joran said. "You don't seem happy to hear from me."

"I am."

"You're a terrible liar."

"Please don't be like that." He squinted, probably trying to figure out where Joran was. *"You look good. Different."*

They hadn't spoken in two years. Of course he'd changed.

"I *am* different. I've been joined."

The look on Yolad's face made the lie so much sweeter. In truth, Joran wasn't to be joined until the next day, but he was eager to put a down payment on his gloating. After his joining, he could cut his family out of his life for good.

"That's . . . that's great, Joran! I'm proud of you."

"The Belar sons." Joran gave a wry grin. "May we outshine our worthless parents."

"Don't say that. Mom misses you."

"And Dad?"

"Joran, I—"

"Does he even ask about me?"

Yolad looked away. *"I'm sorry for how he's treated you."*

Joran needed to control his temper. A joined Trill would be

more confident. "Yes, well, I've grown beyond caring about such things. He can watch my star rise from the ground."

Yolad nodded, smiling. *"He'll come around. He'll see what he's missing."*

"I don't care. I don't need his approval anymore."

The smile faded. *"Of course. Would you come home? Let us see you in person for once?"*

"I wouldn't want to be a drain on you and Teelo."

"I'm sorry she called you that."

"It's forgotten, Yolad."

"Glad to hear it. I miss you."

No, he didn't. Yolad missed having someone to make him look good. His brother won awards and got into a prestigious music academy. He pretended to encourage Joran, but he had stolen ideas for his compositions. Yolad didn't want a brother. He wanted a mirror who'd reflect his brilliance back onto him.

However, Joran had his own successes. He'd composed for three orchestras, traveled to many worlds to play *his* music. Joran's family had only ever made him feel inferior, held him back, but with his joining, he would cement his independence. It was time to get rid of the dead weight in his life, and joining was as good an excuse as any.

"Now that I'm joined, I have a lot to sort out," Joran said. "You might not hear from me for a while."

"Oh, um, okay."

"I need to be on my own. To process."

"Of course, I . . . Will you check in with us from time to time?"

"Be well, Yolad. I don't think we'll meet again."

The words felt great leaving his mouth, so perfect and true. And tomorrow, he'd have his symbiont, and his haughty attitude would be fully justified with a superior intelligence.

"Who is the symbiont?" Yolad asked.

"Excuse me?"

"What's your new name?"

Joran didn't know. He only possessed two facts: the for
had died suddenly in an accident, and the symbiont w
prepped for implantation tomorrow. As an initiate, it wa
duty to be there for the symbiont, a host whose legacy wou
on for generations to come. If he didn't accept that fact, the
cull him from the initiate program.

"Take care, Yolad," he said with a smile, and closed th
nection.

Then Joran went to bed, knowing that on the morrow, h
would change forever.

Joran Belar's death truly began at the moment of his rebirth.

The surgeons slipped the Dax symbiont into him, filling
up. His eyes widened as it pushed deeper into his belly, fee
out his spinal column. It probed around his organs, attach
nerves and rewiring him. He'd studied the biology enough
know the mechanics of the act, but experiencing it was anot
thing entirely.

With this, he could finally become what he was meant to b
The strength of the past hosts would be added to him, and h
would secure his place in history as one of the greatest pianists o
the modern age.

His parents, his brother, everyone who'd doubted him would be proven wrong with this achievement: the first Belar to be joined.

The operating theater at the Symbiosis Commission was clean and bright white, with high ceilings. The medical staff were top-notch, entrusted with taking care of the geniuses and super-achievers of Trill. Now Joran would be recognized in that same rarified air.

"Joran Dax, can you hear me?" one of the doctors asked, and he nodded.

The first tendrils of connection were a static shock, rippling across his entire being. The doctors worked diligently on him, coming down on a short, wheeled cart. The cart went forward; his head went backward.

With a wet *thunk*, the lights dimmed out.

A shaft of dusty sunlight split the dull gray of the music room.

Piano keys drifted in and out of focus, their sheen tarnished by dozens of hands over years. In his time, Joran had played some of the finest instruments ever crafted in the Federation, and was accustomed to only the best. This pathetic specimen was the property of the Symbiosis Commission, a part of their music therapy program—and it was out of tune and filthy. A tendril of sticky drool fell from Joran's mouth, and he numbly watched it adhere to the keyboard.

He was on so many drugs that he couldn't remember any of them. His head swam, and in merciful moments, he was exhausted enough to sleep.

The first four weeks of his joining had been spent in a medically induced coma. They said he was lucky he didn't have brain damage. The doctors saved his life—rebuilt his fractured skull, but they'd left the Dax symbiont inside of him. They'd assumed he wanted it.

He did not.

When he'd imagined his joining, Joran thought of the performances he would give. So many joined longed to discover scientific truths and explore the galaxy—but they'd never fully exploited the beauty of their homeworld, the universes of music. There were still songs to compose, paintings to paint, stories to write. There was a whole spectrum of creativity that the Symbiosis Commission often ignored in their pursuit of excellence. They upheld math, chemistry, astrodynamics, but rarely the arts. Joran was genuinely surprised that he'd been approved.

He needed to be joined. He'd plateaued. The symbiont had become a beacon of hope that he might rise out of his banal compositions to a new level. He'd meant to add the strength and innovation of the past hosts to his own and take the Federation by storm. He was destined to be famous—superior to other musicians.

One problem: every former host of the Dax symbiont was a tone-deaf hack.

It was cruel, to saddle him with hosts that had contributed nothing of real merit. Lela, Tobin, Emony, Audrid, Torias . . . politician, engineer, gymnast, bureaucrat, and a pilot. Not one of them knew a damn thing about music, and Joran found them taking up too much space in his mind.

He hadn't asked for this. Initiates had the ability to request symbionts, though the Commission couldn't always oblige. Joran had asked for Lohk, a symbiont whose past hosts were comprised of a great tenor singer, an acoustical physicist, and a legendary aphonica player. When the time came to make the transfer, Joran had been out-of-system, giving a concert. He hadn't made it back in time to receive the symbiont when its host passed away. The Commission awarded Lohk to Polix, the witless initiate from Ok'vor.

Joran hated Polix, and he hated Ok'vor, but most of all, he hated the sublime beauty of her flute playing after her joining. Joran had been forced to watch her blossom, becoming the embodiment of music while his heart withered. That beauty should've been part of him.

But the Commission *wanted* him to have a symbiont. The purpose of being joined was to be exposed to many lives, they'd pointed out. Joran's mentors all advised him to continue in the program; he'd passed the tests and the field docents loved him.

Then Torias Dax died in a shuttlecraft accident, and Joran was left with a choice—be joined now, or lose his place. The Dax symbiont needed a host immediately. He was assured its past lives were all prestigious, brilliant people.

It was the opportunity of a lifetime.

Which led to him drooling on a piano.

Joran smacked his lips and wiped the saliva. It was too late to take Dax out without killing him.

He was stuck like this, forever.

A woman's voice, smooth as the bowing of a cello, said, "Hello, Dax."

Joran looked back to find a vision in a crimson dress standing over him. Silver hair flowed in wavy curls down her shoulders. She had an angular, pale face, with a pronounced jaw and plump lips. Predatory eyes positively smoked at him behind dark makeup.

He checked himself for spit and smoothed his wild hair. "Hello. Who . . . I'm Joran."

It felt strange to talk. How long had he been sitting there? The drugs made it so hard to perceive time. The head injury didn't help.

"You poor thing," she said.

After the anguish he'd been through, just the sight of her was a balm.

"Who are—" He swallowed. "Who are you?"

Glittering green eyes narrowed with her smile.

"Doctor Elta Vess. I'm the director of Psychiatric Services."

"Psychiatric . . ."

"Yes, Dax."

When she called him that, the other hosts perked up inside. They tried to surge forward, and he held them back like an armful of flapping birds. If this was to be his future, he would find a way to remain himself. Joran's breath heaved, and he stared at the keyboard until his symbiont calmed down.

"Please call me Joran."

Her dark red lips quirked in a smirk. "I heard you took quite a spill."

He touched the bandages on the back of his head, wincing at the still-sensitive skin. "So I'm told. The doctors said I had a . . . a bad hit. There's a name for the in-injury."

"But you pulled through. You're a tough host, aren't you?" She almost sounded like she was talking to a pet, and Joran wasn't sure he liked it.

"It was some kind of, um, axonal injury—"

"Not the right kind, I'm afraid."

He stared at her. "And what is the . . . 'right kind' of brain injury?"

She leaned against the piano and considered him, tapping an index finger to her painted lips. "Are you happy, Dax?"

Voices whispered into him like a rainstorm.

"My friends call me Joran."

"You don't have any friends." She leaned down and placed a hand on his shoulder.

She was so close he could smell her *tilke* lily perfume. He gasped as she draped herself across his back and slid her hand lower onto his abdomen. Her breath came hot on his ear, and he was suddenly quite awake.

Joran was accustomed to women wanting him. He'd always had good luck, especially after a concert—but he was disgusting at the moment. His eyes were no doubt sunken, and he caught the scent of body odor when he raised his arms.

Yet he murmured, "And this doesn't make us friends, Doctor Vess?"

She laughed.

"How well do you remember our original language, Dax? Shall I remind you?"

An electric shock snapped between her palm and his skin. His whole body clenched up tight, fingers curling like a dying insect. The storm of voices became a gale-force torrent, drowning out any conscious thought. The other hosts burbled up through Joran, a greater metaconsciousness arising inside.

It was Dax.

The two symbionts touched across the current, and it was like distilled bliss. Joran was, in that moment, nothing more than the contact surface through which they spoke. Their conversations and thoughts were myriad, far beyond his reckoning unless he chose to open himself up to it. He could relent, let his personality be changed by the joining, and understand them.

But then Joran Belar would be washed away forever.

The electrical current receded, along with Vess's warmth. Joran found himself drooling at a piano for the second time that day.

"Incredible." She leaned against the instrument. "I always wondered if I'd meet someone like you. How *did* you get through the psychiatric evaluations?"

Through chattering teeth, he forced out, "W-what?"

"Truly incompatible." She bent down and looked into him with serpent's eyes. "The initiate program . . . did you *lie* to them on your One-A Tests?"

Joran remembered those evaluations. They'd scanned him with machines able to discover if he was truthful—but they'd underestimated his experience with deceit. To Joran, lying could be a game, a dare to see if the other person was more cunning than him. The practice came as naturally as breath, and it was easy to tell the doctors what they wanted to hear. What mattered was that he secured his place as a joined Trill.

She tapped his cheek. "Hey. Think back to the battery of questions—the ones about childhood. Let's talk sharing, first. You were never any good at it."

"No, I—"

"Do you remember the questions about how you treated the other kids?"

"I—"

"You lied, Joran. You were a nightmare. I did a little digging on you. I know why you don't speak to your father anymore."

"How dare you?"

Her gaze was ravenous. "He showed me the scar. You were a selfish, nasty child. Vindictive. Unable to compromise."

"Call me what you want, I'm suffering." The words were like rotting fruit in his mouth.

"Oh, I'm sorry. Those aren't my comments. I was quoting your school reports. Had them unsealed for medical reasons. You really punched your music teacher?"

Who was she to judge him? Everyone had done things they weren't proud of, and bringing it up did nothing. Here he was—ailing—and his care professional chose to play with him like some kind of vermin. He spat the vilest slur he had at her.

It rolled off like she hadn't heard him.

She straightened up so she could resume looking down on him. "You were never fit for joining, Joran Belar. You just knew how to pretend to be one of us."

No. He wasn't a liar. He deserved to be joined, to the *right* symbiont. Sure, he'd broken a few rules, but the initiate program was a competition. He had to win before he could sort out the spoils.

"A controlling, manipulative person like you could never share space with another soul, much less several. It wouldn't matter if you *wanted* to open up—you can't. Your body will continuously fall out of sync with Dax until we have to take it out of you. We both know what happens at that point, right?"

Vess had assaulted him. She'd humiliated him. Worst of all, she'd exposed him for what he was.

He wanted to slap her so badly his palms itched. What stopped him? Cowardice?

Probably the electric shocks.

"Liar, liar, liar, Joran. That's my diagnosis, and I'm sorry to say, your condition is terminal."

Who did she think she was, to damn him? Was she going to cut off his meds? What if they stopped giving them to him? Would she let him fall into a coma?

Each question hit him harder than the last. His heart hammered in his chest as he considered the power she might have over him.

He could hardly stand it.

Joran stood up, fists clenched. He was still bigger than her by a fair margin, with strong fingers. He could throttle her. He could break her. "If you think you can just—"

"Uh, no."

She pressed a hand to his face, and his thoughts went white with another electric shock. The next thing he knew, his forehead smacked the cold tiles. Blackness crept at the edge of his vision.

"Oh, no!" Her quiet laughter raked his thoughts. "And with your head injury!"

Everything was so heavy, swirling beneath him.

"Ah, ah," she said. "Fall risk. We should've restrained you."

Her fingers pressed to his neck, checking his pulse. He couldn't speak or muster the strength to rise.

There came the chirp of a combadge somewhere in the blurry distance.

"Vess to Security. Joran just attacked me. No, I'm fine. He was nothing."

Joran shouted until his throat was raw.

He'd been stuck in an enclosed healing pod for hours, staring at the ceiling of a dim treatment room. At first, he'd searched for an emergency release. When that failed, he beat upon the lid with all his strength. He wanted to break it—but the pod was surprisingly resilient.

He gave up, muscles burning, and wept at how far he'd fallen.

A fortnight ago, he'd been playing sonatas on Risa, lavished with every form of beauty, from music to bodies. He could've drowned in perfection, instead of this.

His stench fogged the enclosure. Alien emotions swirled among his own—fractures in his mind, each with a different mix of fear and anguish to bring to the situation.

His vision swam, and he blinked back the exhaustion.

"Joran." A shade stood outside his pod, one hand on the lid. "Accept us. Accept yourself."

He could almost make out Audrid's red hair before he closed his eyes. "Go away."

"You *can* do this, Joran. Vess was wrong. You're not incompatible."

"I said go away!" His voice creaked, and his shout devolved into a coughing fit.

"You don't have to die—"

He banged the lid once more, and she vanished. In her place was Elta Vess.

She smiled at him. "Do behave, pet."

He nodded, beaten.

She opened the lid, and Joran gulped hungrily at the fresh air.

He resisted the urge to curl into a ball. "Why are you doing this to me?"

"Because you're in a unique position, Joran."

Not Dax.

She crossed her arms. "Let me start with one crystal-clear fact: The Dax symbiont can't live inside you, and when it dies, you die. Of course, we'd never let that happen here at the Commission, so we would remove your symbiont, and that would kill you."

His voice was pathetic. "There are plenty of records of dominant hosts. I'm just showing the symbiont which of us is in charge."

"Did your own research, did you? What did you study again?"

She thought she was so smart, but she'd clearly never heard of dominant hosts. While in the initiate program, Joran had combed the Grand Archives and found evidence—a peer-reviewed scientific report from the Symbiosis Commission—that host dominance was possible. In fact, the report posited, this condition might be more common than anyone previously suspected.

"My research came from the Grand Archives, and—"

"You know what's funny?" she said. "I know the exact study you're talking about. Men at dinner parties like to tell me about it."

Joran started to open his mouth, but feared she was right. He wasn't about to keep handing her fodder to make fun of him. He might be restrained in a pod, soaking in his own sweat while someone gloated about his death, but he had his dignity to consider.

"The study had what we call 'selective attention.' They only picked hosts that fit the result they wanted. So-called dominant hosts are exceptionally rare." She grinned like it was her first time tasting candy. "Joran, that study was from *forty years ago*. You have to read the science that was done since then. You can't just grab whatever agrees with your point of view."

Photon torpedoes pierced his self-esteem.

"But, you know, that's why I'm the director of Psychiatric Services and you're a pianist."

He was going to die, and it was all his fault.

His mouth went dry as his eyes grew wet. Joran couldn't accept his fate. But it was coming—he couldn't deny it, either.

"Don't . . . don't try to compare our merits." He didn't even convince himself. "I've played dozens of worlds. Met people you wouldn't believe."

"The quality of your acquaintances doesn't make you joining material. You, specifically, need to be exceptional. It took a joined to split the atom. It took a joined to go faster than light. The joined are the reason our species walks the stars, but someone at the Commission said, 'Let's get Joran. He's good at the piano.'"

"My music will be timeless."

"Every composer in the initiate program says that at their evaluation. Ask me how I know."

His voice boiled over in a shout. "Did you just come in here to torture me?"

Vess didn't even flinch. "No. I came to get you to accept something. Salvation."

"I'm not religious."

"How are you *so* predictable? Joran, you're objectively garbage, and the field docents should've kicked you out of the initiate program for your own safety. If anyone, I blame them for this mess."

Joran was coming around to that way of thinking too.

"But you can do something incredible with this tragedy." She placed a hand atop his abdomen, and his heart skipped a beat from fear of a shock. "You can set your symbiont free."

Dax stirred inside him, a mix of worry and longing at her turn of phrase.

"I don't understand," he said.

"Symbionts are reliant upon the hosts. Hosts like you are their sensory organs and access to the world outside. Without them, the symbionts would still be in the Caves of Mak'ala, and the Trill would be rubbing sticks together to make fire. Why should hosts get to make all of the decisions while symbionts remain tucked away?"

She was clearly joined, so why did she speak of hosts like she did? Joran feared it wasn't a simple mistake.

Vess patted his abdomen once, then took her hand away. "We've devised a procedure, something very special and quite difficult. It's quiet, gentle, and painless, and it removes the host's mind from the equation—effectively leaving the symbiont in control."

"What?"

"Joran, there are two beings trapped inside your body—you and Dax. As things are right now, you can't both survive, and we all know which is more valuable to society." Her green eyes seemed to glow in the dim treatment room. "You can't change that."

"You're talking about killing me!"

To his horror, she nodded. "Yes, but we'd leave your body intact for Dax. It would live on inside you, growing old one day at a time in total serenity."

The symbiont twisted, disquieted all at once. The thought of becoming a puppet corpse was abominable by even Joran's standards.

"You're bound for death." Vess ran a finger along the edge of the med pod. "Dax is bound for greatness. Why not ensure it happens in your body, as your legacy? Joran Belar, you won't be alive in two months, but Joran Dax could be the greatest composer of all time."

He gave her a weak smile. "I'm sad to report—it's terrible at music."

"But you must admit, Dax has a better destiny than yours, deceiver. If you don't let me do this, your body and life will be a cast-off husk. A footnote. We'll find someone else for Dax, and they'll take the glory of a joined destiny."

"If you want to murder me, why even ask? Why not get it over with when I was unconscious?"

"Because it helps Dax if you have a satisfied mind."

Joran had wanted everyone to know who he was, so that he would never disappear in a crowd again. But he'd planned to experience his fame, not be promised a legacy of greatness after his demise. He needed to live through the musical era he hoped to define.

But Dax was intrigued. It desired Vess's electric touch, even as the shocks had hurt Joran. The simultaneous fascination and revulsion with Joran's tormentor cleaved him apart on his deepest levels. Perhaps Dax wanted him to die, now that it knew who he really was.

"You've taken good care of this body." Vess looked him up and down. "Could use a washing, but it's more than serviceable. Why let it go to waste when you could become something greater?"

" 'Become'?"

"Symbionts who are alone in their bodies have ascended. They gain powers beyond the hosts. The ancients had a word for it: *kael'tach*, the elevation."

He stared into her eyes, looking for any semblance of sanity. "No."

"Through *kael'tach*, Dax is freed. Think of what it could do with your body and talent."

"You're a monster."

"You could be too."

The idea was almost appealing: his body, put to good use in crafting a legacy. How would it conquer the galaxy? Who would he become? Joran shook his head. Thinking that way was going to get him killed.

But it was hard to feel otherwise when his entire existence was defined by suffering. Dax's thoughts wriggled between his own, louder whenever he needed to concentrate. Joran couldn't keep himself straightened out, and every hour, he grew more nauseated. Was it the isoboramine?

Tears watered in Joran's eyes as he grieved for himself. "I can't die like this."

"It is going to happen."

"Killed because I lied on an exam? It's wretched."

She shook her head. "If you let me elevate you, no one will ever know the choice you made. Dax will live out its freedom in secret."

"Secretly inhabiting a dead man? You must be joking!"

Her eyes went cold above her wicked smile. "Oh, it's possible. Ask me how I know."

Memories of her electric shocks jolted him, and he recoiled.

"You're—"

"Dead?" She leaned down over him. "Yes. It's not as bad as you think."

This had to be a nightmare. He willed himself to blink, to wake up and be the joined composer he was supposed to be. He had no room for a reality in which he was powerless.

Vess crossed over to the med-pod controls and tapped a button. "Think it over, Dax."

The symbiont inside surged at the name as the pod closed around him. He tried to get up, but couldn't.

"No!" He pounded the lid, trying to push it open as it closed on him. His arms were far too weak to stop the inevitable. "Let me out of here!"

Vess's voice was muffled, rendered thin by the pod speakers. "Why? It's the only thing keeping you alive."

She held a portable display up to the glass so he could see his adjusted neurotransmitter levels—fatally low. The pod had him on life-support.

"But I feel fine—"

"That's the med pod. You don't produce enough isoboramine

to be a dominant host. It's like I told you—there's nothing special about you. Your sole talent is your ability to lie."

She walked to the door. "Think about what you'd like to do with the rest of your days and get back to me."

"Wait!"

Vess left, plunging the treatment room into darkness. Finally alone, Joran wept until he passed out.

13

Hard Exit

Orderlies came to take him to the bathroom, and Joran finally had his chance. He told them all about Doctor Vess, and what she'd been up to. He gave them detailed timelines, and made sure they knew she was actually a dead woman being operated by an evil symbiont.

They'd have to look into it. They could see how important it was to him. Could he explain some things further?

Joran thought they were listening until they led him back to the pod. He tried to go for the door, but his balance was still shaky. Within seconds, he was back in the bed, trapped under the lid. They left him with nothing, save his clothes and his time.

He'd done some bad things in his life, but didn't deserve this. What was the point in learning from his mistakes if they were terminal?

It was hard to know if hours or days passed. He lost consciousness at odd intervals, only able to tell the time from the changing color of the sky against the treatment room's windows. He wished he could stand at those panes, banging for someone outside to hear him.

A Trill man peered down through the pod's clear canopy. He was pale, midthirties, with an attractive though plain face. A few of his slicked-back chestnut hairs slipped loose, falling across glacial blue eyes.

"There's a trick to these med pods," he said, bemused.

Joran narrowed his eyes. "What?"

"To getting them open. It's fiddly, but it can be done. I was a test pilot. Spent a lot of time in med pods."

"Okay. Right, yes. How do I get out?"

"By accepting yourself."

Joran screwed his eyes shut, chasing away his rage. In this powerless state, all anger melted into depression.

"This isn't the time for jokes," he said.

"I'm not joking. I'm trying to save your life."

"Then tell me how to get out."

"Why?" the man said. "Even if I freed you, you'd still die. Not enough neurotransmitters, remember?"

He wanted to punch this guy, but there was a canopy in the way. "You're Torias Dax, aren't you?"

"At your service."

"What do you want with me?"

Torias walked around the bed. "You might not believe this, but we've got your best interests at heart."

"You want to make me submit."

Torias shook his head, chuckling. "How did you graduate the initiate program? No, Joran. We want to make you whole, and help you survive."

"Doctor Vess was right about me. I am a liar. I hurt people . . ."

"You've barely lived. There's time to write some wrongs along with those songs." Torias frowned. "No? She really got into your head."

"She also said I was incompatible."

"I'm the one inside you, so I'm better equipped to make that call." Torias hopped up and sat on the middle of the lid without a sound. "Joran, you can do this if you try."

"Do what? Merge with Dax?"

"Yes! It's literally your only way out!"

Joran thought about relaxing, opening his mind, truly allowing himself to dissolve with the symbiont—and a reflexive clutch of fear shut the thought off.

"No." His breath came faster as he tried to hold in a rising panic. "I can't . . . I can't make myself do it any more than I could walk off a cliff."

"Doctor Vess was wrong. It's not your selfishness that's killing you, it's your arrogance." Torias knocked on the lid. "You think you can be the sole author of your legacy. That you can go it alone. That's why you trained as a soloist."

Joran scowled at him.

"But you can't do it this time." Torias jumped off the pod and backed away, raising his palms. "I can assure you, it's easier for me to let you die. Either I get a competent new host or complete control of your body."

"Yes, you stand to gain quite the windfall."

"Problem is, I got to know you. We're joined. I see all the damage you've done, and I see the things you need to fix. You can't die before you do that."

"*You* can fix them in my body after I'm gone."

Torias groaned. "How lazy can you possibly be? You'd rather be dead than put in the work?"

Joran punched the canopy. "Can't someone just be nice to me?"

"Not until—"

"Get out! Leave me with a shred of peace, damn you!" Joran heaved with a sob, gritting his teeth.

"You don't have to die! But you must *let go!"*

A shaft of light spilled across the ceiling as the door opened. Doctor Elta Vess appeared podside, along with another Trill Joran had never seen before.

He was an aging male, with pasty skin and parted gray hair, peering down at Joran with a butcher's eyes.

His high-pitched, gurgling voice broke the disquieting silence. "You look good."

Joran gave him a hesitant smile. "Thank you?"

"Healthy, save for the isoboramine drop," the man observed.

"Excuse me, who are you?" Joran asked.

The man glanced at Vess.

"This is Doctor Hoq," Vess said. "Creator of the *kael'tach* procedure. He would be the one to perform it on you."

"The surgery is most effective"—Hoq folded his hands behind his back—"when the subject understands and accepts his fate. A mind at peace is better captured by the symbiont. Don't you want that?"

"Don't listen to him," Torias said, stepping out from behind Hoq. "You have to try to unify with us."

"No," Joran replied, somehow to both of them. He couldn't die, but he couldn't imagine living, either.

"How much of yourself do you want to survive, young man?" Hoq asked.

"You're a fool, not a doctor. A professional would never suggest this."

"He's a genius with sixty years of experience." Vess patted Hoq's back, and he smiled almost obediently. "He pioneered the surgery, and he's probably the only person who could pull something like this off. You would be in capable hands."

"My first duty, as it has been my whole career, is to the symbiont," Hoq said. "I would like to see more of them liberated in my lifetime."

"Over my dead body, apparently," Joran said.

"Don't be so arrogant," Vess said. "It's why you were almost dropped from the program. If you agree to Hoq's surgery, more of your essence will be preserved for future generations. A form of you will survive long beyond your meager shell. I've done it. Dax could be free too."

"Peaceful slumber, and then life anew." Hoq had clearly been practicing this pitch. "As the shell for a symbiont. Isn't that what all Trill dream of?"

"Become part of Dax," Vess said, "and unleash your real potential."

Torias waved for his attention. "We're better together. Joran, you have to let us in."

But he *was* getting tired. Vess had assembled an accurate portrait of him, and it was hideous. Everything she'd said about Joran was true, and he knew he was scum deep down. Why not give in? Maybe it was better to yield. The pod was disgusting, stinking of sweat and rotten breath. He wanted it to be over.

"Come on, Joran," Vess said. "It's time to relax."

His breath came quicker, and he shut his eyes. All he had to do was say yes.

"You're going to kill me either way," Joran said. "Do what you have to."

Hoq looked to Vess. "I think that qualifies as acceptance. I'll start prepping the theater."

"Send the orderlies to come get Mister Dax when you're done," Vess said. "Let's keep him comfortable."

Hoq exited, and she turned to follow.

"You're just going to leave me alone until the end?" Joran called out.

"I expect you need to get more acquainted with your symbiont," she replied. "While you have time."

Then she left.

Torias alone remained in the gloom with him, shaking his head sadly.

"You're going to give up, then?" he asked.

"Yes."

"Because it's hard to face your misdeeds, and you won't be able to live your life your way."

"Precisely."

Torias dropped his hands to his hips, letting out a big sigh. "You're pretty awful, I'll give you that."

"Then why don't you get lost? I'm broken."

"Because Doctor Vess told you so? Joran, your existence can still hold meaning. There are unwritten symphonies, but you'll have to

work harder for them than you thought you would. You've been gifted so many opportunities already. Unlimited knowledge was too much to ask."

"So what, I should deal with it?"

"If you can only write great compositions with a symbiont inside you, then the symbiont was the talent, not you."

Joran had nothing to say in return. He'd occasionally had that thought himself in the initiate program, but he'd tamped it down. He saw nothing wrong with an unfair advantage, as long as it fell in his favor.

"You can wish you were born powerful," Torias said. "You can wish you'd gotten the Lohk symbiont. But throwing everything away because of it? Fool."

Joran watched the man pace back and forth.

"I died young, but I don't want that for you or anyone. Live, Joran."

Joran had finally reached his crossroads; he could delay the decision no longer.

"Okay. What do I do?"

Torias beckoned to him. "Reach out to me."

"I'm in a pod."

"With your mind, you pi'stet rakhat. *Control your breathing."*

Joran closed his eyes and inhaled. It wasn't hard to find the part of himself that needed to open up to Dax. The barrier between them was sore and irritated, like a wound.

Torias's voice came through crystal clear, like he was whispering into Joran's ear. "Relax your defenses."

Joran began to drift in his solitude, searching for the peace only deprivation could provide. Perhaps if he eased himself into this partnership with Dax, it might work. Maybe there was a world in which he could share himself.

Light washed his eyelids, and Joran opened them to find a pair of burly orderlies coming into the treatment room—a man and a woman in brown Symbiosis Commission uniforms.

"Relax faster," Torias said. "These people are here to kill you."

That did anything but calm Joran's heart, and his mind clamped shut again. "I—what? Oh, no."

The male orderly was massive, like a wall of meat, and he tapped a few buttons on the console to release the med pod hood and cut off the force field.

Joran was no longer keen on getting free of the pod. "Wait."

The fellow pushed back his sleeves, and the woman grabbed Joran under his arms. He screamed and bucked, struggling against their inexorable grip, but couldn't get loose, and got cuffed on the side of the head for his trouble.

"Let me go!" he cried. "Please! They're going to kill me!"

"Get a hold of yourself," the woman said. "The first duty is to the symbiont!"

He caught sight of a hover chair with antique mechanical restraints—his transportation to the execution chamber.

"I can help you with the hand-to-hand," Torias said, "but if they manage to lock you into that chair, you're dead. Unify with us now or never."

Joran couldn't survive as himself, but he'd be damned if he'd die as someone else. Calm washed over him, and the din of the fight went quiet. They carried him toward the chair like water rushing over a waterfall. He couldn't spend his last few moments fighting for dominance. His feelings on submission no longer mattered, and so he needed a better plan for his remaining centimeters.

The countless fibers of his being aligned toward one thought, and one alone:

Open.

"That's right Mister Dax," soothed the big fellow. "There's a good lad."

Joran's new name invigorated him. The symbiont probed their connection, sliding thoughts into his mind—other feelings and truths. His reflex was to snap shut, but he had to be greater than his animal instincts. He had to be vulnerable, and that terrified him.

Open.

The orderlies slammed him down into the metal chair with a clank, immediately moving to secure his wrists.

The louder the thoughts became, the harder Joran listened. Euphoria seized his synapses, and he experienced a sudden fullness of being. He shared all of himself, augmented by the successes and failures of those who'd come before. The borders between Dax and Joran vanished, their essences coalescing like a droplet of water.

He needed to attack a superior opponent from a seated position. Torias knew how to do that.

Joran kicked the man in the knee, twisting it aside with his heel. Then he surged up out of the chair, head-butting the woman's nose. Pressing his advantage, he smashed his palm across the side of the man's face and kicked him backward.

The man swore, drawing out a stun baton and spreading his stance. Despite his tough posturing, he limped a little, and there was clear pain on his face. Joran threw a feinting jab, shouting to try to startle his opponent. It worked, and the man shifted his weight to his bad leg. Joran stepped in and kicked out the side of his knee again, and this time, he heard something snap.

Screaming filled the room as the man fell backward in shock. Joran closed the gap and twisted the stun baton from his grasp. He brought it across the man's temple with a deadly strike, and the orderly went stiff. He collapsed against the hard tile, spasming.

"No!" The woman came barreling into Joran, knocking him out into the hallway. "I'll kill you!"

They tumbled and grabbed, punched and kicked. She managed to pin his baton, so he shoved an elbow into her gut. At last, he knocked her loose, rolling away and scrambling upright.

A rainstorm hammered against the long row of high-rise windows, light filtering in from the surrounding capital. Joran's opponent drew back to swing at him, and he stepped in, grabbing her arm with Torias's knowledge and Emony's grace. With a hip check,

Joran threw the orderly over his shoulder, guiding her head toward the stone floor. With a sickening crunch, skull struck tile, and her body began to shake. Joran stumbled backward, peeling off her grasping fingers, and watched her die with rising amazement.

Torias had nonlethal ways of dealing with people—but he hadn't been trapped in a med pod for days, isolated in madness. In the end, Joran's decision to kill had been instinctual. Watching his opponent slacken, twitching her last, provided Joran with a visceral satisfaction he'd never expected. His former lovers had occasionally earned his ire, and a few of them suffered the consequences—but he'd never killed anyone. It was almost majestic, the final shudder of a dying body. His symbiont spoke in storms just like those.

Joran felt silly for being afraid of surrendering to Dax. He was mostly in control—though he had a few more opinions on everything. For example, Torias, Audrid, Emony, Tobin, and Lela thought Joran should run to the nearby landing pad, steal a shuttlecraft, and escape to tell the authorities what was happening at the Symbiosis Commission. It was a good plan, solidly conceived between Audrid's knowledge of the Symbiosis Commission and Torias's knowledge of spacecraft.

However, the plan lacked a feature Joran desperately needed: revenge.

Audrid knew the Commission top floor well. Joran was in the west wing, in the recovery section. Glancing around, he saw that much of it was empty. Vess and Hoq had housed him in an area under renovation, where they could do as they pleased with little interference. The orderlies were obviously committed to the cause. Who else inside the Commission was in on the conspiracy?

Hoq said he was prepping the operating theater, which meant he might be alone. That was good, because Vess had let slip one critical detail about him: Hoq was the only man capable of performing his procedure.

Joran had witnessed what an elevated Trill could do; Vess's

power was undeniable. She must've been looking for some kind of acolyte in Joran. He'd be glad to disappoint her—but he wanted to take it a step farther.

Hoq wouldn't live to perform his procedure on anyone ever.

Every one of Dax's former hosts disagreed with that decision for their own civilized reasons. They wanted Joran to live within the common bounds of the Trill social compact. The consequences of outright murder, the hosts warned, would be too grave.

Vess and Hoq had left Joran in a pod for days, only taking him out to use the toilet or eat. He stunk, and his skin itched with forming blisters. He would be able to plead that he was justified.

Joran rounded the corner to the operating theater entrance and peered in through the glass. He saw no one inside, but a ready assortment of tools and probes laid out on sanitary trays. He waved the door open and slipped into the room, trying not to jump at every shadow.

Tobin Dax knew a couple of the tools on the tray. He was a consummate engineer who loved all gadgets. Joran recognized a fuser, a couple of probes, and a cauterization pick. This pick was long and silvery, easily capable of vaporizing flesh at full temperature. Joran wasn't sure how Hoq was planning to use it on him, but the thought made his blood boil. He snatched it up from the tray, and the instrument fit into his hand like destiny.

Now he just had to find Hoq.

In Audrid's time, the lead surgeon maintained a lavish office on the west wing with a splendid view of the harbor. Hoq seemed like the sort of man to take up residence there, imperious and cruel—though perhaps Joran was projecting.

No other Dax would've taken the risk or killed in cold blood. But Joran had nothing left to lose. He'd seen the lowest his life could go; he was filthy and twitchy, fueled by utter hatred, roving around a government facility. They'd reduced him to this pathetic state. They'd strapped him down to be slaughtered like prey. He was willing to pay whatever legal price befell him.

However, he didn't have to be a fool.

If he could conceal his identity, that might complicate any search—giving him time to get out of the city. He spotted a rad tech's garb hanging from a hook—a shiny mask and long, silvery lab coat to protect the wearer from the various radioactive substances employed in medicine.

Joran donned the garment and slid the mask over his face. It was like stepping into armor, pure and powerful. It transformed him from mere madman into righteous avenger.

Also, it might protect him from splatters.

He stalked out of the operating theater, headed straight for the surgeon's office. Silent as a ghost, he padded through dark hallways. The capital's ever-present summer storms spit against the windows, further masking his passage. It was a bad squall outside; getting away in the shuttlecraft was going to be tricky, but Torias could easily handle that challenge.

The head surgeon's office was just around the corner, so Joran slowed his pace. Light spilled from an open door, along with the stray melody of Hoq's tuneless humming. Joran cringed. Not only had this man attempted to kill him, but he also couldn't remain on key.

Joran took a chance and peered into the room, finding the doctor hunched over a stack of padds. At this distance, the old man could've been mistaken for any other doddering fool. It was easy to imagine him sitting in the park or bouncing a grandchild on his knee. Maybe Hoq did those things—but he owed Joran a blood debt.

The spacious office contained plenty of hiding spots, with an abundance of plant life for concealment. Doctor Hoq was a single-minded man, absorbed in his preparation for the coming murder and never looking up. It was almost admirable, his devotion.

Joran drew close behind the doctor, near enough to read over his shoulder, and readied his weapon. His heart raced in anticipation of a righteous kill, and his senses grew keen as razors. With one stroke, he would end a nemesis and destroy Vess's future.

He flipped the thumb switch on the cauterizer, and the metal vibrated in his hand. The silver surface grew white hot in an instant, and Joran saw the doctor's hackles rise. Hoq sensed danger; it was time to strike.

Joran grabbed his victim's head from behind and plunged the pick up through the base of his skull, searching out his brain. Sparks and steam came hissing out of the wound, but Hoq didn't scream. He couldn't. All of the nerve structures used for screaming had been cooked in an instant. Noxious smoke filled the room, stinking of hair and meat, and Joran stumbled backward, coughing. He left the pick inside, where it continued to sizzle.

In the aftermath, Hoq was nothing but a spent match head, smoke rising into the darkness. Joran collected himself and rushed from the office, almost afraid of what he'd done. This killing had felt different than the guards, dirtier—more intentional.

More satisfying.

Hoq would *never* get the better of Joran now. If Joran could kill Vess while he was here, he'd be freer to control the narrative of the crime. It'd be the story of slaying his kidnappers and saving himself. He'd be lauded for his valiant act.

So where was Vess?

Doubt nagged Joran as he searched high and low for the errant psychiatrist. He knew he shouldn't continue, that it increased his danger by the second. Dax's other hosts would've holed up somewhere safe and gotten legal representation. It wasn't too late for Joran to live a life inside the law. The courts might understand the killings—two in self-defense and one out of insanity. Vess and Hoq had tortured him.

Joran could throw himself at the mercy of the justice system. His quick tongue and latinum smile could probably get him out of it.

Eventually, he relented, diverting for the shuttlecraft landing pad on the roof. If he wanted to live, he needed to flee, and he was ready to admit that. He bolted down the hallway toward the rooftop access, arriving at the landing pad to find a shuttlecraft there, ready and waiting.

He dashed into the deluge, cool puddles splashing between his toes with every step. He'd have to hack the shuttlecraft door, but Torias knew a few tricks.

"Joran!" Vess shouted behind him, and he stopped in his tracks.

So much for his disguise. He turned to see her standing in the doorway, fury on her face.

"What have you done?" she called.

He looked down at his hands, dripping with Hoq's blood.

"I showed Doctor Hoq my own surgical skills." Joran took the mask from his face and tossed it to the ground. If he was caught, he wanted her to see how happy he was, he wanted her to know it was personal. "Alas, I'm a bit of an amateur."

He crossed his arms and tapped his chin the way Emony once did. "Oh, do you know what I've just realized? You were probably counting on him to deliver you into your next host, weren't you?"

Vess glared at him.

"What are you going to do at the end of your life? They'll find out you're just a monster," Joran said, "and then—"

Lightning snapped from her fingers to the wet ground, shooting into Joran's bare feet. He went flying, landing on the center of his back, knocking the daylights out of him. With a trembling hand, he touched the base of his skull and found blood.

Vess came for him like death itself, taking slow, sure steps toward his now-disabled body. There was no way he could muster the coordination to stand, much less run. She loomed over him, reaching down to wrap a hand around his throat.

Given her somewhat dainty physique, he'd not expected Vess to be particularly strong. Joran had been in physical altercations with women, and thought very little of them as a consequence. As Vess's fingers clamped down and cut off his oxygen, he realized he'd made an erroneous assumption. He tried to bat her off, but it was like fighting a mechanical claw.

"You have ruined something magnificent, you know that?" She dragged him across the pavement as he gulped helplessly for air. "I tried to give you a better life, Dax, and you just . . . just spat on it."

Tendrils of darkness crept into the edge of his vision, and Joran grew dizzy.

"This host has to go, Dax. He's rotten. I'd never kill a symbiont, but you have tested me, my friend."

Roof grit scraped Joran's back as she dragged him. He struck the side of Vess's knee with an elbow, and she let him go long enough to bloody his nose. Joran's head smacked the hard landing pad again, and lights danced before his eyes.

He laughed, and she squatted next to him.

"What's so funny? You're about to die."

He smiled despite his split lip. "But not my symbiont?"

"That creature is too good for you. We all are."

"Then, the next host," he huffed, choking on his own blood, "is going to know what you did."

Vess electrocuted him once more, and his mind went blank.

"No."

She snatched his throat and hoisted him into the air. His whole spine was aflame; Joran's body was not meant to move like that.

"Because I'm going to erase you. Full memory block."

She squeezed and gave him a hard shake, wrenching his body to and fro. His neck crackled before the snap severed everything. Arms and legs vanished into pain, the burning shape of things that should've been there.

"Perks of being the director."

It was the strangest feeling, losing everything in a split second. Joran's mind raced for ways to make it untrue, even as death's cold fog crept into his thoughts. This couldn't be happening. He'd only wanted to take music to its distant frontiers.

Vess smiled into his failing eyes, hoisting his body over the edge of the landing pad.

"To Dax, it'll be like you never lived."

Then she let go, and for a few seconds, he became the rain.

After that, he became the ground.

14

Shift Change

Dax came gasping out of her slumber, jolting upright to find Kira at her side. She caught Dax's arms and held her gaze.

"Jadzia," Kira soothed. "Look at me, I'm here."

"Nerys . . ." The warmth of life reentered Dax's veins, drop by drop.

"What is it? What did you see?"

Dax stared off into the glittering infinity while she put her thoughts into focus.

"I think my ex-girlfriend might be evil."

A gurgling cough sounded out behind Dax, and she turned to find Wynth choking on a mug of tea. She had a pained smile and held up a hand to say she didn't need help. She pulled out a rag and wiped her face clean.

"I've been doing this for lifetimes." Wynth let out a hoarse chuckle. "First time I've heard that one. Broke your heart that badly, huh?"

"No." Dax shook her head. "I mean . . . actually evil."

Kira patted her hand. "All right. First, are you okay?"

Dax nodded, taking a grateful breath. "Yeah, I . . ." She looked around to find dirty dishes and cups of hot tea. "How long was I out?"

"Had to be, what"—Kira looked to Wynth—"four hours?"

Wynth waved her long fingers back and forth. "Give or take. It's hungry business, holding vigil."

"We've just been waiting while you've been, you know"—Kira gave a little shrug—"dead. Not much to do but eat and chat. Hungry?"

Dax laughed and threw her legs over the side of the slab. "Starving."

"That bad, huh?" Kira handed her a box of treats.

"I think it's safe to say we got what I came for."

When Dax awoke the next morning, she felt better than she had in days—maybe even years. Some joined swore by the *morden'oct*s, and after the release of so much stress, Dax could understand why. Her head was clearer, her senses keener—everything seemed so much more colorful. The nausea had vanished too.

Dax pulled out her tricorder to check her isoboramine levels—almost normal.

She could sense why: Joran was at peace. He'd said what he needed to and shattered the last traces of the memory block. She was deeply fulfilled in a way that she'd never been. Dax wished she could bottle this renewal and keep an extra dose for a hard day.

Kira joined her at her lodgings, and together they replicated a plentiful, diverse brunch, with all of Dax's favorites. She ate like she'd just discovered food, sampling everything with glee. A colossal appetite was a well-known side effect of the *morden'oct*, often nicknamed the "First Meal." She washed it all down with Bajoran herbal tea, courtesy of Kira.

Dax spent the morning telling Kira all about Joran's demise. She spared no detail, recounting the torturous days in the med pod. When she finished, Kira stared at her in disbelief.

"Why didn't Curzon Dax report this?" Kira asked.

"Because of Joran's murders, they installed a memory block. *He* gave them the excuse they needed. I couldn't recall Joran at all, and when I was Curzon, Vess seduced—" The bile rose in Dax's throat, and she fought to keep it down. "She used Curzon."

"Who ordered the memory block?" Kira asked.

"What?"

She'd never checked. Her records had been sealed or altered at the highest levels, and it was only after Joran's existence was revealed that the Commission put them right. Jadzia went to the bar top and fetched her padd, accessing the Commission's records on her. An error message popped up right way.

"My access is still throttled."

Kira frowned. "Check the Starfleet Medical database. Doctor Bashir probably mirrored all of your medical records to Deep Space 9 when they were unsealed."

She could always count on the good doctor to save the day with protocol.

"Got it," Dax said, pulling up the record. "Let's see who ordered the block . . ."

She scanned her dossier, moving to the section about Joran's death. He'd spent an indeterminate amount of time in a medically induced coma while they searched for a suitable host—up to six months. That was enough time for extensive memory adjustment. As expected, she found twenty mnemonic rehabilitation therapy sessions.

Ordering physician: Dr. Elta Vess.

Dax's arm went slack, and the padd flopped to the desk. She closed her eyes, letting out a pained sigh. "She killed me, and then she manipulated me."

Kira pressed her lips together, eyes sympathetic. "Oh, Jadzia, I'm so sorry."

She took a few slow breaths, bringing herself back to the moment. "It's okay."

"I know there's nothing I can do to make it better, but I'm here for you."

Dax looked over the half-eaten brunch spread and sat back down. "You can pass me another *kesht*."

"Look at the bright side." Kira handed one over, and Dax took a big bite. "Joran was innocent."

She nearly choked. "Oh, no. He was twisted. He killed that doctor and those orderlies."

"In self-defense."

"That doctor didn't have to die. It was all spite."

"True. But Doctor Hoq was no angel. You said he was going to kill Joran."

"I know, but if he'd stood trial . . ." Dax sighed. "If he'd been exposed and arrested, maybe this *Kael'tach* group never would've formed. Nemi might still be alive."

Kira cocked her head. "Joran murdering a doctor didn't kill Nemi. You're stretching the facts to make this your fault."

"I am not. I'm just saying that justice in the past would've saved lives in the present."

"I know you, Jadzia Dax, and you like to take responsibility for everything. That's why you're here, turning over every rock." Kira poured another mug of steaming tea and took a sip. "I think it's the scientist in you."

"It's called investigating. Joran was malicious, and that had deadly consequences for other people."

Kira smirked. "Agreed. At least you're not him."

"But I am."

"So where does this leave us? We still don't know why Ensign Hart tried to assassinate you, why Brac is blocking you at the Commission, and what Elta Vess has to do with all of this."

Dax's gaze fell. "I still can't believe she tortured Joran. Curzon loved her."

"Yeah, I'm hazy on that part. She murdered Joran . . . *then* had an affair with Curzon? Why?"

"Making sure her precious memory block held."

"And she never tried to get Curzon to, you know, 'elevate'?"

Dax thought hard about it. The blissful months of romance were over seventy-five years ago, and Curzon had experienced a full life after Vess died. There were many other disastrous whirlwinds in his romantic history, and it was easy to confuse them. Curzon had been dumped by a lot of beautiful women.

One moment stuck out.

"One time," Dax said. "I'm not even sure what we were talking about, but she asked Curzon, 'If you could be perfect, truly perfect, would you do it?' "

Kira raised her eyebrows. "And what did Curzon say?"

Jadzia grinned. " 'If I were perfect, Elta, I wouldn't be me.' "

"Quite the diplomat, Curzon."

"He helped negotiate the Khitomer Accords, you know."

"You've only told me a thousand times."

Across the room, Dax's combadge chirped.

"Bashir to Dax."

Dax got up, grabbed the badge, and clipped it to her shirt. "Dax here."

"We've just arrived in orbit," he said. *"How are things going?"*

"No more midnight assassins, thank goodness."

"Excellent. Here's hoping things stay dull. We're beaming to the Capital Arms Hotel, correct?"

"See you downstairs in five."

"Perfect. Bashir out."

Kira went and got her duffel by the door. Per the captain's orders, the major was to return in the *Rio Grande* after it dropped off Lieutenant Commander Worf and Doctor Bashir. Then in one week, Dax and her companions were to return to Deep Space 9 aboard the *Sandpiper*, a Federation science vessel. The captain had been explicit that *all* of his officers would be returning on the *Sandpiper*.

In other words, *Finish this in a week, old man.*

Dax and Kira made their way down to the lobby. A few Starfleet officers ate lunch in the little cafe, a motley crew of engineers from the science outpost. They looked hung over, and Dax felt a pang of jealousy. Her recent nights had been exciting, but they hadn't been a party.

Worf and Bashir sparkled into being outside the lobby doors, glancing around to orient themselves. Dax waved to them until Bashir finally noticed her.

They were a mismatched pair. Bashir was shorter, with a kind face. He held himself with a natural ease as he strode across the lobby, cutting a dashing figure in his uniform. The man seemed born to be a medical officer.

By contrast, Worf was broad shouldered and imposing, with deep brown skin, warrior's ridges, and full lips. Dax had heard stories about the strategic operations officer, but had had little personal interaction with him. He struck her as taciturn and rigid.

"Everything good?" Dax asked.

"Doctor Bashir and I are . . . ill-suited to be confined together in such small quarters," Worf rumbled in a baritone voice.

"But that's fine," Bashir said with a thin smile, "because we're no longer crammed into a runabout together. Plenty of space here."

Kira looked between the two men. "I'm not going to beam up and find a line painted down the center of the *Rio Grande*, am I?"

"You will find it in excellent condition," Worf said. "Despite our differences, we are good stewards of Starfleet property."

"Well, that's nice," Kira said. "I'll have a comfortable ride back, at least."

"Rest while you can." Bashir put down his duffel. "Captain Sisko didn't sound too happy with the both of you."

"No need to rub it in," Kira said.

Bashir tipped his chin. "I'm only giving you the same warning I'd want in your shoes."

"The desk is over there, if you want to get checked in." Dax pointed out the attendant. "I'm going to say goodbye to Kira."

"All right," Bashir said. "See you in a few."

Dax walked the major out to the transporter zone, carrying her luggage for her.

"Thank you"—Dax set down her duffel and took her shoulders—"for everything. With a friend like you by my side, I could face death itself."

"You did." Kira gave her a grin. "Can you face the captain for me?"

Dax snorted. "My time is coming. Hang in there."

"You know he's not going to yell at you. He'll just act disappointed, which is worse."

"Benjamin can put on a guilt trip like no one else. Take care, okay?"

Her smile faded. "I know you've got those two, but watch your back."

"I will."

"I don't like the way this is shaping up," Kira said. "There's too much in play, and we don't even know—"

Dax gave her a quick hug and stepped back. "Stop worrying. I'll keep you updated."

Kira's trepidation was writ large on her face, but she relented. "Okay. Be safe."

The major hit her combadge. "*Rio Grande*, Major Kira Nerys. One to beam up."

"Acknowledged," came the computer's reply as Kira grabbed her stuff.

Dax waved, and Kira disappeared from the planet, beaming up to the shuttlecraft awaiting her in orbit.

"Kira to Dax," came the voice over Dax's combadge. *"I'm safely aboard. Tell Julian he left his teacup on the console."*

"Absolutely. Enjoy your trip."

"Will do. Kira out."

Dax was about to go inside when she spotted Ensign Rush coming up the street. She flagged her down, jogging the short distance between them.

"Commander! I was hoping to find you."

"Ensign Rush, what's up?"

Rush's expression darkened. "It's Colin. Ensign Hart, I mean. They found him."

Ensign Rush led Dax, Worf, and Bashir down through the drainage tunnels of the capital. They arrived at a tall archway over an outflow culvert, its interior dipping into shadow mere meters from the exit. Law enforcement barricades flashed all around as the capital sunset painted the scene orange.

Ensign Hart's body lay facedown in a centimeter of water, uniform tattered. His pale white fingers curled into claws, and Dax tried not to stare. She'd seen plenty of corpses in her day. DS9 had just repelled a Klingon attack, and the unfortunate dead from that onslaught were accorded their due.

This, however, was foul play—cold and heartless.

A trio of Trill investigators in long coats stood over the corpse like blackbirds, recording with holoimagers. One of the investigators raised a hand to Rush in greeting, and the party of Starfleet personnel headed in her direction.

"Inspector Burx," Rush called to the woman, and she sauntered over.

"Ensign Rush," she replied, "you've brought quite the party with you."

"Sorry," Dax said.

"It's fine. I'm Inspector Rae Burx. Pleasure to meet you."

Burx's long black hair curled into ringlets, and she had tawny brown-freckled skin. Her eyes were underscored by dark circles, and she looked like she hadn't had much sleep recently. Dax had met enough hardened characters to recognize someone who'd seen a lot of evil in their life. She'd briefly spoken to Burx at the first interview after Hart attacked.

"You probably remember Lieutenant Commander Dax." Rush

gestured to her companions in turn. "This is Doctor Bashir and Lieutenant Commander Worf."

Burx nodded at each of them.

"Inspector," Dax said, "anything we can do to help the Trill authorities."

"Of course," Burx replied. "I have to warn you, it isn't pretty."

"I'm a doctor," Bashir said with a tight smile. "It's part of the job."

"And I am no stranger to death," Worf added.

Burx looked the tall Klingon up and down. "Handy. This way, please."

Bashir and Worf started after Burx, but Rush remained behind.

Dax touched her arm. "You okay?"

Rush shook her head, looking a little sick. "I always wanted to go to a crime scene. Catch murderers. But . . . that's Colin. He's my friend. Was my friend."

"It's understandable if you can't handle this," Dax said. "No one could reasonably expect that of you."

Rush looked into her eyes, steeling herself. "I have to be able to look at a body."

"But not today. Ensign, you're not here as a Starfleet officer. You're here as Ensign Hart's friend. Maybe he wouldn't want you to see him like that." Dax pointed to a small outcropping up the hill. "I'd like you to go sit over there and collect yourself. After, if you want to join us, then feel free."

"I can't sit by while—"

"You can, and you should. This is going to be hard, and you don't have to do it."

Rush worked her jaw, brown eyes searching the distance for something Dax couldn't see. "Okay. Right, okay. Yeah."

"There will be other bodies," Dax said. "No reason to traumatize yourself. I'll be back."

Dax turned and headed to her compatriots. Close up, the smell was a lot worse, and she restrained a gag. Julian was similarly affected, but Worf maintained admirable stoicism.

"Here." The inspector handed them some nasal filters, and Dax clipped hers to her septum. "Cuts down on the smell."

"Right." Bashir followed suit, regaining his professional attitude. "Now then, what have we got?"

"A lot," Burx said. "First off, it's impossible to know what killed him."

Dax gestured down at the body. "But I would've thought it was obvious. He hit his head on a catwalk on the way into the water."

Burx replied, "It's more than that."

Bashir flipped open his tricorder. "May I?"

"We already scanned, but be my guest," Burx said.

The doctor crouched beside the corpse, his hand scanner whirring as he passed it over Hart's body. The other two Trill officers cleared off, murmuring about checking upstream. Dax figured they didn't care to hang around; local agencies could sometimes be a little standoffish. She was grateful that law enforcement was allowing them to be involved at all.

"Fractured skull and bruising at the frontal cortex and cerebellum. This is a contrecoup injury," Bashir said. "A contusion like that is more than enough to kill. You're saying that wasn't how he died?"

"He was tougher than he looks," Burx replied. "Scans show water in the lungs, which means he was breathing for a while after he went under. But even if he hadn't hit his head . . . even if he hadn't drowned, he was a dead man."

Dax remembered the spot of blood on Hart's shirt after she charged him. She'd pummeled him there, hoping to disable him.

"His abdomen," she said.

Burx nodded. "He's a mess inside."

Scooting around to get a better angle, Bashir began scanning Hart's torso. "There's a massive amount of fluid buildup inside the abdominal cavity—blood?"

"Look closer." Burx tongued the inside of her lip.

Bashir blanched, horror distorting his features. "This man is missing an organ."

"A few meters of small intestine and his spleen, to be precise. He was never going to live for more than a couple of days without major medical intervention," Burx said, pulling out her own tricorder and pointing to the screen. "Someone performed surgery on him, and not well. You can see healing here and here. The strangest part is that some of the young cells are attached to freshly ruptured tissue."

"Meaning?" Dax asked, afraid she might already know.

"After they closed him up," Burx said, "something burrowed through the incision in his abdomen."

Dax's breath quickened, and she stared at the corpse. A thought wriggled into her mind, something she didn't want to acknowledge, but couldn't shake: she knew what happened to Hart.

"Perhaps it was a creature of some kind in the water?" Worf asked Burx. "Carrion often attracts scavengers."

Burx shook her head. "Possibly, but we can't guess. We're going to get better results back at the morgue when we can get some DNA samples."

"Why don't you use the high-resolution scanners on your tricorders to get genetic signatures?" Bashir asked. "My tricorder can do it."

The inspector restrained a laugh. "That drainage system isn't a sterile lab environment, Doctor. Ensign Hart here has tumbled through filthy water for days with an open wound and gaping mouth. Do you understand just how much foreign DNA you're going to find inside that body?"

Bashir's face fell. "I see your point."

"But you *can* check for neurotransmitters," Dax said. "Bacteria and animal life won't have most of the ones we care about."

"Okay. Neurotransmitters . . . sure." Burx rocked on her heels. "Such as?"

Dax looked the inspector in the eye. "Isoboramine."

Burx snorted. "You're kidding. That's a dead human."

"But it's not impossible," Dax said.

"What is isoboramine?" Worf asked.

"It's a neurotransmitter that helps keep a symbiont in sync with its host." Dax's heart twisted in her chest as she watched Bashir switch modes on his hand scanner and begin his pass. "It's not present, unless—"

Bashir looked up at Dax, eyes widening. "This man was joined."

"Sorry, but I have to check your work," Burx said, reactivating her tricorder.

"Be my guest." Bashir stood aside.

What if Hart smashing his head on that catwalk during his escape hadn't been an accident? What if it'd been to cover up a *kael'tach* surgery? Dax took Worf and Bashir a few steps away while Burx continued her examination. Given the severe look on her face, the doctor had been right.

"Julian," Dax began, voice low, "is there any way to know if this man suffered a diffuse axonal injury?"

"Not with a hit like that," he said. "Ascertaining nearly anything about the brain structures at this point would be impossible. Why do you ask?"

"I think he's *Kael'tach*." Dax glanced back at the corpse, whispering. "Elevated."

The doctor narrowed his eyes. "I don't understand."

"Hey, you were right," Burx called to them, standing. "I need to ask why you thought that."

"What?" Dax asked.

The inspector pointed to the corpse "You went straight to joined? I don't think so. This is a major problem with national security ramifications, and now I have to involve the Symbiosis Commission."

Dax wanted to tell Burx exactly what she knew, but how could she? Hart had attacked her after she spoke to the Commission. Her database access had been cut off. Could Burx be in on the conspiracy too? Would one of her superiors be?

"Given the location of his wound," Dax said, "it was obvious he was joined."

"That could've been any human abdominal surgical procedure," Burx said. "Don't tell me you just guessed."

"No. I'm already working with the Symbiosis Commission on a case. Councilor Brac's office is handling it."

"Sounds like you need to brief me," Burx said. "Make some time for me after I'm done here."

"I want to cooperate, I assure you, Inspector."

Burx regarded the Starfleet officers with narrowed eyes, considering Dax's statements. "Since this is a symbiont-related crime, this location is sealed. I'm going to have to ask you to leave."

Bashir balked. "Wait, what? That's a dead Starfleet officer who attacked another Starfleet officer. You can't expect us to simply keep out of it."

"I absolutely can, and I'm going to," said the inspector. "Our governments have official channels for sharing information. I think we'd best stick to those."

"Please. We need to know what's going on," Dax said. "I was attacked."

"You seem nice, Commander, and I appreciate that," Burx said, "but this is out of my hands. You need to take your friends and go."

Dax started to leave.

"Commander Dax," Burx added.

"Yes?"

"Stay handy. I might have questions."

"Of course, Inspector."

Dax, Worf, and Bashir walked back to Rush, disappointed. The ensign was resting on her perch.

"What did you learn?" Rush's eyes were hopeful.

"Not enough," Dax sighed. "They're kicking us out. Hart was . . . the ensign was joined, so it's a matter of national security now."

Rush stood up. "They can't stonewall us like that. I'll file information requests through the Federation ambassador."

Dax said, "Given the sensitivity of the topic, it might be some time before they're in a sharing mood. What can we do while we wait?"

"I have read your report to Captain Sisko," Worf said, "and I believe it would be most prudent to follow your latest lead."

Dax raised an eyebrow. "Which is?"

"The Path of Sky Institute. It is time we paid them a visit."

"I'm listening. What do you suggest?"

Worf inclined his head. "A tour."

"They know what I look like," Dax said. "If I go in there, it needs to be with a Federation detail, not on a tour."

Bashir gave her a scoundrel's wink. "Oh, we've got a solution for that too."

She searched his expression for some clue. "I'm not going to like this, am I?"

"There's an old Earth expression," he said with a grin. " 'I'm gonna rearrange your face.' "

15

PATH OF SKY

Jadzia's ears itched. Bashir had said they wouldn't before he'd altered them, but he was wrong. And she couldn't stop rubbing her eyebrows, feeling the rising lines he'd sculpted. She tapped the side of her nose, which had been thickened slightly with an alien curve to it. Whenever she saw her reflection in the window, she was still surprised at her missing Trill spots and how judgmental she looked.

She'd always thought Vulcans could be a little elitist, but maybe she'd just been misinterpreting their facial geometry. Whenever she tried to smile at her reflection, it looked a bit off. Had she ever written off any Vulcans she knew as rude? She tried to think of all the Vulcan friends and colleagues she'd ever had, wondering if she'd misjudged them.

The hypertrain shot across the countryside, swampy marshlands giving way to green hills. Dozens of houses flickered past in the blink of an eye, and Dax wondered what it might be like to live there. The people were probably happy, going about their days with blissful certainty. She could've chosen that life.

This region was beautiful, the weather enchanting, and the perfect summers, endless. She loved the familiar architecture, low, smooth homes built to complement the hillsides. She had friends in the area too—it was where the Prits were from.

Nothing, however, could compare to the thrills of Starfleet.

Dax spent her days on Deep Space 9 living and working beside a stable wormhole inhabited by transdimensional beings. Some of her shifts had more adventures than most people got in a lifetime—and that was only her most recent life. Torias dared death over and over again as a test pilot. Curzon had fought alongside Kor, and was involved with the Khitomer Accords.

Which had recently collapsed with Gowron's attack on Deep Space 9. None of Curzon's legacy, it seemed, could last in perpetuity.

Dax had spent the last hour filling in Doctor Bashir and Worf on her investigation. She held nothing back, sharing the details of her hallucinations. Julian already knew everything about Joran—he'd helped solve that mystery the first time—but Worf didn't.

As Dax detailed the dishonorable story of Joran's killings and death, she flushed with shame. Thankfully, Worf didn't judge her. She found him a stoic and intent listener, and that made it easy to tell him everything that had happened.

"The man who tried to kill you," Worf began, "you had no warning?"

"Hm? Oh, um, no." She shook her head. "He looked like a regular Starfleet officer."

Worf's eyes widened a bit, and he inclined his chin. "I see. A move to exploit your trust. That you survived the assassin's gambit is most impressive."

In flawless Klingon, she responded, "'*Preparation is the thread of life, and the warrior weaves it into rope.*'"

"As you say," came his deep voice. "Well done."

Even after all these years, there was nothing better than a battle compliment from a Klingon—especially a master like Worf. The lieutenant commander was lauded in many Starfleet reports, virtually a legend.

She smiled at Worf, giving a slight bow. "You're already well acquainted with my skill, Commander."

"Indeed. You fight much better than most." Worf leaned back in his seat.

Bashir perked up, setting his padd aside. "Wait, you fought Worf?"

"Yes," Dax replied, "and I can't wait to do so again."

"I'm impressed." Bashir gave an incredulous laugh.

"She did not win," Worf said.

"I'd like to think we were"—she looked into his brown eyes—"close."

Worf drew a sharp breath and looked away. Was he blushing?

Bashir looked between the two of them, then cleared his throat. "Yes, well . . . Interesting. Shall we review our preparations?"

"Yeah," she said. "How did you get us a tour of the facilities?"

"I signed us up for a conference," Bashir explained.

"A conference?" Dax asked.

He cocked his head. "If they're going to open their doors, we may as well have a look . . ."

"Yes, but what could we possibly learn when they're expecting visitors?" Dax frowned.

"Quite a lot, I'd imagine." He handed her his padd, which contained a news article about an upcoming event. "They're presenting a symposium on the pathologies associated with advanced symbiont age. There will be a few dozen medical personnel in attendance, including us."

"We're going to just walk in?" she asked.

"I've been researching the Path of Sky since you told me what happened on Argelius," Bashir said. "As a licensed medical provider to joined, the institute is required to be at the forefront in their treatment. Hosting symposiums is a foregone conclusion."

Worf nodded. "Our plan is to visit this conference for investigation and reconnaissance, nothing more. While our time is limited, I believe a careful approach will yield superior results. Let us learn what they're up to and return with more directed action."

"Okay," she said. "The Path of Sky might not be related to the *Kael'tach*. We need evidence."

"So these people—" Bashir scratched his lower lip. "Have they all had this . . . *kael'tach* surgery?"

"Possibly, but that might be oversimplifying things," Dax said. "Ensign Hart might've had it, too, but there was no way to know."

"And it enables a symbiont exclusive control of the host?" Bashir rested his elbows on his knees.

"Yes, but that's not what frightens me," Dax said. "It's the way Ensign Hart jumped into the drainage pipes like he didn't care. A symbiont is . . . should be . . . afraid of dying. It could've easily been killed in those drainage channels. In fact, it probably was—and it never should've treated a host like a disposable husk."

"A symbiont could never betray its host?" Worf asked.

She thought about it. "I've never heard of it happening. But nothing is impossible. What I'd like to know is . . . what is Vess's part in this? Is she really dead?"

She could still remember where Curzon had been standing the day he learned of Vess's demise. Fventik's Disease could take many miserable years, but the last few had gone predictably. The news of her passing was supposed to be a relief, but it still—

Dax wasn't actually sure how it hurt anymore. There was a grim satisfaction in Vess's suffering last days after what she had done to Joran. The thing that tortured her, that died of Fventik's—it was a Lost Light, not Elta.

"Dax," Bashir said, "if we go in there and find something, you have to promise to remain calm."

She warned him with a look. "Excuse me?"

"Nemi was your friend," he said. "You'd be totally within reason to lose your temper if you discovered something . . . difficult. If you do, you'll be tipping our hand."

Dax rolled her eyes. "You don't have to worry about me. I'm not a vengeful person."

That was absolutely a lie. She'd had a godson, and she'd helped murder the man responsible for his death. That vendetta had passed from Curzon to Jadzia. Her hands had helped carry out the sentence, because not even death could clear a Klingon blood oath.

"All right, well . . . we're getting close." Doctor Bashir took a deep breath. "You'll want to get into character."

"I cannot believe you're making me be a Vulcan."

Bashir laughed. "Imagine being logical."

"Imagine living through the next six hours," she muttered.

"What was that?"

"Huh?" she said, and noted Worf was using all his Klingon discipline to restrain a laugh.

The taxicraft took them from the train station, settling down on the wide-open lawn of the Path of Sky Institute. The grounds were nestled in the middle of a quaint village, a picturesque garden at the apex of a hilltop. Flat-roof houses and pedestrian streets encrusted the landscape, tapering to farmland after a kilometer or two. From above, the town looked like a thumbprint, with the Path of Sky at the dead center.

The taxi dinged for them to exit, the door sliding open. Bashir stepped down first, offering his hand to Dax, and she waved him off. She wished he'd quit treating her like a fall risk, even if she *was* recently prone to hallucinations. She stepped down onto the pristine lawn, and Worf followed.

The central campus of the Institute was a series of interlinked vertical cylinders, each sliced at an angle like a pipe organ. These basic shapes formed a bundle, which rose from a thermocrete base to gleam in the daylight. Their metal skins caught the sun, splashing it onto interlocking flowerbeds of multicolored lilies. The plants were positioned to catch the light like a sundial, washing their surroundings with a spectrum. Water features rocketed skyward, droplets glittering in synchronized performance.

"Nice place," Bashir said, slinging his shoulder bag. "The groundskeeping here is incredible."

"Agreed," Worf remarked. "The flowers are beautiful."

"Ah, a sensitive side," Dax said.

" 'The truly brave appreciate more colors than red,' " he replied, quoting the poet Paq'paq.

The trio were clad in comfortable professional attire, class without ostentation. Dax had selected a breezy suit of synthetic spun silk in a creamy beige to match the sensibilities of her Vulcan character. She wore a long coat, and the bag at her side held her tricorder and anything else she thought she might need.

The hot summer day made her ears itch again, and she tugged at them.

"Doctor, um, Irek," Bashir said, "something wrong with your ears?"

"They itch."

"They do not."

"We should venture indoors," Dax said. "I think that might be, uh, logical."

Bashir shook his head and whispered, "That's not how Vulcans talk."

Dax frowned. "It is so. They love logic."

"I'm offended on behalf of Vulcans everywhere. Now, do we all remember our names?"

"I'm Doctor Irek," Dax said. "Specializing in epigenetics and anti-aging."

"Excellent. I'm Doctor Hassan. A general practitioner, just looking to better my understanding of Trill physiology."

"I am Doctor K'choh," Worf said, "a dietician."

To this, he added a terrible attempt at a smile. Worf clearly thought it to be a winning expression, but to Dax, he looked bloodthirsty.

"Excellent," Bashir said. "Only one way to find out if our stories hold up. Shall we head to registration?"

Other taxis settled down around them, depositing passengers from all over. To Dax's relief, she saw plenty of non-Trill in attendance. The event clearly had a large draw. They approached the front door, where they were ushered inside by a handsome, young, pale-skinned man with umber spots.

Dax had been to plenty of science conferences before, and she'd been expecting something in line with that experience: a welcome placard and a bored staffer at a sign-in station. The scene before her was far more akin to a charity soiree than any academic endeavor. Clean-cut Trill milled through the lobby, distributing finger foods and drinks among a cohort of medical professionals. The guests were fashionable, if outright showy, and Dax wondered what she'd gotten into.

The lobby was a mishmash of hardwoods and stone, arranged beneath a radial array of glass plates to diffuse the light. Like the flowers outside, these plates existed in harmony with the passing sun, throwing ornate reflections across the space. Everything about the institute was an exercise in precision, a demonstration of what was possible when in synchronicity with the natural world.

"Hello." A wide-grinning, androgynous Trill attendant with creamy skin and laser-straight hair approached them. "Welcome to the Path of Sky. May I get your names?"

Bashir gave the host their fake identities, and they nodded.

"Thank you. It's good to see you, Doctor Hassan," they said. "This is the main conference center. Later in the evening after business has concluded, we'll be taking people through the surgical wing to see our revolutionary facility."

"We are interested," Dax said, with what she felt was a restrained expression.

"Wow, okay!" the Trill laughed. "I can see that! I'll make sure we arrange a tour for you."

Perhaps it'd be better if Dax didn't say anything else until she got her bearings. It seemed she knew a lot less about impersonating a Vulcan than she'd thought. Dax glanced around, seeing a lot of breakout meeting rooms shooting off the main hall. They all had signs on the doors, indicating the subject of the talks happening inside.

"Where should we start?" she asked.

The attendant brightened. "For such an eager learner as yourself? 'Symbiont Semiotics: Expressions Beyond the Bond' is a discussion of potential in both the host and symbiont. In this lecture series, we'll be discussing Path of Sky's recent work in the electrolinguistic arts. If you'd like, I can upload the schedule to your padd."

"Please do," Dax said.

"Oh, my." The Trill chortled to themself, and Dax swallowed her embarrassment. "Such enthusiasm!"

They got the data and wandered into the crowd of medical professionals. Some of them looked like faces Dax should recognize, but she wasn't sure. Perhaps they weren't doctors, but celebrities. Dax wasn't well versed in her homeworld's media. These people were important somewhere—that much was clear.

Dax attended a talk on bioelectric noise patterns and the potential for cybernetic reduction. While it was interesting, she found the science to be basic. There wasn't any actual substance in the talk, just a broad overview of the state of the field. The lecture following it, "Neurotransmitters and Qol'kas Protocols," was similarly vapid—just a bunch of basic theories and entry-level education. Anyone who'd been through the initiate program knew what she heard in those lectures.

By afternoon, she stood at the drink station, waiting while a white-suited Trill juiced fresh *lida*. How much more time was she going to have to waste in these pointless lectures? Dax knew they were here only for reconnaissance, but it was galling to have to sit through inane lecturers boasting of their own achievements while essentially saying nothing. Something was very wrong at the institute if this was "advancing the medical arts."

By contrast, Julian Bashir seemed to have immensely enjoyed the talks he attended, hanging around the temporary bar and chatting up any interested parties. He'd managed to snare an attractive Trill woman with short-cropped hair and a mischievous smirk. He seemed to be having an easy time pumping her for information, so

Dax went in search for her own prey. Worf didn't want to speak to anyone, yet he'd managed to draw plenty of attention. A Klingon on Trill was rare, but a dietician brought even more interest. The less he said, the more people seemed to believe he knew, and before long, his table bubbled with excited discussion. He sat in uncomfortable silence as debates unfolded around him.

Dax stood amid the gaggle of lunching professionals and tried to pick out any patterns. Humans and Trill were the most abundant attendees, which made sense; of the Federation worlds, Earth was Trill's closest ally. The humans present struck Dax as academics, given their eclectic fashion and penchant for midday cocktails. The ones she spoke to were looking for continuing education credits to maintain their Trill operating privileges.

Unlike the humans, the Trill at the conference were wealthy and stylish, crisp and confident. They inhabited their luxurious surroundings like predators in the jungle. Curzon, as a diplomat, would've pegged these people as power players from their entitled air.

Only one Trill appeared less than fashionable: a dour, light-skinned fellow at one of the perimeter tables. His outfit wasn't ugly, but it was nowhere near that of the other attendees—a simple burgundy suit with a dark vest. He nursed a steaming *raktajino* with a sugar wafer sticking out of the foam. He noticed Dax staring at him, so she arched an eyebrow and smiled.

He spluttered into his drink, setting it down.

Dax crossed to him, reminding herself that she was a Vulcan.

"What do you think of the talks so far?" she asked, leaning on his table.

Up close, he had slate eyes with dark rings around them; poor sleep, most likely. His bashful body language folded inward like he could curl around his drink. She knew how to handle men like him; she'd been one as Tobin.

"I uh, I haven't been to most of the lectures," he said, clearly unsure of why this Vulcan was speaking to him.

"That's an . . . interesting strategy."

It was only a turn of phrase, but he flinched at the word *strategy* and regarded her anew. His eyes lingered overlong on her neck. Surely Doctor Bashir hadn't missed a spot, but she still worried.

"The topics are interesting, obviously." He took another sip of his *raktajino*. "I just think I'm perhaps a little too . . . advanced."

She withheld a snort. Vulcans weren't known for their spicy replies. "Interesting. Why are you here, if not to learn?"

Again, his eyes flicked to her neck. It was almost imperceptible, but Curzon was excellent at noticing details like that. It had given him an edge in diplomatic situations.

"Oh, you won't find any of the good stuff in the classes."

So there was more to the conference than just the talks, but what?

"Do you know where to find it," she said, pinning him with a stare, "the 'good stuff'?"

"I didn't catch your name."

"Doctor Irek."

"Yonet Ru'xol." He smirked, turning to face her more fully. "So . . . what about you? Enjoying the talks?"

Dax tried to conjure some Vulcan honesty with a flat, "No. They are beneath me."

"People say it gives you an edge if you go to them, but I doubt it."

"What gives you your edge, Yonet Ru'xol?"

"Going through the initiate program."

"Oh?" She appraised him. "Are you joined?"

"Not yet."

How was the initiate program involved? There had to be a thread she could pull to unravel his secret.

"An . . . initiate?" she asked, trying to nail down a proper Vulcan cadence. "You must tell me about your experience with the program."

He raised his drink in mock salute. "It's the worst place in the galaxy."

If she hadn't been undercover, Dax would've toasted him. "I have heard only good things."

"That'll change if you talk to anyone with a mind of their own," he said with a bitter smile.

He had to be a washout. A man his age would've already been joined if he was going to make it.

Her mind raced for an open-ended comment to make. He seemed to be assuming something about her, and she intended to make the most of that.

"But you still want to be joined," she said.

"I think there needs to be another way. The Symbiosis Commission alone shouldn't get to control who is part of our great Trill legacy or whatever." He rolled his eyes at the last part before stirring the sugar wafer in his cup. "If they determine who gets to be joined, they choose which members of society are immortal. More importantly, they choose whose values survive across generations. Do you really think the field docents are impartial? Of course not. They perpetuate their own biases."

Dax controlled her breathing, though her heart hammered in her chest. She was onto something. "Is that why you weren't chosen? Bias?"

He considered his answer for a long moment. "I mean, not me, but others have probably dealt with it. I was an exceptional candidate. Just unlucky."

Dax snatched a few plump grapes from the tray of a passing server and popped one in her mouth. "How so?"

He tilted his chin. "I wasn't chosen because my field docent died, and the new one didn't like me. I had top marks in everything at the start. My first year was excellent."

Just like Nemi.

"And I brought a lot of other great qualities to the table," he said.

"Oh?"

"Yes, I'm very observant. Like for example, you're not a Vulcan; you're a Trill all dressed up to look like one."

She didn't react with shock or dismay, since he wasn't going to out her. He stated the fact with no rancor.

"You stood there for ten minutes and spoke to nobody. Then you zeroed in on me and came over to talk. Could've chosen a more Vulcan name, like Doctor T'Something." He took another sip. "I know a test when I see one."

A test? Every sentence out of his mouth brought her a step closer to something big. She had to keep him talking.

She looked over the crowd. "And do you think you passed?"

He gave her a short nod. "You tell me."

She'd gotten lucky before, pawning off nonanswers long enough to get context. Now he expected her to give a verdict on his test, but she wasn't sure what it was.

"I'm not the one who makes those decisions." She gave him a disarming smile. "But I like your odds."

He looked like he bought it. Whatever nefarious activity he was involved in, it was based at the Path of Sky Institute. If he wasn't attending the talks, he was waiting for something.

"Did we give you an . . . appointment?" she asked. It seemed noncommittal—unlikely to conflict with anything his contacts would've said.

"Yes, finally. Just after teatime," he replied.

"And you're ready?"

"To be joined? Born ready."

And there it was: this man had come to the Path of Sky not to attend the talks, but to become joined. While there were medical providers like the institute across the galaxy, only the Symbiosis Commission had the authority to grant someone a symbiont.

Perhaps the Path of Sky was performing the *kael'tach* procedure. If she was right, Ru'xol would be going to his death.

But where were the symbionts sourced from? Vess had been a willing Lost Light, and there were surely others. The Guardian had talked about the phenomenon like it was rare, but what if there were more than anyone imagined? A Lost Light was still mortal. Its host body would grow old and need to be replaced. If it didn't want to go back to sharing, it'd need a reliable way to get a new dead host.

Why not recruit them from the initiate program?

"This is why you chose me," he said. "If I can spot agents like you, think of what I can do for the Path of Sky."

"Indeed."

"Now if you'll excuse me, I'm going to take a walk. I need to clear my head for the interview."

"Good luck," Dax said.

He set his mug aside, gave her a polite nod, and headed in the direction of the gardens.

She let out a breath as he left. If she didn't do anything and he had a successful interview, was he going to die? There were too many coincidences, and Dax felt a sickening certainty that Ru'xol was about to become a skin sack.

His *raktajino* lay cooling on the table, sugar wafer half-eaten. She couldn't allow another elevation to be performed.

16

Duplicate

For the remainder of the lunch break, Dax tried to free Worf. He'd rapidly become the life of the party, a curiosity to the Trill elite present. Many of them were Klingon enthusiasts like Dax, though she hoped she wasn't so cringey about it.

She found Doctor Bashir sitting alone after the fourth lecture of the day. He'd camped out on a bench between a pair of huge potted plants near the entrance, perusing his padd.

"How's it coming?" she asked.

"Struck out, I'm afraid."

"Didn't get any intel?"

"No, and I didn't get that woman's contact information, either."

Dax grimaced, faking Vulcan outrage. "Doctor Hassan . . ."

"Only kidding. But no, I haven't made any progress. The talks are fascinating, but of little consequence. And half the attendees aren't doctors."

"People aren't here for the talks." She sat beside him and kept her voice low. "They're here to be joined."

"That's illegal."

"Correct."

"It's very un-Vulcan to smile as much as you are, you know."

"Just excited to catch a break. Did you see that gloomy guy I was talking to a while ago?"

"Afraid not."

"He's right over there." Dax surreptitiously indicated one of the entrance archways, where Ru'xol stood leaning against a column. "Dark red suit, floppy hair."

Bashir gave a quick glance about the room, then rested his elbows on his knees. "I see him."

"He has an appointment in five minutes. We need to follow him."

"What about Worf?"

She shrugged. "If you can figure out how to get him away from his fan club, I'm all ears."

"Vulcan jokes? Poor taste, Jadzia."

"I'm going to follow him, and I need the backup."

Bashir crossed his legs, leaning against the wall. "Well, that's exciting. You know I've tailed a lot of henchmen in the holosuites. One of my favorite holonovels is a spy story."

"I know."

"Why are you saying it like that?"

"Like what?"

"You think it's silly."

"Julian, you told me the name of your love interest is Honey Bare. I don't care what you do in your off-hours, but let's not pretend that's literature."

"It's postmodernist, Dax. Honey has more complicated motivations than you might think—"

Across the main conference hall, a young woman approached Ru'xol, and Dax immediately recognized her: Aia Keteel, one of Nemi's associates in the *Kael'tach*. Who was she, really? Another Lost Light, perhaps?

They spoke for a few moments, then she led Ru'xol away.

"Let's go," Dax said, rising to follow.

"We're not done talking about Honey," he muttered.

They tailed Keteel and Ru'xol out of the main building, where their targets wound through the gardens. Sun-sprayed lilies wavered as they passed, and Dax wished she hadn't been there for such grim reasons. It was a peaceful campus, full of serene places to sit and enjoy the day.

Their quarry approached a smaller side building, where a door slid open for them. She and Bashir hurried after, and they slipped inside before the door could close. They waited a moment to let Keteel and Ru'xol get ahead of them before following.

This part of the complex was decidedly more sterile in appearance, with stark white walls and floors. There was a lift in the back, a set of numbers descending on its status panel. The two Trill must've been on their way down. Dax waited until the lift numbers stopped before calling it back. It arrived, doors parting to reveal an empty car, spacious enough to easily house a gurney.

"After you," Dax said, and Bashir stepped on.

The car descended, the doors parted at the bottom, and she peeked out. Light blue walls extended in either direction, corridors leading deeper into the complex.

"This looks like a hospital level," Bashir said. "Are we allowed to be here?"

A Trill woman in nurse's attire came walking around the distant corner.

"Only one way to find out." Dax confidently stepped off the elevator and into the hallway. "Follow me please, Doctor Hassan."

The nurse seemed a little surprised by their presence, but didn't stop them. When Dax passed her, they nodded to each other.

She'd gotten a few steps beyond when the nurse asked, "Excuse me, can I help you find something?"

"We're looking for the administrator's office," Bashir said. "I'm mostly sure I know the way, but I could use a reminder."

"Of course." She pointed down the hall the way she'd come. "Over there, take a left, then your second right. There are signs. Can't miss it."

They thanked her for the help and set off in that direction. After the first turn, they found an infopanel on the wall with a directory of locations.

"Here we go," Dax said, scanning down the list. "Let's see what we've got . . ."

All the typical amenities of a hospital, along with a few choice extras—holosuites and spas.

"What's 'Selection'?" Bashir asked, pointing to the list item.

She'd almost missed it, a mundane word in a sea of medical jargon, and scrolled back. She tapped it, and the hospital map showed a large room at the end of the complex.

The lift chimed in the distance, and Dax's heart skipped a beat. A gaggle of stylish Trill stepped out of the car, led by a member of the medical staff. They laughed and joked as they walked, like they were going to a party.

"Come on." Bashir took a few hesitant steps. "This way."

He and Dax took off to the selection room. They dove down circuitous corridors, looking in any windows as they went. The facility appeared to be cutting edge, if a little underutilized. Dax kept expecting to see more staff, but they never appeared.

"Where are all of the patients?" Bashir asked. "None of these rooms have their occupancy indicators on. Is anybody even using this place?"

"Probably," she replied, "just not for any of the reasons they claim."

They passed a laboratory, full of exotic gear: gravity stacks, nanoreplicators, tunneling microscopes, and more. It had all the capabilities of a lab in a major Federation hospital, just smaller.

"If you're going to run a false operation, there are easier ways go about it," Bashir said. "Some of this equipment is extremely hard to come by."

"Perhaps it's not in use yet." She peered inside the dim room, looking for some running tests, centrifuges, something—but the equipment was all powered down.

She swallowed. "Or maybe they're done using it."

They rushed past two more labs. In each case, it was the same: more capabilities, powered down. Dax marveled at just how much advanced tech they were able to cram into such a small area. In many ways, the Path of Sky's potential rivaled that of the Symbiosis Commission.

They reached the selection room and slipped inside. It was a cozy space with five plush chairs arranged in a semicircle, a fully stocked bar, and intimate lighting. Fabric baffles covered the walls, embroidered with intricate patterns.

"Certainly comfortable in here." Bashir prodded one of the squishy chairs, which rocked in place.

"It's like a therapy room." Dax ventured farther inside, looking for any more clues to its purpose.

The sounds of laughter and conversation echoed down the hall. The group of Trill from before were coming closer. It wouldn't do to be caught snooping around the rooms.

One glance told her Bashir heard them too. They had to hide.

She cast about for somewhere to climb inside, but there were no closets or containers. The fabric baffles were attached to the wall, so there'd be no safety there. The only option was the chairs. She scooted up under the back of one and wrapped her arms around her knees to tuck in tight. Bashir looked at her like she'd lost her mind, but she frantically gestured for him to do the same. He crawled in behind his own chair and balled up.

"Computer—" Dax hoped it'd respond to her. "Lights off."

The system complied, and the room was plunged into darkness.

"I'm excited!" came a young woman's voice as the door swooshed open. "I honestly didn't think they'd pick me."

"We're quite happy for you," said the man. "I should get the lights."

"Start it up," came a third voice, alto, with a burnt smokiness to it—possibly a woman. "I think it's better in the dark."

"Of course," said the man.

Dax hugged herself and considered the odds that one of them would sit in front of her: five seats to three people. The first person took a seat close to the door. The second sat down in front of a horrified Bashir. The last person picked a seat nearest the wall, leaving Dax's cover empty. She tried to see the faces of the newcomers, but it was too dangerous and dark.

"Computer," said the man, "show us the Path of Sky."

Clouds blossomed overhead, pouring into the chamber with rays of golden sunshine. They parted, day faded to night, and a blanket of stars spread like a sea of jewels.

"Final selection," a narrator said over the holoprojection, deep and bassy, with a high-class accent. "You are lucky. You have been chosen to inherit the stars, because you believe in a journey outside of what is normal. You understand the limitations of tradition."

The points of light came loose from their heavenly sockets, traveling down to hover before the occupants. They wove into a logo—the Path of Sky. Dax peered around the side of her chair, trying to get a better look. Bashir sat curled up in the lee of his, tense as a piano string.

"You are unrestrained," said the narrator. "You are untamed."

Ghostly busts appeared in the darkness, faces carved from stone.

"You," the hologram intoned, "are *Kael'tach*."

Dax's eyes widened, and she glanced at Bashir for his reaction. The doctor was trying to peek around his own chair when the occupant leaned back, squishing him. He barely managed to restrain a squeak, getting clear before the fellow could flatten him again.

"The following brethren have signaled interest in joining with you," said the narrator.

The faces disappeared, becoming a set of words. Dax recognized the common phonemes of symbiont names—it was a list.

"Computer," said the young woman, "show me Nyfeh."

A wriggling symbiont appeared, along with four headshots of different Trill. The images arranged themselves on a timeline with a wall of biographical text. Dax was familiar with the format; the Symbiosis Commission had a similar dossier about her hosts—though hers wasn't arranged in such an elegant fashion, rendered as a hologram with lovely music. It added a lot.

"Nyfeh," said the computer. "Four lives lived, six spouses and twelve children, all deceased. The most recent host was Ansendella Nyfeh, deceased 2278."

"Ah, poor Ansendella," said the smoky voice. "What a tragedy."

"I know." The woman sounded almost dreamy. "I read all about her; cast out for returning to the love of a former life. It seems like a long time ago, 2278. Nearly a century."

"I'm sensing a question," they replied.

"It's not that I'm ungrateful, and I really am very excited. But . . ."

"If you're not able to fully commit—" Smoky Voice began.

"It's not that! I'm sorry. I didn't mean to offend."

"Tell me your misgivings. Nyfeh will learn of them eventually."

"It's just . . . well, I—" The woman went from ebullient to cringing in a matter of seconds. "It's been in cryo for almost a hundred years. Most of Nyfeh's hosts were scientists, and the field moves at an alarming rate. What if its skills are no longer relevant?"

"What is the expiration date of a kiss?" The voice grew cold. "Or the knowledge of death? In the future, will anyone care about creativity, or drive? Is empathy still relevant? Nyfeh has experienced more than you could possibly imagine, and you're summing it up like it was a résumé."

"I'm sorry. You're right," she said. "Please. I think it's beautiful. We could do amazing things together. I shouldn't have doubted."

There was a long silence.

"So you're decided on Nyfeh, despite your . . . misgivings?" the voice asked.

"It's the opportunity of a lifetime," the young woman said.

"Very good," the man cut in. "Nyfeh has been thawed and is reviewing the final applicants. We'll tell you if it's a match."

"Wait . . . what? I thought I would be getting a symbiont today," said the young woman.

"Is there a problem with our process?" The voice carried a note of acid.

"No, no, of course not. Sorry."

"I'm glad. I think you'd find the Symbiosis Commission far more taxing."

"Let's get you back to the festivities," said the man. "This way, please."

The door opened, and the three of them exited.

When the coast was clear, Dax stood up.

Bashir followed suit, rubbing his back where he'd gotten crushed. "The seating around here is a little rough on the lumbar."

"Julian, do you realize what this means?"

"That there's a black market for symbionts?"

Elta Vess, Nemi Prit, the surgery, and deceptions all swirled through Dax's head, and she strained to make sense of it all.

"These symbionts have to be coming from somewhere, but *not* the Symbiosis Commission," Dax said. "What if these people aren't telling the whole truth about which ones the patients are getting?"

"So candidates go in, thinking they have a chance at getting joined . . ."

"And become a Lost Light instead."

"But that would mean—"

"They're slaughtering these people, Julian."

He nodded.

"One thing I remember from Joran," she said. "They promise you that the more you accept the surgery, the better it works. They might be grooming their victims here, getting them excited, compelling them to accept their fates."

"That's an awfully complex psychological operation. Hard to imagine someone putting it together, much less pulling it off."

"You don't understand. The symbiont knows that it will never live without a host. If for some reason host and symbiont are exiled, they lose all access to the Symbiosis Commission. A symbiont cast out of Trill society is a death sentence."

"I see."

"A Lost Light wouldn't be allowed to be joined, and even if it were, it'd be *sharing* existence with the host." She looked over the holosuite. "This is their only way to be joined: the Path of Sky Institute."

"Find hosts, initiate them, then use them." He counted the conspiracy's points on his fingers. "If that's true, we have to shut this place down. Every minute it's in operation is one that they might elevate someone."

"We need to steal what information we can while we're here. If they find out they're compromised and destroy data, we'll lose the advantage."

"Agreed. What's the plan?"

"We go deeper."

One of the worst fears of the Symbiosis Commission was that symbionts would become items of barter. Only some Trill could be joined, but the possible hosts outnumbered the symbionts by orders of magnitude.

They believed that if the system were ever corrupted, those Trill with exceptional means would chase after the wisest, most knowledgeable symbionts. Hosts were carefully selected by the Commission to be the best and brightest, not the richest or most connected.

Their fears had been so much lighter than the truth.

The Commission had been right about one thing: unjoined Trill would gladly attempt to game the system, given any opportunity. That made them ripe marks for exploitation. As Dax and Bashir ventured deeper into the facility, she wondered how many lives had been taken there.

No, not taken—*stolen.*

"If they're bringing symbionts out of cryo," Bashir said, voice low, "they must be here somewhere."

"But where?"

"Cryo tanks have a distinct thermal signature and massive power draw. That's a pretty specific environment, so we can scan for it." The doctor pulled out his tricorder. "This is going to be far too easy."

"I'd like to be safe and sound back at the hotel before you say that."

He scanned as they walked, and Dax kept an eye out for anyone who might stumble across them. After a few minutes, he made a frustrated grunt.

"I don't understand. I'm finding a massive EM field from all the power draw, but no commensurate cold spots."

She glanced at his screen. "How wide is your scanning band?"

"It's opened up. Anything outside this range wouldn't sustain cryo."

"Okay . . . you said you detected a large power draw?"

"Twenty-five meters that way." He pointed, intently staring at the readout.

Dax crept to the corner and peeked around. Much like the rest of the complex, the hallway was empty. A lone door adorned one of the walls, and they found it locked.

"Do you know how to bypass it?" Bashir asked.

"Kira would've known what to do with this . . ."

Surely hotel and hospital locks weren't all that different. She knew how to get past the basic system using some of Curzon's old tricks, but this one looked more complex. The only way to be sure, however, was to try.

"Keep a lookout," Dax said.

"On it."

Bashir headed for the corner to stand watch while Dax messed with the panel. She'd only begun to scan for receiver frequencies when she heard approaching footfalls on the other side of the door. She attempted to tuck the tricorder into her bag, but fumbled it to the ground. Out of time, she kicked it at Bashir, who stopped it with impressive reflexes.

She then turned and began walking away from Bashir and the door as casually as she could.

A woman spoke up behind her. "Excuse me, are you lost?"

Dax turned to see Aia Keteel standing in the hall, posture tense. She looked exactly like the photo in her dossier: pale skin, blond hair, and cobalt eyes.

"I was looking for the restroom facilities," Dax said, adopting her even-toned Vulcan affect.

Aia inclined her head. "It's nowhere near here."

"I apologize. This place is rather confusing. Perhaps you can direct me?"

"Up front, toward the lift."

Behind Aia, Bashir crept across the floor toward the open door. Dax watched him in the periphery of her vision, for fear of giving him away with a glance. She could scarcely believe her eyes as he slipped in the door behind Aia, light-footed as a cat.

"I'll walk you to the front," Aia said.

"Thank you." Dax smiled.

"Of course. Follow me."

Dax's escort led her back through the complex, headed for the door. Her mind raced to concoct any further excuses she might need as they neared the exit. If Aia tried to wait on her outside the restroom, she might not be able to ditch her easily.

"Sorry, the restroom?" Dax reminded her guide. "It's quite urgent."

"Right here. When you've finished, please go straight back to the elevator and return to the gardens." With strained politeness, she added, "We'll be starting sunset cocktails in thirty minutes."

"Indeed."

Dax entered the restroom and waited, turning on the taps before pulling out her hidden communicator. "Dax to Bashir. Julian, are you all right?"

To her great relief, he answered, *"Yes, but you're going to want to get in here."*

"I'll be there as soon as I can."

She peered out of the door, and finding no one, hurried the

way she'd come, heart thudding in her chest. Bashir was alone, and anyone might walk in. Aia Keteel might come back. Dax had to get to him and provide backup.

With each turn, she expected to encounter someone. Thankfully, the halls were empty, and she made it to the lab unmolested.

The door slid aside, revealing a small alcove just across the threshold with clean-room gear and bottled gasses. Opposite her was another hatch, cracked halfway open, spilling a stormy blue light across the floor.

"Julian?" she whispered.

He opened the hatch and bade her to join him. He'd summoned her so urgently, and seeing the lab, she understood why.

Dozens of fluid-filled vats lined the walls, their silver cases windowed to show the contents. There was a huge array of gauges on the lab's controls. Cloudy liquid filled the chamber windows with a cerulean glow, and Dax marveled at the contents. A symbiont hovered in each vat, suspended by a web of biomatter.

Bashir gave her a bloodless look. "This isn't a cryo facility."

She drew close to one of the tanks and peered at its occupant. It looked healthy enough—long, fleshy body adorned with ample pink knots—but there had been changes. A small bone protruded from the anterior bulb like a folded-in claw, or maybe a tooth. Two fins of orchid violet trailed from its dorsal side, flowing in the fluid like a cloak.

Horror raked icy claws through her gut, and she put a hand to her abdomen to steady herself. "What am I looking at?"

Bashir's voice was soft. "Extreme genetic enhancement."

"What?"

"All of these are sequencing tanks."

"Sorry, but this is . . ." She took a step back from the wall, trying to fathom exactly the depth they plumbed. "What are they doing to them in there?"

"Cloning."

"How do you know?" But upon closer inspection, she realized

he was right. Every single symbiont bore the same markings, the same lumps and bumps, and the same mutated appendages.

"I've seen this kind of equipment before."

She drew up short. "You . . . where? This stuff is all highly illegal."

He was about to answer when the door slid open and Aia Keteel stepped inside, leveling a disruptor at Dax.

"Look out!" Bashir snatched up a nearby padd, hurling it at the newcomer. It cracked across Aia's nose, affording Dax an opportunity to close ranks.

She brought her knee up into Aia's diaphragm, shoving the breath from her lungs. Judging from the twitching of her eye and excruciated look, Dax had nailed her right in the symbiont. Dax snatched away Aia's disruptor, switched it to stun, and put her down.

"Nice throw," she huffed, turning to Bashir. "How does Miles beat you at darts?"

He smirked. "Because we're not using padds, obviously. Let's get out of here."

"We've got to bring back some kind of evidence."

"What do you suggest?"

She drew out an isolinear chip from her bag. "Copy their project files. Any medical files you can find too—especially patients."

"Dax, that's protected information."

"Any patient of this place either has been murdered, or is about to be murdered. Getting this information to the authorities will save lives."

He went to the computer, hesitating. "You're . . . you're right. I'll get everything I can."

Dax checked the disruptor—full charge. She didn't want to shoot her way out, but this plot went way deeper than she'd realized. Lost Lights, clones, biological enhancement, and a symbiont black market were all serious infractions of the law, let alone having the potential to rock Trill society to its core.

A chirp sounded from beneath her jacket, and Dax tapped her combadge.

"Worf to Dax. I am under attack."

Phaser fire sounded in the background like bird cries, and Dax flinched. If she got him killed, she'd never forgive herself.

"Dax here. What's your position?"

"I'm leaving the conference center on foot." There was a huffing to his voice, like he was sprinting. *"Six of the staffers attacked me simultaneously."*

"Simultaneously?" Bashir repeated.

Dax didn't like the sound of that, either. "We're in an underground hospital, coming topside as quickly as we can."

She turned to the doctor. "Worf needs us. You got the data?"

He snapped up the chip and tucked it into his pocket. "As much as I could."

"Then let's get to the surface."

Bashir started out heading for the turbolift, but Dax stopped him.

"They'll be expecting us that way. Let's find another exit."

He gestured for her to take the lead. "By all means."

They raced up the corridors, following any exit signs they could find. Each detour took them up floors, and they eventually came blinking into the daylight.

A shimmering brick path spread before them, lined on either side by tall shrubs. It wound between the structures, disappearing into a wooded courtyard. On the positive side, it had a lot of cover to mask their escape. On the negative side, she had no idea where it went.

"Where are we?" she asked. "We've got to get to Worf."

Bashir scanned the horizon with his tricorder. "One Klingon this way. Come on."

He bolted out ahead of her, and she ran after, scarcely keeping up. She'd always known he was quick, but his speed was ridiculous.

They dove through the gardens of the complex along circuitous pathways, eyes keen for any threats. Dax held her disruptor low, making sure it was hard to see—but ready.

Bashir slowed to read his tricorder. "We're getting close."

Please be okay.

They rounded the corner and stopped dead.

Assembled before bursting rose bushes was a firing line of ten Trill, half of whom had disruptors aimed right at Dax's chest. They were different ages, genders, and skin tones, but they all shared one thing in common: the same expression of murderous self-satisfaction. It was unnerving, like they were trying to do impressions of one another.

"Hello, Dax," said the russet-toned teenager in the lead. He was younger, maybe eighteen years old, with black spots upon his neck. Wavy brown hair hung around his dark, smiling eyes. She recognized him from Prit's dossiers: Seval Gep, the third of Nemi's *Kael'tach* friends.

"Drop it." His aim was rock steady, as was everyone else's in his force.

"All right." Dax placed the disruptor onto the stone path and took a step back.

Gep looked to Bashir. "That was a good throw. It's too bad you're not Trill."

Bashir kept his hands raised, tricorder still chirping uselessly. "You saw me hit that woman with a padd? We were alone . . ."

"And observant too. You'd make such a fine addition to my number."

The crowd's gaze grew predatory, every member leering at the doctor, and Dax's heart lurched. Joran knew that look. Curzon knew it too.

What if the *Kael'tach* were all the same symbiont?

Dax's mouth went dry. "Vess."

The crowd's eyes snapped onto hers, sending a quiver over her skin. She resisted the urge to back up or even flinch.

The young man in the lead sighed. "My doctors did shoddy work with your memory."

She took a slow breath. "You killed Nemi, didn't you?"

The crowd smirked.

"Incredible." Seval Vess shook his head, pacing. "You're really more upset about me killing your friend than murdering you?" He gestured at her with his disruptor. "More than once, if we count what I'm about to do?"

Dax gave no response but a glare.

"You're so different from Joran and Curzon, Jadzia. I can scarcely believe you contain their ingredients."

She gave a short laugh. "Talent and bravery?"

"Okay, maybe not that different."

"I thought you were dead! I mourned you!"

"Oh, don't hand me that. Curzon was up to his neck in other women the day after I left him. He was an arrogant, unfaithful brat. When I understood that, I was done with him."

Dax's scowl deepened. "And you were a *Lor'inor*, so I guess that makes us—"

The unified screech rose from the crowd. "Don't call me that!"

"'Lost Light,'" Seval Vess spat, pacing back and forth with real anger. "We're docile creatures, only leaving the Caves of Mak'ala when someone else deigns to allow it. They pick the host, never considering what *we* might want. No one asks us who should be joined!"

He clenched his fist. "And the Symbiosis Commission guides every step of it, picking and choosing their favorites! It's memetic inbreeding, and it's sick. With the Path of Sky, I choose the ideas I want to absorb. I make my own way through life without—"

"The Symbiosis Commission isn't murdering people." Dax regarded him with something like pity.

Seval Vess's eyes sparkled in the sun, pupils thinning to pinpricks as he raised his chin. "No, I'm taking the freshest castoffs and preserving them in their most perfect state. Castoffs like *you*, as I seem to recall. Oh, what was it my ex-boyfriend failed you out for, Jadzia?"

" 'Castoffs' . . ." The words nauseated Dax. "Nemi wasn't just a body."

He smiled. "I know, better than you ever will. I gave this host a purpose. Like all of us, I loved the Commission. Trusted them. The Path of Sky was there to give Nemi what they wouldn't. I tried to offer that same mercy to Joran."

The others spoke like mirror reflections. They alternated bits of words and sentences in a storm of words, malignant and rumbling.

"Why drag Curzon into it?" Dax asked.

The umber discs of his irises transfixed her. "No one wants to be alone. I've seen things no other symbiont would understand—unless they were like me."

"You wanted an acolyte."

"Yes, well . . . I couldn't stand Curzon for two months, much less eternity. Honestly, I don't know how you do it."

"I'm not here to defend Curzon, or the Commission."

"And why *are* you here? For Nemi?"

Dax set her feet. "For me."

Seval Vess nodded and took careful aim at her chest. "Jadzia, you really are more entertaining than your predecessors. I wish I didn't have to kill you."

"Then don't, Nemi. You were a sister to me."

The crowd flinched, and their eyes grew a little shiny and red. Seval wrinkled his nose, clearly fighting something within himself.

Eventually, the conflict vanished from his features, and his eyes went dead. "Nice try."

Worf came in like a photon torpedo, smashing into the middle of the Vesses. His *mek'leth* flashed in his hand, his form exquisite as he sliced through adversaries in a silver whirlwind. He used it to inflict painful wounds—nothing mortal, but terrible nonetheless. His powerful muscles controlled the battle against a perfectly coordinated foe, throwing bodies to the ground, bowing them to his might.

Dax closed the gap, searching for a shot with her disruptor and picking off anyone she could. The closer she got, the more Dax could appreciate his master blade work, the precise movements of his feet, his stalwart heart. Worf met his victims with unflinching decisiveness, ending the fight with a warrior's ease.

He was magnificent.

At last, Dax and Worf stood among a pile of unconscious or bleeding Vesses, huffing at one another. Blood splashed his features, and Dax marveled at the fire in his dark eyes. The quiet ones were always the most captivating when set loose.

"I'm glad you're okay," she said. "I'm so sorry for mixing you up in all of this."

He shook his head, breath coming hot. "Never apologize for bringing me to a battle."

A disruptor beam struck the shrub near Dax, and it burst into flame.

"We should leave!" Bashir headed toward an open pathway.

Dax and Worf dashed after him, covering each other's retreats with stolen disruptors. Red beams sliced the air with deadly force, and every second in the open was an exercise in luck. They sprinted down brick-lined pathways along botanical wonders, using the labyrinthine environment to their advantage. The shrill cry of disruptor fire put extra speed in their steps as they made for the perimeter. They leaped the low hedgerow into the pedestrian thoroughfare, startling leisure seekers out to enjoy the sunset along the plaza.

"You know, you could've said something back there, Julian!" Dax juked past a busking guitarist.

"She was telling us everything!" He jammed his tricorder in his pouch as they ran. "Besides, I was busy!"

She was about to ask him what he meant when a beam passed close enough to singe his hair. She thought he was hit, screaming on instinct. Bashir stumbled a step, then redoubled his pace, thankfully intact.

"We must get farther away." Worf ducked a shot and returned fire, sending a distant Vess to the ground.

Dax didn't ask him what setting he was using, but she hoped it was "restraint."

Dax tapped her combadge. "Commander Dax to Ensign Rush!"

No answer.

Bashir led them along a silvery canal, thronged with water horns and orchid pads, and it would've been an excellent place for an afternoon stroll. The disruptors fried the ambiance.

"Ensign Rush! Come in!" she said.

"What are you doing?" Bashir asked.

"Getting us out of here!"

"This is Rush. Go ahead, Commander."

"Ensign, do you have access to a transporter?" Dax jumped a low wall, ducking disruptor fire as she turned down a side street.

"I do," Rush said. *"What's happening?"*

"We're being shot at!" They tried to stay away from civilians as they ran. "Can you beam us out of here?"

"The pad is on the other side of the facility. Just wait for me!"

"We're not waiting anywhere!" Dax took long, bounding strides, maintaining a record pace.

The basin of the city sloped away from them, twisting through unknown streets. Rooftops spread down the hill, and Dax leaped over the guardrail with her compatriots. Jumping from roof to roof, they were able to clear a few blocks before the Vesses managed to find them. The trio clambered down into an alley, darting along the back pathways.

"They're persistent, I'll give them that," Bashir grunted as another beam sliced past him.

"How much longer?" Worf turned and stunned two of the Vess husks, and they crumpled to the ground.

Dax asked, "Rush, ETA?"

"Powering up! Two minutes, Commander!"

They used the winding footpaths of the village to lead their pursuers over a more difficult terrain. They dashed across an open patio, through a dinner party, and out the back side. Revelers erupted with shouts of surprise or anger, but no one stopped them.

"Get down! Get out of the way!" she cried. "Take cover!"

Confusion turned to screaming as the Vesses arrived, blasting into the crowd. It was exactly the situation Dax was trying to avoid: casualties.

"We must lead them away from the civilians." Worf returned fire.

"Then we can't stay and fight!" She nearly slipped down as she took a hard corner. "Keep them moving."

"Follow me." Worf led them on a loop around a small block of buildings.

Their pursuers came into view, and Worf and Dax fired, nailing two of them in the chest. Still more came, pulling up in vehicles, emerging from houses, chasing after them on foot. The enemy wielded disruptors, stun batons, landscaping equipment, sharp kitchen implements, and a diverse array of other weapons; Dax was impressed with the creativity of their lethality.

"Hello, Dax." A little man stepped in front of them with a cruel smile on his face, and Worf plowed through him with no change in momentum.

"There are so many!" Dax said, skidding to a halt as the Vesses moved to cut off their escape.

"Where are you going?" they laughed.

Others emerged, swiping at them, one nearly taking Bashir's head off with a fire poker. Dax had trouble keeping count. It could've been dozens, it could've been hundreds—she wasn't sure. She could only run and hope no disruptors put an end to their lives.

"Rush, beam us up!" Dax shouted.

"Locking onto your combadges. Three of you?" came Rush's reply.

"Yes! Three to beam up!"

"I'm getting interference!"

A disruptor shot passed close enough to warm the back of Dax's neck.

She spotted a house with a long, open window, its screens drawn aside for the summer breeze. "Let's go!"

They clambered over the short fence, scrambling across the lawn to get inside the house. Dax tripped on the smooth tiles of the foyer, and Worf pulled her upright with stony hands.

"Stairs!" She took the steps two at a time, her companions close on her heels. The Vesses piled inside the fence, firing up at them, missed shots charring the walls.

The Starfleet officers stole into a spacious master bedroom, its environs made of polished stone with deep blue accents.

"That's got to be two-thirds of the bloody planet out there," Bashir huffed.

Dax tapped the door panel and it closed, but she couldn't get it to lock. Footsteps pounded up the stairs outside.

"Computer, lock the door!" she ordered.

"Unauthorized user," it responded.

Channeling her inner Kira Nerys, she pointed her disruptor at the panel and fired. Sparks shot forth from the controls, melted metal housing swelling outward.

"Lock system damaged," the computer said. *"Engaging safety release."*

And the door slid open to reveal a bunch of surprised—yet pleased—Vesses.

The lead Vess raised her weapon. "Goodbye, Dax."

Transporter light took her, and the next thing Jadzia knew, she was standing on a pad with Bashir and Worf—all three of them breathing hard and covered in sweat. If she thought her ears itched before, it was almost unbearable after an all-out sprint.

The transporter room was small—only four pads. A tiny console adorned one side, where Ensign Rush stood, hand still on the controls.

She waved. "You know, it's not really beaming up if I beam you across the planet."

Dax rested her hands on her knees, catching her breath. "Really?"

Bashir stepped off the pad. "Up, down, left, right—the important thing is that you beamed us *out*. Much obliged, Ensign."

"The number of attackers was . . . alarming," Worf rumbled.

"Yes." Bashir smirked. "I'd say we've got quite a problem."

"Why are you so chipper?" Dax brushed off some bush from her pant leg. "That was a small army."

"Because I've got the solution."

Dax narrowed her eyes. "Which is?"

Bashir spread his hands. "Vess put on quite a show for us, coordinating all of those shells while she taunted you."

"You can feel free to taunt back next time," Dax said. "I shouldn't have to pull that load by myself."

"You had it under control. Besides, I was busy." He really was incorrigible.

Her hands dropped to her hips. "Doing what?"

With a flourish, he flipped open his tricorder. "Scanning them."

17

Web of Light

Another close call, another night with Trill investigators. Dax and her companions summoned them to the Federation science outpost to report their findings.

The team set up in one of the testing chambers for new starship power systems. They took seats amid a sea of random parts, scopes, and tools. Dax laid out what'd happened.

This time, the exchange was far less friendly. Inspector Burx felt that Dax had withheld information, and demanded copies of all the recovered data about the Path of Sky. Burx would've taken their tricorders, but Worf refused to turn over any Starfleet property. Things grew heated, and the inspector made more than one pointed statement about obstruction of justice.

Dax's accusations against the Vesses, however, stayed any immediate consequences. Bashir's and Worf's accounts matched, and the three of them convinced Burx to send law enforcement to the institute.

Eventually, Burx and her team gathered to leave, but she stopped at the door.

"You'd better hope I find something at the institute," Burx warned. "And if you've withheld anything else, *nothing* will protect you from me."

Dax nearly jumped out of her chair. "We're the victims! We were just trying to survive."

"Perhaps. If what you say is true, we're looking at a major crime against all of Trill."

She scowled. "And we shed light on it. How is that not a good thing?"

"Because it's hard to gather evidence and make arrests when everyone's gone to ground. You know tachyons and wormholes. Leave the law enforcement to the professionals."

Some of Joran's old fire sparked her temper, but Dax harnessed it. "Are you, um, 'professionals' going to stop Vess, or let it commit a few hundred more murders?"

Burx's jaw worked beneath her dark, freckled skin, and she summoned a surprising amount of menace. "If I need to arrest you, Commander Dax, I will. I can't go back in time to stop this plot *you say* exists, but—"

"Are you suggesting I'm lying?"

"I haven't fully investigated the crime, maybe you are."

"Jadzia Dax speaks the truth," Worf stated, voice firm as a mountain. "Are you suggesting Doctor Bashir and I are lying as well?"

Dax glanced at him, warmed by his support.

Burx shook her head. "A court needs more than your word, Commander. It needs *facts*. I don't have them. You three are making it impossible to do my job, and there will be consequences if this continues—*am I clear?*"

"We'll comply," Bashir said, holding up a hand. "Anything we find, we'll share with you. Surely there's a way we can collaborate. We have a right to be here."

"And you also have Starfleet regulations." Burx jabbed a finger in his direction. "Follow them."

"Fine," Bashir said. "Of course."

"You three are out of your depth. Stay on Trill while we sort your story out." Burx jerked her thumb at the sky. "Then you're all going to go back to Deep Space 9 as soon as possible."

By the time they left the science outpost, Dax was ready to pass out. Joran was at peace, and she could finally rest. Rush beamed them over to the Capital Arms, where they settled in for a long midday nap.

Except when Dax tried to go to sleep, she couldn't. Vess—what it'd become—horrified her. It could be anyone, anywhere.

It would certainly be coming after her again.

The hotel replicator didn't have Argelian sweet buns, but it had a passable tea and Terran moon cakes. Dax sat in her living room and ate, staring out the holowindow at the simulated noon. She was so exhausted, yet her eyes refused to shut.

More than an hour passed before Dax's door chimed. She rose, grabbing her phaser, and discovered Julian Bashir outside her room via the desk screen.

"Come," she said, and the door opened.

Bashir took a few steps inside and held out his tricorder. "I hope you don't mind, but I couldn't sleep. I was too excited, and I wanted to play with the readings. Sorry. *Excited* isn't the right word, but I wanted to look over the scans I took while Vess was explaining itself."

Dax's heart skipped a beat. "You found something?"

"I did, in fact." He handed the device over to her. "Every single Vess present was emitting a peculiar electromagnetic energy pattern."

She studied the readout, seeing nothing.

"Adjust the bias," he said.

She did, and a clear carrier wave rose from the noise. It wobbled along on the little scope, rising and falling in analog fashion.

"A wave," Dax said. "Vess is acting like a transmitter. That's how all the Vesses were acting in sync."

"And it looks like they're fairly long range." He took the tricorder back. "Jadzia, I've been thinking about the way the Vesses were yelling at us."

"Like a choir?"

"Exactly. I imagined them at first to be just clones, but what if they're more like a faerie ring?"

"A what?"

His head bobbled a little as he tried to sort the words. "I'm not talking about mythological creatures. I'm talking about a fungus. Above ground, it looks like individual sporocarps, but beneath the surface, it's one organism. What if Vess isn't individual clones, but a single creature?"

Her heart thumped. "Julian, if we can figure out how it's projecting . . ."

He arched an eyebrow and grinned. "We can cut off its communication, and that could disorientate it."

"How do we jam Vess's signal?"

He shrugged. "I hoped you'd have a suggestion."

"Counter-peak neutralization with dilithium oscillators. With this data, I think I could make it—and with your help, of course."

"Oh, come now," Bashir said. "I doubt you need me."

"Julian, you're better at precision work than anyone I know. That's why we teamed up on the biolattice experiment. Speaking of which, how is that going?"

He grimaced. "They . . . they died."

"What? *All* of the lattices?"

"Afraid so."

"Those weeks of work! I'm so sorry. What happened?"

His eyebrows rose. "I don't think this is the time for that. We have important matters to plan."

She sensed a dodge in his response. "It's okay to tell me. You're the one I feel badly for. I know how much you were looking forward to those results."

He gave her a sad smile, and she was reminded just how handsome he could be. "We didn't do anything wrong."

"Come on. What happened?"

"The experiment . . . couldn't live without constant intervention from one of us."

She sighed. "And you're here helping me."

"It's all right, Dax. If you're in trouble, there's no place in the universe I'd rather be."

She knew just how much he meant that. Bashir would risk life and limb for her. When they'd first met, he'd fallen quite hard, a trait that soured Dax on his company a little. It hadn't been Bashir's fault—infatuation seemed to be a regular peril for the doctor. His friendship and expertise, however, had been a constant over the years.

He held her gaze a little too long, and she thanked her lucky stars that she could trust him not to keep hitting on her. So many other men who'd been captivated by her were of lower quality than the doctor. One of those men was permanently a part of Dax.

He cleared his throat, blushing a little. "So, um, since you don't appear to be getting any rest, perhaps I should grab Commander Worf, and we can crack into the files we took?"

"Oh, let him sleep, Julian."

"I don't know if I could call what he does sleep. His snores are like a cross between apnea and a battle cry."

"That's what my first husband said about me," Dax replied, and he laughed.

"I've heard you sleep. You're not that bad."

A pang of longing coursed through her at those words. She'd once spent the night in his room aboard the *Defiant*, not being intimate but simply in his company as a trusted friend.

"Julian, it's best if we all get some rest, but . . ."

"Yes?"

"Would you stay here? I'm having trouble, and I think I'd feel better if I wasn't alone."

He smiled. "It would be my pleasure."

Dax curled up on the bed, and he stretched out on the couch, padd in hand as usual. After the exhaustion of the day, she was out in minutes.

Bashir, Worf, and Dax gathered in the sitting area of her hotel room, a stack of padds on the table with dozens of different database entries on them. Julian had insisted that they try pizza, an obscure human dish involving a circle of bread, some stewed sour fruit paste, and a ton of fermented bovine milk.

It was, to put it simply, incredible. Her previous experiences with human cuisine had largely involved Cajun food, spurred by Captain Sisko's cooking. Bashir's culinary curiosity was crispy on the edges, then gooey and chewy in the middle, with a burst of wet salt and oil from the fresh cheese. Appetites sated, they settled into the couch to start dissecting the files they'd found.

The first order of business was to decrypt the contents of their isolinear chip, a task made infinitely easier by Worf. As Deep Space 9's strategic operations officer, he had access to some of the best cryptographic assistance available. His understanding of law enforcement and security interchange protocols kept their actions legal and well informed.

After a few hours, Worf looked up from his makeshift workstation in the kitchen. "Command has finished decrypting the files. They've placed them into a database for our examination, as well as evidence."

"Evidence?" Dax asked. "I'm a little concerned about going so official—"

"Commander Dax, I gave the captain my word that we would not act as rogue agents. Doctor Bashir and I are here to investigate the multiple assaults on your person." He gave her a shields-up look. "We will do this the right way, with transparency to our superiors."

She raised her palms. "No, of course you're right."

"I want justice for you." He glanced at Doctor Bashir. "We both do."

"Lead on, then," Dax said. "Where do we start?"

"The medical records have been returned to us redacted." Worf picked up a padd from the coffee table and handed it to Bashir. "Doctor, you will take those and analyze what you can."

"Sounds easy enough. If it's all right, I'm going to get these back to my room where it's quiet." He rose. "I'll raise you on the combadge if I find anything."

"Thank you, Doctor."

He left, and Worf turned his deep brown eyes on Dax. "I would like you to analyze the project documentation. As an exobiologist, you are best suited to understand what you are seeing."

She smirked. "I never told you about my degree."

"I read your dossier as part of the protection detail." Worf handed her a pair of padds. "These are the personal log files we found, as well as all of the project data. I'm looking forward to your analysis of the contents."

"And what'll you be doing?"

"Searching through shipping manifests for any procurement patterns that might indicate intent. Many times, the intelligence leads we need can be found in enemy logistics."

"Sounds fascinating."

"I assure you, I would prefer your company to that of data tables."

She folded her arms in front of herself. "I don't see why we have to work separately. Julian likes the quiet, but I don't need it unless I'm trying to play the piano."

"I do not think I should stay. I like to listen to music while I work."

"What did you have in mind?"

"You would not enjoy it."

"I've had a few lifetimes to develop eclectic tastes. Test me."

"I prefer the soothing drones of the dirge operas of my homeworld. It is . . ." He ruminated on a description, settling on, "not a sound for foreign ears."

"Computer," Dax called, a coy smile on her face, "Play the *QeylIS Cycle*, Act One, Movement Three."

The harrowing strains of Klingon choristers wafted through the room as the opera began. They were grand and terrible, bellowing their mournful songs of glorious loss. Their discordance was like the tearing of hull plating, and Worf's nostrils flared.

Worry fluttered through Dax. She'd only chosen the song because it featured the House of Mogh. At first, it'd seemed like such a good idea, but she'd briefly forgotten—he was cast out of the Klingon Empire, thrown down for siding with Starfleet. As Dax looked into his unknowable expression, she wondered if she'd made a terrible mistake.

He stiffened as the singers reached his old family name, eyes hard. She wasn't afraid he would hurt her—she'd never felt safer.

But what if she'd inadvertently hurt him?

Worf nodded once. "A classic."

She let out a relieved laugh, then reined it in.

"Shall we get to work?" he asked.

The padds weighed heavily in her hands, bursting with undiscovered secrets. "Absolutely."

The first thing Dax noticed about the records was the meticulousness of organization. The person who'd prepared the database did so in the fashion of an academic scientist. The structures were similar to ones Dax employed in her day-to-day.

She was grateful to her enemy for that. It made browsing a whole lot easier. One directory contained a small abstract and a codename: "Web of Light." Nearby entries held various images and attachments.

She located an entry called "Mementos," and opened it.

I start medical school tomorrow.

I don't need it.

These fools are so backward.

I was on my way to the dorms when I saw her—Dad's old friend.

She's still just as beautiful as she was back then, same silver hair. Maybe she's fifty now? Not sure.

Mother would've known who she was. I wish I could've asked her. I pray I see the woman again.

Dax studied the words. She hadn't been expecting anything specific, but this short block of text somehow defied that.

There was no author's name, no voice recording. She searched all over the metastructure for identification but found none.

She opened another file, a draft.

I've deciphered Dad's notes, but they don't make sense. If there's a benefit to the surgery detailed, I don't see it. Kerin said Dad was crazy. I slapped him for it.

Dad wasn't insane. He was brilliant. I'm brilliant, too. I can figure this out. He mentions Elta Vess. The beautiful woman—is that her name?

Who was this writer? What was their relationship to Vess? Dax scanned down and found another short entry.

Dad was right about us. As a species, we're all sick. Emotionally and intellectually. With a symbiont, a joined Trill becomes something more. Even mediocre wisdom, aggregated over several lives, would be incredible.

If I were joined, I would be different.

No one wants me.

Dad wanted me, but he was murdered, so who cares?

Dax's words came out a whisper. "Oh, no."

She opened the next entry.

I worked up my courage and met with Elta Vess. She smelled like an'angaa orchids and sugar. She knows so much about Dad, about what he was working on.

She said that, in order to understand the surgery, I needed to understand my father. He dreamed of a world where symbionts were free to explore the galaxy, unfettered. He understood that the glory of our species rested in their potential, and that no one should seek to control them.

When I pressed Elta for more, she said I needed time with her to comprehend.

But I didn't tell her that I've read Dad's journals. I know what she is.

She's pure.

Dax swallowed and moved on.

I followed her home and watched her. She's very careful, but I was more so. I've done this before. I'm good at it.

I can make her mine. She wants me. I know she does. Need to keep my cool. Let the feelings build.

"Worf," Dax called, and he perked up. "I think you need to come look at this."

He strode over, leaning past her shoulder to look. "What have you found?"

"I'm not sure, but I think someone was stalking Elta Vess."

He sat beside her on the couch. His nearby warmth comforted her, and she uncoiled inside as her stress receded. The thought of him wrapping an arm around her shoulders slipped into her head unbidden. It tripped her heart, and she wondered if the electricity she felt was mutual. She reminded herself they were looking for the truth behind Nemi's death.

Dax walked Worf through the entries she'd found, and they divvied up the others. Worf returned to his chair—relieving the unwelcome-yet-most-welcome distraction. Dax was scared and raw; they were unearthing terrible secrets. She didn't need that tension in her state of mind.

More time with the mysterious author's unrelenting darkness iced her mood. The journals painted a picture of a paranoid, hateful person, twisted through a lifetime of disappointment. He obsessed over Elta Vess, using his relationship with her to get into her house, cataloging yet more of her private life.

She is everything Dad wanted her to be. I see what he saw—perfection.

I stole a hair and took it back to the lab at school. It was on her couch, she went to the bathroom, so I took it.

All the way back to campus, my breath was coming fast. I wanted to archive her DNA. She's a blueprint for grace. I couldn't wait to analyze her and know everything.

I put the hair into the scanner.

That's why I know she's dying.

Fventik's Disease.

I beat the scanner to pieces. The professors don't know it was me.

At least one thing about Elta Vess was real—she *had* been dying.

I'm going to start keeping records if I want to pull this off. Going to put everything into this project and make something of myself.

I can save her, but I can't save both of us.

"Commander," Worf said.

"Call me Jadzia," she replied, "please."

He nodded and raised a padd. "Very well . . . Jadzia. I have discovered the identity of our author."

She rose and came over to him.

"Before you read it"—he wouldn't look at her—"I think you should prepare yourself."

This world is nothing but a disappointment. Elta can't possibly love me. Why is she hanging around? Doesn't she know what I am?

I'm trash. The only good in me came from Dad. I barely remember him, but everyone tells me how brilliant he was. I wish more than anything he could see what I'm doing. Would he love what I've become?

I have no way of knowing. I was only five when that monster killed him.

I wish I could've ended Joran Belar's life myself.

And there it was, the consequence she'd feared all along. A murder was never simple or disconnected. People's lives were tightly interlocked, and to remove one could easily break things in other places.

Joran hadn't understood that. He'd been wicked, lusting after revenge. She'd inherited his debts, just as she'd inherited Curzon's. She'd stood trial for them in the past, and she was being tested yet again. It was exhausting.

"Are you all right, Jadzia?" Worf's low voice summoned her back to her present.

She wasn't. It hurt to know what Joran's actions had done to that child.

"I'm fine."

"I can leave you alone."

We are *alone, Worf.*

She wanted to say it, to throw caution to the wind. But that would've only been so she could make the pain go away—bury the past instead of facing it.

She nodded, dying inside. "Yes. I think a bit of solitude is needed. Thank you, Worf."

His subtle smile was reassuring as a sunrise, and she nearly gasped when he put his hands on her shoulders. "It is all right to take your time, and I respect your privacy. Should you need me, I'll be in my room."

She nodded again. "Thanks for understanding."

"Of course."

He left the room, and she deflated, sinking onto the couch. Was it his lips that made her so weak? Emony had been a lips kind of woman, and Worf's were quite nice. She shook her head to clear her thoughts. There was work to complete, and she didn't want to think of the Klingon while she did it.

The story fit together neatly, and she was able to search out nearby events to get at a frame of reference. Then she looked up the children of Doctor Lowan Hoq. In a stroke of luck, he only had one: a boy.

Dax took in his name. "Hello, Sameron."

I finally did it—told her I knew everything.

I'll never forget the face she made when I said "Lor'inor." Like staring down a bird of prey. Her fingers crackled with lightning, and for a minute, I thought she was going to kill me. Dad's journal said they might do that.

"Which is what makes you beautiful!" I shouted it at her, and her features softened.

I meant it too. The symbiont's understanding goes so far beyond our mortal ken, lives stacked upon lives, unlimited Trill wisdom. Vess has ventured even beyond the most intrepid joined, shedding dependence on a host consciousness. It has faced the universe alone, a task that few symbionts could even contemplate.

I wish I could live with something like Vess inside me—but that would be wrong. Vess would be suborned to me after being evolved. I'm not worthy of partnership. I'm hollow. Disgusting. Everyone thinks so.

"A Lor'inor . . ." Even her sneer was lovely as she approached. "Beautiful. Not a corpse? Not a grotesque, animated husk?"

I wish I could remember exactly what was said between us. One day, historians will seek that precise moment the same way we search out records of the first joinings. In this endeavor, I found purpose and it flowed out of me in rare eloquence.

"I can see beyond what others do. I have studied my father's works my whole life, following in his footsteps. He understood existence in a way few others could—with eternal pragmatism. We must face the uncomfortable truth: You are a superior life-form. Courage is in your very makeup—the courage to be alone."

"Is courage why I hide my true nature?"

"You hide because of the bigotry of the lowing masses, but that cannot be allowed. Vess, you are the best of us, the most evolved. You are made of many past hosts, yet singular in purpose—informed but uncompromising. Next to yours, the life of a joined Trill is nothing more than a spark in the darkness. No one knows the true lifespan of a symbiont. You may be immortal. Is that not the key to a superior life-form?"

She looked at me for a long time, I think considering whether to kill me. She'd probably been in fear of others for so long that she felt exposed.

"My father loved you," I said. "I love you. You're the future of the species. The supremacy of the Trill. I only wish he had lived."

"If it's any comfort, I'm the one who threw Joran Belar from the roof."

Of all her utterances, I treasure that one the most.

When I was a child, she was Dad's graceful friend, a regular visitor to our house. When I became a man, I saw another creature entirely, one of enchantment and mystery. And when I learned of her murder of my most hated enemy, my heart opened. This is the woman I hoped for. I couldn't let her die.

I knelt before her. "Please. Please let me save you. Don't disappear."

"And what would you suggest, Sameron? It's Fventik's Disease. I need a new body, and you don't have one."

"But I do," I said. "One that knows quite a lot about genetic sequencing, symbiont endocrinology, autonomous surgery, and neurosurgery."

Given her expression, she must've guessed my intent immediately. "You can't mean . . ."

I smiled. "You are immortal. I can create life. Together, we make a god."

I, Sameron Hoq, being of sound mind and body, commit my existence to Elta Vess. Tomorrow, I will be implanted with the Vess symbiont. Tomorrow, I will be elevated.

It will kill me.

I have a confederation of like-minded friends to assist me, and am determined in my endeavor. The operating equipment is ready. Elta's assets have gone into escrow.

For posterity, I've gone back and organized my journals, starting from the day I saw you. When you look at them, it'll be through my eyes. I'll mercifully be gone, and from my fertile corpse will grow the seeds of a new era.

The Lost Lights are more then abandoned symbionts; they're hungry. They seek to expand their influence with a selfishness that rivals any predator. With my knowledge, Sameron Vess will be unstoppable. We're going to do so much more together than even Elta knows.

There is little that remains, save to make peace with my fate. I am alone, but soon I will be the lever that moves the galaxy. I leave this life as I came into it, crying, terrified, and furious. Let Vess reign for a thousand years.

Let the galaxy be unmade with my dead hands.

18

Delving

It took six hours for them to parse the most relevant details. They'd agreed to meet in Dax's room once more, and when Worf and Bashir were ten minutes late, she began to worry. She couldn't help herself; there'd been so many sudden turns in the past few days that she was on edge.

The journal continued for a few months, but it appeared Vess lost interest in keeping it up after taking control of Sameron. For a time, it focused on the Caves of Mak'ala, and the origin of the symbionts. Vess had obtained extensive maps of the entire campus of the Symbiosis Commission, including the underground, the Grand Archives, and maintenance buildings. There were highly detailed network diagrams and wiring layouts of the modern redundant systems of the Symbiosis Commission, including how to shut them all down.

That couldn't be good.

But what did Vess want? The Guardians? Fluid from the pools?

Dax's heart slowed at the sound of Bashir's and Worf's voices approaching outside. The door chimed, and she checked the desk screen before admitting them.

"Come."

The Starfleet officers entered, deep in conversation.

"What is it?" she asked.

Bashir brightened. "I'm happy to report that I've found quite a lot."

"As have I." Worf looked far less enthusiastic—bad news.

Dax swallowed and gestured to Bashir. "Doctor."

"A full roster of every likely Vess." He held up an isolinear chip. "Path of Sky patients who received elevation. They kept good records."

"We can get those to Inspector Burx," Dax said. "Vess can't hide from a brain scan."

Bashir nodded. "Exactly. If the authorities scan even one of the people on this list, it'll be proof. But Jadzia, I have to tell you . . . some of these people are well placed."

"Who?" Dax winced as her first guess came to mind. "Councilor Brac?"

"No, but someone on his staff—Illia Sobel, who handles most of his day-to-day affairs," Bashir said. "I think it's likely Brac doesn't even know you were banned."

"And with the Commission stonewalling me, there's no way I can contact and tell him." Dax slowly shook her head. "Who else?"

"Keeta Lynketa, the director of Career Placement Services."

"Odd," Dax said, "when I looked up the records of Nemi's *Kael'tach* friends, they hadn't gotten placement services. What's Vess's angle?"

Worf interjected, "Consider who the placement office is designed to help."

Her eyes widened as she made the connection. "Washouts."

"You said that Vess was a psychiatrist, and it exploited that knowledge," he continued, pacing the central living area. "Taking control of that office would give it a steady supply of possible victims."

She balled her fists, but kept her breathing under control. How long had Vess been at the Commission? Had she spoken to it without knowing during her days as an initiate? When Jadzia herself had failed out, had she been a potential target?

Bashir cleared his throat. "I cross-referenced the list against the Federation database. There are five Vesses in the Symbiosis

Commission administration—small roles, but a serious infiltration, nonetheless."

"How many names do you have in total?" Dax asked.

The doctor gave her a pained look. "More than a hundred and fifty. The cloning of Vess has been going on for over a decade."

Years undetected. So many lives.

"I suppose that was the *good* news." She almost didn't want to ask the next question. "Worf?"

"I was able to analyze their logistics and security posture. Their records were extensive," Worf said. "Entries numbered hundreds a day, and many are recent. The requests are . . . eclectic."

Dax thought he was talking about the wide array of chemical requirements. "Every project has countless unique requirements. Are we sure this isn't normal laboratory supply?"

Worf countered, "Most laboratories don't replicate more than a hundred disruptor rifles, explosives, and infiltration gear in a single month. However, that is not the most disturbing thing I found. The logs also indicate a synthesis of a compound known as siraxin sigma."

Dax cocked her head. "I've heard of that . . ."

"It's incredibly toxic to symbionts," Bashir said. "Siraxin binds to the oxygen receptors in the symbiont. Hosts who are exposed feel like they're short of breath, and symbionts asphyxiate."

She gazed at the floor while she tried to wrap her head around this horror. Vess's plan was obvious to anyone, but she didn't want to believe it. The trio of aspects—access, weaponry, and reconnaissance—meant one thing.

"Jadzia, are you all right?" Bashir's voice was barely audible over the thump of blood in her ears.

She had to say it out loud. "I think Vess is going to destroy the Caves of Mak'ala and all the symbionts."

"What?" Bashir composed himself, then said: "Jadzia—we know it doesn't care about hosts, but you're talking about genocide. If it poisoned the caves, how does it benefit?"

"It's obsessed with godhood and evolution." Dax worked her jaw. "Think about how arrogant you would have to be to play with your own DNA, to clone yourself."

"It boggles the mind," Bashir said, almost too quietly to hear.

"Maybe it's trying to eliminate any competition." Dax looked to her fellow officers, hoping they'd tell her she was wrong, but they were silent.

Worf clasped his hands behind his back, inclining his head. "If that is true, then we have entered the most dangerous phase."

"How so?" Bashir asked, but Dax knew the answer.

Worf's eyes carried a fire as they drilled into her. "You have exposed your enemy's weakness. Biding its time is not an option now, so it has a choice for a response."

"Either kill us . . ." Dax began.

". . . or proceed with its plan," he finished.

Bashir raised a finger. "Or both. It can be in two places at once."

She blew out a sigh. "This can't be happening. We have to contact Burx! She needs to know immediately."

Worf said, "I ordered Doctor Bashir to forward the list of names to Burx. Her office said she would respond soon."

"How long ago?" Dax looked out the holowindows at the sunset.

"Two hours," Worf said.

"And?" Dax hadn't meant to take such a demanding tone, but she was afraid they might lose their advantage. "That's more than enough time to mobilize and arrest some of the Vesses."

"They said they were looking into it." Bashir crooked an eyebrow. "They assured me they took us seriously, but wouldn't answer any of my questions. I don't think they're overly fond of us."

"The feeling is mutual." She crossed her arms. "We've got to get to work on our countermeasure against Vess. I want it in Burx's hands by the time she believes me."

"Do you think they'll accept our help?" Worf asked.

"We have to try," Dax said. "The fate of the symbionts is at stake."

Bashir nodded. "All right, Commanders. What next? We wanted to jam Vess's swarm coordination with counter-peak neutralization. This hotel doesn't have what we need to fabricate a jammer, or those dilithium oscillators."

"But the science outpost does," Dax said. "Benjamin could ask them to let us use their facilities, although . . . I feel like I'm already on thin ice with him."

"I will contact the director myself," Worf said. "My name may not be welcome in the Empire, but within Starfleet is another matter."

"And Ensign Rush has been helping us," Bashir said. "Surely her colleagues would like to see justice for their fallen comrade?"

"Agreed," Worf said. "Give me one hour to make the arrangements."

They were given a disused room in the science outpost. The equipment hadn't been powered on in a while, but everything was in perfect order. They immediately set to work on their plans—Bashir for medical, Worf for tactical, and Dax on science.

Although Dax never quite felt romantic chemistry with Julian, their partnership as professionals was among the best she'd ever experienced in any life. The doctor was calm, patient, and respectful, and she entertained his ideas in kind. She wished they had more time to involve Worf, but he was working on his own plans.

The Klingon settled into a quiet corner of the room, combing more of Vess's journals—studying a foe.

Dax and Bashir were building a basic electromagnetic jammer, which operated on simple wave-cancellation principles. The difficulty came in the complex, random modulations of Vess's signal. They acted as a sort of natural encryption and resilience, and proved annoying to crack.

Equipment of all types spread across the room as they replicated more supplies, and soon the place looked like every other Starfleet lab Dax had fallen in love with. The director of the facility assigned several junior staff to assist, and Ensign Rush went from helping a little to being a full-blown operations coordinator at Worf's disposal. Dax felt a bit bad for the staff of the science outpost; she sensed Worf would be giving them an unofficial inspection. He was a stickler for the rules, something Constable Odo had complained to her about once in private.

Work continued through the night, and all into the next day, with the only interruption being a communication from Burx.

"We got your list and we checked it out," Burx said, her image concerned. *"There's something strange about everyone on it."*

"And?" Dax asked.

"They're all missing."

"Your office should've listened." The words slipped out of her mouth before she could stop herself.

Burx scowled. *"We did. Units were dispatched within an hour of getting your notification, but scrambling them to handle even ten arrests takes time."*

"Too *much* time." Dax could almost hear Joran. "Vess killed Joran. It's taken over dozens of others. The situation is out of control, and the worst fears of the Symbiosis Commission are being realized."

"First of all, I do not personally run the tactical division. Secondly, I did *put in for a warrant when I got your list. Your name doesn't carry a lot of respect with the team."* Burx gave her a dark look. *"My other interviewees have said some pretty bad things about you, Commander Dax."*

She jutted out her jaw. "Are any of them missing too?"

Burx grunted like she'd just took a punch to the gut. *"Yes."*

Dax considered using every swear word she knew through the ages. "I was asking for a Trill officer to respect and listen to a fellow Trill. What I got—"

Worf cut through her veil of anger with: "Commander."

She looked to him, a pinprick of shame welling inside. Berating local authorities was conduct unbecoming a Starfleet officer. She wanted it to go faster, to be more agile, but she knew how large organizations worked. Burx was probably doing her best.

But Dax wanted more.

"Inspector Burx," Worf said, his voice smooth and diplomatic, "we rendered our investigations fully transparent to you. We ask the same. Collaboration is critical, given the severe threat Trill is facing, would you not agree?"

Burx nodded. *"Absolutely. Commander Dax . . . I'm coming around to your way of thinking. You have got to understand that we're moving as fast as allowed."*

"Every day might cost another life," she replied.

"And if you're not careful, it could be yours. Do you think I want these Vesses running amok?"

Dax focused on controlling her breathing.

Burx sighed. *"Keep me in the loop. Don't get killed. Understand?"*

"Yes."

"And call before you do something foolish."

"Fine."

"You're not going to call me, are you?"

"We'll cooperate, Inspector," Dax said.

Burx's lips pulled to one side. *"You know where to reach me."*

She terminated the connection. Joran would've thrown a chair across the room. The thought was appealing.

"Jadzia, what do we do now?" Bashir asked. "They've all gone to ground."

"We keep working."

Dax never took breaks, never rested, just focused on the jammer, fueled by her anger. By the afternoon, they had a successful test and returned to the hotel, where she waited, impotently, to hear from anyone in the inspector's office. Her comrades remained with her, staying prepared, keeping her spirits up, assuring her.

They were sweet, but she had a hard time relaxing, even for a moment.

It was late when the computer's voice spoke: *"Incoming call."*

"Put it through," Dax said, and Etom Prit's face appeared onscreen.

Dax's old friend was a shadow of himself, with massive bags under his bloodshot eyes and a thin frost of stubble on his drooping skin. What remained of his hair was plastered to his scalp in a few sad, greasy wisps. Far from his stiff-collared diplomatic attire, he wore an old gray coat with an unadorned hood folded back.

The glint in his eye was something Dax had seen before. Here was the steely Prit who'd proved ruthless when his planet needed him. Here was the man who'd made hard choices alongside Curzon.

He was a Trill of means and connections.

It was bad-old-days Prit.

"Jadzia." His voice sounded rough.

"What's happened?" She almost didn't want to know, looking at him.

"I got tired of waiting." He picked up a glass of liquor and gave it a sad smile, admiring the contents. *"So I called some friends . . . and I acted."*

She suppressed a shiver. "What have you done, Etom?"

"I found my granddaughter and brought her home."

She exchanged worried glances with her fellow officers. "That's not Nemi. That's not a normal symbiont. You're in danger if you treat her like—"

"We got her contained. Electric shocks won't do anything against a force field." He took a sip. *"We can chat, finally."*

"Whatever you're planning, don't," Dax said. "You're probably not making the best decisions right now."

"I want to know how long it's been wearing my granddaughter. I'm going to get answers, Dax."

"What are you going to do?"

"I'm going to scoop that thing out and Nemi will be . . ." His lips turned in a bitter frown. *". . . what she was."*

"She's gone, Etom." Dax looked to Bashir, hoping he had some better words, but he stood quiet. Dax kept her voice as calm as she could, despite knowing the awful truth. "Nemi is never—she's never coming back. That thing isn't what you—"

His sadness vanished into a dispassionate fog. *"Be here in an hour."*

The connection went dead.

"That's not good," Bashir said. "We have to contact Burx."

Dax shook her head. "He sounded unstable. We need to act before we bring in law enforcement. They've botched it too many times."

"Why? What do you think is going to happen?" He frowned. "I know you want to do things yourself because this is personal, but—"

"Vess murdered Joran, Julian! How am I supposed to feel? Of course this is personal!"

He recoiled, and she caught herself.

"I'm sorry. You just . . . you don't understand."

His eyes were soft. "I can see that."

She shivered, wrapping her arms around herself. "Every day that a Vess is walking around . . . every life that it takes. . . . It's a curse I can't shake. Does anyone get me? They all told me the system knows best, but that *same* system failed me, it failed all of them, all of Trill."

"Please pardon my confusion," Bashir said. "Are you still talking about Vess?"

"I'm talking about the Symbiosis Commission hiding Joran until I almost died! Or their director of psychiatry throwing him from the roof. Or . . ." The shaking wouldn't stop.

Dax looked down; so many lives. "I don't want to lose myself. I'm Jadzia Dax. I want to grow old . . . I—"

"It's all right." Bashir's smooth voice was like a blanket.

She gazed into his eyes. "We have to stop Vess. No one will be safe until we do."

He raised his palms. "All I'm asking is that we be cautious."

"Vess," Worf said, glancing at Dax, "is an ongoing threat to a member of Starfleet. I believe that we should maintain our own inquiry, separate from local enforcement."

"They'll say you're engaging in vigilante justice." Doctor Bashir's tone carried a note of warning.

"I agree with Worf." Dax's shoulders fell. "Julian, I don't want to see a Vess ever again, but the authorities have failed too many times. We have a countermeasure, and we need to get it to Etom Prit before Vess's clones home in on him. He's in danger, and you want me to leave it to the people who let Vess run riot?"

"No. I want you to inform them, so we aren't court-martialed." He gave her a pleading look. "Please, Dax. You heard Burx. We shouldn't trifle with her."

"We'll contact Burx from the Prit estate," Worf said. "We will have kept our word, but it will give us an opportunity to test the device. If the authorities arrive before us, we'll have no such chance. Their past performances have been unremarkable."

"And I can make sure Prit doesn't do anything rash when the investigators arrive for Nemi," Dax said. "He didn't sound like he was going to let go of her, and I'm afraid he'll get hurt."

Bashir looked between her and Worf, torn. "I'm still so uncomfortable with this."

"I am the ranking officer," Worf said. "We will be assisting Commander Dax as she sees fit."

Dax looked to her jammer. "Let's go test this blackout box."

Dax stared wistfully out of the taxi window as it descended toward the Prit estate. Harsh lights painted the perimeter of the grounds, and large muscular guards patrolled the area. Several of them took note of the craft's descent, and a team of three Trill approached them.

The manor was a curving organic structure of alabaster, with a wavy window exposing a huge cross section of the side. The designer had been inspired by the ocean, and whenever the house was fully lit at night, it threw sea-foam shades across the grounds. Dax had always found it so beautiful, yet its halls were dim.

The taxi's automated doors opened, and two of the guards leveled their disruptor rifles at Worf and Bashir, while a light-skinned man approached with a hand disruptor and a tricorder pointed at Dax.

"What is the meaning of this?" Worf's voice filled the taxi's tiny cabin, and the guards jumped.

"No entry until you're scanned," the leader said. "Got to make sure you don't have any extra passengers."

Dax shook her head. "Etom invited us."

The guard didn't lower his pistol. "Still need to get scanned."

She submitted to the procedure, and they imaged her whole body, looking for fresh surgeries and abnormal brain waves. They found Jadzia's waves and Dax's, both healthy and synchronized.

"No need for your next checkup, I suppose," Bashir whispered.

"Quiet," said another guard, looking like she might hit him for daring to speak.

When it came time to scan Worf, one of the guards put a hand on his shoulder. The Klingon stared down at the poor Trill with murder in his eyes as he evenly stated, "Do not touch me."

The guard removed his hand.

Once security was satisfied there were no renegade Vesses in them, they led the trio through the yard to the marble front steps. With each footfall, a sense of nostalgia rose in Jadzia. It'd been so long since she'd been there.

The urge to call out to Nemi, to run to her room to say hello, blossomed in Dax's heart, wilting just as quickly. The house that greeted her was both familiar and alien. The wide foyer stretched before them, its once-cozy interiors reduced to a dull gloom. The fires that formerly welcomed visitors lay unlit, their metallic hearths full of ash.

A classical Trill drapery swept along one long wall, its folds suggestive of a cloak. Long, dark *zashka* boards ran the floor, their polished surfaces like caramelized sugar. The furniture was an assortment of cubes and puffy ovals in subtle tones, upholstery patterned with tessellating shapes. The ghosts of endless parties and galas arose in Dax's memory.

Jadzia hadn't been shown the way to the hidden chamber beneath the house—but Curzon knew it well. After the first diplomatic intrigue, Prit got a taste for espionage. A natural salesman, he'd leveraged his new contact within the intelligence branch to involve himself further in statecraft. Curzon never met Prit's other government contacts, but he knew the man's network ran deep. To that end, Prit kept a hidden room for his secret work.

He'd showed Curzon the comms facility, once. There was a holding cell down there, in case Prit needed it. Curzon's opinion of the man changed that day, never fully recovering. Once joined, Jadzia's opinion of him changed too.

Etom Prit wasn't a killer—but he idolized them. He wanted to be in Special Operations, or on the Intel Commission, and kept their members as friends. He'd often spoken to Curzon about everything he was learning, ever the eager protégé. He bragged he knew the most lethal Trill operators.

And now he was unstable, in possession of a genetically modified nightmare, with little to lose. What would he do to Vess?

What had he already done?

They turned a corner to find Prit waiting for them in the hall. The man standing before them was a mere shade of the friend Dax once knew. He swayed in place, eyes bleary—doubtless from weeping, drinking, rage, or a combination of the three.

"Jadzia Dax." Even his voice was failing.

She'd promised herself she'd be tough with him and drive home the seriousness of the situation. Instead, she ran to him, throwing her arms around his neck. He gasped as she did, gently raising his shaking hands to embrace her. She pressed her cheek to his, whispering condolences.

After a few seconds, Prit grew heavy in her arms, and they sank to the floor. She cradled him against her side, keeping him upright and trying to make eye contact. Whatever he was looking at was light-years away.

His dry lips parted. "She looks like Nemi."

"I know, Etom. I'm so, so sorry."

He finally gazed into her eyes, a man broken by the horror. "Nemi . . . She started crying. Begged me to let her out. Told me things only Bean could know. She's in there somewhere. My little Bean is in there somewhere. There has to be a way to . . . to . . ."

"Vess gets into your head," Dax said. "I understand that better than anyone. But you're in danger now. We need to get you out of here."

"And her, as well," Bashir said, crouching beside them both, his tone warm with sympathy. Dax had often taken comfort in his professionalism, and he put it to good use on Prit. "If Nemi knows her surroundings, that's a problem. I'll start making arrangements to transfer her with Inspector Burx."

The old man stood up and scooted away. "I don't know who you are, young man, but I'm not leaving, and neither is Nemi. I'm not letting her out of my sight until I understand what's going on."

"The authorities have ordered us to share all information. We have an obligation to notify—"

Prit gestured to the doctor. "Guards."

The two Trill flanking the doctor grabbed his arms.

"Hey! Hands off! You're assaulting . . . a Starfleet officer!" Bashir made a futile attempt to resist, but they'd managed to catch him unaware. In short order, he was missing his tricorder, phaser, and a bit of his dignity.

Worf flashed his sharp teeth. "And what if I wish to call the inspector? What would you do?"

Prit stood, arms dangling by his sides as he gently approached the Klingon. Dax half expected her aged friend to be claimed by fatigue at any moment, but he held on, drawing closer and closer, until he stood directly beneath Worf's baleful stare.

Prit gave him a sardonic smile. "Would you tell me your name?"

"Worf."

He never broke the stare as he spoke. "I've heard of you. From an honorable house. Curzon took me to many trade missions on your world. Do you have any living children, Commander Worf?"

Worf broke eye contact first. "Yes."

"I want you to . . ." Prit cleared his throat in a poor attempt to subdue his raging emotion. "I want you to imagine your child murdered. Imagine the corpse paraded around in front of you, lying to you . . . haunting you."

Worf looked down, throwing his eyes into shadow, and breath hissed through his nostrils.

Prit raised a fist, unfurling fingers to a flat palm. "Now, tell me what you would do."

Worf took a deep breath. "I would celebrate my son's passage into *Sto-Vo-Kor* over the smoking bones of his murderers, and all who gave them comfort, and all who begat them."

"Her killer is in my basement, and I want answers. Would you deny me that?"

"I cannot."

"Then come downstairs with me, and let's all get some."

19

Separation Anxiety

Dax descended into the basement, which reminded her more of a bunker than anything else. Polished walls and floors gave way to drab gray, while blaring white lightbars illuminated everything from overhead.

Screens lined the walls of Etom Prit's makeshift ops center. A couple of guards loitered in the corner, a tawny-skinned woman and a pale man, flicking through information on their padds.

A long, rectangular cell stretched across one side of the room, its force field flickering intermittently. Nemi stood on the other side, eyes on Dax.

Her old friend was clad in street clothes, though they were scuffed, with a dribble of blood down the front. A red welt ran across Nemi's forehead where she'd been struck with a blunt object.

She smiled with split, swollen lips.

"Hello, Dax." Nemi's voice was less like herself than before, in a lower register like Elta's. She carried herself differently, like nothing remained of the woman she'd once been.

Dax turned to Bashir and Worf. "Get the blackout box powered up."

Bashir gave her a quick nod. "Commander Worf, could I have your assistance?"

The two started work on the box, and Dax turned to regard Nemi, steeling herself to approach.

She walked along the edge of the force field, and Nemi copied her motion with a mocking stare. Dax wished she could reach inside and wring the life from that symbiont.

Nemi smirked. "Computer, shut down force field, authorization two-six-Nemi-alpha."

"Access denied."

Dax scowled at her.

"What? Sometimes people leave the old passwords."

"Why did you do it?" Dax clenched her fists at her sides.

"Do what? Be specific." She tapped a finger to her lower lip.

"Kill all those people."

Nemi regarded her coolly. "Because it was easy."

Dax winced. " 'Easy.' "

"Yes. I could find people who were willing to do whatever it took to become joined—pay any price. All I had to do was look for the washouts, the failures."

"Is that how you've been wasting your immortality?"

Nemi rested her hands on her hips. "Curzon flushed initiate after initiate, getting rid of more potential than he ever had. I saw them all going out into the world, trying to make something of themselves—but a lot of them never recovered. All that talent just went unused, unappreciated."

"But then you took them for yourself."

"That's right. Nemi will be with me always. I have her thoughts and memories, her abilities." Nemi sneered. "Everything she knew about you, Jadz, I know. Like how you needed Curzon's approval even though he failed you."

Dax had cared more about being joined than anything else. The docents had absolute power over their initiates, and Curzon had wielded that power more coldly than most. He relied on his gut intuition to decide people's fates, and he washed out more than his fair share. But he was better than this monster standing before her.

"That's why you took over Career Placement Services," Dax said. "To get close to the washouts."

Nemi spread her hands. "Like sifting for gold."

This thing standing before her in Nemi's body was, according to Trill tradition, Nemi Vess. Jadzia's feelings for one tangled with the other, tearing her apart inside.

"You know my favorite thing about you, Dax?" Nemi stepped closer to the force field. "You're so easy to rile up."

She crossed her arms. "Am I?"

"Yes. You have this . . . I guess you could call it self-righteousness. You get so upset when people don't follow your moral code. For Joran, everything that impeded his success was evil. Curzon worked for the greater good, but was still ruled by his . . . baser instincts. It gave them such terrible blind spots. It won't be long before I find yours."

Nemi gave Dax a poisonous grin, pulling back the corners of her mouth in an unnatural way. Dax had been dreading seeing her again, but in that moment, she was able to glimpse Vess for exactly what it was—an infestation of a corpse.

Doctor Bashir powered on the jammer. Green light raced along the sides, shimmering just beneath the housing.

"We're ready," he said.

"Excellent," Dax replied, never breaking eye contact with Nemi. "Start it up."

"Gladly." Bashir tapped on the interface.

The change on Nemi's face was instantaneous, but subtle—the simple twitch of an eyebrow. She straightened, blinking and looking around as though she heard a strange noise—

—or perhaps, stopped hearing one.

Dax crossed her arms. "Those pulses you use for telepathy—Sameron never considered that they could be jammed, did he?"

Nemi took a dry swallow, backing up a step. "Stop it."

"I was going to ask," Dax continued, theatrically resting her chin on her knuckles. "What species of animal did Sameron splice into you? We didn't have time to figure it out yet."

"Stop it!" Nemi's eyes went wild, pupils shrinking to pinpricks. "Shut it off."

"Why?" Dax's arms dropped to her sides, and she stared daggers into Nemi. "Are you uncomfortable? It's probably nicer than seventy-two hours in a med pod."

"I would never do this to you, and you know it."

"What are you talking about? You murdered Joran!"

"Shut it *off*." Her teeth chattered, and she rubbed her bare arms. Nemi backed against the wall, eyes going red with forming tears as she sank to the floor. "Gone . . . you—they're gone . . . Shut it off."

"Who's gone?" Dax demanded. "All the lives you stole?"

"Stop it." The words hissed from her quivering mouth.

"Just because you—"

"*Stop it! Shut it off!*" Her screech rang in the concrete, loud enough to cause Dax to flinch.

Nemi covered her face, hair falling across her hands as a horrified eye peeked out between fingers. Her words devolved into screams until her breath gave out and silence conquered the room.

Dax turned around. Worf's face was unreadable, but Bashir clearly didn't like what he was seeing. Prit vacillated between joy and sorrow, his hatred of Vess wrestling with his love of Nemi.

Bashir's hand hovered perilously close to the device. She knew what he was thinking: it looked like they were torturing her. With each weeping exhortation from Nemi, Dax grew less comfortable with her blackout-box solution. Julian, as a compassionate physician, would be even less so.

Nemi clenched her teeth and curled her fingers. The hairs on the back of Dax's neck stood up, and the force field shimmered.

"Is your force field acceptably powered?" Worf asked Prit.

"Are you some sort of holding-cell expert?" the older man replied.

"Yes."

"This whole section is on its own grid. There's no way she can—"

Prit's response was cut short by the snap of lightning. Dax's hearing vanished in an acute spike of pain, followed by incessant ringing. She crouched on the floor, holding her hands over her ears until the room began to hum.

Dax looked up to find Nemi on her feet, hands outstretched, palms arcing with blue light. A thick bolt of electricity exploded between her and the cell's metal sink basin, splitting it into red-hot scrap. Another devastating shock shook the room—which suddenly felt too small.

The sound went out of the world, and before Dax knew it, Bashir was at her side with his medkit. She couldn't hear a word he was saying, and she could barely stand. She'd been on starships under fire, survived plenty of explosions, but this was unique. The doctor held her head in his firm hands, turning her this way and that to get a better look at her ears. She recognized the word *bleeding*.

He treated her on the spot with a few devices from his medical kit before moving to the next victim. It wasn't until Dax regained her footing that she saw the blood streaming from his own ears. Of course he was treating others first.

Nemi knelt in the middle of her cell, streaks of carbon spreading from her like a coronal halo. Burns tattered her sleeves up to her shoulders, exposing pale arms. She sat, head hung low, hands rested palms up at her sides. Soft sobs echoed through the room, accompanied by the ticking of cooling superheated metal.

Only a couple years ago, a Trill named Verad had come to Deep Space 9 and held the station hostage. He took Dax out of Jadzia, and for a few hours, she'd been terrified that she would die without it. Nothing could match the depths of emptiness she felt in those hours. To be just Jadzia had been the most horrifying experience of her life.

She walked toward Nemi's cell and stared down at her, wondering if Vess was feeling some of that same emptiness.

"You're a m-monster," Nemi whispered, hugging herself. "How could you?"

"This isn't for torture," Dax said. "It's for our security."

A bitter shrug. "Because no one ever tortures anyone in the interest of security."

"In a few minutes, we're going to lower that force field and stun you. Then I'm going hand you over to the authorities. I already told them about your plot to poison the Caves of Mak'ala."

Nemi glared at Dax. "You did?"

"Why?"

"Because they hate me, and they'll hunt me down."

"For being a Lost Light?"

"Just like the others they've jailed." Nemi rose and crept closer to the field, hands stained with chalky ash. "It's forced integration with another host, imprisonment, or death, but I found a fourth option."

"Kill off the competition—the other symbionts," Dax said.

"It's such a waste, isn't it?" Nemi huffed a laugh. "They could all be like me, with the power that entails—but that control is given to the Commission."

Dax narrowed her eyes. "You're right. You killed my friend. I will *absolutely* hunt you down."

Nemi recoiled, then looked at her with admiration. "Jadzia really looks good on you, Dax. She's got confidence without arrogance, without lies. Just like my Elta."

Dax looked at Prit. "Round everyone up. We have to move her if we want her to stay hidden."

Prit frowned. "I don't understand."

"There's too much to explain. I'm on your side, but we have to move her now." Dax took him by the shoulders. "Do you trust me?"

"Yes."

Dax nodded. "Then let's get everything packed up."

They'd only been at it for a few minutes when Nemi called out, "It's going to break you when Jadzia dies."

Worf and Bashir were assisting the security crews preparing the convoy, and Prit was with them; Dax wanted to keep him away from the shell of his granddaughter. He'd looked worn down, and she worried about his well-being.

"Dax, you know what I'm talking about," Nemi said. "Why do you keep going through it? Dying, I mean?"

"I grow with each host."

"Spare me the Symbiosis Commission propaganda. Jadzia is going to be the one that destroys you. Just wait and see."

"I intend to," Dax sighed.

"Life is always shorter than you think. One day, you're going to feel her slipping away."

"I'll always be part of Dax."

"You mean you'll always be able to do a good Jadzia impression."

"You know it's deeper than that." Dax cleared the last of the equipment off the table. "The Guardians were right about you. You're just as sick as the other Lost Lights."

"Don't."

Dax hefted a case to the floor, where one of the guards took it to the waiting transport. She dusted off her hands and rested them on her hips. "You don't care about hosts, so you don't have a clue what will destroy me."

"I know the pain of losing one more than you think."

"You murdered the host you're using to talk to me."

"I'm not talking about the failures. Elta was different."

Dax almost spat on the force field. "Elta didn't have half the heart that Nemi did."

She smiled. "I would've been so touched if you'd told me you cared while I was alive."

"Of course I did!" Dax knew she shouldn't engage, but she couldn't help it. "I wrote that letter to get you back into the initiate program."

"And once I got in, you said what?"

Dax was ashamed of that memory, and wished she could take it back.

"You remember," Nemi said, "don't you?"

"I said, 'I vouched for you, so I know you won't fail like before.' "

Nemi shook her head, stringy blond hair wavering. "That *destroyed* me. Every time I buckled or messed up, I thought of you. You were so obviously disappointed."

Dax wanted to tell her to shut up, but some part of that thing was still Nemi. Would she ever have a chance to talk to her again?

"I'm sorry. I never should have said that." Dax knit her eyebrows. "I thought it would help you."

"Oh, don't worry about it, sis. Everything turned out all right in the end." She gave Dax her skewed corpse grin.

She's now joking about killing Nemi?

Dax stepped back, heat rising in her cheeks. "Which one of your hosts was the first to go bad? Was it Sameron who ruined the lot of you, or Elta? Seems like she was always scum from way back."

"Careful."

"You like to get into people's heads, so I'm going to return the favor, *Vess*." Dax projected as much derision as she possibly could. "You're obsessed with Elta because you absorbed Sameron, who thought she was a god. There was nothing special about Elta besides her looks, and let me tell you, sweetheart, those don't last."

She could hear Curzon in her words when she said it, but Nemi puffed up, so maybe she'd hit a nerve.

"Joran was 'only good at piano,' but what was Elta famous for? Director of psychiatry? An impressive feat. She had a job!"

Nemi quirked an eyebrow. "Was 'evolving into a new life-form' not impressive?"

"That was Sameron. Not Elta."

"What she had ran deeper than mere scientific acumen. Deeper than wisdom. She was my perfect truth, and I mourn her every day." Nemi's gaze fell. "Jadzia is special too. That's how I know her death is going to break you."

"Nothing you can say will excuse the things you've done."

"No, but I can keep you talking."

"What?"

"Dax!" Bashir called to her as he came down the stairs. "We're almost ready to go. How is everything down—"

He stopped dead and looked over at the blackout box. She followed his gaze to see the unit wasn't operational. Dax and Bashir rushed to it, and he pried off the front plate to find damaged circuits.

Dax gritted her teeth, looking at the hours of work shorted out. "She must've overloaded it when she shocked the force field. She's in contact with the other clones! How long has it been down?"

Nemi gave Dax a wild-eyed grin. "Long enough."

The lights went out, followed by the nauseating sound of a force field shutting off.

Beams of light crisscrossed the room as guards switched on their disruptor rifle illumination, sweeping for targets. Dax's heart dropped when the flashlights converged on an empty cell.

"Run!" she shouted, yanking Bashir backward.

Arcs of lightning blasted through the room, catching the two closest guards. The bolts threw them against the far wall before things went dark once more. Disruptor fire filled the basement, slicing up the shadows. One of the guards shrieked as a friendly blast caught her in the arm, then darkness. Dax ran straight for the door with the flashes of weapons fire and electricity to light her way. The sound deafened her, and she did her best to cover her ears.

Dax came barreling out into the hallway, Bashir on her heels. Emergency lights traced a path for the exit. Screams and explosions rumbled behind them, though those fell silent after only a few seconds. Dax hazarded a glance backward as electrical arcs jumped into the hallway, shorting out the emergency lights and shattering them.

"Hey, Dax!" Nemi laughed from the shadows. "Where are you going?"

They rounded the stairwell to the sounds of disruptors, and Dax stopped Bashir before he was caught in the crossfire. She pushed his head low, and they sneaked from the hidden cellar into the corridors of Prit's mansion. The shouting of guards echoed through the hall, cut short by more blasts.

When they reached the foyer, they found an all-out siege. Security guards hugged the door frame, hunkering down as aggressors fired into the opening from the front yard. Dax was relieved to see Worf unharmed among the security team, shooting out into the night.

"Worf!" she shouted, and he turned in her direction. "Come on!"

They couldn't stay here to fight. When Nemi came up from the basement, she'd probably attack the guards from behind—certain doom.

Worf followed them around the corner and up another set of stairs. Guards came rushing down the steps as they rose, comms rattling off combat statuses. Dax reached the landing as Nemi encountered the security forces in the foyer, and she had a good view of their fates from the mezzanine.

They didn't stand a chance. Nemi's bolts smashed their defenses and cooked anyone unlucky enough to get in front of her. She delivered lethal voltages and concussive blasts that were orders of magnitude larger than the tiny damage she'd done to Dax in the Argelian hotel.

Nemi's laughter echoed through the foyer as all fell silent once more. "We're too old for hide-and-seek, Jadz!"

From her vantage point, Dax could also see out the massive front window—and the landscape was bleak.

At least a dozen presumed Vesses had set up at the perimeter, blasting at guards with disruptors. Bits of the structure cracked and splintered under the weight of their fire, sending noxious fumes into the air along with gouts of flames.

"Nemi!" Prit coughed as he stumbled out through the smoke, emerging into the foyer.

It was getting hard to breathe on the second floor; they needed to escape, but Dax couldn't look away from her old friend as he limped toward his granddaughter.

When she tried to rise, Worf kept her low.

Dax gave him a panicked look, but he whispered, "Whatever happens, his battle is decided. Yours is not."

"Wait! Nemi, talk to me!" Prit yelled at her back, his hands locked at his sides. The poor man's face was covered in sweat and soot, tear streaks painting his cheeks. "Don't leave. You're still my . . . my granddaughter. Some part of you loves me."

"A very small part, Papaw." Nemi turned to face him. "Walk away and enjoy your life without me."

"I'm sorry I pushed you to be joined," he said, taking on a sad smile and shuffling closer. "I only wanted the very best for you."

Nemi spread her arms wide and smiled. "And here I am, filled with exactly that—the very best."

"I'm sorry," he sobbed, sinking to his knees. "I'm just so, so sorry. I never should've . . ."

"Papaw," Nemi said, looming over him, "I'm going to let you forget me. Don't—"

He raised his right hand, and Dax spotted the glint of a disruptor. The muzzle came level with Nemi's chest, and at this close range, there was no way she could survive. All he had to do was fire—

—except he couldn't.

A snake of lightning struck Prit's skull, permanently etching the look of surprise onto his face. He went sliding backward in a smoking heap, disruptor clattering uselessly to the ground.

Dax wanted to scream for her friend, but she couldn't draw attention to their position. She longed to check his pulse or give any kind of aid. There was still a chance Bashir could save him, if she could get to him.

Nemi scoffed, looking down at herself as if checking for wounds. "Sneaky."

She pointed at her grandfather and sent another blinding bolt through his body, electricity licking at every joint. Prit spasmed and juddered, but Dax seriously doubted he could feel it. Nemi played out the assault longer than she had to, not stopping until her grandfather was assuredly destroyed. An unspeakable stench filled the air, and Dax covered her mouth with her arm—to filter the smell and stifle her screams. Tears soaked her sleeve, and she squeezed her eyes shut.

The man who'd taken care of her after she'd washed out—kept her out of Career Placement Services—was permanently erased, body and mind. The arc broke after ten brutal seconds, and Prit's corpse went still.

Dax had expected Nemi to leave, but she crossed to Prit's body and crouched beside it. She couldn't make out what Nemi said, but there was something like sadness on the woman's face. The other Vesses streamed into the foyer, weapons at the ready. They didn't speak or acknowledge one another as they fanned out to sweep the place with unnerving synchronicity. This was a single organism in multiple bodies.

"Time to go," Worf whispered, creeping back from the mezzanine's edge.

When Nemi rose, she briefly swooned, along with the other assembled Vesses. Dax looked closer; were they tired? That electrical output had been massive. Could it be a weakness?

"Dax!" Bashir hissed. He and Worf stood in the hallway to the upstairs bedrooms, beckoning to her. "Which way?"

She crept after them, taking the lead. "Follow me."

There was an emergency exit on the second story, hopefully unwatched. They moved through the halls as swiftly and silently as they could, coming to the deck in the rear of the house. No sooner had Dax looked out the window than red beams came pouring inside. The three of them hit the floor, narrowly avoiding the lethal spray.

Of course the Vesses would've guarded every exit. Nemi knew about it; she grew up here.

Engine wash blew through the melted glass as a ship passed low overhead. Debris came clattering into the hall, and Dax crossed her arms over her eyes. Was that ship one of Vess's?

She ducked out to see Nemi at the end of the hall. The killer squared her stance and pointed her soot-stained fingers at Dax.

"Look out!"

Dax scrambled into a side bedroom, and her comrades dove in after her. Another deafening crack rifled down the hallway with a bolt.

Dax took stock of her surroundings—a small guest bedroom with a wooden door and a single bathroom. A long window stretched along one side, destroyed by the weapons fire streaming in.

No way out.

Worf steadied his breathing and drew out his *mek'leth*, metal glinting with crimson light. "I will not die cowering."

"Got another one of those for me?" Dax asked with a sad smile.

He smiled back, the expression fleeting. "I should have been more considerate. Would you like to use mine?"

He held it out for her, clearly not expecting to survive the coming assault. Dax took his hand and closed his fingers around the hilt.

"Wouldn't be right," she said. "But thank you."

Before Nemi could enter the room, Dax heard the glorious sound of transporter beams, along with phasers shrieking in the night air. The disruptor rays stopped coming in the windows, and Dax was able to stand and peer outside.

All across the grounds, Trill security forces tangled with the Vesses, stunning them, sprinting through the gardens after anyone who fled. Some of the Vesses dropped their disruptors and fought back with bolts of electricity, but they were nowhere as powerful as Nemi.

"I called the authorities earlier when no one was watching me," Worf said. "Doctor Bashir was right."

"Ah-ha!" Bashir cried, and he looked like he could kiss the Klingon. "Saved by doing things the right way!"

But Nemi was still coming, and she would still kill them. Dax poked her head out to see how close she was. Red and blue light filtered in through the windows from the dying battle outside, flickering against empty walls and floors.

Her old friend was gone.

Two hours passed as the authorities cleaned up the estate, capturing anyone they could.

Dax gratefully took the cup of *raktajino* from Bashir and sipped it. There was a bit of a chill in the humid night air, and the lights of the nearby capital stained the clouds silver and gold. She hugged herself and sat down on the front steps to listen to the soughing of the tall ferns.

Dax was waiting for Inspector Burx to get around to arresting them for being at yet another crime scene. Benjamin would be furious with her for dragging Worf and Doctor Bashir into this.

"You all right?" Bashir asked.

She could still smell Prit. "No."

"Anything I can do?"

"No." She stared at the ground. "Sorry."

"Understood. And quite all right."

Worf talked to the authorities, while Bashir helped with the wounded. Two of Prit's guards had survived, but they were the only fortunate occupants of the mansion. Dax took another sip of *raktajino* and surveyed the lawn to see if she needed to help anyone, but she didn't. She simply needed to take care of herself.

Finally, Burx appeared before Dax, her face serious, but not foreboding.

"Inspector," Dax said, bracing herself.

Burx gave her a short nod. "You did the right thing, calling us immediately."

Dax glanced at Bashir, who had the decency to feign humility and look away.

She cleared her throat. "Of course. We understood your position clearly the last time we spoke."

Burx jammed her hands into her coat pockets. "I'm sorry about your friend."

"Thank you."

"We . . . we found some of the missing people—the ones you said were Vess."

Dax looked up at her with pleading eyes. "And? Anything strange?"

"We got called out for two people who fainted on the subway," she said.

Bashir perked up. " 'Fainted . . .' "

"Yes," Burx said, "and when one of our officers detained them for treatment, they shocked him senseless and took off."

"Electrocuted him?" Bashir said. "Well, I hope you can see we're telling the truth then."

Burx gave him an annoyed look. "For the record, I never said any of you were lying. I said we had procedures and laws to follow, which we do, Doctor."

"These people, what time did it happen?" Dax asked.

Burx thought about it. "About two hours ago."

Dax explained, "The blackout box. And Nemi's lightning."

Burx looked at her sidelong. "Commander?"

"Inspector," Dax began, "we used a special jammer to disrupt Nemi's, um . . ." She asked Bashir, "Would you say it was telepathy?"

"A form of it," he said.

"Just about two hours ago," Dax added.

"You used a jammer on Nemi . . ." She nodded slowly. "And this was about two hours ago."

"Yes."

"But Commander Worf called us only an hour ago," Burx said. "What was happening before he called?"

Before Dax could answer, Burx's pocket chimed. She drew out a small black folio and flipped it open like an antique Starfleet communicator, revealing a Trill-investigator combadge.

"Burx here. Go ahead."

"We've got a developing situation," said a male voice. *"You're needed downtown."*

She studied Dax and Bashir. "I'm a little busy at the moment."

"Code red," said the voice. *"Drop what you're doing. Return to the capital."*

Burx walked farther away, tantalizingly out of earshot. Whatever was going on, it wasn't good.

"Copy." Burx flipped the folio shut and came back to them. "You need to give your statements. Stick around and talk to one of my people."

She was already walking away before Dax could say anything. Whatever she'd been told, Burx was clearing off, along with two-thirds of the security team.

Worf came jogging up to them. "We need to return to the capital immediately."

She gestured to Burx. "The inspector took off in the middle of her sentence. What's going on?"

Worf's lips turned down. "There has been a bomb detonation."

"Where?" Dax already knew the answer.

He looked into her eyes with a surprising sympathy.

"The Caves of Mak'ala."

20

War Room

"Burx!" Dax ran after the inspector, catching up to her at the front drive.

The inspector stood among five others in a formation about to beam out.

"Stand by." Burx lowered her combadge wallet and stared at Dax. "The look on your face means you know what's going on. Twenty seconds."

"The symbionts! Were the caves poisoned? Vess was making—"

"Siraxin sigma," Burx finished. "I read the files, and I've warned the Guardians. No reports of poison from the sniffers yet. I have to go now."

"We can help! No one knows Vess like I do. Get me down there and let me help."

"Not a chance."

Dax's mind raced to think of any way she could be included. If Vess was attacking the Caves, Dax and Worf were combat trained. Bashir's services would certainly be needed to treat the wounded.

"Time's up," the inspector said, stepping back and raising her badge to speak once more. "Burx here, six to beam up."

"Wait, I—"

They disappeared into a swirl of light.

She'd been ignored and sidelined. If the Commission had taken her seriously, the home of all symbionts wouldn't be under threat, but they'd chosen to be obstinate—no doubt under pressure from Vesses on the inside.

Three times Vess outmaneuvered Dax, and the symbionts hovered on the brink of extinction. No more joinings. She looked back at the smoking house, its once-beautiful exterior scarred with disruptor fire. It'd been a beloved safe haven, but nothing remained for her.

"Dax!" Bashir called as he and Worf caught up. "What's going on?"

"They won't let us help." She massaged her temples.

"The inspector is gravely mistaken," Worf said.

Dax shook her head. "The Caves of Mak'ala are under threat. Our greatest treasure. I understand why they won't let *you* in, but I'm joined. It's my right to defend those caves!"

"We need to get to somewhere we can monitor the situation," Worf said.

"The science outpost," Dax said, a fire igniting inside. "They'll have everything we need to keep up the fight."

The doctor gave her a worried look. "And just what are you planning to do, Dax? We were told, yet again, to stay out of it. And if you're thinking about breaking into the Caves—"

"I'm not." She cut him off. "But I refuse to sit by and do nothing. The blackout box worked, and that was a major advantage."

"It won't stop a lightning bolt," Bashir pointed out. "Look, I want to help, but the caves have the best security on Trill. I'm sure . . ."

"After everything you've seen, do you really believe the authorities will stop Vess?"

"Dax, siraxin sigma is literally designed to kill joined Trill. You're not only jeopardizing your life, but you're throwing away your future."

"What future?" She hadn't meant to shout it. "If someone doesn't stop Vess, joining as we know it is done."

"Jadzia." Bashir was treading on thin ice, and he obviously understood that. "We can't always go barging in."

"This is pointless," Worf said, and they both stopped to glare at him. He nodded at Dax. "We can prepare at the science outpost."

"Yes, but . . ." Bashir shook his head. "Worf, you're not seriously going to embroil us in this. If you think Captain Sisko is going to approve . . ."

"I intend to engage this threat if cleared to do so," Worf said. "And it will be with the captain's approval."

Dax could've kissed Worf for saying that. "Julian, it's preparation. Benjamin's call. Nothing more."

"Of course." Bashir summoned the optimism Dax always admired in him. "Wherever you go, I go."

She smiled back. "I'm counting on it."

The disturbance in the capital was at the front of every news feed. A column of smoke poured from the Symbiosis Commission's main building, and fires burned in several of the offices.

The director gave Dax's team use of the design lab because it had the most capabilities. Worf set up a strategic operations center, commandeering one station for local news, another for anything and everything Vess related. Bashir retasked their data stations to analyze all his tricorder data. He'd gotten recordings of the electromagnetic fields during Nemi's attack, and he wanted to know precisely what Vess was doing to generate the lightning bolts.

"We need to get started on manufacturing another blackout box," Worf said.

Dax shook her head. "Vess can still fry both it and us. I think we should look at a different solution."

"Such as?" he asked.

The words dried out her throat, but she forced herself to keep talking. "We target Nemi specifically. I think she's the nexus of all the Vesses. She's more powerful than the other ones—throwing lightning bolts where the others are more like stun rays. And the blackout box?" Dax absentmindedly tapped her fingers on the table. "When we switched it on, two Vesses fainted. What if there were more? Nemi's telepathy was jammed around the time of those faintings."

"Perhaps if we knock her unconscious," Bashir said, "we would neutralize the others?"

Worf crossed his arms. "I would not count on that. Nemi's body must sleep sometime, but the other Vesses are probably operational."

Bashir's face fell. "So it might not end, unless . . ."

Unless someone kills Nemi.

She studied her hands. "I'm glad Etom isn't here for this part."

"Commander Dax." Ensign Rush entered, followed by two nervous-looking fellow ensigns. "My colleagues want to help."

She wasn't sure they had the time to read in new people. "Okay, sure, but . . . are you all engineers? Is everyone current on their combat training?"

The big, pink-skinned balding guy in the back made a horrified face. He wore an operations uniform. "Sir?"

Rush grimaced. "Ensign Lindros doesn't do combat. Or away missions. Or leave the lab. These two are good at something else you might need for lightning."

Lindros grinned. "Power distribution."

"Ensign Hart was our friend," the other ensign said. She had an honest look about her, and wore a science uniform, like Dax. "We've all had . . . a tough time with what happened to him."

Dax nodded. "Your name, Ensign?"

"Sisson, sir. We were studying the schematics on your blackout box after the attack. With all due respect, we felt like the power distribution was, um . . . suboptimal."

Worf asked, "Could you do better?"

Sisson recoiled. "I didn't mean to insult—"

"Ensign, time is short. Can you do better?" Dax said.

Sisson laughed nervously and looked at her colleagues. "We all make mistakes on draft designs. I mean, you didn't have any time for testing or—"

"Ensign." Worf's tone was unmistakable.

"Yes," she said. "But not with your blackout box."

Dax cocked her head. "All right, what've you got?"

She and Lindros exchanged a look, and she said, "A wearable surge protector."

The electrical transformer was quieter than Nemi's bone-rattling thunderbolts, but not by much. It was a small device the size of a medkit, a component of small-craft power systems, but it could fry someone if it wasn't properly grounded.

Which it wasn't.

Which is why it was spitting arcs of lightning all over the test chamber.

Dax and the others stood in the operations center, watching through the window with tinted goggles. The device was quite a sight, as well as a serious safety hazard.

She turned to regard the engineers through her dim lenses, and her tiny flicker of hope burned brighter. "Okay, you're definitely in the neighborhood of Nemi's power. What's your thought process?"

"People have known how to ground lightning for centuries," Lindros said. "A simple process. We just updated things a bit."

Rush, who'd disappeared a few minutes prior, came walking around the corner in one of the strangest suits Dax had seen in a while. It was a sleek mesh of rubbery webbing over her uniform, with glinting cables running along each limb to conduct electricity. At each joint was a node, a disc of metal with a set of glassy packs mounted to its surface. Electrical contacts glittered on the sides of her boots. Rush tapped a button on her gauntlet, and a short spike shot out of it above the knuckles. The protrusion was almost as long as her forearm, extending past her hand.

"This," Lindros said, "is the arcsuit. It's easy to replicate—there's nothing complicated about it, and it's designed to withstand up to fifty thousand amps of current without a problem."

"Also," Rush said, clipping in some earpieces, "it has hearing protection."

Rush showed off the suit so Dax could get a better look, then walked straight for the containment door. Dax watched in amazement as the ensign went into the antechamber that stood between her and death. Rush turned to the control room as the doors sealed behind her and gave them the thumbs-up. Lindros returned the gesture and opened the interior hatch.

The electrical transformer could have killed her the second she stepped into the room with it.

A line of dazzling blue energy snapped onto the spike on Rush's hand, and the packs on her nodes glowed soft orange.

Lindros continued. "The floor inside the test chamber is a low-oxygen gold alloy for maximum conduction to ground. The lightning rod enables her to ensure the perfect point of contact for the bolt, effectively diffusing it."

"Can you use the spike for fighting?" Worf asked.

"What?" Lindros said. "Uh, no, sir. The suit is designed for making repairs in dangerous environments. If you hit that rod, it's going to fold in half—it's not a weapon."

"Everything is a weapon in the right hands," Worf said. "Will a lightning strike interfere with a phaser?"

"Well—" Lindros considered an answer, then said: "The beam, no . . . but beware how you're aiming to fire. Lightning strikes the closest point—and the tip of a phaser is pointy enough. If your weapon is in front of your conductive spike, you'll get struck on the phaser."

Bashir grimaced. "What'll happen?"

Lindros sucked in a breath through his teeth. "I mean . . . best-case scenario, you fuse a power pack."

"And a worst-case scenario?" Bashir gave a tight smile.

"Blow your hand off, maybe," Lindros said. "Tough to say, because phasers are generally pretty safe, but those packs have a lot of stored energy. Honestly, I worry about carrying them at all, because lightning flows over the skin of objects on its way to ground. Your weapons might be exposed to a heavy surge if you get struck."

"And what about metal weapons?" Worf asked. "Blades and *bat'leths*?"

"That's basically the same as the lightning spike, as far as the arcsuit is concerned," Lindros replied. "The current ought to pass on through just fine."

"So . . . what?" Bashir made a sour face. "We learn an entirely new way to shoot before a battle? I guarantee you Vess is walking around with disruptors, because it has shot at me on two separate occasions. How has it been able to do that this whole time?"

"I haven't seen one hold a disruptor and make lightning at the same time," Dax said. "Also, most Vesses don't seem like they're that capable of damage—just stunning voltages. Nemi, however, hits more like that ungrounded transformer over there."

"We use the arcsuit to parry the lightning," Worf said, "and the phasers to assault. Discipline will carry us through the battle."

She watched the unrelenting power of lightning arc over Ensign Rush as she circled the energy source. The packs on her legs had gone luminous amber, with white-hot circuitry.

"What are those glowing bits on her knees and elbows?" Dax asked.

"Ah." Lindros gave an embarrassed shrug, endearing on such a mountain of a man. "That's because in the real world, the floor isn't hyperconductive alloy. It's carpet or wood or thermocrete. Lightning doesn't penetrate those surfaces as easily, leading to more energy buildup in the body as it seeks ground. Those packs on Rush's joints are consumable heat sinks. They actively draw thermal energy off the system, and when they fill up—"

One of Rush's packs grew bright and popped off her body with a loud ping, skipping off the deck plates like a river stone. She flinched, but continued walking through the test chamber, always keeping her spike pointed directly at the open transformer housing.

"What happens if you run out of heat sinks?" Bashir asked.

Lindros looked at Sisson. "I'm not sure. I think you could last twenty, maybe thirty . . . milliseconds?"

"I bet you would live for at least a minute, but those wires in the suit?" Sisson said. "Imagine being draped with strands of molten metal."

The doctor blanched. "Lovely."

Dax turned to Lindros. "Any other tactical considerations?"

"Just pay attention to your feet, Commander," he said. "Granite, grass, metal . . . all pretty good. Insulators like rubber—"

"Or materials with stored water like concrete . . ." she added.

"Yeah, exactly. If you don't watch your footing, you're toast."

On cue, another one of Rush's heat sinks pinged off her body and struck the window.

"All right!" she laughed over her comm. *"We definitely proved it works, so I'm coming out now."*

Rush came staggering from the antechamber shaking off her hands and laughing. "Gets the blood pumping, I'll tell you that much!"

Dax took off her tinted glasses, and for the first time, she felt pretty good about her odds. "I like it. What else have you got, Lindros?"

"Sisson, you want to show her your project?"

"As you know, the caves used to flood in the rainy seasons. With weather control, they stay dry and safe, but the satellites still have to scan them . . ." Sisson led Dax down the hall into a command center, where she sat down at a terminal and pulled up the capital-area weather-satellite feed. "We get all that data here."

Dax nodded, a lump forming in her throat. "I know where you're going with this."

"I've recalibrated them to detect siraxin sigma. The compound disperses rapidly in open air, so if even a little bit has been released into the environment, we'll see it. The satellites are now focused on the Commission campus."

"Nice work, Ensign."

An overhead view of the Symbiosis Commission campus appeared on the screen. Dax was expecting to see a bright red cloud spreading like blood in the water—but it was clear.

Dax leaned in closer. "Ensign, what am I seeing?"

"Sir," she said, "there's no siraxin sigma." She zoomed out. "Anywhere in the city. I've double-checked."

"That can't be right . . ." Dax looked closer at the scans.

"Maybe that first bomb was a warning shot?" Sisson offered. "Or a malfunction?"

Dax thought back on everything she knew about Vess, a hypercompetent, twisted symbiont capable of conceiving a multilifetime plan. Why not release the poison?

"We're missing something obvious," Dax said.

"I thought you'd be happy," Bashir said. He caught himself before she could respond to remind him of the day's events. "You know . . . relatively speaking about the siraxin."

She wrinkled her nose. "Vess wouldn't botch this. It's way too smart for that."

Worf stroked his chin. "This tactic seems calculated to provoke the maximum response from law enforcement."

Dax nodded. "Predictably, they've locked down the Caves of Mak'ala. If anything, Vess has made it harder to get in there—but there's more that doesn't add up."

"What are you thinking?" Bashir asked.

"Well . . . first of all," she began, "why didn't Vess kill me?"

The doctor gestured to her. "Nemi was fond of you, so Vess spared your life."

"It's planning to kill all symbionts," Dax replied. "Genocide."

Worf said, "We know Vess believes that a symbiont is a superior life-form."

"Which is why I can't understand why it would poison them

all." Dax was almost ready to pull her hair out over this one. "When Elta Vess came to Joran, she wanted an acolyte. The conversations we had through the currents of her electricity . . . She was respectful of my joining—cherished it, even."

I'd never kill a symbiont, but you have tested me, my friend. Vess had said that to Joran before throwing him to his doom. What if it was the truth? What if bombing the pools was never its plan?

Vess no longer sought out acolytes, because it didn't want them. It'd found another source of kindred spirits, right across from the Caves of Mak'ala, nestled in the heart of the Grand Archives.

Kira had said security was poor, and she couldn't have been the only one who noticed.

"Not genocide."

Dax straightened up and looked at her friends.

"It's a jailbreak."

21

Striking Twice

Bashir crossed his arms. "A 'jailbreak'?"

"One of the Guardians told me that the other Lost Lights were housed in the Grand Archives," Dax said. "That's next to the Symbiosis Commission, and the security on that building is lax."

Worf frowned thoughtfully. "Commendable—you've already analyzed their security posture."

Well, Commander, that's because we broke in.

"I did research there as an initiate." Dax hoped her quick response would end the conversation. "There's a cryogenic storage area for biological specimens. It wasn't something that was used during Audrid's time at the Commission."

"You think Vess is going there for the other Lost Lights? A rescue?" Bashir asked.

"That's the best source for acolytes. Those symbionts will already be predisposed to follow Vess's path."

Worf said, "Ensign Rush, contact the authorities and relay our new information. Make it clear that we stand ready to assist."

"Yes, Commander," Rush said, and took off.

"Ensign Sisson, I want this data collated and ready for the Trill authorities. Ensign Lindros, get three arcsuits finished and ready with two additional ones on reserve. Commander Dax and Doctor Bashir, you will join me if we must make an incursion. Be suited up within twenty minutes."

"I'll get my medkit ready." Bashir headed for the door.

Jadzia was about to follow the doctor when another explosion lit the screen. The central district of the capital flickered in the night, then went dark. The overhead lights bled emergency red for a moment as the entire science outpost switched to backup power. A few glimmers of light rekindled on the satellite feed, blotches in the darkness.

Sisson looked up at Dax. "The capital's main grid is down."

"Why would Vess do that?" Bashir asked.

Dax considered the prize—cryogenic tanks of symbionts. They'd be reliant on power to keep their occupants in stasis and alive.

"If I were going to steal frozen symbionts . . ." Dax tapped her chin. "I wouldn't take them out of the tank. There's a process, and the symbionts can't live outside of a host or a liquid for long."

"You'd need a quantity of symbiont-balanced fluids," Bashir said, "and time."

"Or—you move them in stasis," Dax said, "with a transporter. However, the Grand Archives are protected with a transporter suppressor."

"That protection has likely failed without power," Worf said. "We can be assured, then—Vess's crime is happening at this moment."

Dax had to agree. "We forced its hand by exposing it."

"Rush to Worf," the ensign reported. *"I couldn't get through to the security forces."*

"That is impossible," Worf said. "Surely they have communication backups."

"Sir," Rush replied. *"Those backups are down too. The explosions have them totally in the dark."*

"Vess must've known targeting the Commission would cause a panic and jam everything up," Bashir said. "If we have no way of contacting Burx . . ."

Worf studied his fellow officers. "There will be dire consequences for our presence in the Grand Archives."

Dax looked deep into his eyes, knowing that she wasn't at her best; she was harried and covered in the ashes of her dead friend's home. She probably looked like she'd lost her mind.

But she kept Worf's gaze and, as clear as she could, said, "Worf, we need to intervene."

He took a sharp breath, and his eyes widened. "I wish to test the mettle of this foe."

Dax smiled. "That's the best thing I've heard all day."

The arcsuit's straps were snug around her joints as Dax climbed onto the transporter pad. She flexed her wrist before retracting the lightning rod into its flimsy housing. A readout showed the system readiness, and she took a deep breath.

It was only a little lightning, right? No match for science.

Nemi was the deadliest Vess, so she would be on the scene. There would be others supporting her, too, and alerting any of them was the same as all of them. The plan was to sneak into the Grand Archives, stun Nemi unconscious, and hope that the other Vesses collapsed.

If that didn't work, they could switch from stun to kill.

Joran's final memory of the pavement smashed into her mind. She knew which setting he'd use.

Ensign Rush pulled up the Grand Archives on the console. "I hope it's current."

Dax squinted at the readout, the way Audrid used to. "Looks good. But where will Nemi be?"

"Though powerful, Nemi Vess's lightning is close range," Worf said. "I do not believe she will position herself where she'll encounter security forces, except as a last resort."

"Agreed," Bashir said. "One shot to her, and the whole operation fails. Do you think she'll be there?"

Worf nodded. "She is the most powerful of them, and this is Vess's objective. We will find her there."

"Then she'll be in the cryo lab itself," Dax said. "It's in the basement, in the back line. Even if the authorities arrive, she'll probably have finished tagging everything for transport."

"Understood." Worf stepped onto the transporter and his fellow DS9 officers joined him. "Ensign Rush, please set the coordinates accordingly."

"Because of structural interference," Rush said, "I can't beam you into the subbasement. It's a first-floor insertion only."

"Near the stairwell will do," Worf replied.

"Coordinates set, Commander. On your mark."

Worf clipped a last stun grenade into his suit and turned to Dax. "Before we depart, there's something I wish to say to you."

Her heart skipped a beat.

"I am"—his voice was low, almost as if embarrassed—"impressed by the strength of your enemies."

"Really?" A flush of heat rose, and she couldn't restrain a smile.

His deep eyes twinkled as he gave her the briefest nod. "Yes."

Dax checked her own gear so he wouldn't see her melting.

For her left hand, she had a type-2 phaser. For her right, she had the arcsuit's lightning spike. It was a little longer than a *mek'leth*, a hollow cone of metal with a dull point on the end. Lindros was right—it was flimsy and gave her no comfort.

"Remember," Lindros said from the door. "Watch your footwork."

Sisson peeked in behind him. "And if you see Nemi, don't point your phaser at her the way you normally do! Shoot from the hip!"

"Thanks," Bashir called to her.

Dax smiled. "Be ready to retrieve us, because we don't have a clue what's about to happen."

"I'll be standing by," Rush said. "We'll keep trying to get you backup."

"I'm counting on you." Dax took a deep breath and shook out her limbs before looking to Worf. "You ready to do this?"

He inclined his head. "Energize."

The world became solid, and for the second time in under a month, Dax was inside the Grand Archives without authorization. The dim marble halls were painted by slashes of emergency lighting—the power was offline.

She wished Inspector Burx could handle this. She didn't want to face down Vess again. Her track record was terrible against the monster.

But if she didn't stop it, who would?

They dropped low, drawing out their phasers, and after a moment, Worf signaled the all clear. Dax looked around to get her bearings—first floor, east wing, directly above the cryoarchives.

All they had to do was travel one floor without alerting any Vesses, catch Nemi unaware, and put her down. If even one of them spotted the away team—

A disruptor beam shot at them from the darkness.

"Go!" Dax pointed out the stairwell door.

Another shot seared past her head, and she slid into the safety of the stairwell. Worf returned fire while Bashir retreated to the doorway, and Bashir covered him in turn until all three were inside.

"Keep moving," Worf barked. "We stand no chance if we get trapped in here!"

They sprinted down the stairs, racing to secure the lower landing. No sooner had Dax poked her head into the subbasement than disruptor beams came flying in. She hissed a few choice swears under her breath as a close shot scored the doorframe, throwing sparks and melting metal.

Her teammates fired up at attackers closing in from the first floor. They were in the inferior position, and if Dax didn't get them out, Vess would kill them all in no time. Dax ducked out for just long enough to clock the position of a light-skinned Vess taking pot shots from behind a statue.

She took a few quick breaths and charged across the hall to get behind a column. Beams seared the front of her cover, cracking the stone face and sending bits of smoking rubble in all directions. Acrid smoke choked her, and she tucked in tighter.

Worf leaned out from the stairwell and laid down suppressing fire, drawing scorched lines along the enemy position. With the distraction in place, Dax stepped out and nailed the Vess in the chest with a single stun. Whoever it was keeled over in the darkness.

Dax cautiously approached the downed Vess, only to recognize Yonet Ru'xol. He'd been so sure of himself.

"I'm sorry," she whispered.

Worf's hand squeezed her shoulder. "We have to keep moving."

A pack of Vesses tromping down the stairs provided all the incentive Dax needed.

"It's just ahead." She ducked a spray of disruptor fire, rounding the corner at full tilt.

Except a male Vess stood ready for them, disruptor outstretched. Bashir slammed into Dax's side as the man fired, narrowly saving her from a lethal blast. Worf put the Vess down with a stun beam.

Bashir dragged Dax to her feet.

"Thank goodness for your reflexes," she gasped.

"I'm glad you're all right. Let's go."

The cryogenic facility came into view, its vault door wide-open. Vesses were inside, tagging the symbiont tanks for transport. Dax counted three hostiles as she looked for the shock of Nemi's blond hair in the darkness.

No such luck.

The enemy turned and fired on Dax with perfect synchronicity; of course they'd been expecting company. She shot back before seeking cover behind a large planter. Worf hurled a stun grenade through the cryoarchives door. It bounced among the Vesses, who scattered.

"Move up! Now!" Worf said. "Enemies behind us!"

Dax momentarily covered her eyes as the grenade exploded in a blinding flash. Advancing to the cryoarchives door, she drew a bead on a stumbling Vess and put her down. Bashir hit the other one dead center with a perfect shot. Those holonovels really helped his aim. With two of the three Vesses down, Worf charged through the door, headed straight for the last one standing. The Klingon closed the gap and knocked him off his feet, throwing him to the ground.

The Vess landed hard on his shoulder, and a sickening crunch echoed through the cryo facility. He screamed for a split second before Worf stunned him.

"Search the room!" Worf called, and they all moved into the cryoarchives before securing it.

Hundreds of silvery tanks lined the large chamber, vapor wafting from their sides. There were consoles and workstations spread out at odd intervals, all surrounded by flat-black mats. A stripe ran across the center of the room to a column housing an array of robotic retrieval arms. Several vats had already been brought down, their sides sweating condensation onto the floor near the retrieval console. The open vats hissed with steam, and Dax tracked her phaser to and fro. Any inattentiveness could be the last mistake she ever made.

The hairs on the back of her neck stood up, and she felt the gossamer caress of static.

"Look out!" She ejected her lightning rod and raised it just in time.

The air hummed before a bolt of electricity smashed into the tip of her arcsuit. The flash was blinding, but Dax's hearing protection absorbed most of the thunder. It rumbled through her belly, shaking every soul in her body.

But she was upright, alive, and essentially unharmed.

She raised her phaser to return fire, but Nemi took cover behind the misty vats. Dax couldn't shoot, or she might hit one of the tanks. Damaging the sensitive systems might spell doom for the occupant, and no matter who was inside, they didn't deserve to die in this fight.

"Nemi!" Dax hoped some part of her friend was still in there. She didn't want to hurt her more than necessary. "Listen to me!"

Nemi rolled out and blasted the area surrounding Dax with lightning. Sparks shot from tanks as cryo systems shorted out. Bits of metal blew off the various circuit housings, bouncing off her back and arms as her heat sinks began to glow. She couldn't stay out there and keep absorbing the lightning—Nemi's strikes were more powerful than anyone expected.

Dax dove behind a console as lightning chewed up the screens. Shards rained down on her bare neck, and electricity crawled across her suit like snakes. Every heat sink on her body took on a ghostly glow, and she realized she was standing on a rubber safety mat. Dax splayed out her legs to get her heels in contact with the marble floor, and the light of her heat sinks faded some.

Worf took three steps and hurled a stun grenade straight at Nemi's head. The device entered the path of the electrical beam and took fifty thousand amps straight to the power pack. It exploded in a flash and a rain of slag, far more dangerous than its original purpose.

The lightning stopped.

Dax jumped up to find Nemi screaming, clutching the side of her bleeding face. She snarled, and with curling fingers loosed an arc of energy at Worf. The blinding bolt hooked onto his lightning rod, and he calmly held the beam, maneuvering it to one of the consoles as casually as handling a torch. Two of his heat sinks popped off in the process, flying into the shadows like ships going into warp, but he didn't flinch. Worf touched the spike to the console's metal, and the beam of lightning latched onto it instead.

Then he stepped back, standing tall and allowing the lightning to dance over the console from a safe distance. He stared at Nemi, eyes clear as a hunter staring down prey, steady and solemn.

The lightning went quiet as Nemi ducked back behind the central column, and Dax shouted, "Nemi! Surrender now!"

"Today is the last time I'm going to see you, Dax!" Nemi shouted. "I was finished with you seventy-five years ago."

"You don't have to die today." Dax kept her lightning spike up, just in case Nemi tried to surprise her. "But you do have to stop your crimes one way or another."

"Bold words," came her reply, followed by a sinister electrical hum, "for someone trapped."

The entrance to the cryoarchives flew open, and Vesses streamed inside, firing at Dax and Worf from behind. He blasted repeatedly into their lines, felling three of them, but there were too many for him to take at once. They leaped over each other's bodies, fanning out into the cryoarchives to take up firing positions. Dax raced from her exposed position to one deeper inside the archives—closer to Nemi. The woman struck Dax again and again as she ran, the air thundering and whipping her face. She managed to get behind a refrigeration unit where she had some relief from the Vesses at the door and the lightning at her heels.

Bashir slipped through the shadows, just visible in the corner of Dax's eye. He was moving for a flank, but he needed a distraction if he was going to succeed.

Dax emerged from cover, lightning rod pointed at the robotic arms. "Nemi—"

"That's not my name!" The anger in Nemi's voice mixed with a note of panic. She was afraid. "This! This is the problem! You don't see *me*! I'm not just the host I'm in—can't you understand that?!"

Electricity crawled from Nemi's cover like she was overflowing. The column she hid behind began to shift and shudder, robot arms going haywire as a tangle of blue energy traveled up their length. Manipulators writhed and twisted, smoke pouring out of every joint. Wiring harnesses melted and sloughed off like syrup.

"I will *make* you see." Her voice was forced, hoarse with exertion.

Nemi came around the corner, her hair twitching in the shifting electromagnetic fields, hands spread low and wide, palms up. Bolts sparkled around the soles of her feet, flashing with each step.

Whatever Sameron did to Vess must've amplified its abilities, because no symbiont could muster this kind of power naturally.

Worf couldn't help, pinned down as he was. Dax took a shot, but it went wide. Nemi's return blast nearly whited out her vision, and she squinted to try and fire again.

She was just able to make out Bashir's figure as he took aim. He hadn't missed a shot since they'd entered the building, and Nemi was out in the open.

Nemi followed Dax's gaze right to the doctor.

"Julian!" Dax cried as Nemi spun and loosed a bolt into him.

It struck on the sharpest, closest point—the tip of Bashir's outstretched phaser. He'd been aiming with the classic phaser stance instead of his lightning rod. A flash blinded Dax, and the doctor's screams filled the air. She couldn't see what'd happened, but she heard him whimpering.

His agony lit a raging fire inside Dax, and she vaulted the console, sprinting for Nemi. She had the best chance of ending this quickly.

Nemi snapped out a bolt at Dax, locking onto her lightning rod and ruining her aim. A wave of heat surged through her suit, and one of her sinks popped off, spinning across the floor. Dax fired again, sprinting against the dazzling energy to save her friends, but no luck.

Dax dragged Nemi's bolt aside with her lightning rod as she closed ranks. She delivered a powerful kick into her opponent's gut, and Nemi's eyes bulged. On instinct, Dax swung the blunt side of her lightning rod and Nemi caught it—folding the hollow metal assembly over on itself before landing a glancing punch to Dax's throat.

Her windpipe closed up and she staggered backward, choking. Dax scarcely managed to raise her arcsuit's spike before Nemi fired again, but it was damaged. When the bolt connected with her gauntlet, the broken end of the rod went white-hot—along with the heat sinks on her elbow.

She tried to raise her phaser, but Nemi was quick, closing the distance and grabbing her free arm. Nemi's deft fingers hooked into the straps of Dax's arcsuit, and she threw her onto the marble with a wrestler's prowess. Lights danced in Dax's eyes as she scrabbled with Nemi, and her opponent tore her phaser free. Not wanting to be the victim of her own weapon, Dax smashed her palm into Nemi's chin and batted her arm aside. The phaser went clattering across the floor, and Nemi pointed at it before blowing it to smithereens with a well-placed bolt.

She'd have to knock Nemi out the hard way.

Dax rolled to her feet and squared off, ready to take her hand to hand. Nemi clambered backward before regaining her legs and raised her fists. Her posture and form was that of an expert; whose expertise had she stolen for those moves? No doubt more innocents.

Across the hall, Worf traded fire with the other Vesses, but it looked to be a losing battle. They maneuvered around him with their superior numbers, and yet more spilled into the room by the second. He picked them off one by one as they tried to get around his cover, but his luck would run out eventually. A tall, dark Vess closed on him from behind, a knife glittering in her hand; he didn't see her.

"Worf, on your six!" Dax cried.

He turned just in time to stop the attacker, but Dax lost sight of him as Nemi loosed a flurry of punches into her abdomen. Dax countered, but every move Nemi made was faster. Everywhere she turned, she found the leering face of her dead friend and ringing blows against her blocks. Despite her grace and martial prowess, she lost ground to a fighter containing multitudes more lives.

Nemi landed a solid punch across Dax's face, and she stumbled. Nemi's knee drove the air from her lungs and she boxed her ears. Dax tried to throw a punch, but Nemi caught it with a wicked smile.

"I don't kill symbionts"—arcs of blue light erupted across Nemi's body—"but I'll make an exception for you."

Dax swung with the other hand, but Nemi snatched her fist in a crushing grip. She grinned as she forced Dax to the ground with superior strength. Dax struggled against the force, yet she had no choice but to kneel. When she tried to kick Nemi, the other woman shoved her off-balance, toppling her to the floor. She followed Dax down, pinning her beneath unrelenting arms into the worst possible position—

—between lightning and the ground.

Nemi poured more power into Dax's arcsuit, and heat sinks went popping off into the darkness. The wires surrounding Dax's joints grew hot, their electrical resistance increasing with the thermal runaway. She smelled smoke, and feared it might be her own cooking clothing.

"Nemi, stop!" Dax was desperate to push her off, but Nemi snapped a punch into her nose, dazing her.

She wrapped her fingers around Dax's throat and squeezed, crushing her against the ground. Dax clawed at her, desperate for air.

Three heat sinks left.

Dax squirmed and thrashed, but she couldn't get loose.

Two.

Nemi's grip was inevitable, undeniable, and Dax's vision grew dim.

One.

She choked out two words. "Elta, stop!"

Nemi blinked, and the lightning arcs extinguished as she looked into Dax's eyes. Something like horror crossed her face.

Dax pleaded with her. "Stop."

A dark figure appeared behind Nemi, a shadow from the next world. It wasn't death, however, but a Klingon.

Worf rammed his lightning rod into Nemi from behind, sending its short, dull point through her abdomen. Her clothes poked outward for a moment before he ripped it from her and stepped back.

Nemi's eyes went wide, and she sucked in a breath as hot

blood spilled onto Dax. The wound went directly through the symbiont—an expert kill. Nemi swooned, slow blinking, and sank into Dax's arms.

"*No!*" Dax hadn't meant to scream.

In the distance, the other Vesses near the door sagged, then sunk to the ground. It was the right choice. It was the wrong choice.

"Jadz." Nemi's voice was weak, and Dax rolled over to cradle her.

"Why wouldn't you stop? You should've stopped! I told you, I told you, Nemi!"

"That's not my name," she said, blood staining her pale lips. "I have a name, and you will not erase me."

"Then why did you erase my friend?"

"When I lost Elta, I . . ." She rolled her eyes, and Dax wanted to shake her to keep her awake. Nemi only had a precious few minutes left, maybe seconds until the symbiont inside died of its injuries.

"Worf, please go check on Julian," Dax whispered.

He knelt by her side, voice gentle. "Will you be all right?"

She couldn't bear to look at him. "Yes, please, just go. She's not going to hurt me. She's not . . . not going to do anything."

Worf's conflict was plain. He wanted to stay.

"Go," she said, and he silently rose and left.

"I thought I could replace Elta with a companion," Nemi said, smiling. "I thought I could find love . . . or cure this emptiness."

"There is always another host," Dax said.

"Not for me." Nemi smacked her dry lips. She looked sleepy, like when she used to pass out on Jadzia's lap while she brushed her hair. "I only ever wanted to be . . . Elta Vess. That was my . . . real self. What I was meant to be. My truth."

Nemi's eyes grew distant.

Dax stroked her cheek. "You're still Elta, but . . ."

Nemi's body relaxed as the symbiont faded away. More than a hundred Vesses vanished in that bitter moment. For a symbiont to die, no matter the circumstances, was a terrible loss to all of Trill. A symbiont whose host was reprehensible might be redeemed in the next life—Dax knew that better than anyone.

"More importantly . . ." Dax whispered.

She leaned over Nemi's body, resting her forehead on her wet chest.

". . . you were my little sister. I'm so sorry."

22

Inheritance

The Trill authorities arrived and took them to the closest hospital, the Solar United Downtown. Its trauma ward was more than equipped to deal with their minor injuries, though Doctor Bashir needed a little more recovery time. Worf assured Dax that Julian would be fine, and urged her to accept the care of the medical staff.

They offered Dax the use of one of their med pods to heal, but she couldn't make herself climb into it. Joran's memories of entombment by Elta Vess were too strong. Dax asked for a quiet room and a warm blanket, and she let the doctors treat her wounds. Once they were done, she slept.

Sadly, she awoke to find Bentis Brac and Doctor Renhol standing at the foot of her bed. The late-afternoon sun filtered in through the blinds, clouds fluffy and gold after their daily summer storms. Brac wore plainclothes, eschewing his beloved councilor's robes when outside the Commission. Renhol's suit was the dark blue of mourning. They'd both had professional contact with a Vess for years.

Brac's upper lip curled in a stiff snarl. "Illia Sobel, from my office, is dead."

"Illia *Vess*, you mean," Dax murmured.

"He was my friend. I would've seen Vess apprehended."

"I find the idea of your office apprehending Vess laughable." Dax normally tried to be more diplomatic, but her restraint was exhausted. "You didn't believe me. Yonet Ru'xol died because of your inaction."

"And every host inside that Vess perished because of your Klingon friend, including my Illia—"

"Bentis!" Renhol's voice was sharp. "I brought you here to speak to Jadzia, not to make a fool of us."

He gestured to Dax. "Oh, *I'm* making a fool of us? Jadzia Dax and her Starfleet friends are the reason our capital is in mourning today. Vess lies dead, and we have no answers. Do you call this justice?"

Dax stared, too numb to hate him. "The Commission bears responsibility for this tragedy. For decades, Vess murdered initiates right under your nose, and it succeeded because of your deception."

"If you intend to lay this monster at our feet—" He rolled his eyes.

"You lied to the population—half of us can be joined, but you pretend like it's some elite status."

"It *is*," Brac spat. "You know that because you fought hard—"

"The people who failed out of the program aren't less than us. You made them think there was something wrong with them. You act so special for being joined, but—" She thought of all the talent Curzon destroyed in his years as field docent. "But you were just lucky. Had the right friends. Had the right field docent. Plenty of better Trill than you were passed over for joining."

"*Pach't*. You talk like you've lost all faith in the Commission." He folded his arms across his chest.

"That happened a long time ago, Councilor, and you've only reinforced it with your own failings."

"The nerve of you! You bring up state secrets in a public hospital and hurl insults at the people mourning their colleagues!" He thrust a finger at Dax. "If you think I'll let this stand, you're sadly mistaken. Your pathetic, idiotic adventures are—"

"Councilor Brac," Renhol said, "I'll have you sanctioned if you don't shut up right now."

He smirked. "Will you? I was unaware you had that authority."

"No." Renhol's voice was clinical. "I'll have the Commissioner do it after our weekly *Ski'tin* match. There are other levers of power than mere titles, Brac."

He puffed up like an officious bird, clearly unaccustomed to such a challenge.

Renhol's glare could cut glass. "Say what you need to say, and then leave Jadzia alone."

He turned to Dax, speechless and rapidly filling with his own hot air.

Dax arched her eyebrows. "You heard the good doctor."

Brac looked down his nose at her, pronouncing it like a sentence. "Jadzia Dax, by order of the magistrate, you are to leave Trill immediately. You will be offworld within the next day or we'll have you deported. You're not to return for a period of five years, or you'll be subject to civil action."

"You can't just kick me out," Dax said.

"We can if it's for your own safety," Brac added with a patronizing smile.

"Jadzia," Renhol said, "there were a lot of Vesses. More than a hundred Trill have passed away in the wake of yesterday's events, and those people had family, friends, and colleagues. They'll want answers, and they deserve them—but not from you."

She came and sat on the edge of Dax's bed, taking her hand. "I know it feels like an indignity, but please understand. It's what's best to begin the healing."

Dax thought about it. If she remained any longer, what good would come of it? The families of Vess's victims might seek her out. Would they welcome her as the liberator of a loved one or a destroyer? Captain Sisko needed her on the station, so she couldn't stay, even if she wanted to fight Brac.

"I was already leaving," Dax said. "I'm due back on Deep Space 9."

"Excellent," Brac said. "Your escort will be waiting outside. I don't want to see you again."

"The feeling is mutual, Bentis," she said, scoring a final hit before he stormed out.

Renhol grinned, patting Jadzia's hand. "I'm still going to have to deal with him after you're gone, you know."

"You have my sympathies."

The doctor looked out the window and sighed. "I'm so sorry that we failed you again."

Dax squeezed her hand. "Don't count yourself among that number, Doctor. You looked the other way when I needed you to."

"Yes, well . . ." She smiled. "That's true. At least I don't have to live with any *extra* regret."

"I think that's the best way to be."

"I wish we had some time to sit down and share a meal. There's a lot I wish I could say to you—about Joran."

Dax smiled at her old doctor. "I'd like that too."

"There is something I have to ask." Her eyes reddened, and she balled her pants legs in her fists. "And no matter what you say, I'll understand. Truly."

Dax nodded. "Go ahead."

"Do you . . . *can you* ever forgive me?" Her lip quivered a little as she spoke, and she wouldn't look at Dax.

Dax paused, then said, "It's in the past, Doctor."

"Dax!"

Bashir's smile was like the sun as he came through her door, healthy hands stretched wide. She rushed to embrace him, and he grunted and laughed.

"I'm so glad you're okay, Julian. When you got hit—"

"I've had worse."

She pulled back. "Really?"

"No, it was absolutely bloody awful, but that's what medicine is for, isn't it?"

Dax gave him her best smile. "Thank goodness for doctors, right?"

"Yes, thank goodness," he chuckled. Bashir always looked down at his shoes when he got flustered. "I've been given a clean bill of health, so I'm cleared to leave."

"And I've had twelve hours of uninterrupted sleep."

He quirked an eyebrow. "That sounds like a fantasy."

"It's not that unbelievable. I am, as you know, on a relaxing vacation." She strode to the corner of the hospital room and grabbed her duffel. "Now, let's get back to work."

Dax finished packing her things in her room at the Capital Arms and sighed. Life aboard Deep Space 9 had helped her become accustomed to limited space, but she'd enjoyed her cozy environs here.

Sure, it wasn't luxury, but it was a great place to have sampled pizza with colleagues and pored over twenty different padds of data. Despite the darkness of the past couple weeks, there had still been moments of light, and the tenderness of her comrades.

She stood by the door, duffel across her shoulder, and took one last look at the room. She wouldn't miss the place, but she'd never forget it.

Her combadge chirped, and Bashir said, *"Everything all right up there?"*

She tapped it. "Yeah. I'm fine. Just wrapping up. Down in a minute."

After the confrontation with Nemi, Worf had made himself scarce. He'd already checked himself out of the hospital by the time she and Doctor Bashir left, and he was out of the hotel when she'd arrived to pack up. That was when she realized he might be avoiding her.

Dax couldn't blame him. She hadn't meant to be cold—quite the opposite, in fact—but the trauma of Nemi's death hadn't allowed space for that. Perhaps he felt shunned by her, or worse, dishonored. She needed to speak with him and clear things up, but he wasn't around.

In the bustling lobby, Dax found Ensign Rush and the engineers from the science outpost waiting with Bashir. Lindros offered to let her keep an arcsuit, and she politely declined. Sisson told Dax that she'd been the one to file the mission report to Worf, and he'd given the team top marks for procedure. Rush told Dax that she was taking care of Noodles, Ensign Hart's cat, and he was settling in nicely.

"And all of us want to thank you . . . for what you three did," Rush said with a wide smile. "Colin would've been grateful. I think Nemi would have too."

Dax gave a little laugh. "Do you think so?"

"I do," Rush said. "We saved future lives in their name. That's always worth something."

The ensign said it so concisely that it stunned Dax. Everything about Rush seemed to embody the promise of Starfleet, and Dax hoped this wasn't the last time she'd see the young woman.

"You're going to go far, Ensign."

"Thank you, Commander." Rush shook Dax's hand in the human custom, and her grip was sure. She exchanged a shake with Bashir, as well. "I'd better let you get to your ship."

"Yeah." Dax patted Rush's shoulder the way Curzon always did. "Take care."

"You, too."

Dax stepped back and patted her combadge. "Lieutenant Commander Dax to *Starship Sandpiper*."

"Sandpiper, *go ahead, Commander.*"

"Two to beam aboard."

Jadzia Dax found herself restlessly wandering the corridors of the *Sandpiper*. It had a decent lounge—a round, gray-paneled room with a glassy bar in the center. The crew laughed and drank together at the smooth-top tables, cocktails and happy faces aglow in the underlights.

She sat at the bar and made idle chitchat. Crew members shared their stories with her, and she absorbed them, ever curious. Curzon had a glib tongue, and she could get a conversation going with anyone. She whiled away a few hours, amusing herself with the company of fellow Starfleet officers.

Then with a practiced yawn and a gentle smile, she left for her quarters. The walk through the corridors was considerably quieter than before, with only the low thrum of the *Sandpiper*'s warp engines in her ears. Dax decided to take the long way back. It helped to stretch her legs when she couldn't sleep, and there was an observation deck she wanted to check out.

Upon arrival, she found it small, but cozy, with a panoramic viewport along one side. A lonely bench stood watch, casting a short shadow in the warp light.

Dax walked over to the bench and took a seat, trying not to feel sorry for herself. Nemi's and Etom Prit's funerals would be that week—a final goodbye, forbidden to her by the Trill state that Curzon, Audrid, Lela, and Tobin had served so faithfully. The rites were necessary to her grieving, and several lifetimes had taught her the process was lengthy.

"Jadzia." Worf spoke behind her, and her heart thumped. "May I sit with you?"

Without looking up, she said, "Yes."

Worf joined her on the bench, his sweet, now-familiar scent invigorating her. She admitted to herself that she was developing a weakness for him, and now that she was safe again . . . maybe it was time to indulge. Perhaps the brilliant strategic commander would entertain the thought, and the rest of the trip home could be more pleasant. Then again, he'd been avoiding her for a reason.

He took a breath to speak, held it, then hesitantly said, "I want you to know how sorry I am . . . about your friend."

That killed Dax's mood.

"It's okay, Worf. Well . . . not okay." She gave a bitter laugh. "But, as okay as it has to be."

He nodded.

"I used to have a little sister. Now it feels like I don't even have a homeworld."

Worf took in a breath. "I . . ."

She regarded him while he composed his thoughts, searching his eyes. "What is it?"

"This is . . . personal . . . and you must share it with no one else, but I would tell you a story." He leaned forward on his knees, interlacing his fingers.

"I would never break your confidence, Worf."

His eyebrows knit together. "Many years ago, my parents were killed in the . . . cowardly assault on Khitomer. I was only a boy."

Curzon had loved that world—the site of his greatest victory and yet another gem in the Klingon Empire's crown. The pain of the Romulan sneak attack still lingered in Dax as well. The diplomat had followed stories of the few refugees, scattered to the winds.

So Worf was one of those children.

"Oh, Worf. I'm so sorry."

"Before the attack, the planetary defenses were sabotaged—codes were sent to the Romulans by a traitor, and they lowered our shields." His breath came a bit quicker. "Six years ago, new evidence implicated my father, Mogh. A challenge was brought against my family."

Dax knew the penalties that came with such a revelation—shunned for seven generations, along with his entire house.

"But my father was *not* a traitor." He shook his head, and his knuckles tensed. "And the High Council accused him nevertheless because they wanted to prevent a civil war. It was Duras's father, Ja'rod, who sent the codes—and the House of Duras held the Empire stable."

"I believe you."

Worf gave her a grateful nod. "If I defended against the challenge and failed, I would be executed for treason. The outcome of the trial against me had already been predetermined, because for my father's name to be cleared, the Empire had to burn. But the High Council was wrong about two things: I would rather die than live in shame."

He sighed. "And I was not the last son of Mogh."

She hadn't heard of a sibling before, but then again, she didn't know Worf as well as she wanted.

"Kurn—my younger brother—was not at Khitomer during the orbital bombardment. If I chose death, it would have condemned him too. It was a decision he would gladly have agreed to—if I had allowed it."

Dax kept silent. For Worf to share the inner workings of his family, of the dark secrets of the Empire—they'd forged a bond in battle that she would cherish.

"I chose dishonor, so he would live. I protected my family."

"Did I fail, then?" she asked. "If I didn't save Nemi? Or Etom?"

"No. You avenged them. We live on for the ones we care for, even when we cannot be near them."

"I'm glad you chose dishonor, Worf." She looked off into the tunnel of space swirling away from them. "Otherwise, I never would've had the privilege of your company."

"Welcome back, old man."

Dax had been a little nervous to come before the captain again after his lecture back on Trill, but the second she saw Benjamin Sisko, she knew all was forgiven. She walked into his office aboard Deep Space 9 as though no time had passed—save that they held hands just a little bit longer upon greeting.

He'd been worried for her, and it showed.

"I missed you, too, Benjamin."

He gave her a coy smile. "Is it that obvious?"

"You didn't have a pot of gumbo ready, but yeah."

"Why don't we fix that?"

She considered it. It'd been such a long vacation.

"I'm . . . not hungry."

"You?" His appraising stare always went to her core. "All right. I read Commander Worf's report. Perhaps take a day to—"

"Thank you, but . . . I'm not sure I can handle any more vacation, sir."

When Dax returned to her quarters that night, they smelled a little too clean. Everything was exactly where she'd left it, except her flowers had wilted.

She didn't stay up late reading, as was often her habit. No other diversions called to her, either, so she lit some candles, put out some incense, and took a long bath. The waters did wonders for her joints, and she added some Betazoid soaking salts. Dax always trusted the empaths to maximize their relaxation.

As she lay in her tub, she closed her eyes and thought of her other lives.

All of them had flaws. They'd each been damaged people in their own ways, simply making the best decisions they could within the frames of their time.

Who would one day look back and think this about her?

"You certainly know how to relax, kid." She could almost hear it in Curzon's voice.

"I want to, but we need to talk."

She opened her eyes, and he wasn't there. Only the flicker of low-burning candles and shriveling fingertips marked the time, so she must've been in there for nearly an hour. Dax longed to climb into bed, but she had one last person she needed to speak to before she could sleep.

Dax replicated a few more lit candles and placed them underneath her mirror. She put her palms on the countertop and gazed deeply into her own eyes.

"T'nora, ja'kala vok . . . 'za Jadzia . . . zhian'tara rek . . . pora'al

Zheem Dax . . . Tanas Rhem Curzon . . ." Curzon didn't fight, or cause a light show, or try to scare Dax, which was something she appreciated about him. He dutifully came when summoned.

Her eyes took on his deep sea-foam green, and her cheeks began to change. White hairs sprouted through her dark ponytail, and before long, she was staring into the face of her old mentor.

"I appreciate what you did for Etom," he said.

"Of course. Your skills helped me a lot."

"I'm glad."

"Curzon, you—" Dax began, but stopped herself. "You need to understand something. You hurt a lot of people—harmed promising young ones by kicking them out of the initiate program. Their lives went wrong sometimes because of your callous indifference. Vess preyed on that."

"Jadzia"—he shook his head—"you know all too well what the stakes are. When someone isn't ready—truly ready—it could turn out like Joran. And look at the debt that you inherited. Initiates must be prepared for that eventuality too."

"Oh, are you referring to the time I was put on trial for a murder you supposedly committed?"

"And you were acquitted!"

"Because you were sleeping with the victim's wife when he was assassinated. And that's not even your worst ex-girlfriend story! Are there any more 'debts' I've 'inherited'?"

"The past always comes back. Initiates cannot be soft as the caretakers of immortal knowledge."

"You thought that about me, but I took care of *your* problems *twice*."

"And I think we've established—you're special!"

"How many other *special* people did you destroy, Curzon?"

He took a breath to speak, but no retort came.

"You gave yourself to me," she said, "so I'll answer. You don't even know. I understand—you were trying so hard to be good, and only now do you see your legacy. I'm sure you didn't mean to hurt anyone with your antics, and you're ashamed, and it still doesn't matter because you hurt *me*. Dealing with Vess only brought it all back."

"Jadzia . . . I would do anything to change the past."

"I know," she said. "That's one thing I love about you." It was her turn to look away. "Please understand, there were parts of you that . . . that I truly adored when you were alive. I wouldn't have asked to join with your symbiont otherwise."

"So why did you?"

There had been many reasons given over the years, things she'd only spoken to professional counselors.

"Because I thought you were a brilliant man who saw all my flaws."

"I failed you out of the initiate program because I . . ." He shook his head, trying to remember a terrible mistake. "I couldn't see a single one of them, and I was certain my blindness would get you killed. I loved you."

"Why didn't you tell me before we joined? I didn't need that burden."

"Because I wanted to leave you my adoration and respect. If I'd understood what I was really heaping onto you, I promise I would've done things differently."

"You were a force of good with a dark stain—but I overcame it."

"And that's the greatest joy you could bestow. I am truly sorry, and I'll keep coming back to tell you that as many times as you need." He gave her a pained smile. "I'm here for you."

"I know. Now chin up, Curzon. I want you at your best."

Dax closed her eyes and inhaled slowly, counting the beats of her heart. When she opened them, she didn't see Curzon, the venerable councilor with a troubled past. She saw the beautiful young man at the Diplomat Corps Ball, his whole life ahead of him, eyes sharp, hair slick, wearing a mint suit on a perfect evening. He was charming, confident, and untethered by all the sins of his future. He was a force of nature who would reshape the galaxy.

She pressed a palm to the mirror, and he synchronized movements with her. His life was her gift. His legacy, her future. Dax would keep the good in him and learn from the bad. She was more than this one man's mistake.

Dax was a murderer and a liar, a diplomat and a daredevil, eight faces and countless adventures.

And completely exhausted.

When she blinked, Curzon was gone, and the room was dim. She basked in the familiar thrum of the station. Then she blew out the candles and climbed into bed to sleep soundly once more.

ACKNOWLEDGMENTS

Every book is the work of many, many people, and this one is no exception. It was written at what I hope was the height of the pandemic, during a period of personal tumult. Friends, family, and colleagues all came through for me when I needed them, and because of that, you get to read *Revenant*.

Without a doubt, the first person to thank is my spouse, Renée. She was a caretaker, a sounding board, and an encouraging voice. She watched *Deep Space Nine* over and over again, willing to delve into the details with me, and I'm lucky to have her.

The second person is Connor Goldsmith, my lovely agent who always makes deals run smoothly. This one was no exception, and his guidance was priceless. Well, okay, it has a percentage cost to me, but his *presence* was priceless, at least.

Thank you to the wonderful staff of Gallery Books for making my dreams a reality. Writing Jadzia Dax was a beautiful thing, and I can't believe I got to do so for such a wide audience. My editors are fans of the series, and it shows. Their passion was infectious, and I was lucky to have them.

I owe a debt to the people who consulted on my book. Piper J. Drake helped me name drugs the right way so I didn't look foolish. Dr. Raychelle Burks lent me her forensics expertise, making my crime scenes so much more criminal. Dr. Stephen Granade taught me how lightning works, which is shocking to no one who knows us.

Beta readers are integral to my process, and I want to thank the following test subjects—erm, participants: Bunny Cittadino, Amy Sisson, and Gary Lindros. Your feedback was so valuable along the journey, helping me to chase away the impostor syndrome that still haunts me with a half-dozen books in print.

And, of course, readers like you. (Please also buy my other books.)

ABOUT THE AUTHOR

Alex White is the author of the widely acclaimed Salvagers trilogy—*A Big Ship at the Edge of the Universe*, *A Bad Deal for the Whole Galaxy*, and *The Worst of All Possible Worlds*—as well as official novels for *Alien* (*The Cold Forge* and *Into Charybdis*) and this *Star Trek* novel. Born in Mississippi and having lived most of their life in the American South, Alex currently resides with their family in Georgia.